Praise for *A Fine Romance* by Christi Barth

"[A] fun book with a great story
and wonderful characters. I'd recommend this to
anyone who's a fan of contemporary romance."
—*Kindles and Wine*

"I don't know whose story is next
but I know I'll be one of the first to read it.
I'm really enjoying the series with its eclectic mix
of personalities and sexy heroes,
and this one was hard to put down."
—*The Book Nympho*

"*A Fine Romance* was sexy and romantic,
and everything I look for in a plot as far as
contemporary romances go."
—*Sizzling Hot Books*

"If you like a fun contemporary romance, you
will like *A Fine Romance* by Christi Barth."
—*Harlequin Junkie*

"It was a cute, easy read. Something to relax with
and dream of chocolate sexcapades."
—*Reading Between the Wines*

"With enjoyable characters, a well developed and
nicely written plot, sparkling sensuality including
some lovely food play, *A Fine Romance* is just
that. Christi Barth has created another winning
installment in this fun series and
I'm already looking forward to the next one!"
—*Guilty Pleasures Book Reviews*

**Also available from Christi Barth
and Carina Press**

Planning for Love
Ask Her at Christmas
Love at High Tide
Friends to Lovers
Tinsel My Heart
A Matchless Romance

**Coming soon from Christi Barth
and Carina Press**

Up to Me

Christi Barth

A Fine Romance

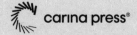

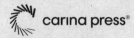

carina press®

ISBN-13: 978-0-373-00235-1

A FINE ROMANCE

Recycling programs
for this product may
not exist in your area.

www.CarinaPress.com

Printed in U.S.A.

Dear Reader,

I'm thrilled to welcome you back to the Aisle Bound series. My hope is that you'll adore book two, *A Fine Romance*, as much as I do. Mira is my überdetermined heroine who wants to put a string of failures behind her and make a success of her new Chicago romance store. If only it wasn't located next to a bakery owned by Sam, the absentminded hunk who abandoned her at the airport. Not only a baker, Sam's also an aspiring chocolatier who can't understand why Mira hates chocolate. They've got a handful of quirky, funny friends you'll recognize from book one, *Planning For Love*. And then there's the chocolate. This story is drenched in chocolate. Seriously, you'd better keep emergency chocolate next to you every time you open this book. You'll need it.

I'll bet quite a few of you are wondering where I got this idea. When I got married, a friend gave me a pack of date-night cards—fun, inexpensive and slightly offbeat things to do. One suggestion was to picnic in the same place every season and take a picture. We jumped on that. Food, wine and smooches at the edge of Lake Michigan sounded like a great combo. The Chicago lakefront park was a great backdrop, and showed off the change from verdant leaves to knee-high piles of snow. But as we lugged our jam-packed picnic hamper onto the El and then walked blocks upon blocks to the park, I got an idea. What if there was a store downtown where you could grab all the trappings for a spontaneous date? Great snacks, picnic backpacks and hampers, cards, romantic little gifts to tuck in as a surprise... I'm still convinced it's a great idea. But the lease on a downtown storefront is astronomical. So I created it between the pages of this book instead.

If you've got a sweet tooth and like a sassy and sexy happily ever after, this is the book for you. Along with the rest of the series! In case you missed it, book one, *Planning For Love*, shows how under the harsh spotlight of reality television, a romance-a-holic wedding planner tries to snare the anti-Cupid. Book three, *Friends to Lovers*, follows Daphne the florist and Gib the British lothario as they journey from—well, friends to lovers! And in book four, *A Matchless Romance*, a matchmaker transforms an awkward nerd into a sexy stud, and is sorely tempted to keep him for herself! But first, enjoy *A Fine Romance*. And if you do, please let me know at www.christibarth.com—I'd love to hear from you!

Christi

Thanks so much to all the MRW Scribblers
for pushing me to be a better writer.
Thanks to Lea Nolan, Eliza Knight, Joya Fields
and Stephanie Draven for performing the
critical beta reads. I owe you one, ladies!

Immense gratitude for Angela James and her sage
wisdom. She keeps me out of potential litigation,
reminds me that the hero's motivation can't
remain a secret in my head but must make it onto
the page, and champions my books at every turn.

A Fine Romance

For my beloved husband,
who, after fifteen glorious years of marriage,
still romances me every single day.

ONE

So far, Chicago sucked. Thanks to her parents' wanderlust (aka their addiction to hedonistic parties that required passport stamps for entry), Mira Parrish had seen much of the world in her twenty-nine years. A slide show of exotic locations flashed through her mind. Topless parties on yachts under Monte Carlo's blazing sun...which left her with horrid memories of her mother's uncovered breasts bouncing around. Annual beach parties in Brazil's sweltering heat...which left her with even more horrid memories of her father in a thong. Ski-boots-and-sun-tan spring parties in Switzerland's melting snow. Well, that one was a good memory of Yves, a Nordic god who gave Mira an excuse to avoid the slopes. Yves preferred to focus his attention on the moguls *beneath* her sweaters.

Familiar with almost every corner of the globe, and its peculiarities of inclement weather, Mira knew very well that Chicago didn't have monsoons. Yet here she was, drenched beyond belief, smack in the middle of a humid downpour violent enough to be quantified as nothing else but a monsoon. It didn't make any sense. Why would Fate import India's worst weather here, to the middle of the United States? Mira bit her lip. Clearly this Biblical rain was an omen. A dire warning she'd made an epic mistake with her brand-new life direction.

Shifting her aching shoulder so her three bags didn't slip any farther down her arm, she rang the bell on the tall, brick triplex. While waiting, Mira did a quick assessment. Her shoulder-length brown hair hung in wet, ropy strands down her back. Blisters piggybacked upon throbbing blisters caused by her sodden navy pumps. The blue pants she'd chosen specifically to endure the chill of an airplane clung to her thighs like a second skin. Brown streaks slashed across her white top from the river of muddy water a bus sprayed over her at the corner. Mira gritted her teeth. Always mindful of first impressions, she wished she didn't have to meet her new roommate while looking like a flood victim.

The front door swung open to reveal a smiling woman in a daisy dotted tank top and shorts. "Hi, I'm Daphne Lovell. You must be—wow, a freaking mess. You poor thing! What happened to you?" A blond ponytail whipped over Daphne's shoulder as she grabbed for Mira's matching green brocade (and soaked through) suitcases.

"Nice to meet you." Mira jerked her chin toward the fast-flowing river at the edge of the curb. "Your weather caught me by surprise. Does it monsoon often here in August?"

"Nope. Just today. Maybe you imported the bad weather from Vermont." Daphne snickered as she climbed the flight of narrow, wooden stairs.

Probably. It made sense to blame the recipient of an omen for the omen's wrath. "Stranger things have happened."

"Welcome to your new home sweet home." Kicking open the door with her foot, Daphne dropped the suitcases by the door and ushered her inside. Mira stopped only a few steps in, not wanting to drip on anything.

"I'm so grateful you're letting me stay here, Daphne. I know we've got Ivy as a mutual friend, but the bottom line is that you've never met me. Taking on a roommate sight unseen is a huge leap of faith on your part." Not to mention her own. But Mira couldn't afford to live in a hotel for the next who knew how long.

Her all-consuming new job wouldn't leave any time to search for an apartment for at least six months. And searching for a good roommate could be more difficult—and scarier—than searching for a boyfriend. Mira hoped that Daphne didn't have any weird quirks, such as sleepwalking naked (like her sophomore-year roommate) or only washing dishes at the full moon (her officially pagan roommate in Boston tied everything to cycles of the moon, from cleaning to job hunting. Mira discovered the hard way rent didn't come in reliably when someone only answered help wanted ads four days a month to coincide with each quarter rise of the moon).

Daphne hurried down the hall, voice raised. "You're one of Ivy's closest friends. That makes you a safe bet. I figure she'd have mentioned at some point in the past few years any huge character flaws. Like if you were an alcoholic ax-murderer."

That teased a smile out of her. Apparently Daphne set a low bar for roommate qualifications. "I'm not."

"Glad we've cleared that up. Anyway, taking you in isn't a completely selfless act. Now that Ivy's moved out to live in connubial bliss with Ben, her empty room certainly isn't bringing in any rent. And I like having company around the place. If I don't have someone to talk to, I'll start having conversations with my flowers. Word of my craziness would spread. Small children would run away in fear." She reappeared with a fluffy purple bath sheet. "Dry off and get your bearings," she ordered. "I'll get you a drink."

"Thanks." The towel blotted the worst of the drips from her hair, but Mira's clothes still clung to her in wet bunches. She craved a hot shower, but didn't want to appear unfriendly. Ten minutes of getting-to-know-you chitchat, one drink, and then she'd be able to politely excuse herself to change. Until then, she took stock of her new home.

Close-up photographs of individual flowers dotted the pale lavender walls. Extra-wide chairs covered in a watercolory print of lilac sprays looked super comfortable for reading away an afternoon. Not that Mira anticipated much free time in the next few months. Her new position as manager of A Fine Romance required her to put together a romance store from nothing and get it up and running in less than two months. While she thrived under pressure, the next few weeks would be brutal in terms of both time and energy.

A deep purple velvet sofa dominated the living room. Probably chosen for its make-out potential, it was more than long enough for a tall man to stretch out full length. Although Mira in no way anticipated any of that type of action in the foreseeable future, she loved the dramatic flair it brought to the room. The sorry state of her clothes made her bypass the comfort of the couch and wander straight to the fireplace. Flanked by built-in bookcases, the wide white mantel held a whimsically mismatched collection of picture frames.

"Here you go. I made you a Dark and Stormy. It seemed fitting, given the weather." Daphne handed over a tall glass, already frosted down the sides with condensation.

Mira took a sip. The mellow kick of the rum soothed, while the ginger beer's bite cut straight through her exhaustion. "Yum. I think you just turned my whole day around."

"I thought you were supposed to land a couple of hours ago. Was your plane late?"

She savored another smooth sip before answering. "No, the plane was on time. Everything went downhill after we landed. The man Ivy said would pick me up and bring me here—"

"Sam? Sam Lyons?" Daphne frowned.

At this point in her difficult afternoon, his very name skittered sharp prongs of anger across her temples. "He never showed up."

Daphne waved a hand, cutting her off. "Wait. Ivy texted him a reminder. Sam promised us that he'd take care of getting you home. Are you sure you didn't miss him?"

"Well, I waited for an hour on the curb. Even went back inside the airport and had him paged, in case I was waiting in the wrong place. The only phone numbers I had were for you and Ivy, and I knew you were still working today's wedding." In a perfect world, Mira wouldn't have scheduled her arrival in the middle of her friend's workday. But as a wedding planner, Ivy worked crazy hours all weekend, and Mira wanted to be able to start her new job bright and early Monday morning.

"Crap, we should've given you Sam's number, too. I'm so sorry about that." Daphne bit her lip. "Ivy and I felt awful that we couldn't meet you at the airport ourselves, but there was no way to leave the wedding early. This is Aisle Bound's busiest season. I did the flowers for all four of Ivy's weddings this weekend. This afternoon's was the worst because of the crazy-heavy candelabras the last bride rented from us for the centerpieces. Who needs candles at a Sunday-afternoon wedding in August? I thought we'd never be able to pick them up and get out of there."

No matter how miserable she felt, Mira knew she couldn't lay a guilt trip on this friendly woman who'd opened her home to a complete stranger. "Don't apologize. It's not your fault this Sam guy forgot about me." His name fell from her lips like a curse.

"He'd better have a damn good excuse, or I'll rip him a new one," Daphne said with a scowl.

Mira certainly wouldn't object. The only person she knew in this city of eight million people was her grad school roommate, Ivy. A fresh start meant being open and friendly to everyone, because literally anyone could be a new best friend or a business contact. However, she pretty much wanted to do something to the no-show Mr. Lyons. Maybe go all old-school and toss a drink in his face.

"I don't really know my way around Chicago. I've only visited for a few nights, and that was years ago." The easiest solution, that of a taxi all the way into the city from O'Hare, got crossed off her list immediately. It would've cost precious dollars Mira wouldn't have until she cashed her last, meager paycheck. "But Ivy mentioned your apartment was only two blocks from the El. I figured I'd deal with being stranded like a real Chicago native and use the transit system." Except for not thinking through the fact that El stood for elevated. Halfway down its two flights of rickety wooden stairs she slipped in a puddle. Of course she dropped all her luggage, which magically landed in more puddles. Five minutes later, a bus sprayed her with filthy, disgusting street water right at the corner. "It's…different than the subway in Boston."

"You poor thing." A knock sounded on the front door. Daphne set her drink on the coffee table, then shuffled off in fuzzy slippers sporting the head of Disney's Beast. She cracked the door.

"What the hell are you doing here?" she demanded.

A pleasant baritone voice answered. "Geez, why the attitude? I come bearing gifts. Mom played around with the special blend Ivy sent over and made these chai tea scones. You know, for that high tea reception in October? She wanted Ivy to taste them while they're fresh. Bestow her seal of approval."

"*Ivy* moved out yesterday, you moron. *Ivy* doesn't live here anymore, Sam." Daphne threw the door open all the way and jerked her thumb at Mira. "She does."

Sam? So this was the guy who forgot about her. The first thing Mira saw was a shock of jet-black hair. Thick eyebrows slashed across his forehead above electric blue eyes which squinted at her. Late-afternoon scruff covered his strong, square jaw. If she wasn't so royally pissed, she'd probably rate him as off-the-charts sexy. But looks weren't everything.

"Geez, Daph, why didn't you tell me about your

gorgeous new roommate? Or did Gib already call dibs?" Sam closed the door and shifted his box of scones from one hand to the other. "I'm Sam Lyons. And wow, you're soaked through. Get caught in the rain?" He picked up the towel she'd discarded on top of her luggage pile and held it out to her.

"Not exactly. A thoughtless jerk left me stuck in the rain, to be precise." When no comprehension lit his eyes, she continued. "At O'Hare. Where he was supposed to pick me up over two hours ago." Her eighth grade etiquette teacher, Miss Duvalier, would be disappointed if she could hear her favorite student railing at a stranger so rudely. Mira knew her inner whiny bitch had taken over. She also knew she'd regret the harsh words later. But looking at her ruined luggage, which she could in no way afford to replace, she didn't care.

"Oh." He blinked twice, with lashes so long and thick it'd take her four coats of mascara to replicate. "Oh! You're Ivy's friend. Mira, right? Great to finally meet you. Guess Ivy's the one I should poke about hiding her gorgeous friends from me."

Too little recognition, way too late. "So you're able to remember my name, but not your promise to pick me up?"

When she made no move to take the towel, he dropped his outstretched hand. Looked down at the growing puddle on the floor. Scrunched his face into a pained grimace. "Shit. No wonder you're drenched. Sorry about that. I planned to go get you. Ivy reminded me a dozen times. Here, let me help." Sam squeezed the towel around the ends of her hair. His closeness made Mira super aware of the wide breadth of his shoulders. But an awesome set of pecs didn't make up for how utterly alone she'd felt, standing on the curb of the second-busiest airport in the world.

No, his weak apology didn't even approach the realm of good enough. Or maybe she was overly sensitive from exhaustion, and he was a handy place to vent the frustrations of her day. Either way, she needed to hear more. "But?" she prompted, wondering if he'd work up at least a shred of a decent excuse.

Sam put down the towel after a final pat at her neck. "But then my mom called. She was shopping downtown when the storm started. So of course I had to go get her. You know what? Let me set you up with a scone. You'll feel better after you try one. Just ask Daph." He ambled into the kitchen, as though the conversation had come to a logical conclusion. Clearly at home, he pulled a plate out of the cupboard and set it on the wide counter. Methodically, he began transferring the scones out of the box.

Mira rushed after him, hitching herself onto a stool on the other side of the counter. She couldn't believe he was trying to justify his behavior. Pathetic that he used his mother as an excuse instead of just owning up to his mistake. Even if his well-muscled forearms, covered with a fine layer of dark hair, emitted an almost magnetic pull to her own fingers. The need to caress him from wrist to elbow, to fruitlessly attempt to wrap her hands around that thick masculinity, pulsed deep inside her. Instead, she fisted her hands on her hips. "So?"

"God, Sam," Daphne exclaimed, "you're thirty-one, not eleven. Don't hide behind your mother's apron strings." She perched on the stool next to Mira's.

"I'm not hiding. I'm responsible for her. There's a difference." The scone in his hand was reduced to crumbs as he curled his fingers tight. Interesting. Clearly she and Daphne had hit a nerve. "You know she's not well. Her bone scan results only came back last week." His voice deepened, head swinging side to side. A frown almost pulled his eyebrows into a single slash of dark worry across his forehead.

Guilt oozed through the cracks in Mira's armor of righteous anger. How could she fault the guy for taking care of his sick mother? A bone scan sounded scary, like the poor woman could have leukemia or cancer. What were a couple of pieces of wet luggage compared to a fatal disease?

Daphne rolled her eyes. "Geez, cut the dramatics. Sam, she's got mild osteoporosis, not a death sentence. I talk to your mom just about every day too, remember? The doctor actually urged Kathleen to get out and walk more."

Maybe exhaustion slowed her synapses. Mira had worked a fourteen-hour day, stayed awake all night full of excitement and jitters, rushed through packing, then hopped a plane. Right now her thoughts were moving at about the same speed as a herd of jet-lagged snails. But she could swear Sam had left her to fend for herself at the busiest airport in America just because his mother should eat a few extra slices of cheese a day? Hysterical laughter tickled the back of her throat like champagne bubbles, but she fought it back. There simply had to be more to his story.

Sam set his jaw. "Sure, she should walk more, but

only at a gym. A nice, smooth track. She's worried about slipping in the rain, down stairs, on uneven pavement."

Hopping off the stool, Daphne blew a raspberry. "She's worried?" She rounded the counter to poke a finger dead center in his chest. "Or you are?"

Another long, slow sip of her drink only made Mira feel better for a moment. Heat from the rum coiled inside her chest. It gave her something to concentrate on besides the urge to keep arguing with the man in front of her. Well, that and the almost equally strong urge to trail her fingers over the tuft of dark hair peeking out from the collar of his white T-shirt. A chest hair sighting nowadays was rare and lust-inducing.

"I can't let anything happen to her. I promised—" He broke off. Crumbled another scone to pieces. The vein at his temple bulged. Stress and guilt were written all over his face. His gorgeous, sexy face.

Mira got the feeling there was more to his concern about his mother. Maybe the doctor had delivered a worse diagnosis, and they were keeping it a secret? Maybe Sam was about to donate a kidney to her? Okay, that was probably an over-the-top idea brought on by exhaustion. But she wanted to dig deeper and find out. Something about the way he'd categorically stated he was responsible for her strummed a chord deep in her psyche. After all, no one in Mira's family had ever taken a stand like that for her.

"Look, it was lunchtime." Sam pushed Daphne's accusatory finger away. "Pouring cats and dogs out there. I couldn't leave her stranded, could I?"

Another raspberry blurted from Daphne's lips. "Your mother is wonderfully self-sufficient. A trait you rarely let her exercise. I guarantee she would've made it home just fine, rain or no rain."

"Funny, she said the same thing when I offered to get her. Tried to talk me out of it." He leaned against the refrigerator, arms folded across his chest.

Wait a minute. His mom hadn't snapped her fingers in the expectation her baby boy would come rescue her and thereby strand Mira? Even the view of his T-shirt pulled taut across his eye-popping pecs didn't stall the runaway train of righteous pissiness barreling to the surface. Spurred on by the cold trail of water trickling from her scalp down to the small of her back. Mira stood, gripping her glass. "Do you mean to tell me that your mother didn't call to ask for your help?"

The right corner of his mouth pulled down. "Of course not. She only called to tell me it was raining so I'd remember to run up and shut the windows in my apartment."

Unbelievable. The man had all the sense of a drunken turtle. It frayed the very last nerve Mira had left. On the bright side, if she got all the irritation out of her system now, they could start fresh whenever they next met. Hopefully then she could just concentrate on his utterly tempting body. "Which means we're back to my thesis statement. You're thoughtless."

"Look, I'm sorry I didn't get you. Stranding you at O'Hare was a crappy thing to do. I get that. But I had a reason." He smiled down at her with the patience of a venerable priest explaining the mysteries of the catechism to a child. "I worry about my mom all the time. Today, I worried about her slipping down the steps of the El and breaking a hip. If she'd gotten stuck walking in the rain? I can't imagine how wet and miserable she would have been."

"Well, in case this visual isn't enough to clue you in," Mira gestured at her still-sopping clothes, "let me help you wonder no more." She gave in to impulse, surged forward, and dumped the icy, wet contents of her glass over his head. Then immediately gasped, shocked by her own over-the-top behavior. How could she rail at Sam for being rude when she acted so childishly? Did temporary, exhaustion-induced insanity account for being a full-on brat? Probably not.

For a second he stood still, blinking away the rivulets of sticky soda. But then Sam twitched. Knees bent, he slapped his hands against his back while his feet shuffled in a weird, contorted dance.

Mira guessed that a couple of the ice cubes must've slithered down his collar. She should apologize. But instead, she giggled. As he continued to claw at his back, feet jerking in a small circle between the fridge and the stove, she rolled into a full-out guffaw. Watching his obvious discomfort went a long way to making up for her wreck of an afternoon. Mira looked over her shoulder to see that Daphne had both hands clamped over her mouth, but laughter still escaped.

"This is stupid," Sam declared. He grabbed the back of his collar and pulled his shirt over his head. Six ice cubes landed at Mira's feet. She gulped at seeing the toned expanse of his back. It was a smooth, tan canvas she longed to paint with the tips of her fingers. Impossibly broad shoulders tapered to a narrow vee at his waistband. And when he turned around, her mouth went dry. A mat of dark hair stretched across his chest, down over an honest-to-God six-pack, then disappeared into his shorts in a fine line. Sam's half-naked body packed the sexual explosiveness of a Molotov cocktail, and Mira was ready to burst into flames.

Sam wiped his eyes with his shirt, then made a quick pass across his hair. "Are we even now? Or do I need to keep my guard up every time you've got a drink in your hand?"

Her mouth didn't remember how to form words. As if all those sexy pecs weren't enough to drive her crazy, she'd swear a faint scent of cinnamon and sugar surrounded him. The aroma pooled the moisture back in her mouth. She wanted nothing more than to lick a path through the fine pattern of chest hair across and see if he tasted as good as he smelled. Mira stopped herself about a second—and a single inch—away from sniffing him. She attributed her overreaction to exhaustion, and took a big step back. Then another. The farther away she got from his overwhelming manliness, the better her neurons seemed to function. When she turned away from Sam to put her empty glass in the sink, the power of speech miraculously returned.

"Are we even? Not by a long shot. But do you need to worry about me seeking further retribution?" Mira paused to give him a minute to wonder just how far she might go. She had the upper hand now, and wasn't willing to relinquish it that quickly. Even though most of her anger had whooshed away with her laughter. "I guess time will tell."

Metal screeched against the wood floors as Daphne pushed her stool back. "On that well-deservedly ominous note, I'm kicking you out, Sam. You've caused enough trouble here for one day. Thank your mother for the scones. I'll take them over to Ivy's new place tomorrow." Putting a hand in the small of his back, she shoved him toward the front door.

"Quit the manhandling. You want to grope me, do it when we don't have an audience." He planted his feet and tugged his shirt back on.

"Fat chance, Lyons." Daphne snickered. "The only things I want to squeeze around you are your amazing doughnuts. A good apple fritter's a lot harder to find than a nice set of abs."

"Don't I at least get a beer for my trouble? I did rush those scones over the minute they came out of the oven." A quick up and down once-over of Mira, then Sam lifted an eyebrow. "Maybe get to know the new roomie?"

Was he oblivious? When someone poured a drink over your head, in what possible way did that indicate they were in the mood to chat? Apparently his brains and personality didn't quite measure up to his off-the-charts gorgeous body. It'd make it easier to ignore the low-grade lust she'd been infected with since the moment she laid eyes on the tall, dark and yummy Mr. Lyons. Because the longer she stared at him, and was tempted by him, the more Mira knew that both lust and love were complications she didn't have time for in her new life.

Daphne shoved him once more. "You drove six blocks. It doesn't qualify you for a medal of honor. Now scram."

"All right, I can take a hint." He paused halfway out the door. "Welcome to Chicago, Mira. Sorry for the bad start, but I bet you'll like it here."

Daphne slammed the door behind him. "I'm sorry about that."

"No, I'm sorry. I made a mess of your kitchen." Mira grabbed an arm's length of paper towels off the counter and wiped up the puddled remains of her drink. "Honestly, I don't usually toss drinks on people. I keep my temper under a pretty tight lid." Because she'd learned long ago that her volatile temper shouldn't be let loose. Today being a perfect example of the bad things that could happen if she let her emotions have free rein. Mira lived by reason and practicality. Far safer to let her logical brain do the driving, and make her heart a mute, backseat passenger.

Daphne crouched next to her and picked up the half-melted ice cubes. "Sam's a sweetie, but he sometimes gets this single-minded focus that shuts him off from everything else. Today you were its unintended victim." She took the wet towels and tossed them into the sink. "You're off to kind of a crappy start here, aren't you?"

Yep. It'd be way too easy to look at today as a harbinger, turn tail and run right back home. But Mira didn't take the easy way out. For the past ten years, she'd avoided the easy path offered to her and struck out in the opposite direction. Why stop now? She shook her head and forced a smile. "A long, hot shower should be all it takes to turn the day around."

"Right this way." Daphne grabbed two of Mira's bags and led her down the hallway.

"Looking on the bright side, I lucked out in the roommate department, and this apartment is terrific." Mira stepped into her new bedroom and grinned. Without being told, she knew it used to be Ivy's room. It bore her über-girly stamp from curtains to carpet. Either that, or a Disney princess came to life and decorated it. The walls were covered with wide pink-and-white stripes. The curlicued white ironwork headboard barely showed from behind a mound of pink throw pillows. A pink dust ruffle peeked out beneath the white comforter. White curtains were tied back with floppy pink bows, and the throw rugs by the bed and in front of the dresser were cotton-candy pink as well.

"Are you sure this is okay? I mean, I think it looks like a package of bubble gum exploded in here. I know it probably isn't what you're used to…" Daphne trailed off.

"Used to? I just spent six weeks sharing a cabin in the woods with a dozen teenage girls who never stopped talking. Our camp is great, but it's far from fancy. Having a room all to myself again—especially one without bunk beds—is sheer bliss." The indulgence of absolute quiet once she turned out the light made her want to dive into bed right away.

"But you're only a camp counselor in the summer. The rest of the time, well," leaning in, Daphne switched to a loud whisper, "I heard you're rich. Crazy rich. Mansions in three states rich. My place has to feel like you're living in a matchbox in comparison."

Mira cocked her head to the side. "Ivy told you I'm rich?"

"No. Well, not in so many words. I pieced it together from stories over the years. All your world traveling, the ski lodge in Aspen, the beach house in Key West, the house in Connecticut—"

"Let me stop you right there. Those all belong to

my parents. As does all the money." Mira dug into her purse and pulled out the crumpled dampness of her last camp paycheck. "See this? Aside from the eleven dollars currently in my wallet, this whopping $475 is all I've got to my name until Ivy puts me on her payroll. My last apartment was a tiny studio. I've got drive and determination, but I sure don't have any money."

"Oh. Wow." Daphne crinkled her nose. "You're really taking a chance opening this store with Ivy, aren't you? If it fails, you're screwed."

Mira rubbed her temples at the spot where she knew her stress headache would manifest any second. It happened with disturbing regularity whenever she thought about the maybe-bold-maybe-stupid leap she'd just made by going into business with Ivy. "You have no idea."

Sam pressed his ear to the back door of Lyons Bakery. He knew it was ridiculous for a grown man to try to sneak into his own damn apartment. But he just didn't want to rehash the scene at Daphne's place. Hell, he didn't want to talk to anyone. This morning he'd visited his father's grave. That always sucked. The grief of losing him was still raw after only two years. Talking to a headstone didn't get any easier, no matter how often he went.

The visits were always the same. He took a handful of sunflowers—the least girly flower he could think of—and trimmed the grass around the vase sunk into the earth. Squatted on his haunches to trace the words *Beloved Father*. Then launched into a monologue that never failed to leave him feeling slightly

stupid. But his father hadn't left any room for interpretation in his single deathbed request to his son.
Kathleen Lyons was now, and forever, Sam's responsibility. You couldn't say no to a man's dying wish.
You couldn't do anything but accept it and treat it as
law. As the number one priority.

So he made biweekly visits to the cemetery, and
delivered updates on his mom to a freaking headstone.
They left him wrung out every time. From trying in
some way, although fruitlessly, to make a connection
with his father. And from the heavy weight that covered him from being responsible for his mom. Atlas
had it easy, just carrying the world on his shoulders.
Sam would trade jobs with him in an instant.

Hearing nothing, Sam eased the door open. Slid in
sideways and ended up face-to-face with his mother.
Crap.

In the middle of hanging her brown apron on the
hook, Kathleen froze. "What happened to you, honey?
You're sopping wet. Didn't it stop raining before you
left?"

"Yeah." This was the problem with living above
the bakery. No damn privacy. If Sam wanted to bring
two hookers in zebra-striped lingerie home for a
nooner, he should be able to. Even though all Sam
really wanted right now was to collapse in front of
C-SPAN with a beer. Other guys relaxed over Xbox,
or in front of mindless horror flicks. As a political
news junkie, nothing made Sam happier than a couple of hours of talking heads going at each other. A
man's apartment was supposed to be his castle. Unless said man lived above the family business where
his mom still held the reins.

"Did you get in a water-balloon fight?"

Sam didn't hold back the impulse to roll his eyes. "I'm not twelve, Mom. Why do you think I'd spend a Sunday having a water-balloon fight?"

"Exactly what I was wondering," she said crisply. Then she smoothed a hand over her short white hair… and waited. Wielding silence like a battering ram in that way all mothers had.

Might as well get it over with. "I met our new neighbor."

"Ivy's friend from grad school?" Her eyes, just a few shades paler than his, sparkled with curiosity. Kathleen adored new people. "The one who's going to run the store?"

"Yeah." Right next door. Sam thought about the off-the-charts hotness of his new neighbor. How hard it would be to have someone that beautiful just on the other side of the wall, every day. Someone he couldn't possibly date. Not least of all, because he'd royally fucked up the all-important first impression.

Kathleen stepped out of the bright green clogs that helped her survive the long days of standing behind the counter. "Is she nice?"

He gestured at his drenched shirt. "Well, she did this to me. What do you think?"

"I think she needs some manners."

Yeah, it felt good to have his mom leap to his defense after the way Mira had slapped at him. Of course, they would be working side by side. Probably a good idea not to start her off on the wrong foot with *all* the Lyons. "It wasn't completely her fault."

She dragged him down the narrow hallway to the

front counter. Grabbed a dish towel and rubbed it over his wet hair. "What happened?"

Sam wanted to tell her. 'Cause he did feel guilty as hell for leaving Mira to fend for herself at the airport. Wanted to tell his mother that worrying about her had caused it. But he couldn't. Couldn't lay that burden on her for fear she'd break...again.

At first he hadn't thought taking care of his mom would be any big deal. Figured his dad's request would be more of an honorary thing. Kathleen already ran the bakery. Was a magician with pie crusts. Had a huge circle of friends—his mom never met a stranger she didn't squeeze the life story out of in ten minutes flat. She reminded him of a cheerful little steam engine, puffing straight ahead through life. Sam hadn't anticipated what would happen when she ran out of fuel.

It had only been a year since seeing his mom's number on his phone spelled disaster. That some kind stranger had called her pre-programmed *in case of emergency* number because she'd broken down into a sobbing heap at the grocery store, or the sidewalk. Or, one memorable time, stopped her car in the middle of freaking Clybourn St. during rush hour, lay down on the seats and cried for half an hour until the police showed up.

Now, they worked side by side all day in the bakery. Kathleen didn't have much need to ever call him. So when her number popped up in his phone, it still induced gut-clenching fear. That she'd fallen apart again. That this time, she'd been dragged off—again!—to the emergency room. That yet again, his mother's physical and mental deterioration proved that Sam had failed his father.

Kathleen looked better on the outside. Seemed fine. But who could tell, really? Who knew what might set off another downward spiral? Sam couldn't, wouldn't let it happen again. Couldn't let his mother suffer or let down his father. If that meant turning his life upside down to keep her protected, so be it.

He sank onto a chair by one of the bistro tables. Stared at the brown, dotted Swiss curtains but instead saw Mira's face. Even surrounded by wet streaks of mascara, her eyes caught his attention right off. No, she didn't deserve to be stranded by him like that. But his mom didn't deserve—and probably couldn't handle—the guilt of knowing she'd caused the snafu, even indirectly. And God, Sam was tired of running everything he said or did through that filter.

"It was just a misunderstanding, Mom."

"Oh. Well, then." She bustled behind the counter and rummaged in the display case. "Give her this."

A glossy stripe of chocolate rose out of a ruffled paper border. "An éclair?"

Kathleen shook her head. "Lyons' famous triple-chocolate éclair. You of all people know that chocolate makes everything better." She came around, kissed him on the head, then dug her fingers into his armpit. Sam jerked out of reach, almost tipping over the chair. He hated being tickled. "Tell her it's a peace offering. We don't want to start off on bad terms with our neighbor."

He watched her leave. Heard the drone of the washing machine she must've started. Smelled the faint tang of yeast in the air from all the dough she'd prepped for the morning. All evidence pointed to his mother being a wholly normal, productive member of society. That maybe Sam could dial back the constant worry and overprotectiveness a couple of notches. And yet…he couldn't. Not yet. Not if there was the slightest chance his heightened alert could prevent another incident. So Sam would continue to put her first. No matter what.

TWO

"I'M SO THRILLED you're here." Ivy gave Mira a one-armed hug, then quickly separated before they walked into a gingko tree on the edge of the sidewalk. As usual, Ivy looked perfect. A wide, hot-pink sash drew attention to her tiny waist. Below, her blush-pink sundress belled out like an open tulip. Matching sandals with ankle ties pulled the ensemble straight into magazine worthiness. She was about one pink hair bow away from impersonating a cake topper. Chirping birds should circle her head. Except that the concerto of honking horns of Chicago's morning rush hour drowned out the possibility of hearing any birdsong.

Mira looked down at her own faded black workout shorts and bilious green Camp Ticonderoga tee. She'd dressed to unpack boxes of inventory rather than impress on her first day of work. Staring at the closet this morning, it seemed the proactive, professional approach. A way to show her new boss just how ready she was to push up her own proverbial sleeves. But next to Ivy's crisp appearance, Mira knew the only thing she looked ready for was a marathon day of soap operas on the couch with perhaps a silver foil sash to proclaim her queen of the slobs.

Determined not to let self-consciousness ruin her first-day buzz, Mira squeezed back. "I've missed you, too. But you've got to stop hugging me every ten steps. We look ridiculous. Like drunks just staggering home after an all-nighter. I'm supposed to be a respected member of the business community here, as of, well, right about now."

Ivy laughed and let go. "If I promise to take you to the next neighborhood association meeting, will you let me keep hugging you? You can wear a very serious suit and impress everyone with your business acumen. Nobody will recognize you as the possible sloppy drunk doing the walk of shame her first day in the city."

"Aww, how could I turn down such a professional and heartfelt invitation?"

"Besides, I owe you about two hundred more hugs, and it's going to be hard to squeeze those in before I leave."

Two months had passed since that first rushed and excited phone call when Ivy asked her to manage the store. In the back would be all the ingredients for the perfect spontaneous picnic; wine, cheese, bread, gourmet finger food. Upfront, an array of picnic baskets, blankets, wineglasses, vases, and all sorts of romantic tchotchkes. At that time, A Fine Romance existed only in Ivy's head. But the idea of it alone was enough to get Mira on board. And every single day since, Ivy had emailed or called to thank her for taking the leap. It astonished her Ivy didn't realize *she* was the one giving *Mira* an amazing opportunity, not the other way around. Especially after the string of bad luck she'd had with her last few jobs.

"Ivy, I know you're glad I'm here, but you don't owe me anything. Except for a paycheck every two weeks, with the upgrade to profit sharing after our wildly successful first year."

Those dainty sandals skidded to a halt. Ivy's mouth rounded into comical chagrin. "Are you kidding? You are saving my bacon here, kiddo. The idea for a romance store's been dripping into my head with the persistence of Chinese water torture for a few years. Two things stopped me from moving forward, though. Even though I talked myself hoarse at every bank in town, I couldn't finagle a loan."

"That still shocks me. You can talk anyone into anything. Isn't that how you manage to coax your brides away from their tackier decorating ideas, like the photo place cards? Oh, and the ball and chain groom's cake?"

"I try to use my powers of persuasion for good," Ivy said with a deceptively modest smile. "Which was the second problem. I already own Aisle Bound. My job as a wedding planner is full-time, and then some. The idea for A Fine Romance was too special, too dear to me to hand over to just anyone. You're the only person I trust to bring my dream to life. Once the start-up money fell in my lap, it was a dream come true."

No pressure or anything. "Since he's not here to stand up for himself, I'd like to point out that your starring role on a reality television show led you straight into Ben's arms. Meeting the love of your life was the real dream come true. Taking obscene amounts of money to let people film your every working moment was merely good business sense."

"Ben's going to love you." Ivy steered Mira around the corner. One block off the main drag, the noise level dropped by half. Birds warbled in the leafy tree-tops. The buildings were less obviously commercial, with a row of converted brownstones housing boutiques and two art galleries. The neighborhood looked both affluent and inviting. It guaranteed their store would get lots of foot traffic. Even the wet mantle of late-August humidity steamed a tad less ferociously on this shady street.

Talking about Ben was a surefire way to get Ivy off the unrelenting string of thanks. Mira couldn't wait to meet the man who'd so thoroughly enamored her friend. "He's got good taste. Case in point, that two-carat stunner weighing down your left hand. Show me again."

With an actual squeal of delight, Ivy thrust out her hand and waggled her ring finger. "Isn't it beautiful? I catch myself staring at it so many times during the day. As a wedding planner, I watch brides flash their engagement rings all the time, so I thought I'd be immune. But when the sparkle's on your own finger, it's irresistible."

Mira had seen enough fancy jewelry in her mother's safe to know the real deal. Ivy's new fiancé had exquisite taste. Two carats, flawless cushion cut with impeccable clarity. "It's the most beautiful ring I've ever seen. But—" She broke off, unsure of how to proceed. She and Ivy had forged an unbreakable bond in grad school, and the intervening years hadn't weakened their friendship in the slightest. Sharing secrets and venting frustrations over midnight cell phone calls was easy. Asking the hard questions face-to-face while still adjusting to the transition of friends to friend-and-boss might be trickier.

"What is it? You know you can ask me anything."

"This whole thing with you and Ben. The engagement—you know I'm thrilled. Nobody's looked harder for happiness than you."

"Want to know a secret?" Ivy swiveled her head from side to side, as if checking for the reality show cameras, which were on a break this month. "Looking for love didn't work. What did work was being open to the possibility when I landed at its feet."

The very Zen approach clashed with Ivy's history of blatant husband hunting. Ivy threw herself headlong into relationships. She could downhill slalom her way through anything a guy (or as Ivy called all her dates, a potential husband) threw at her. No matter how weird his hobbies—including turtle racing—or strange his family—goat herders—Ivy viewed every first date as the first step toward the altar. Adorable in high school, cute in college, but a fault that led to a train wreck of adult relationships.

"It's just that, well, I feel like I'd be remiss in my friendship duties if I didn't ask you this horrible, intrusive question. Ben proposed to you after only a couple of months. It happened so fast. How can you be sure?"

"Believe it or not, you aren't the first person to question our speed match. Especially given my track record of falling head over heels for every guy I ever dated.

"Love, true love, feels different. I can't explain it."

Neither the reasoned or impassioned answer Mira expected to hear. "You, of all people, are at a loss for words about love?"

Ivy grinned. "Yep. Ben leaves me speechless with happiness."

"Wow. I can't wait to meet this paragon of manliness."

"Oh, he's no paragon, trust me. After traveling the world living in hotels for a decade, Ben's not used to having a kitchen. Something as simple as making a sandwich results in an average of four plates, an arm's length of paper towels and a slew of topless jars. A toddler would make less of a mess. Drives me absolutely bonkers." She clasped her hands to her chest and batted her eyelashes. "But he's all mine. And when it comes to our relationship, he can be even sappier than me."

"Not possible. An injection of straight-up insulin has less sugar in it than you do. Hearts and flowers are your thing, Ivy."

"And now they're your thing. Here we are." Ivy stopped in front of a storefront with large windows covered in brown butcher paper. Across the top of the door was stenciled A Fine Romance. Mira recognized the font as the same as Ivy's purple logo for Aisle Bound, but this one was in bright red. Seeing the logo made it all so real. It would be on business cards, stationery, gift bags, receipts. This was her chance to get in on the ground floor of a business, truly shape it from day one, and Mira couldn't possibly be more excited. Her heart thumped in triple time as Ivy pressed a key ring into Mira's palm. A large silver heart weighted down the circle of four keys.

"Okay, one more hug, and then I have to run."

A second reference to leaving. She'd ignored the first one, but now Ivy sounded serious. Sure, day-today control belonged to her now, but there were things on which Mira needed to be brought up to speed. How did the security system work? Did Chicago delivery men expect to be tipped, or not? Where did they keep the petty cash for tips? In the dangerous, albeit unlikely event one of their new shelving systems fell over, where was the nearest urgent-care clinic? At least a dozen more questions scrolled through her mind in an eye blink.

"What are you talking about? You can't go anywhere. It's my first day." Although she'd aimed for a playful tone, bordering on nonchalance, Mira feared a quaver of panic had slipped through.

Ivy worried her lip between her two front teeth. "Yes, well, that's why I owe you so many hugs. You see, I have to pick Ben up from the airport."

"Today?" Still smarting from her own lack of a pickup yesterday, Mira couldn't understand Ivy's desertion on such a momentous day. Ben lived here now. Certainly he knew how to use the El. Why couldn't he get himself home? This was a new beginning, a new life. And now she'd have to start it alone? Without anyone to ooh and ahh over the beautiful stock as they unpacked it? Without anyone to share her barely containable excitement and dance around the big, empty space in sheer joy at the possibilities ahead of them?

It was subtle, but Mira caught Ivy's surreptitious eye flick to the watch on her left wrist. Apparently there wouldn't even be a happy-first-day shared coffee and muffin before she got abandoned. All the more upsetting to contemplate because a rich butter and sugar aroma wafted through the air, teasing her nostrils.

"Right now," Ivy said. "Ben's been gone all week at headquarters in New York doing preproduction. Or maybe post-production. Between you and me, I tune out some of the time when he gets into work details. He's got some funny stories, but he's also full of dull rants about digital conversion points and lighting issues and a host of camera things that fly right over my head." She took a breath, smiled at Mira and grabbed her hands. "The point is that he's coming home, and I've missed him terribly. So I'm going to battle rush-hour traffic to pick him up at O'Hare and greet him with a barrage of smooches. You can handle this. You're on your own here this morning."

"Ivy, it's too much. I wouldn't know where to begin." Not actually true. Mira knew she'd figure it out once she got in the door. The component she'd miss was her friend Ivy, not Ivy as a boss.

"Don't be ridiculous. Next to me, you're the most ruthlessly organized person on the planet. It's one of the reasons I hired you. The preliminary stock you ordered began rolling in a few days ago. You'll have plenty to do unpacking it and figuring out where you want to put it all. I promise I'll be back this afternoon to go over all of the nitty-gritty details. And draft an ad for a part-time cook." Ivy cocked her head and gave a quick, double-handed squeeze. "I'm so sorry to leave you in the thick of it."

Mira stood up a little straighter, firming her spine both physically and emotionally. The last few moments of panic could be explained as typical new-city jitters. And she'd shake them off here and now. No more clinging to Ivy, or counting on her to introduce her to the ins and outs of the city. Not even to point her toward the nearest coffee shop. She'd strike out on her own. Maybe map out a route to run in the morning and explore the city from its sidewalks. Mira reached back to caress the smooth, solid doorknob. It gave her the strength to flash a confident smile.

"Nope. I refuse to let you apologize for letting me in on this amazing opportunity. You had the bright idea. Now it's up to me to bring it to life." And after she'd unpacked five boxes, she'd reward herself by tracking down the source of that heavenly, sweet scent.

"Are you sure you don't need a day to recover from your stint at camp? I hear wrangling teenagers can be exhausting."

Mira laughed. "Very true, but I can't wait to dig in. I'm on the clock, boss."

As promised, Ivy leaned in for another hug, this time with both arms. "Enjoy your new kingdom."

"I like the sound of that. We should consider tiaras as part of the uniform."

"You get this store up and running, I'll bring you a tiara for opening day."

"Deal. You should know that I prefer pearls over diamonds. Now go get that wonderful man of yours."

With Ivy gone, Mira realized she sort of liked the idea of tackling the store by herself on the first day. Begin as you mean to go on. If only her life came with a soundtrack, there'd be a big swell of music as she put the key in the lock. This could be the first day of the rest of her life. No, that wasn't any good. It made it sound like she'd been shipped straight from an intervention to rehab. This could be the first day of a grand adventure. Much better, she grinned, and slipped inside *her* store.

Thanks to the morning brightness outside, even after slipping off her sunglasses Mira couldn't see anything but shadowy shapes. She groped along the wall for a light switch as she waited for her eyes to adjust. Finding nothing, she wondered if Ivy had turned on the electricity yet. One of what was to be sure a hundred burning questions.

Before taking another step, she reached into her bag. Better to jot down each concern immediately, than risk forgetting it. Lists were her life. They gave her structure, order and at least the illusion of sanity no matter how much chaos swirled around her. Each new job didn't really begin until she'd purchased a planner, complete with multiple tabs, pockets and lots of pages. This one was lipstick red, to match the store's logo. Sure, some of it ended up on a computer eventually, but you couldn't slip a computer into your back pocket.

A shuffling noise at the back of the store brought her head up with a snap. Either they had supersized rats here in Chicago, or another person was in the store with her. Her fight-or-flight response bobbled back and forth as adrenaline juiced her like a thousand volts of electricity. Oddly enough, she landed on the side of running from a rat, but staying to fight a burglar for her store. A drawer swished open, then slammed shut. That negated the possibility of a rat, so Mira crept forward on tiptoe.

On top of what must be the sales counter sat a crystal vase, filled with tall, sweet-smelling stock and roses. Probably a welcome-to-your-new-store present from Ivy. Thoughtful and pretty, the bouquet just might be her best weapon. After all, she couldn't use a packing box in self-defense, which were the only other things Mira saw scattered throughout the store.

Behind the back counter, a figure stood, his back and broad shoulders to Mira. This could be her best chance. Running the last few feet, she hefted the vase overhead before slamming it with all her might onto the intruder's head. Flowers and water cascaded everywhere, and the man swayed, but didn't crumple to the floor as she'd hoped. Undaunted, Mira lifted the vase again for a second thwack. At the last second he spun around and grabbed it from her. The outrage in his scowl was as frigid as all the lake-effect snow she'd been warned about.

"What the hell do you think you're doing?"

Oh no. Definitely not a burglar. Instead, she'd bashed in the skull of one of Ivy's closest friends. Sam Lyons stood in front of her, soaking wet, with blood gushing from his head. All of Mira's fear-based adrenaline melted from her system, leaving behind only a lead ball of guilt in her stomach. Mouth dry, she knew she'd have to stammer out a doozy of an apology, and cross her fingers that he wouldn't press assault charges.

Except…what gave him the right to be so mad? Apart from the whole streaming blood issue, of course. Although cuts on the head always seemed to bleed twice as much as anywhere else. As manager, she had every right to be here, baseball bat in hand, if necessary, to protect the place. Sam was the trespasser. How did he even get in—the front door had definitely been locked when she entered.

"Why'd you clock me in the head? God, I know I forgot to pick you up at O'Hare, but I don't think that gives you the right to inflict bodily harm." He kept hold of the vase, as if worried she might snatch it back and hit him with it again. His other hand lifted to his head, gingerly assessing the damage she'd wrought.

Wasn't it obvious? Gosh, how badly had she scrambled his brains? She should scoot closer and see if the pupils of his brilliant blue eyes were enlarged. "I thought you were a burglar."

"You'd be in a world of hurt by now if I was a burglar. Some kid, keyed up on meth and looking for cash, isn't going to be stopped by a bang on the head."

Now he was just being pissy. But with a bleeding head wound, she'd cut him a little slack. "You're not a meth-head. I presume Ivy wouldn't have roped you in to play chauffeur for me if you had a drug problem."

"I could be. You certainly didn't know one way or the other when you barged in here instead of doing the sensible thing and calling the police. If you plan to make a habit of being stupidly brave instead of a smart coward, you should take some self-defense classes. Maybe aikido—there's a studio just a few blocks away."

Mira refused to stand there and debate her choice to hit him on the head. Especially because a little voice in her head whispered that he was probably right. She should have gotten out and called the police. His rightness irked her even more. "Keep your unsolicited advice. Why did you break into my store?"

"I didn't break in." Sam put down the vase, tore off a length of paper towels and pressed them to his head. "Geez, you really see me as one step above pond scum, don't you?"

"Pond scum doesn't skulk around, uninvited, in the shadows."

"Ivy gave me a key." Sam fished it out of his pocket and twisted it in the air with all the melodrama of a blood-stained knife being exhibited at a trial. "So I could accept all the deliveries. Boxes have been coming in at a steady clip for about a week now."

She didn't understand. Once, sure. But to do it for a week? That was a favor of enormous proportion. "You just drop everything and pop over?"

"Sure. Not an inconvenience to walk ten steps and unlock a door." He pointed across from them at a door she hadn't noticed yet in the middle of the wall. "My shop's right through there. I hear the doorbell, and I take a five-minute break. No big deal."

"You can come and go, into my store, whenever you like?" The idea of someone essentially trespassing at will snapped her back teeth into a grind. Even if that someone stood more than six feet and had biceps that bulged out of his T-shirt.

"I call it being neighborly." He shrugged, then immediately winced. Blood still dripped at a shockingly steady rate down his neck. A guillotine victim probably had less bloodstains than Sam's shirt. The poor man might need stitches, or even have a concussion. Guilt swamped Mira. Her privacy tirade could wait. She'd inflicted the injury to him, so it fell to her to clean him up. Just like she'd have to clean the red smears on the beautiful pine floor.

"I'm sorry I hit you. And I'm worried about how much you're bleeding. Let's get you to the bathroom and assess the damage. Maybe I should take you to a hospital?"

"Thought you didn't have a car." He sounded a little sulky, but calmer.

"I don't. But I'm not going to let you bleed to death on the floor, either. Calling a cab is not outside the realm of my abilities."

Sam waved a hand in the air as if erasing the suggestion. "I used to play hockey. This is just a scratch. Slap a bandage on it and I'll be okay. Although I might have to add in a couple of drinks tonight to offset the massive headache that's settling in." Groaning, he bent over and grabbed a first-aid kit from under the sink. Great. He even knew his way around the place. Mira didn't know they owned a first-aid kit, let alone where it lived. Sam was single-handedly taking the brand-new luster off of her shop.

Remembering the layout from the floor plan Ivy had sent, Mira tromped down the hall to the bathroom. With Sam in and out on a daily basis, she assumed the electricity was, indeed, working. A flick of a switch illuminated the tiny room, painted crimson with black trim. It dripped with all the dark sensuality of a vampire's lair. Sam loped in behind her and took a seat on the black toilet lid.

Up close and in full light, the injury looked worse than she'd realized. A long gash slanted diagonally from his temple to just below his ear on the back of his head. On the plus side, it did give her hope that one more good swing would've taken him—or an actual burglar—down. Mira popped open the box he handed her and pulled out a fistful of gauze.

"Hold this on your head while I get the antiseptic."

"Hang on." In one smooth yank, Sam pulled off his shirt. She understood why. It was wet and sticky with his blood. What she couldn't understand was how she was supposed to help him when all she could do was stare at the… God, the magnificence he'd revealed. Dark hair dusted each manly pec. Biceps that were too big to wrap her hand around rose to thickly muscled shoulders. Tanned skin stretched across tightly defined abs, bisected by a thick, dark, sexy line leading straight into the waistband of his black running shorts. Sure, she'd seen him shirtless just yesterday, but the impact today was just as powerful. Maybe more so, since he sat a mere two inches away. Close enough that she caught a faint whiff of cinnamon sugar again off his skin.

Mira wanted him. Not just because she'd spent the last two months at a camp full of nothing but teenage girls, and he was the first man she'd seen unclothed in twice as many months. No, she wanted Sam because his chest was the most arousing and appealing she'd ever seen. She was drawn to his skin, yearned to rake her nails down the middle, and then circle her palms over his nipples, just to start. Touch wouldn't be enough. Tasting him, that would be next on the list. Licking every inch of that cinnamon sugar tan until he shivered beneath her tongue. Without conscious thought, Mira reached out a single finger and stroked a soft line down the side of his corded neck.

He jerked away, as if she'd trailed a red-hot skewer across his skin. "What are you doing?"

Good question. Making a fool out of herself? Making an already awkward situation ten times worse? Stroking a man she barely knew and could barely resist in the hopes he'd stroke her back? The red walls closed in on her. In a room this small, if she tried to look at anything besides Sam, she'd catch her red-faced reflection in the ebony-framed mirror. Neither visual appealed to her.

"Just wiping up some blood." Mira thrust her finger into a wad of paper towels, pretending to dry it. "Let's get you tidied up."

Embarrassment slowed her movements. She fumbled in the box, dropping the bottle of antiseptic spray on the floor. They both bent to pick it up. Mira's shoulder banged into Sam's knee, and he grabbed her arm to steady her. His palm seared her skin, big and rough and with a ridge of calluses at the base of his fingers. How good would that roughness feel, stroking across her breasts? God. She had to get out of this bathroom, away from the wall of naked sensuality that sucked every bit of air out of the tiny space.

"You have a shop next door?" Mira asked. Nice, innocuous chitchat. Her mother always said, when in doubt, make small talk. The sink acted as a handy barrier. As long as she stayed in front of it, she couldn't accidentally brush against his strong, muscular thighs. It strained her back to lean over far enough to clean his wound, but it was a small price to pay. Maybe ask Ivy to share one of her fancy yoga moves to stretch it out tomorrow.

"Not just me. Lyons Bakery belongs to my family." He shot her an inviting smile. "Come on over any time for a sugar rush."

Nooooo. Not fair. Nobody should be forced to work next to a bakery or a coffee shop. The temptation was too constant, too great. Mira itched to grab her planner and add *find a gym* to the top of her to-do list. "A family business? They say many hands make light work."

"Not so many, unfortunately. My parents used to run it, but Dad died a few years ago. Now I'm the only one to help out my mom. But if either of us needs to—" He broke off. Opened and closed his mouth, as though starting to speak but then re-choosing his words. "—take some personal time, it leads to long hours for the other one. Well, you run a shop. You know what I'm talking about."

Sam shifted, wincing as she dabbed at the edges of the cut. A few stitches might not be out of place, but she didn't want to insist on a trip to the E.R. and annoy him any further. Any scar would blend into his hairline, so as long as he kept it covered, it should be fine. He leaned an elbow on the sink. His hand floated onto her hip. To steady himself? Or something else? Something…flirtier? Warmth seeped into the sliver of skin between her shorts and shirt where his thumb rested.

"My sister's supposed to be here by now, pulling her weight."

"Where is she?" Mira asked.

He shrugged, sending a waterfall of ripples through his muscles. Mira caught her breath, then swallowed hard. "No idea. Somewhere in Europe. Depends on the day of the week, and which exotic accent catches her fancy. Sorry, I won't bore you with our family drama."

"Don't stop. It sounds like an interesting story." Any family drama interested her—as long as it wasn't *her* family. That's why she adored reality television.

Those shows gave her glimpses into other people's wildly messed-up or (less often) staidly normal lives. Mira hungered for family, since hers contributed almost nothing to her life.

"Interesting to an outsider. Nothing but a pain in the ass to live through."

"Doesn't everyone feel that way about their family?" Mira shook the bottle. "This might sting a little."

Sam caught her wrist, stopping her from spraying the antiseptic. Midnight-blue eyes locked on hers with the magnetic pull of a tractor beam. "If it does, will you blow on it?"

First the touching. His blunt fingertips gently curving into the top of her ass. Now…what *was* that? A come-on? An invitation? A biological response to the pheromones she must be pumping out at an astronomical rate? Or should she take it at face value, as a simple, teasing question with no seductive double entendre? Mira flipped through the options, didn't see any of them as viable enough to act on, and merely squirted him without further comment.

Predictably, like all men, he hissed and growled as if she'd lopped off a toe instead of just sterilized a cut. Mira slapped tape across a couple of fresh gauze pads and hustled out of the room. When he followed, he was still shirtless. Weren't bakers supposed to wear chef's coats? Or aprons?

Great. Now her mind went *there*. She pictured him completely naked. Lots of ripped muscles covered by velvety skin, except for where a long white apron covered the strategic bits. Mira paused at the kitchen counter, braced her palms on it and took a few deep breaths. This was the man who abandoned her at the second-largest airport in America, in the middle of a monsoon. This man who intruded into her store and completely ruined her first morning in her new little kingdom. And yet, none of those facts diminished her physical attraction to him in the slightest.

"What were you doing when I found you? Why are you here?"

Sam tossed his ruined shirt in the trash can by the sink. "We'll be working side by side. I wanted to smooth over our rough start from yesterday."

Sweet, but misdirected. "Mission not accomplished. Scaring me half to death doesn't go a long way to making me feel warm and fuzzy toward you."

"Trust me, I didn't intend to frighten you." Sam pointed at his bandage. "This wasn't in my plan for today. I brought you a present, a peace offering."

Who didn't like presents? Perhaps she had misjudged his apparent skulking. "I appreciate the gesture, but you don't have to bribe me into maintaining a professional relationship with a neighbor."

Sam reached under the counter, the same position as when she'd first entered the store. "I wanted to use one of your own napkins, since it is your first day here." He put a plate down in front of her, draped with a white napkin stamped with her store's red logo. "I hope this sweetens your feelings toward me. Enjoy."

Intrigued, and more than a little charmed, Mira lifted the corner of the napkin. Underneath sat the richest, most decadent-looking breakfast pastry she'd ever seen. It did not, however, appeal to her in the slightest. She dropped the napkin and pushed the plate back at him.

"Thank you, but I'll pass."

His eyebrows shot skyward. "You're kidding. On Saturday mornings, we have people lined up for twenty minutes waiting to buy one of these."

"Then I'm sure you won't have any trouble selling it today."

Sam shook his head, then whipped off the napkin. "You're new here, so you don't know that Lyons Bakery is famous for its triple-chocolate éclairs. We've been written up in national food magazines for these. Chocolate pastry, filled with cocoa and hazelnut pastry cream, and covered in a dark chocolate glaze." He pushed the plate back in front of her with an expectant nod.

It was like playing air hockey, but in slow motion. Mira shoved the plate with a tad more force so it slid almost past him. "It looks lovely. But I don't eat chocolate. Ever."

Staggering backward, Sam slammed into the refrigerator handle, and his openmouthed gape turned into a tight-lipped grimace. "You can't be serious."

"I don't like chocolate."

"But it's the food of the gods. Literally." He paced the narrow strip between appliances and counter. One hand rubbed at his still-bare chest, as if she'd punched him right in the sternum. "The Mayans honored a cacao god, Quetzalcoatl. The Aztecs used it as money, and Cortez took it to Spain, where the nobility used it as medicine. It spurs on the heart as an aphrodisiac, and can help prevent heart disease. It is an eight-billion-dollar industry worldwide. Everyone likes chocolate." As his argument gathered steam, his voice steadily rose. Sexily shirtless and eyes bright with enthusiasm, Sam became more irresistible every

second. It was all too easy to transpose his passionate state into a vision of him in bed, equally flushed
and missing more than just his shirt.

"I need to get to work. Thank you for stopping
by." Mira remembered his all-access pass. The last
thing she needed was Sam stirring up her hormones
with unscheduled visits. "Oh, could I have the key to
my store back?"

"What? Why?"

"So I don't accidentally take a chunk out of the
other side of your head. I'll be here every day to accept deliveries. You won't need to come over anymore."

Sam stalked around the counter until he loomed
over her, a breath away. "Our businesses don't just
coexist. The plan is to leave the door open between
here and the bakery. Your customers can purchase
desserts for their romantic picnics from us, and bakery customers will wander in and buy whatever romantic crap you're pushing that day."

Looked like he hadn't let go of the temper she'd
riled by turning down his éclair. Wow. The guy really
cared about chocolate. "We're not open yet. I don't
need random people wandering in while I'm doing inventory and organizing our carefully chosen romantic
crap. That's an open invitation to shoplift."

"Of course. Because people who want a dozen
cookies from me will get all wild on a sugar high,
come in here, stuff a foot-high vase down their pants
and try to sneak off with it?" Sam fished the key out
of his pocket and slammed it down. Every muscle in
his body, from his pecs to his biceps to his abs, were
as rigid as his clenched jaw. "Dark chocolate boosts

serotonin and releases endorphins, which lifts your mood. In other words, if you ate a truffle, you might not be such an uptight bitch. Welcome to the neighborhood."

Sam stalked out, slamming the connecting door to the bakery behind him. Wow. The sexy stud had a seriously short fuse. The mama's boy who blew off his promise to pick her up at the airport and barely apologized, then all but broke into her store actually had the nerve to call *her* names? Mira looked around at the empty shelves, stacks of boxes, and wondered if it was too late to find a different location for A Fine Romance.

THREE

CLIMBING THAT FOURTH flight of stairs to Ben and Ivy's roof deck reminded Sam he'd been on his feet since the wrong side of dawn. He'd almost given in to the temptation to stay home and fall asleep in front of a Cubs game. But the lovebirds were excited to show off their new nest, and it was rare at the height of wedding season for their whole group to have a night off. So he manned up, bringing a housewarming present of a six-pack of Goose Island beer for Ben and six kir royale truffles for Ivy.

"Welcome to Casa Westcott," Milo said, greeting him with a tray of drinks at the top of the stairs. Despite the August humidity, a white linen jacket topped off Milo's shirt and white slacks. Whenever he acted as bartender, he liked to dress the part, although Sam had yet to encounter a real bartender who tied a sequined white scarf around his neck.

"They're not married yet. Why assume Ivy'll take Ben's name?" Sam set his presents down on a glass-topped table.

"Because saying welcome to Casa Rhodes-Westcott doesn't have the same panache. You know I'm all about the panache."

"True." Flamboyant was Milo's middle name. The only time he dropped the swishy shtick was in their monthly poker games. There he chomped on a cigar, drank scotch straight and routinely took all of their money. Or at least he had until Ben joined their group.

"Have a gin rickey. It'll cool you down."

Sam looked at the sweating glass. Milo liked to experiment with girly drinks. Tonight's cocktail might be sweeter than Lyons Bakery's famous cherry fritters. A sugar-bomb drink pretty much guaranteed a hangover, and Sam was just getting over his headache from Mira's unwarranted attack.

"Try one." Milo fisted a hand on one hip and sighed. "I promise there's beer in the cooler to go with dinner."

"You said the magic words." He could drink one glass of anything as long as there was beer to wash it down. Too bad he couldn't hold his nose and throw it back like a shot of Jäger without hurting Milo's feelings. Sam took a cautious sip.

"Well?"

"Not bad. The lime juice curls the tongue enough to balance the simple syrup."

Another huff from the drama queen. "Trust a baker to analyze the sugar content. Most people would call it refreshing and delicious."

"So go hawk your wares to them." Sam grinned and walked away. He only made it a few more feet onto the deck before a bundle of fabric hit him in the chest.

"Got a wardrobe upgrade for you. It'll get you in a party mood." Ben Westcott flashed an evil grin. "Or it'll put you in the mood to drink heavily."

Sam looked at his friend. Although Ben spent his life behind a video camera, the women in their group swore he was gorgeous enough to pose in front of one. Sure, he was tall, with surfer-blond looks and lankiness. But Sam didn't usually spend any time thinking about how Ben looked. Tonight, though, he couldn't tear his eyes away from the party's host. He wore a bright turquoise shirt printed with rows of thatched umbrellas, tiki torches and crashing ocean surf. It was the tackiest, most garish piece of clothing he'd ever seen.

"Why the hell do you look like a reject from an Elvis movie?"

Ben grimaced and plucked the front of his shirt away from his body as though it was made of acid-dipped sandpaper. "Leftover favors from a Hawaiian-themed wedding Ivy did last weekend."

"Somebody forked over the cash to hand out shirts as favors?" The amount of money the über-rich were willing to waste constantly amazed Sam. He charged a fair price for his cakes and truffles, even though he knew good word of mouth meant he could probably ask twice as much. In fact, charging more might net him more business from the idiots who bought things just *because* they were expensive. The idiotic wealthy class pissed him off. Sam took another sip of the surprisingly tasty drink to cool down.

"For the guys. The girls got leis," Ben held up a hand, forestalling the inevitable, "and don't make the obvious joke, because I spent three days straight doing it. I'm done with leis."

Sam struggled to keep a straight face. "I hear that happens once you're engaged."

"Very funny. You won't be laughing once you put yours on." Ben slapped the back of his hand against the shirt Sam had caught one-handed.

"You're kidding." Setting his drink on the wooden railing, Sam unfolded the shirt. This one was toxic-waste green, and covered with hot-pink hibiscus flowers as big as his palm. "What have I ever done to you to deserve this?"

"Besides the fifty dollars you stole off my ace-high full house last month?"

God, that had felt good. He still remembered the look of utter shock that replaced the cocky grin on Ben's face when he laid down his cards. "Four of a kind always beats a full house. Period."

"But it never comes around. I'm supposed to feel secure and joyful with a full house."

Sam shrugged. "Keep telling yourself that. And keep your ugly shirt, too." He tried to hand it back, but Ben refused to take it.

"Sorry, but Ivy insists. To get everyone in 'a festive mood,'" he said, bending his fingers into quotation marks. "Humor her? Throw it on over your T-shirt, and then burn it tomorrow, for all I care. It's our first party in the new digs, and it means a lot to her."

"For Ivy," Sam agreed. He loved her like a sister, and as long as all the other guys would look equally ridiculous, he could deal.

Ben pointed at the still-fierce sun, which had turned Chicago as steamy as a guy's pits after basketball. The humidity made rolling out his trademark fondant icing a struggle for Sam, even with the air-conditioning blasting. "Since we're dressing you, do you want to borrow a baseball hat? There isn't much shade up here on the deck."

One more reason to be mad at the crazy-hot girl next door. And that's what pissed him off the most.

Mira was annoying and had a stick up her ass bigger than the Sears tower, but she was gorgeous. Sam couldn't deny that despite her peevishness and the two-inch dent she put in his skull, he wanted to wrap his hands around that curtain of dark brown hair and kiss her until the only thing out of those lips was his name. If he hadn't been covered in blood and woozy, he'd have pulled her onto his lap in that bathroom and made his move.

"No can do." As he pulled on the shirt, Sam turned sideways to show the raised scab across his head.

A long, low whistle split the air. Gibson Moore, looking like a suave idiot in tailored suit pants, suspenders and a Hawaiian shirt with sunsets splashed across it, pointed at Sam's cut. "Looks painful. Did a dissatisfied bride come at you with a cake knife?"

"Sam doesn't leave any women dissatisfied, clients or otherwise," said Milo with a wink and a hip shake.

Truer words were never spoken—although Sam didn't need Milo, of all people, talking about his prowess in the sack. "A client would be easier to handle. This is the handiwork of my new neighbor."

Ben coughed, spraying his gin rickey across the deck. "Mira Parrish split your head open like a cantaloupe?"

"Yeah."

"I don't believe it. I've met her. Heard plenty more stories. Mira comes from old-school money. She's got class up the wazoo."

"She's uptight, snippy and is convinced the world revolves around her. This woman wouldn't know real class if it bit her on the nose." As he warmed to the topic of the most annoying woman ever, Sam began to pace. "She tried to knock me out. Worst of all, she doesn't eat chocolate." He threw his hands up in the air. "There's got to be something wired wrong in her head, like a serial killer. Chocolate makes everyone happy. Or maybe she really does like it, and just wanted to piss me off?"

His friends stood in a loose circle, looking at him with identical squints of confusion.

"That's the most words I've heard you put together at once in the four months I've known you," said Ben.

"Well, I've known him for four *years*, and I've never heard him rant like that," Milo piped in, extending the pitcher for refills. Sam didn't know when he'd drained his drink, but he did know he needed more. Or maybe just straight shots. Four in a row, one for every day of irritation and frustration he'd suffered since meeting Mira.

"She coshed you on the head—" Gib's British accent made even a bloody wound sound like a costume ball invitation.

"With a crystal vase. So sure, I guess that makes it classy." Sam drained his second glass in one long gulp. Why'd Ben stick up for Mira? *She's* not the one who walked away from their conversation with a scalp lac. Where was the sympathy for the pal who kept them in a steady supply of muffins most mornings? Ben slipped in at least once a week for a slice of cake, too. Didn't that earn him a little loyalty?

Gib waved his hand as if erasing Sam's comment off a chalkboard. "—but you're most upset that she doesn't care for chocolate?"

"Yeah. It's just wrong." In so many ways. Sure, he knew people who were allergic to it, or dropped it for Lent or a diet. All that made sense. But to flat-out not *like* it? Impossible. Might as well say she didn't like oxygen, or water. And yeah, Sam knew he was probably overreacting. He'd let her pissy attitude get under his skin. So if Mira said the sky was blue, he'd probably argue back that it was really zebra-striped. Because chocolate wasn't just his livelihood. It was his passion, his religion. How could she dismiss it, with a cool nod and a glare that dripped off her nose like an icicle? It made no sense.

"So is equating her to a serial killer for not liking chocolate," Gib pointed out.

Gib called every couple of months, needing an emergency cake at the fancy hotel he managed. Next time, Sam might not be so quick to answer the call. Where'd he get off taking her side when he hadn't even met Mira yet? "She *did* hit me. Maybe she's got violent tendencies."

"*Why* did she hit you with the vase? What the hell did you do?" Ben spread his hands at his waist, palms up. "Ivy's going to grill me for details. Easier for you to spill to me than to have her hammer away at you."

Sam propped his forearms on the railing and stared at the city skyline. He could just catch a glimpse of Lake Michigan. Too bad they weren't close enough to catch the breeze off the water. Sweat already glued both shirts to the small of his back. "She thought I broke into her store," he muttered.

Behind him, the guys all laughed. Milo's titter rang out a little higher, and stopped first as he broke into a barrage of questions. "Didn't Ivy give you a key? What did you do—throw a brick through the window? Trash the place?"

The stench of inevitability grew stronger. His friends wouldn't lay off until he spilled everything. Sam hoped the brats and burgers were as good as the lemon meringue pie he'd left down in the kitchen. He hadn't planned on being forced to sing for his supper. This interrogation would cost Ben no less than three brats *and* a burger.

"I spooked her. You know, her first time in the store. Mira didn't know I had a key. It was dark. But she didn't give me a chance to say anything—just came in swinging." Sam spun around, full of righteous indignation.

One of Gib's eyebrows shot skyward faster than a fly ball at Wrigley Field. "A woman alone, in an unfamiliar city, wouldn't pause to ask a burglar for his identification and three references before defending herself. I'd say she behaved sensibly." Gib swirled the ice cubes in his glass. "In fact, this Mira Parrish sounds like a delightful handful. I can't wait to meet her. Is she attractive?"

"Hands off," Sam snarled.

Gib backed up a couple steps. "Whoa. You called the lady a psycho. Forgive me for assuming that means you don't want to sleep with her. I thought she was fair game."

The guy had a point. Especially since Sam wasn't sure why he'd reacted so strongly. Just because Mira had all the right parts didn't mean he'd take his life in his hands and try to rub up against that short-fused stick of dynamite in a dress. But he wanted the conversation to be done, so he pulled out tried-and-true ammunition.

"You don't sleep with women. You pop them like

Tic-Tacs. Since we all have to work together, you probably shouldn't pull your usual screw-and-scram routine."

Gibson Moore had elevated the casual hookup to an art form. They had a running joke it was a good thing he managed the Cavendish Grand. That way he'd always have a steady stream of new women, along with four hundred and twenty beds to choose from with clean sheets every day. Amazing how fast women dropped their panties for a guy who sounded like Prince William.

"Follow your own advice, Lyons," Ben warned. "Sleeping with the girl next door's never a good idea. Sleeping with a business associate's even worse."

"Dangerous as juggling best friends in your bed." Gib winked. "Trust me on that one."

"Ivy needs Mira focused and happy to get her shop off the ground. Don't mess with that plan." Ben soft-balled a punch into Sam's arm.

"No worries," Sam said. "She hasn't spoken to me in three days. Even though I only scared her because I was trying to apologize. The lady can sure hold a grudge."

"Wait, there's more? You've had two altercations with the untouchable Ms. Parrish?" Gib asked.

Of course Milo chimed in with the missing piece. At Aisle Bound, he was equal parts office manager and gossip sniffer. "He forgot to pick her up at O'Hare. She got caught in that massive storm on Sunday. *She* was pissed. *Daphne* and *Ivy* were pissed. Many snarky things were said about Sam at our staff meeting. You are deep in the doghouse, buddy."

"Damn it, I apologized. More than once." Sam

knew he fucked up. Didn't even mind apologizing. But since he had...repeatedly...he expected Mira to get over it. "My mom needed me. It was only about twenty percent forgetting, and eighty percent re-prioritizing." Again, the circle of confused squints aimed his way. From the unanimous disapproval of his friends, Sam could either think two things. That they'd all turned in their balls in exchange for the fluorescent shirts, or maybe, just maybe, he'd jumped the gun on his assessment of Mira. After all, he did feel bad about leaving her at O'Hare. Maybe he should forget about trying to smooth over their rocky start, and make an entirely fresh start.

Ben shook his head. "Sam, you need to cut the apron strings."

"Just because your dad died doesn't mean you have to fill in all his footsteps." Gib used his straw for emphasis, flicking it in the air as he made each point. "Bad enough you had to take over his job at the bakery. You don't have to give up your life to take care of your mom, too. She's a tough old broad."

"Like Ethel Merman," piped in Milo.

Sam didn't need anyone telling him how to deal with his mother. Especially people who didn't know the whole story. "Look, you may have crossed the entire Atlantic Ocean to get away from your family, but not everyone needs that distance." Gib and his family were a complicated mess. Nobody knew the whole story, since he refused to talk about it. And from what they could tell, he refused to talk to his family, too. Not the kind of person who should be giving advice on dealing with parents.

Dunking the straw, Gib used it to blow a stream of

liquid at Sam. "Cool it, Lyons. Don't lash out at me with your sublimated maternal resentment."

"You sound like a psychiatrist. Did you screw a shrink last night?" Milo asked with a jab to Gib's ribs.

Sam didn't wait for him to answer. He didn't care. "I don't have resentment. Except toward Mira. But I hear you, okay?" Sam handed his empty glass to Milo. It was good to hang with friends, even when they annoyed the shit out of him. Who else could you trust to dish it out, and then laugh with you over beers? "God, I'm glad Mira's not here tonight. I need a break from her wall of silence. All that churned-up, buttoned-up energy of hers is probably seeping through the walls and souring my whipping cream. Plus, I've got a twitch from ducking every time I hear her walk by." He curled in his shoulders and fig-leafed his hands, as though protecting himself from an errant tennis ball.

Ben snickered. "Then you'd better hope you wore your cup tonight, 'cause she just got here."

Sam twisted to face the door. "What?" Sure enough, she stood at the top of the stairs, smiling as Ivy dropped a pink-and-white lei over her head. Mira looked amazing. He'd caught glimpses of her the past couple of days, always in grungy clothes appropriate for unpacking. But tonight she'd dolled herself up, and the effect rattled his knees. She wore a short white skirt that showed off miles and miles of tan legs that ended in some wedgy white shoe. Milo probably knew what to call it. Her blue-and-white-striped top clung to every curve like it was painted on.

His mouth went dry. And she'd left all that dark hair down and free, hanging down to her breasts. God, he wanted to touch it, see if it was as soft as it looked. He remembered from when she bandaged him how it smelled. Like fresh-cut grapefruit, sweet and bright. Maybe she tasted that way, too. Not that he'd ever find out. "Why'd you invite her?"

"Uh, the same reason we invited you. Longtime friend sound like a familiar category?" Ben elbowed him as he loped over to the barbecue. The other guys followed, leaving Sam alone to bear the wrath of women wronged. Ivy and Mira bore down on him. The swingy white sundress didn't make Ivy look any less formidable because of the serious frown topping off the outfit.

"I heard you got beat up by a girl, Sam. Is that true?" Ivy asked.

Crap. Now that they were closer, he saw the giggle peeking out of her hazel eyes. Mira pressed her lips together, not out of anger, but also trying to hide a smirk. Great party. First the guys ganged up on him, then the girls. What would happen next—maybe an overconfident pigeon would swoop down and steal one of his brats right out of the bun?

"Let's be clear. Mira attacked me from behind with a weapon. It's not like she took me down in three rounds of a cage match."

Ivy crossed her arms. "Sounds to me like the sour grapes of a sore loser."

"Oh, I'm sore, all right." Once more, Sam turned to show off his scab.

Both women gasped. Mira's hand flew to her mouth. "Sam, I'm so sorry. You really should've let me take you to a hospital. I'll bet it did need stitches."

The tremble in her voice marked her concern as sincere. It made all the difference. His resentment dropped from a full boil to barely lukewarm. "Don't worry about it. I didn't have any plans to be a scalp model."

"Mira told me the whole story. I'm disappointed in you, Sam. Working right next door with Mira, I'd hoped you'd be a friendly resource she could call on. Offer her the strong, silent shoulder you always offer me—and instead you've already got two big strikes against you." Ivy circled him, giving him the once-over from head to toe.

Sam was willing to concede he hadn't rolled out his A game. "First impressions are rough."

"However, you are wearing the party shirt, which makes me super happy. So I'll give you one last chance to redeem yourself."

Why did women always make men jump through hoops? Men would grunt, nod, and the whole thing would be over. Ivy could be one hell of a whip cracker. "Christ, I brought pie. Your favorite, as a matter of fact, even though Ben begged me to make him chocolate pecan. Doesn't that earn me any points?"

"Oh, I saw the pie on the counter. That's why I didn't start by whacking you across the ass."

"Get rid of Ben and we'll revisit that scenario," he said, wriggling his eyebrows and leering. Sure enough, it sent her into a peal of laughter.

"In your dreams, Mr. Lyons."

"Every night, Ms. Rhodes." Out of the corner of his eye, Sam noticed Mira following their interplay very closely. Didn't she have a sense of humor at all?

"That's the soon-to-be Mrs. Westcott," Ben corrected, throwing an arm around Ivy's waist. "How about you stop hitting on my woman?"

"Hard to do. You snagged a good one." Although he didn't know how Ben dealt with Ivy's obsession with planning and lists. She probably made a list of what order to move through foreplay.

Ivy melted against Ben's side like thick caramel over toffee. "Here's the deal, Sam. I want you to show Mira the city on Saturday."

"Can't do it." He hated playing tour guide. Mira hated him. Talk about a recipe for disaster.

"Why not? Your mom told me that you're free on Saturday afternoon."

Mom needed a lesson in the interpretation of the word *free*. She had a bad habit of thinking his free time equaled the perfect opportunity to re-tar her roof, or paint the kitchen. Volunteering him to babysit Mira didn't sound like any less work. "I've got three weddings Friday and a bar mitzvah on Saturday morning. I'll be comatose by noon. Ask Daphne when she gets here."

"Nope. Daphne's got her own string of weddings with me this weekend. Think of this as your second chance at a first impression. Show Mira Chicago. I need her to be very happy with her choice to move here and help me out. Make her fall in love with it the way we all did."

Sam's idea of a fresh start was saying hello in the mornings, and *not* offering her a chocolate éclair. "That's a tall order for one afternoon."

"Don't be an idiot," Ben snapped. "Do the Shedd Aquarium, or the Field Museum. Take a carriage ride down the Magnificent Mile. Hell, go to a street festival."

"Excuse me, but did I suddenly turn invisible?

You're all discussing my Saturday as though I don't have a say in it." Mira glared at each one of them in turn. It was an expression already quite familiar to Sam. "Perhaps I'd like to arrange my own plans."

The fact that she hated the idea as much as he did cheered Sam up a bit. At least they were finally on the same page. "You're right. Twenty-first century, free will, a woman's right to choose—all good things."

"Individually, yes. But not in this case." Ivy flipped into full wedding-planner mode, which turned her into a velvet-covered steamroller. "Mira, you're wonderfully independent, but you need to learn to lean on other people. Chicago's too big to take on by yourself. Let Sam show you around. Time together away from work will lead to better working conditions when you're coexisting five feet away from each other. Do this for the good of the store." Ivy finished with an imploring smile that didn't at all reveal she knew Mira and Sam had no choice but to fall in with her plan. Everyone always did. If she ever used her persuasive powers for evil, the world would be in big trouble.

"Fine. Anything for the store." Mira turned to Sam with a smile less believable than a crisp three-dollar bill. "I'm all yours."

Her words blasted an image into his head with the focused heat of a crème brûlée torch. Mira, back in that sexy red bathroom at her store, only this time she straddled his lap. Hands on his knees, she leaned back, thrusting her breasts at him, with a what-are-you-waiting-for look inviting him from beneath half-lowered eyelids to take everything she offered. The warmth in between her widespread legs seeped into his skin. Sam reached out to grab her waist and pull her closer—

And realized he'd actually reached out with both hands toward Mira. Here, on the deck, in front of everyone. Good thing Ben foisted that extra shirt on him, because it flapped low enough to cover the rock-hard bulge straining the front of his shorts. Nothing short of a jump into Lake Michigan would put out the fire she'd unknowingly lit. Wait. There was the solution to his problem.

Smoothly, he kept reaching forward as if he'd intended to all along, and took Mira's hands. They were as soft as he remembered, and it took all his concentration not to rub his thumb in small circles over the top. "Let me take you on the architectural river cruise. You'll get to see all the historic buildings and end up in Lake Michigan with a view of the city that can't be beat."

"Sam, that's perfect," said Ivy.

So perfect. He'd get to sit down the whole time, which was halfway to napping in his book. The tour guide would keep up a steady chatter during the whole boat ride, which meant he wouldn't have to say a word. "I'll pick you up at two-thirty."

"Oh, no. I'm not falling for that again." Mira snatched back her hands. "Besides, I need to start learning how to get around this city on the El. I'll meet you there."

Yep, a serious grudge-holder. Their fresh start was already tarnished. He hoped Ivy still gave him full credit for trying. "Fine," Sam snapped. "Take the red line to Lake Street. Once you get off, walk two blocks to the dock at the Michigan Avenue bridge."

Mira inclined her head into a nod stiffer than one of his wedding cake dowels. "It's a date." Without waiting for a response, she broke away to greet Daphne.

Sam waved his hands in a crisscross pattern. "Did you hear that? What the hell, Ivy? This isn't a date. Nobody offered a date. There's a whole set of expectations built into a date. He," with a vicious stab of his finger in Ben's direction, "specifically ordered me not to date Mira."

For the third time in less than an hour, identical looks of confusion targeted Sam. Ben threw in a bemused head tilt. "Wow. How many of your own doughnuts did you eat today? You're jacked higher than a kid who mainlined a whole pack of Pixy Stix."

"It's nothing more than a figure of speech," Ivy soothed, with a gentle pat on his arm. "Mira has no intention of dating you, and absolutely no expectations."

"Good." Although he didn't care for how quickly Ivy ruled him out. She could do worse, right? Sam might not have fresh notches on his bedpost every week like Gib, but he knew how to treat a woman right. Did Ivy think he wasn't good enough for her friend? Her super classy, apparently wealthy friend? Was Mira a blue-blooded snob who'd turn up her pert nose at his flour- and chocolate-covered hands?

Well, she'd better leave her uppity attitude at home on Saturday. He'd show her such a good time she wouldn't know what hit her. By the time they got off that boat, Mira Parrish would be head over heels with Chicago, and label Sam Lyons her new best friend. Her report back to Ivy would be filled with awe and wonder. Then all of his friends would get off his back about being nice to the new girl.

And he could get back to worrying about his real problems: namely his mother, his sister, and how his entire life might be decided in the next two months.

FOUR

BE NICE. BE CHARMING. Sam repeated the words over
and over in his head as he paced the length of the
ship. For some reason, Mira brought out the worst
in him. Weird, since he'd always thought of himself
as a pretty laid-back guy. It took a lot to ruffle his
feathers. Or, for the past week, a little over a hundred
pounds of smoking-hot brunette with eyes as blue as
the pilot light in his oven. Maybe if he concentrated
on her very agreeable looks, he could ignore whatever
disagreeable things came out of her mouth.

"Ahoy!" Mira waved at him from the dock. Sam
nodded at the captain, indicating she was with him.
The man helped her across the gangplank. Then Sam
noticed him stare another minute at her ass as she
boarded. Not that he blamed him. Mira looked adorable in tight white jeans and a bright red shirt that
dipped low over her breasts. A ponytail swung back
and forth out the back of a ball cap. Good thing she
hadn't worn something fancy and expensive. High
heels like she'd worn the other night and the pitch of
a boat didn't go together well. He'd give her credit for
dressing sensibly. Maybe this cruise wouldn't turn
out so badly.

Mira gestured at the gangplank, then back to his
spot at the rail. "I know I said I could get here on

my own, but really? You couldn't wait for me on the dock?"

Not even a hello before she laid into him. This voyage was going to feel as long as the entire three-year run of *Gilligan's Island*. "Expecting a red carpet, princess? Maybe a glass of champagne and a welcome from the cruise director? It's a sightseeing boat, not a honeymoon cruise."

"The boat is fine." She tipped down her sunglasses to glare at him over the rims. "However pie-in-the-sky it might be, I was hoping for some common courtesy. Since you agreed to be my escort on this excursion, I assumed we'd board together." As she snarked at him, Mira widened her stance and planted her hands on her hips. "Isn't us getting to know each other Ivy's grand yet transparent scheme for today? Because I'm more than capable of taking in the sights by myself."

If only she would. Sam shrugged. "You're here now. We'll cast off any minute. What's the problem?"

His calm seemed to only provoke her more. Mira swung her arm wide, first at the rail, then back to him. "It's not like you have a track record of being reliable with me. If I hadn't seen you at the rail, I would've stood down there, wasting my entire afternoon waiting for you. Oh, and wasted thirty dollars I can't spare when you'd already purchased the tickets."

"You're welcome, by the way." Come tax time, he'd deduct both tickets as a business expense. She'd made it damn clear there wasn't an ounce of pleasure to be had this afternoon.

Basic manners finally poked a hole through her abrasive demeanor. Mira sucked in a short breath, then a long, slow exhale. "Sorry. I appreciate the ticket. But why on earth didn't you wait for me?"

Sam tried to turn his gritted teeth into more of a grin than a grimace. He pointed to the rows of folding chairs along the top deck. "I wanted to save us the best seats. Got here half an hour ago to score them. On a day this nice they tend to sell out, and people are stuck sitting indoors."

"Oh." She looked down at the sweater she clutched with both hands. "Thank you."

"My pleasure." Sam put his hand in the small of her back to guide her. Spine as rigid as a granite countertop, Mira walked silently beside him. "Here we are. Smack dab in the middle for a smooth ride." He picked up the backpack and baseball cap holding their place.

"I'm sorry," she blurted out as she sank onto the plastic chair. "Reserving our seats was very thoughtful. I shouldn't have snapped at you."

Snapped? He'd feel less beat up if the entire Bears defense had tackled him. "Why should today be any different?" Then it hit him. "Oh. Did Ivy give you the same lecture about getting along that she gave me?"

Mira tilted her head, perusing him from under the brim of her cap. "No. I'm delightful. I get along with everybody."

He'd believe it if he ever saw it. "Right." Sam stretched the word out slowly. "You dumped a drink on me and hit me over the head because we've taken such a shine to each other so far."

"Mitigating circumstances, both times." She dismissed the encounters with a lazy hand wave as she hooked her sunglasses in a belt loop. "Did Ivy really have to order you to get along with me?"

"Maybe." How much should he admit? After talking to the guys, he'd been willing to take the lion's share of the blame for his two less than great encounters with Mira. On the other hand, she'd just verbally eviscerated him. That kind of attack made a guy unwilling to fall on the sword. "Let's just say I agreed a fresh start might be in order. But I'll take an extra dollop of delightful if you're offering it today."

Mira smiled. For the first time, she smiled full force straight at him. Good thing he was sitting down, because the power of it would've dropped him on his ass. Her face transformed with that smile, and her eyes lit up. She looked genuinely happy, approachable and downright beautiful. A smile like that could practically be weaponized. It could make men leap tall buildings, or at least feel like they could, as long as she kept smiling.

"You know what?" She stretched out her arms along the backs of the seats and lifted her face to the sun. "It is a spectacular summer day. This morning's shower cleared out most of the humidity, and I'm on a river on my first day off from my fabulous new job. Delightful doesn't begin to describe it."

Something was off. Sure, he liked this version of Mira about a thousand percent better than the one who'd boarded the ship five minutes ago. But the change was too abrupt, as though she'd flicked a switch. While Sam had as little understanding as most men of a woman's mind, it was obvious something was off. He'd rather deal with it now than spend the afternoon braced for the next unpredictable mood swing.

"What's wrong?" he asked. "When you bit my head

off without meaning to—was there another reason? Did you get turned around on the El and have to backtrack a few stops?"

"No. The city of Chicago didn't invent public transportation, you know. It isn't that complicated."

Okay, now her sass was back, but at an acceptable level. "Spill," he ordered.

Her prim and proper side took the lead and straightened in her seat, crossing her ankles. "We're practically strangers. It wouldn't be appropriate for me to burden you with my problems."

"Sounds like a line from a soap opera." His mother kept a tiny set in the back of the bakery just to stay current with her soaps. The number of times she manufactured an excuse to hustle to the kitchen and catch a few minutes astounded him. Whenever possible, Sam turned it to C-SPAN, but a lot of daytime drama had trickled into his brain nonetheless. "Look, everyone has problems. They tend to get better if you share them."

Mira shifted again. She fiddled with the bill of her cap, then tucked her hands under her thighs. The engines rumbled to life, but the noise didn't fill the empty thought balloon hanging over her head. As they pulled into the grayish-green center of the Chicago River, the other fifty passengers cheered and clapped. And still Sam waited. The sound system let out an earsplitting whine. After a couple of thumps on the microphone, the guide started his practiced spiel. Facts, figures and historical tidbits came fast and furious.

"My parents called," Mira said in a quiet voice.

That was her big mood-killer? Sam worked elbow

to elbow with his mom ten hours a day, and he didn't go around biting off people's heads. Not even when said mother offered up his only free afternoon to babysit the snippy new girl. "Oh, the horror."

"Obviously you and your mother have a close relationship." She slid him a knowing, sidelong glance. "Maybe too close, according to Gib."

"I object. Hearsay." Everyone said the British were reserved and tight-lipped. So how come Gib flapped his jaws nonstop? The man was almost as bad a gossip as Milo. They both could chitchat the girls in their group under the table.

"Well, consider yourself lucky. Not everyone enjoys that level of closeness." Mira looked away again. Was it an interest in the glass-and-steel skyscrapers along the water's edge, or simply a desire not to look at him? "I don't get along with my parents. At all. And I assure you, the feeling is mutual."

"That's too bad." Sam couldn't imagine living like that. His family had always been so tight-knit. The bottom dropped out of his world when his dad died, and they were all still struggling two years later to pick up the pieces. Out of that encompassing sadness, the one bright spot was that he and his mom grew even closer. The flip side was his worsening relationship with his sister, Diana. She who was the black hole currently sucking his life and his future away. "Do you have any brothers or sisters?"

"Nope. The family's hopes and dreams are all riding on me. Or, if you believe my parents, the hopes and dreams were buried a few years ago under the crushing disappointment I turned out to be. They call every six months or so to layer on the guilt. It never goes well. I usually dive for ice cream or wine as soon as they hang up." She flashed him another determined smile. "But today, I get to go on a boat ride instead."

"No reason to skip a good coping mechanism." Sam dug in his pack. He produced two plastic glasses and what Gib had promised was a more than decent bottle of Riesling. "I brought provisions."

"I'm impressed." She took the glasses so he could pour.

He paused after filling only one glass. "I should probably check before I ply you with alcohol. Do you know if you get seasick?"

Mira sipped quickly from the filled glass, as if concerned he'd take it back. "No worries in that department. I got my sea legs before I could walk. We'd yacht around the Côte d'Azur or the Greek islands over spring break. What I liked better, though, were the summers at our house on the Cape when I raced sailboats."

"Wow." Sam almost dropped the wine bottle. They weren't from two different worlds. They were from two different universes. He recorked it and stowed his bag below his seat. Then he took a long, slow swallow to buy time while he recalculated everything she'd done and said so far.

When Ben mentioned at the party that Mira came from old money, he'd dismissed the information. Coming from money wasn't the same as having it now, in this century. Chicago was chock-full of people related to railroad or stockyard barons. Thanks to wars and the Depression, all that many in this generation had left were a bunch of swanky stories. But Mira sounded like she was loaded. Hell, yachting and summer houses? Make that wipes-her-ass-with-hundred-dollar-bills loaded.

He hadn't started the day expecting them to have much to chat about. Now Sam was positive they had less than nothing in common. Aside from a single connecting door between their shops. And how long could you talk about a door?

Mira elbowed him. "What?"

No point dancing around it. "You're crazy rich, aren't you?"

"You mean you didn't know?"

Surprisingly, she looked embarrassed. Since when didn't the rich love to brag about themselves? Sam met new clients every week who insisted on bragging how many thousands of dollars the flowers and the photographer and the dress cost before they'd pipe down long enough to sample his gourmet wedding cakes. In his experience, the bigger the price tag, the more they wanted to tell everyone. It drove him nuts. He far preferred the everyday bakery clientele, who came in for cookies or a birthday tart. They always had a smile, and bothered to ask after his mom if she wasn't around. Real people, not walking bank accounts who measured everything by their net worth.

Sam scratched the back of his neck. "How would I know something like that? You don't walk around with a giant green dollar sign across your back."

Wine sloshed over the edge of her glass, and he nipped it out of her unsteady hands. Mira's words tumbled out so fast he could barely keep up. "I thought you all knew. Daphne said Ivy told her all these stories about me over the years—where I went and what I did."

"I'm a guy. There's every chance Ivy mentioned you and I tuned it out. Ivy talks a lot. If I paid attention to everything she said, my brain would've filled up two weeks after I met her."

Her cheeks reddened. Mira bit her bottom lip, but it still trembled. Embarrassment morphed into— oh God, was she about to cry? Sam panicked. He'd brought wine and sunscreen, not Valium and a box of tissues. Then he noticed all the heads swiveled in their direction, rather than facing out at the historic architecture along the riverbank.

"Come with me." Sam took her slender wrist and led her down the stairs to the very front of the boat. It gave them privacy, aside from the circling seagulls. Plus, the gusty wind at the prow might whip away those tears hovering on her lashes. He couldn't tell if she wanted to talk about it or not. Should he leave her in peace and retreat to the upper deck? Christ, if Ivy found out he made her friend cry, his life wouldn't be worth two cents. How the heck did you comfort someone who yachted around the world?

Mira shifted out of his grip to hang on to the railing with both hands. "I'm so sorry."

Not at all what he expected to hear. "For what?"

"For sounding like an idiot. I never should've mentioned those trips. But I figured that for once I didn't have to hide my background. The cat was already out of the bag."

"Mira, you don't have to hide who you are. You don't have to hide anything."

"Yes, I do. Trust me. I've been doing it for years. Do you think I didn't see the expression on your face? The disbelief, followed by an immediate layer of glacial frost? The automatic *she must think she's too good for me* reaction I've encountered a thousand times? When people immediately stop seeing me and only see money?"

Sam didn't know what to say. She was right. Once he figured out her net worth hovered near the level of a small country's GNP, it put a filter on everything Mira said. That filter was based on his experience with the über-wealthy, as well as stories from his friends. Gib's job as manager of the swankiest hotel in town provided an endless fodder of bad attitudes coupled with over-the-top excess.

It was easy to write off an entire social group—until one of them stood before you, sniffling and teary. It was also dead wrong. His mother would probably lecture him for two days straight if she found out he'd been such a judgmental prick. Sam passed over the paper napkin he'd grabbed from his pack. In that odd way of all women, Mira dabbed the corners of her eyes, and then underneath.

"Ivy never cared about my background. She never made a big deal about it. Daphne cracked jokes, so I knew she'd be cool." With a head shake that sent her ponytail horizontal into the wind, Mira's spine straightened back to its familiar, ramrod position. "I guess I shouldn't have leapt to the assumption the rest of their friends could handle it so well."

An hour ago Sam would've slapped back at her high-handed insult. But now he'd seen a glimpse of the complicated, vulnerable woman beneath the ice princess facade. Worse, he knew he deserved the dig. His response had nothing to do with possible recrimination from Ivy for making her friend cry. It had everything to do with his genuine regret at hurting Mira. He cupped his hands lightly around her upper arms.

"You're right."

Her toned muscles tensed beneath his palms. "What?"

"I made a snap judgment. It was stupid. I'm sorry." Thick-lashed blue eyes widened at his words, but he couldn't tell if it was from surprise or disbelief. Funny how her eyes were the same color as the miles of lake surrounding them. A man could drown in eyes that deep blue. "You don't deserve to be judged on anything more than who you are, right now, in front of me."

At that, her biceps softened. Her entire demeanor softened, and even her lips fell into an open circle. "Oh."

Sam wiped away the last teardrop glistening on her lashes. As his thumb grazed the softness of her skin, he couldn't resist feathering the back of his knuckles down her cheek. It made those bright red lips purse into a tighter circle, that drew him like a tempting target. One that drove away all thoughts of why this might be the worst idea ever. He dipped his head and kissed her.

It only took a second to realize one kiss wouldn't be nearly enough. Mira's lips were cool from the wind and spray at first, but quickly warmed beneath his. Soft and pliable, they melded against his the same way her body leaned into him. Eagerly he wrapped his arms around her waist, drawing her even closer. It lined everything up in a way that jacked his desire from hot to supernova. He bracketed her legs with his, making sure to keep contact with their long, smooth length. It made it easier to turn her, angle her back against the rail. He caught one last glimpse of those alluring eyes before they fluttered shut.

"This is…" she whispered, barely able to be heard over the slap of the water against the hull.

Sam didn't like where that sentence might be going, so he kissed her again. "…terrific," he said.

Not satisfied with slow nibbles, Sam deepened the kiss. She tasted sweeter than his honey truffles. Mira moaned as his tongue swirled, learning the secrets of her mouth. Learning just where to apply pressure, where to linger that made her clutch at his back. Her long nails dug through the thin cotton of his shirt, but he didn't care. Sam relished the proof he'd roused her. All he wanted was to seduce more moans, more sexy little gasps out of her.

He wrapped his hand around her ponytail and tugged her head to the side. There, on the side of her neck, he licked at the spot where her pulse fluttered against the surface in a rapid triple time that matched his own. Mira wriggled, a move that threatened to pop his dick right through his shorts. The way she flowed against him, with the sinuous ease of perfectly tempered melted chocolate, made him want to drop to the deck, rip off all of her clothes and bury himself deep inside her. Another few minutes, and he wouldn't have a choice in the matter. His below-the-belt brain would take over completely if they kept up this level of foreplay.

Hell, he hadn't even touched her breasts yet. And that was a treat he refused to skip or rush. Or short-change her the pleasure he had every intention of bestowing. No, they wouldn't have sex until she begged.

Until she wrapped those chorus-girl legs around his waist and joined them herself. Until he'd worked her into such a frenzy that she quivered at the touch of a single finger, and screamed his name to the heavens as he lapped at her—

Obnoxiously loud, the ship's foghorn split the air. Mira's eyes flew open. Her arms dropped to her sides.

"Don't worry. Nothing's wrong. The captain's just saying hello to the bridge operator." He eased back a bit so she could take in the first of a series of high drawbridges that spanned the river. "It's a waterway tradition here in Chicago. Like how they kiss under bridges in Venice, but not nearly as fun." Sam cupped her cheek, then traced her generous bottom lip with his thumb. "And speaking of kisses, where were we?"

Mira twisted her head away. Her ponytail lightly slapped his cheek. "Oh, I don't know. Out of our minds, perhaps?"

How did she do it? How did she burrow under his skin like a fire ant with just a sentence? "Don't do that. Don't pretend for a second you aren't as revved up as I am right now." He lowered his hand from her waist to her sweetly curved ass and squeezed. "Or do you need me to prove it?" Sure enough, she twitched, grinding her hips into his.

"No. Stop that!" Mira pushed at his chest, breathless. "Enough already."

"You don't mean that."

"For now, I do," she hissed. "Don't be an idiot. With moves as smooth as yours, you must know full well how effective a kisser you are."

"Effective? Way to damn me with faint praise."

Sam made sure not to let a smug smile get any further than his eyes. But he knew he had her.

She rolled her eyes, but stopped pushing him away. "Okay, you were fabulous. Will that do? Your lips deserve a gold medal. Your technique is flawless. Sam Lyons should be listed as a must-do attraction on all the Chicago sightseeing maps."

"That's more like it."

"What I meant was that we were out of our minds to grope each other on a fully packed boat. I think our fellow passengers wanted to take in the sights, not a sex show."

"Trust me, no one can see us. Except maybe the captain, and he deserves a little excitement. Poor guy pilots in the same straight line three times a day. Must be like throwing a bowling ball with the bumpers up."

Mira pointed off to the side, where two tricked-out powerboats bobbed very close. Both were full of water-skiers in trunks and minuscule bikinis, clapping, hooting and waving at Mira and Sam. "I don't want one of them to video us. With my luck they'd post it on the web and it'd go viral by the time we docked. I'm quite sure that's not the sort of free publicity Ivy wants me to drum up for the store."

"What happened to *there's no such thing as bad publicity?*" But Sam saw her point. And he backed off a few steps, leaning against the wheelhouse with his legs crossed at his ankles. He didn't really want to be the feature of the day on YouTube, either. The guys would never let him hear the end of it.

"Soooo." She let the word unfurl slowly, like a birthday horn. Then she fiddled with her shirt, and tightened her ponytail. Stretched her arms out along the rail, and crossed her ankles, mirroring his pose.

It only took until her third deep inhale for him to figure it out. Mira was nervous. She'd liked his kisses. Hell, she'd bent over backward explaining just how much she liked them. And now she had no idea what came next.

Well, neither did Sam. It's not like he'd planned to kiss her. He didn't have a rule about it or anything, but it struck him as wise to steer clear of women who practically scalped him. Not to mention women who took everything he said the wrong way. Life was too short to waste on high-maintenance, snippy women.

However, life was also too short to waste by not kissing this particular vibrant, beautiful woman right in front of him. Especially when being with her distracted him so thoroughly from the looming question of his future. It wasn't much of a plan, but Sam could think on his feet. "We should go on a date."

"Should we?" The thin slash of just her right eyebrow arced up into a half moon. "What gives you that idea?"

Sam wasn't ready to lay out a firm case. This was more of an itch between his shoulder blades. The kind that wouldn't let you concentrate on anything else until you scratched it. Call it a hunch that he needed to spend more time with her, even if he couldn't fully explain why. "I've discovered there's more to you than the annoying princess veneer. I'd like to find out what else you've got hidden under there?"

"Interesting premise. Or, maybe this is a monumentally stupid idea."

He chose to ignore the stupid comment, and latch

on to the fact she found the suggestion interesting. "Not at all. As you pointed out, we're on a full boat, shouting to be heard over the engines and the rushing water. Not the ideal circumstances for a first date. I didn't even wear my lucky blue first-date shirt." She'd stopped fidgeting. He'd take it as a good sign.

"What makes it lucky?"

Gotcha. He had her on the line, and it wouldn't be too hard to reel her in. Well, for the date, at least. Sam had no doubt Mira was nothing if not full of complications. "I always get a second date when I wear it."

"You sound like a girl, Sam. I never would've imagined you to be a fan of fashion."

"I'm not." Snorting, he waved his hand at his one hundred percent non-name-brand outfit. "I'm a big fan of second dates, though."

Mira laughed. "I like your honesty. So I'll admit I like second dates, too. Of course, the third date is where things really get exciting."

"Come on, give me a chance to take you out and get to know the real you. You had fun today, right?" Shit. All she'd done so far was cry and kiss him. Probably the wrong thing to ask.

"The last five minutes weren't so bad."

She was like the rainbow trouts he hooked in this very lake, fighting against every attempt to be reeled in. Except Sam knew he had her on the line. Tire her out, and he'd get her eventually. "Well, I put zero effort into this excursion. Imagine how much fun you'll have once I buckle down and put serious thought into impressing you?"

Mira batted her lashes in double time. "Be still my heart."

"Plus, we're pretty good at the kissing part. Don't you want to find out how good we'd be at the rest of it?"

"Mr. Lyons, are you trying to seduce me?"

"Ivy did tell me to be nice to you. I'm just following orders."

Long, red-tipped fingers drifted to her lips. "I'd say you went above and beyond the call of duty."

"True. This isn't my standard welcome-to-the-neighborhood approach."

Her hand fell to her side. "You know, maybe we shouldn't go on a real date. After all, we work with each other."

That thought had already taken up residence in his brain like a pulsing neon sign. Ben would probably skin him alive if he found out he'd already rounded first base with the newest member of Ivy's team. Was this smart? He couldn't say for sure one way or the other. But the longer he stood there, staring at Mira's lips, still plump and moist from his mouth, the more he knew he couldn't walk away. She'd burrowed under his skin, all right. In a good way, this time. A couple of kisses hadn't slaked his raging bonfire of desire. They'd stoked it. As long as she didn't belt him in the head again, nothing would stop him from getting another taste.

"We work next to each other," he corrected. "The customers will have free rein to shop in both of our stores. But what if we don't?"

"I don't understand."

"We'll keep it all business when we're at our stores. That door will stay shut, and you and I won't walk through it. No fraternizing. No singing along to the other person's radio. Definitely no flirting."

That made a saucy smile brighten her eyes. "Where's the fun in that?"

Sam agreed, but he knew his plan had merit. Both their businesses were too important to risk on one kiss. "Anticipation heightens the payoff. No one has to know. We'll try one date. Wednesday night. If it doesn't go well, no harm, no foul."

"And if it goes well? It'll be like the Great Wall of China between Lyons Bakery and A Fine Romance?"

His version ran more along the lines of a picket fence made of dominoes. So he could knock it down with one sharp poke. "Something like that. What do you say?"

"Don't rush me. In fact, in the spirit of exchanging basic first-date information, here's the first thing you should know about me. I'm very methodical. I like to weigh the pros and cons."

Sam dug another napkin out of his pocket. "Do you want to make a list?"

"The fact that you offered gets you a check in the pro column."

"What if I sweeten the pot?" He bridged the distance between them in two long strides, and captured her mouth once more. Hard and fast, he laid claim to it, making sure she could feel how much he wanted her to say yes.

Panting, she broke away. "The funny thing about bribery? It's got a bad rap, but it works. I'll go out with you, Sam."

"You won't regret it."

"Make sure I don't."

That sassiness, dialed back from the sharp-as-glass version she first used on him, made him want to smile and smother her with more kisses. She wasn't the only one who made lists. And first thing on his would be to wash his lucky shirt.

FIVE

MIRA PUSHED OPEN the back door with her butt and dragged the giant box of cut-down boxes into the alley behind the store. It was her third trip of the day. Unpacking inventory was the fun part. Dealing with the shipping boxes, packing peanuts, miles of plastic wrap, bubble wrap and bags that swathed seemingly every item she unwrapped was a tedious workout. She'd need to take a long shower before her date with Sam tonight. And not just to get clean. Mira loved the ritual of getting ready for a date.

Using the good shower gel the same flowery scent as the expensive lotion from Provence (only pulled out on special occasions). Flinging twenty different outfits on the bed until settling on one that made her feel delightfully feminine. Dawdling over hair and makeup while wondering if she'd get a kiss at the front door. Or would he make her wait all night?

This was pointless. She'd spent more of the afternoon daydreaming about the dreamy boy next door than actually working. And there was a strong possibility she'd gotten a crick in her neck from glancing over at the closed connecting door every five minutes. Wondering what Sam was doing on the other side of it. Wondering if his rock-hard forearms covered in dark hair sparkled with a dusting of sugar. Or if his hips swiveled to the radio's beat. Mira bet he swiveled his hips really well. Yikes. Mira popped her eyelids open, appalled they'd drifted shut mid-reverie, while gripping a box of trash, of all things. Might as well stop kidding herself and call it a day.

"Need some help, lady?" A tall, rail-thin teenager jittered a few steps toward her. He was part of a group clustered by the Dumpster, all shoving cookies in their mouths. Had they scavenged the bakery's discarded cookies from the Dumpster? She'd seen them a few other days, hanging out back here, always with cheeks full of cookies. Baggy jeans so low they seemed to mock gravity, oversized jackets, hoodies and Cubs caps made up a sort of uniform.

Warning bells rang in her head. She didn't have a good read on Chicago's vibe yet, but good kids didn't hang out in alleys. Were they a gang? Their eyes were hard. Too hard, too knowledgeable for kids that age. They carried themselves with real swagger, not the puffed-up pretense of innocent youth. To her mind, they were far too loud and animated. Maybe because she'd spent the last few months at camp surrounded by just girls? Or because they were strung out on drugs? Oddly territorial, she didn't like them gorging on Sam's cookies, even if he had thrown them out.

"I'm fine, thanks." The circle of boys laughed, elbowing each other. Mira didn't know what set them off, but she didn't want to stick around and find out. She'd finish with the trash later. Hurrying inside, she quickly locked the door behind her. It looked like a nice enough neighborhood, and she didn't have any solid proof the boys were up to no good. But as a single woman alone, Mira didn't want to take any chances. Getting the security system online zoomed from number fourteen on her to-do list straight to the top.

A loud knock at the front of the store whipped her head around, and her heart leapt into her throat. Was she really going to have to use the crystal vase again to defend herself? Mira inserted *sign up for self-defense class* somewhere into the middle of her to-do list. The vase wasn't a practical long-term solution, although it was still her best option. On the other hand, would a burglar be so polite as to knock? Mira crept down the hall. From the counter she palmed her cell phone, and hit the speed dial for the police. Her thumb hovered over the send button. Better to be paranoid and prepared than caught off guard.

On the other side of the glass door stood a middle-aged woman clutching a picnic basket. No-nonsense short gray hair—the real kind, not fashionably streaked—contrasted with the high-end St. John knit suit. And a fabulous pair of Prada platform pumps. Mira may have walked away from her parents' money, but the love of shoes her mother had instilled wasn't so easy to dismiss. She still eagerly eyeballed the new collections at the start of each season. And her mom loved her enough to throw at least a few pairs of Louboutins into the birthday box that arrived every year, in lieu of her parents actually showing up and spending time with her.

Nerves a little less jangly, Mira put down her phone and eased open the door a crack. "I'm sorry, but we don't open for a few more weeks. If you'd like to leave me your email address, I'll be sure to send you information about the grand opening."

"Goodness, I know you aren't open yet. That's why I'm here. I'd like to apply for a job."

"Really? The sales clerk position?"

"Nope. I'm a cook." She pointed to her basket. "If you'd indulge me for a few minutes, I brought a résumé, of sorts." When Mira hesitated, the woman put down the basket and rummaged in her purse. "I almost forgot. If there's one thing my husband's hammered home to me about the business world, it's that connections are everything. I don't mind shamelessly using mine to open the door. After that, I'm confident my food will speak for itself." She handed Mira a glossy program.

"What's this?"

"My letter of introduction. Not as professional as I'd like, but it's remarkably hard to find stationery in the middle of a gala."

Mira unfolded the program. The splashy purple-and-white cover indicated it was from last night's Minds Matter gala to benefit Northwestern Hospital's Brain Tumor Institute. Scribbled in the margin was a single sentence: *Give her a try!* It was signed by Samantha Rhodes, Ivy's mother. Which made it practically a royal edict. Samantha was a force of nature, not to mention a big mover and shaker in Chicago's elite social circles. The mystery woman was right. Dropping that name was all it took for Mira to swing open the door and usher her inside.

"Well, if you cook half as well as you network, you'll be a shoo-in for the job." There. With a touch of humor, she'd established the blatant name-dropping was acknowledged, but not enough to hand her the job on a silver platter. "I'm Mira Parrish. Welcome to what will soon be A Fine Romance."

"Helen Warrington." After setting the basket on the floor, she shook Mira's hand. "And all I want is a fair shot." They both sat on the stools by the front counter. Helen crossed her legs and beamed a warm smile.

Mira glanced at her watch, trying to figure out how much behind this would set her pre-date routine. "I'm afraid this will be a brief interview. I need to head out shortly."

"Do you have a hot date lined up?"

The professional side of Mira was prepared to shake off the question, but surprisingly, a different answer popped out when she opened her mouth. "As a matter of fact, I do." It must be because they'd agreed to keep it under wraps. Letting the whole gang know just cranked up the expectation level. After one real date, she and Sam would be able to ascertain if this thing was just a crazed spurt of lust-on-the-lake, or something worth pursuing. Then they could share the news. But it had been driving her crazy not to be able to gush to Ivy or Daphne. Part of the fun of anticipation was anticipating with others. So out of the blue, she'd blurted it out to a total stranger.

"Good for you. You're young and pretty. You should be out breaking hearts left and right." Helen leaned forward, one elbow on the counter. "Is he a thoroughly gorgeous specimen?"

Mira choked on a laugh. "Why yes, he is. But… it's complicated."

"Take it from me, dear. The best ones always are."

Helen's congenial openness was very appealing. She'd made a strong always-important first impression. Mira liked her right off the bat. However, she still presented a mystery. The upper-crust clothes didn't mesh with a burning desire for a job slaving away over a hot stove. Resisting the urge to gush about Sam, Mira grabbed her pad to take notes. "Do you have experience?"

"Yes." Helen settled her hands in her lap. "I worked in my family's restaurant down in Champaign growing up. My grandmother switched out my pacifier for a wooden spoon before I was even on solid foods. I loved it. Loved it so much I refused to go away to college, even after I won a scholarship. But then, one fateful day, Dan Warrington walked in the door."

"Was he gorgeous and complicated?" Mira teased.

"Right on both counts. Pretty soon I had to choose between my love of cooking and my love for Dan. They ran neck and neck for a while, but once he sweetened the deal with burn-up-the-sheets sex, the decision was easy."

Okay, she didn't just like this woman. Mira had a full-blown girl crush on Helen. It took a certain fearlessness and self-assurance to mention premarital sex in a job interview. She took a pointed glance at Helen's left hand, weighted down with what had to be a four-carat diamond. "Let me guess. You lived happily ever after?"

With a fond smile, Helen too looked down at her ring. "So far, anyway. I married him, moved to Chicago and had two beautiful babies. And before you ask why I'm boring you with my life story, my point is that I never stopped cooking."

Although Mira liked her, and the early restaurant experience was a plus, it sounded like she'd taken about a twenty-year break from creating enough food to satisfy throngs of customers. It would require all her delicacy to politely turn down this delightful woman. "While I don't discount the enormous amount of work it takes to keep a family fed, it is different from the sort of cooking we'll require here."

Helen shook her head and held up one hand, palm up, to stop Mira. "Don't I know it! There's more to my tale, I promise."

It would be important to report back to Ivy, and subsequently her mother, that she'd given Helen every opportunity. Mira nodded. "Go on."

"At first, my addiction to cooking drove all my friends nuts. Dan moves in a very socially aware group, shall we say."

Oh yes, Mira knew exactly the type. She'd grown up surrounded by people like that. People to whom status was practically a religion. For a while, as a teenager, it had been easy to get sucked into games of social excess. Easy to stop talking to a girl when she wore the wrong brand of shoe to school. Or shun a boy who couldn't afford tickets to the hottest rock concert of the year. But in college, surrounded by people of so many different social strata, Mira came to her senses. She learned to judge people on who they were, not what they were worth. And most of all, she'd learned that distancing herself from her parents' wealth made her a better person.

With the demeanor of a stern teacher, Helen brandished her index finger. "Don't get me wrong—I've made some great friends amidst Chicago's elite. But people who are thoughtful and tell a wicked joke and helped nurse my daughter through chicken pox are often the same people who like to brag about how much they spent on the caterer, and who look down their noses at a batch of homemade cookies." A smug smirk tightened her lips. "Or at least, they did until they tasted my cookies."

Mira crossed to the fridge and brought back two bottles of water. She liked where this story was headed. "Did you make them eat their words?"

"Ha! Good one." Helen took a long sip. After she recapped the bottle, she continued to run her finger around the cap. "I'll never forget the first Junior League committee meeting I hosted. I talk a good game, but my stomach had about a hundred flocks of butterflies. Even though I'd dithered over the menu for weeks, sent Dan to work laden with some of my test runs for his staff, it is a whole different proposition to serve a score of people rather than the four of us."

"What did you make? When I think of a committee meeting, I envision pretzels, or maybe a plate of cookies."

A deep belly laugh rolled out, with the strength of the wake behind an ocean liner. "Well, that's why *you're* not interviewing right now to be a cook! I served an authentic high tea, complete with five kinds of sandwiches, scones, pastries, you name it. The women couldn't rave enough, and begged for the name of my caterer. When I told them I made everything, you could've heard a pin drop in that room. I honestly thought they were going to walk out in a huff, insulted to the quick I'd dared to serve them homemade food."

"Did they?"

"Only one. Ruth Carlin. You know, to this day, she

still demurs if I offer her anything. Just purses those thin lips of hers and insists she already ate. Which is weird, since that stick on stilettos looks like she hasn't eaten in about two decades. I suppose I'd rather have her not eat my food than eat it and regift it to the toilet gods ten minutes later."

Mira bit the inside of her cheek to keep from bursting into unprofessional giggles. "Sounds like it's her loss."

Shrugging through another sip, Helen forged ahead. "The upshot was that I became known as the quirky one who always cooked. And oh boy, did I ever. Of course Noah and Lucy came first. I was a room mother, and a Girl Scout den leader. To my children's great chagrin, I chaperoned every school event from field trips to dances, and I shouted myself hoarse at swim meets and lacrosse games. Those two are the sunshine in my day."

Wow. Mira knew her parents loved her. Or at least, they loved the idea of a daughter, someone to carry on the family name. But never once had she seen her mother's face light up like Helen's at any of Mira's accomplishments. The boarding schools they shuttled her between didn't have room mothers. Her parents hadn't come to watch any of her speech tournaments, or her misbegotten half year on the track team in junior high. They hadn't even made it to her high school graduation. It conflicted with the Cannes Film Festival, which was a must-see-and-be-seen week of events. She'd hungered for the kind of love Helen described so effortlessly.

"It doesn't sound like you had any spare time to cook."

"Oh, I carved out precious moments here and there. As they got older, it grew easier. I was always in the kitchen, tinkering with recipes, putting my own spin on things or dreaming up new ones. Soon my friends not only accepted my odd habit, but they embraced it. I cooked for committee meetings, for birthday parties, first communions, bridal showers, you name it. I even helped out my nephew with an engagement picnic."

Which reminded Mira about her fast-approaching date. She didn't want to cut Helen short, but she didn't want to deprive Sam of the full effects of a leisurely *toilette*. "What brings you here today?"

"As a proud mother, I'm tickled to report that Noah graduated from Stanford in May, and Lucy's starting her sophomore year at Cornell. However, woman to woman? Last year was miserable. That empty-nest syndrome you hear about? It is real, and brutal."

"I'm sorry. You must miss them terribly." Mira knew it to be true, because she'd witnessed the almost daily calls from Ivy's mom when they roomed together. Just because her parents lived the mantra *out of sight, out of mind* didn't meant that other parents shared their viewpoint.

Helen slid off the stool and began to pace across the width of the front room. Her footsteps clattered on the hardwood floors, the sound bouncing off the empty walls. "After a quarter of a century, I suddenly had no reason to get up in the morning. No driving force in my life at all. It was a hard adjustment." She shook her head, hard and fast. "No, to be fair, I didn't adjust at all. That's why I'm here."

"I don't understand." Mira slipped off her stool as well, wanting Helen to know they were on an even level. The older woman whirled around, hands at her sides, clenching and unclenching, as though trying to grasp something.

"I don't want the money."

Her candidness threw Mira for a loop. "That's an unusual approach to take in a job interview."

"Honesty is everything, right? What would I gain by beating around the bush? My clothes don't look like hand-me-downs. And you hid it well, but I saw the way you eyeballed my wedding set. Whatever your story is, you certainly recognize fine jewelry." Helen began worrying those same rings, sliding them up to her knuckle and then back down. "I want a purpose, a passion. Something more than shopping for gala dresses, salon trips to prep for said galas, and talking with the same sixty people at every damn gala. I'm on boards and committees, but volunteering seems to be more about who wore what to the committee meetings than actually helping people."

It sounded all too familiar to Mira. It was the life she'd fled. "I understand."

Helen barreled on. "I need a reason to get up in the morning beyond having dinner with my husband twelve hours later. And cooking is truly my passion. I'd love it if you would give me the chance to pursue it."

The impassioned speech tugged at Mira's heartstrings with the keening delicacy of a master harpist. She sat back down, and patted the other stool. "Why don't you show me what's hiding in that basket?"

Gratefulness—or possibly unshed tears—sparkled in Helen's eyes. "Now that you've heard my story, you see that while I do have experience, it isn't the kind of thing that fills a résumé. So I decided the best thing to do is wow you with samples." She lifted the cover and pulled out a bottle of white wine. "I know drinking is usually frowned upon in interviews, but this sauvignon blanc would be a perfect accompaniment to my food. And I wasn't sure if you planned to sell alcohol."

"I'll apply for a liquor license eventually, but we don't have one at the moment. I do appreciate a well-paired wine. Unfortunately, as I mentioned, I have to leave for my date soon, so I'll abstain."

"As I didn't stomp the grapes or bottle them, it makes no never mind to me." Helen pushed it off to the side and lifted out a series of plastic containers. "Samantha and I didn't have the chance to go into details, so I'm not sure if this is exactly what you had in mind to serve to your customers."

"Nothing's set in stone. I'd hoped whoever we hire would take the lead on menu planning."

"Great. Let me start by saying I can make anything you want. But I did burn the midnight oil thinking about the sorts of romantic situations your customers needed as a light repast. That was the key for me. Keep it light. Nobody feels sexy after filling up on a huge porterhouse and loaded baked potato. Satisfied, sure, but not in the mood for nooky."

Mira ignored the urge to glance at her watch. As eager as she was to see Sam, she couldn't wait to taste the delicious tidbits in front of her. Helen unfurled a lacy place mat and fussed with each morsel, positioning them just so on gold-rimmed plates. "I agree. In that refrigerated case we'll carry a small but varied selection of cheeses, and the shelf below will hold crackers. But the daily specials should lean more toward delicious than hearty."

"My example of an appetizer is a goat cheese tartlet with roasted zucchini and parmesan curls."

The phyllo shells oozed with creamy cheese, contrasted beautifully with the bright green zucchini ribbon and golden toasted pine nuts. "Helen, you've brought enough to feed at least four people."

"I wasn't sure if you'd hired an assistant sales clerk yet, and wanted everyone to be able to have a taste."

"You're going to tempt me to ruin my dinner." Mira took a bite and knew she'd hit the mother lode. The flavors melded into a single burst of deliciousness that melted on her tongue. If the rest of the food was as good as this one bite, Helen would be a huge asset to the store. "I like this. I especially like that it's finger food. It's easy to picture a couple lying on the lawn, feeding each other bites."

"I'd keep the focus seasonal, so we can work with farmers' markets." She arranged the plates in a semicircle, and pointed to each one in turn. "As summer wanes, I'd serve this chicken and couscous salad with tomatillo sauce. The citrus kick gives it zest, and the salad can be served at room temperature. Instead of a sandwich, I went with the more compact and less messy wrap, of rare roast beef, spinach, blue cheese and a drizzle of horseradish."

Mira finished her tart and resisted with all her might the urge to go back for seconds. "This is a very thoughtful presentation. The needs of our customers are balanced with a variety of tastes and textures." She wrinkled her nose. "I'm sorry, I sound like a food critic, and a stuffy one at that. It all looks wonderful."

"Wait, let me get this all out. I rehearsed, after all."
Helen sucked in a deep breath while Mira dug into
the salad. "I'm a big fan of Lyons Bakery. Samantha
explained your two stores plan to have a symbiotic
relationship, urging customers to sample the wares of
the neighboring shop. It'll provide both of you with
a constant influx of new customers. That being said,
I think A Fine Romance needs to offer a single, signature dessert item. I'm leaning toward chocolate-
covered macaroons or chocolate-covered shortbread.
I brought both, just to be on the safe side."

It was a smart idea, and Mira liked it. She still
wouldn't touch anything covered in chocolate with
a ten-foot pole, however. But if she took them home,
chances were good Daphne could be convinced to
take one for the team and sample them. Mira bit back
a moan as she bit into the roast beef wrap. There
wasn't a person alive who wouldn't wolf it down. Samantha Rhodes had sent her a kitchen magician. Not
to mention considerably shortening her to-do list by
shaving off days' worth of calls and interviews in the
ever-tedious hiring process.

"You've got an impeccable reference. More to the
point, your food is divine." A breath away from offering her the job, Mira's phone rang and vibrated its
way across the counter. "I'm sorry, I need to check
this. I'm waiting to hear from a glassblower in Ala-
bama who might work with us."

"Please, you already let me hijack your afternoon.
Take your time."

It took no time at all to read the four-line text.
*Sorry. Emergency. Mom needs help for bunko night.
Rain check?* Mira set the phone down slowly, but

didn't let go. Her thoughts spiraled, all the different emotions mixing into a giant black funnel cloud. The first hit, the real left jab into her solar plexus that sucked away her breath, was disappointment.

For four days, not to mention sleepless-with-excitement nights, she'd looked forward to their date. She and Sam had shared an honest, deep moment on that boat. The kind of connection that usually doesn't spring up until several weeks into a relationship, if ever. For some completely unknowable reason, she'd dropped her defenses and revealed her vulnerability. He hadn't mocked or turned away. What he did do was listen, and thoughtfully respond. Follow up that emotional honesty with one of the best kisses of her twenty-nine years, and she was hooked.

Mira hadn't stopped thinking about him. Which was odd, since she'd nursed a grudge as strong as a double shot of tequila against Sam for the entire first week of their acquaintance. They'd stuck to their guns and not opened the door between their stores even once. Since one last, scorching kiss when the ship docked, she hadn't seen him at all.

So the thought of not seeing him tonight, of not running her fingers through that thick, dark lock of hair that kept slipping onto his forehead, of not splaying her hand across his super-defined lats as hard as the tectonic plates below L.A....well, it was a letdown.

Vying for equal time in her pout zone was disbelief. Mrs. Lyons wasn't in any danger. She wasn't sick. She wasn't only here for the night before embarking on a two-year trip around the world. No, Sam stood her up to help his mom with a stupid game. What sort of emergency was even possible during an evening of brownies, cider and dice rolling?

And what about sex? Mira knew men, at least as well as any other woman. The whole "men think about sex every three seconds" stat might be a bit excessive, but it did rule their world. She didn't assume they'd have sex tonight, not on their first official date. But a serious make-out session had definitely been an agenda item. What kind of guy walked away from any amount of potential sex…for his mom?

That's where she made a hard turn straight into righteous pissiness. Mira knew she had better than average looks, a good figure, and she'd planned to spend more than an hour buffing and polishing everything to be at her best for Sam. For a guy she thought wanted her right back. How could he cancel on her to—what—help his mom fold napkins? Properly plate the cookies?

"Mira?"

"Hmm?" She looked down to watch Helen tug the phone away.

"You sort of zoned out on me there for a minute. Do you feel okay? Do you need some water?"

"Water? No, water won't fix this." Mira reached for the wine bottle. "Before my phone rang, I was about to offer you a job. But it is important to note that I have not yet done so."

Helen furrowed her salt-and-pepper brows. "I don't entirely understand. If it would help, I can come back tomorrow with more samples?"

"No need. I want you to come back tomorrow, when I will officially ask you to join our team." Mira got up, walked around Helen to rummage in her picnic basket until she triumphantly brandished a corkscrew. "Tonight, however, I'd like to ask you to stay and help me eat these orgasmically delicious tidbits. If you're willing, I'd also like you to help me with this bottle of wine, so I don't have to drink alone. I need a friend right now, more than I need a new employee. And if you look at this place," she waved her arm at the piles of inventory in the middle of the floor, "you'll know that's saying quite a bit."

"I can't pinpoint if it's my mother's or women's intuition, but one of them just kicked into high gear." Helen pulled out two wineglasses. Then she gently took the corkscrew from Mira and deftly opened the bottle. "Let me guess. Bad news?"

"On several different levels."

"And if you want me to stay longer, I suppose that means Mr. Gorgeous and Complicated won't be enjoying the pleasure of your company tonight?"

Why couldn't she stay focused on the righteous anger? Why did it have to feel so lousy? "Right again." In one long glug, she drained her glass and pushed it forward for a refill. "The short version, as Oedipal as it sounds, is that he stood me up for his mother." Mira popped two more tartlets. Even through her haze of emotions, the flavors sparkled in her mouth and gave her pause. "Are you interested in the long version?"

"You couldn't pay me to leave without hearing it."

"I love that you turn my money away at every chance. This is going to be fun."

SIX

"ARE WE DONE yet?" Ben Westcott wore the downtrodden air of a man being marched to his own execution. Head bowed, his feet barely shuffled, his eyes were downcast, and an unattractive grimace marred his otherwise handsome face.

Gib, moving beside him with the effortless grace of a panther, snorted. "We've been jogging for five whole minutes. And calling it jogging is generous, as two power walkers just passed us. You're an embarrassment, Westcott. I don't know why I bother with you."

"I'm confused." Mira bumped her way in between the two men. It was a beautiful morning for a jog. With the sun glinting off of it, Lake Michigan was the color of a Tiffany's box. A wide swath of white sand bordered their running path. Loads of toned, muscular men passed them with regularity, giving her plenty of eye candy to distract her from the repetitive slap of her shoes against the blacktop. Of course, none of them was as attractive as Sam, but she was trying not to sully her brain with thoughts of that mama's boy.

"Ben, you look like you're about to need an oxygen tank." She'd hoped to take advantage of this time to get to know Ivy's fiancé better. Hard to do if they'd have to haul him to the nearest emergency room to check on his imminent heart attack. Ben's entire face was the same color as the tomato atop her morning breakfast bagel. "But when you invited me to come running with you, I got the impression it was a regular thing." Or could this be an initiation ritual? In order to be accepted by Ivy's friends, did she have to pass a test? Were they going to push her in the lake? Run away and make her find her way home?

"Oh, indeed it is. You'll find me running along here at least twice a week," Gib said. He waved a hand down the expanse of his torso. Being shirtless, the move showed off every rippling muscle, and there were plenty. "One of the many ways I keep myself in performance-ready shape. Because you—"

Ben interrupted. "Because you never know when a beautiful woman will need a round of slap-and-tickle. We've heard you say it a million times."

"See, when you say it, Ben, you sound ridiculous. But I bet if Gib said it in that lovely, plummy accent of his, I might very well be interested." Mira gave him an exaggerated, Marx brothers leer. He responded with a dexterous eyebrow waggle.

"Stupid British euphemisms," Ben groused. "Your people are always trying to make things sound proper, even when they aren't. Why is it, in your country, you politely *pinch* things instead of *stealing* them? Or go to see a man about a dog, instead of admitting you're headed to the bathroom. Mira's a big girl. Tell her what you really mean. You exercise twenty-five hours out of the day in case a hot chick—"

"—needs a shag?" Gib finished the sentence for him.

These guys were funny. Mira could picture them leaning against a fireplace mantel, dressed in tuxedos, each holding a scotch and hurling wisecracks at each other. Gib's dark hair set off eyes a deep indigo. Even though he'd been in this country more than ten years, he still had the classic pale English complexion. Ben projected an air of careless ease with shaggy blond hair and a tan that could fit in on the beaches of Saint-Tropez. The contrast between the two gorgeous specimens, both showing off more muscles than she could count, would make any girl's thoughts head straight to the bedroom. Or at least, any girl who hadn't been kissed boneless by Sam Lyons.

"Sorry, but I have to tell you that from a woman's perspective, Gib's the real deal. Anything sounds dreamy with a British accent. The way he says the word *shag* makes even the prospect of a filthy quickie in a bathroom stall sound appealing."

Ben threw his hands in the air. "I give up."

Gib slowed down enough to drop behind Mira. He switched places with her to elbow Ben in the ribs. "If you gave up talking, you'd have the breath to pick up the pace." He returned to Mira's side. "I started Ben on an exercise regimen a few months ago. But he's been zipping around the country for his show the past couple of weeks, and it's obvious he never once darkened the door of a hotel gym in all his travels."

Ben produced a reality television show about wedding consultants, called *Planning for Love.* He and Ivy fell in love while he taped her first season, which Mira found to be blissfully romantic. While her friend loathed being the center of attention, Ivy agreed to do the show in order to raise the capital to open A Fine Romance. Mira couldn't wait to watch their romance unfold on the small screen. Plus, if it wasn't for the show, she wouldn't have a job now. Gratitude alone would make her a hard-core fan.

"I pumped some weights." Ben flexed a bicep in his own defense. "In every city I hit, I left my sweat on the weight rack. Does that satisfy you?"

Gib shook his head, utterly unimpressed. "Not in the least. You've always pumped weights. I'm trying to train you that cardio is just as important. Look at Mira, here. She's got great form, a healthy glow and she breathes right. Do you do marathons?"

"Are you nuts?" Mira shuddered in mock horror. "All those people crowded together, the pressure to finish no matter what—sucks all the joy out of it. I just like to run."

Back when her parents first had her delivered to Camp Ticonderoga, it only took her a day to discover she was attending a fat camp. Not just from the array of similarly chubby girls, but because they exercised nonstop. As the counselors tried every possible way to get her to drop the pounds, they'd introduced her to running. Mira didn't want to like it. She didn't want to do anything but sit on her bunk and read comic books.

But even during those first few attempts when she lurched along like an elephant rather than a gazelle, she loved it. Her mind didn't wander and zip to a hundred different topics like normal. When she ran, it was all about one foot in front of the other, making her oblivious to everything else. As she grew older, she realized that clearing of the mind, the meditation of it, was a remarkable stress reliever. To Mira, running became more than just another way to work out. Running kept her sane, kept her grounded. Which is why she'd been thrilled when Gib offered to show her some jogging trails.

"Good to hear. Once this miserable blighter next to me loses interest, perhaps you and I can set up a regular schedule." Gib picked up the pace a bit. Mira had no trouble matching him, but Ben muttered something very nasty under his breath.

"I'd like that. I'm looking for things that will make me fall in love with Chicago. A few good places to run will be a step in the right direction."

"Perfect, as we're about to hit one of Chicago's most famous landmarks. I guarantee you'll take one look at Buckingham Fountain and fall in love."

"Hey, don't shut me out." Ben put on a burst of speed to get in front of them. Then he turned to face them and kept jogging, backward. "I want to come along. This is way better than when Gib sticks me on the treadmill at his hotel. At least out here he can't push a button and increase my rate to just short of the speed of sound. He may look all civilized, but Gibson Moore is a holy terror of a trainer."

Ben's whining cracked her up. No matter how much he complained, it couldn't be more obvious the two men shared a serious bromance. She turned to look at Gib. "You live in a hotel?"

"I manage one. The Cavendish Grand, over on Michigan Avenue."

Wow. Mira would give anything to be able to sink into one of their famous marble bathtubs right about now. Unfortunately, she hadn't been able to afford to darken the door of a Cavendish since she walked away from her family and its stupid, condition-laden trust… and all its attendant money. "I'm impressed. I haven't been to yours yet, but I'm a big fan of the Cavendish brand worldwide. It's always the best hotel in the city, no matter what country you're in. The Egyptian cotton sheets, heated towel racks—such a high and reliable standard of luxury."

Gib's eyes lit up. "Funny you mention that. We're brainstorming ideas for a new motto, and the frontrunner is *Limitless Luxury*."

"It would certainly entice me to check in." If, and it was a big if, she had the limitless funds to subsidize such a wildly expensive treat. The last time Mira stayed in a hotel, it had one-ply toilet paper. 'Nuff said.

Gib swiped at the sweat gluing his bangs to his forehead. "I let Ben use the gym facilities. Mostly because he lived in the hotel for three months, but also because it makes me laugh to watch him suffer and sweat. You're welcome to swing by and use them, too. Unless you've already joined a health club?"

"Not yet. I've been too busy to do anything but go to work and crawl home at the end of the day. Lots of quality time zonked out on the couch watching movies with Daphne." Not to mention the tricky business of not being able to afford a gym membership at the moment. One of the best things about running was that it was free.

"All work and no play makes Mira stressed out and boring," said Ben. "You need to get out and meet people. Start dating all the decent guys around town who are pining away now that I've taken Ivy off the market."

Dating. Right. That thing she and Sam were *supposed* to do. Mira's frustration, not at all eased by her heart-to-heart with Helen, burned at the base of her throat like the remnants of a bad Mexican meal. Yes, they'd agreed to keep their first date a secret. But as far as she was concerned, Sam gave up that privilege the moment he stood her up.

"Getting a date hasn't been hard so far," she said. "Getting the guy to actually show up, now, that's a level I haven't cracked."

Gib put a hand on Mira's arm, pulling them both to a stop. "Do you mean to say some wanker stood you up? You of the flowing locks and eyes as seductive as a siren's song?"

Wow. Over the past few years, she'd heard scores of stories from Ivy about Gib's legendary charm with the ladies. Seeing it up close and personal was something else altogether. "Why do I get the vague sensation that you're hitting on me?"

"No idea. Several reasons, really. The first being that if I chose to set my sights on you, as it were, there'd be nothing vague about it." He trailed a finger softly down her cheek, the merest hint of a caress. It set every nerve in Mira's body into the upright position, grabbing for a seat belt and bracing for one heck of a ride. He finished by tracing the bottom edge of her lower lip. "And you'd have already said yes."

Well, he was right about that. Gibson Moore was a consummate seducer. Mira couldn't imagine any woman saying no to him. "How about we leave that as a possibility down the road?"

"Ah, how I'd like to, but as I said, there are multiple reasons why you're surrounded by metaphorical caution tape." He started jogging again. "Secondly, Ben here informed us in no uncertain terms that your loveliness is off-limits. Something about keeping harmonious working relationships within our little group."

"Wait a minute. I call foul on that one." Mira ran a lazy circle around Ben. "Not only did you and Ivy date while you filmed her show, but your first kiss with her was on the job. Or did you think she wouldn't tell me about you smooching her on the balcony with wedding guests right downstairs?"

He grimaced, flattening out the dimples that usually flashed in his cheeks. "Precisely why I know it is a bad idea to mix work and wooing. We've got a tight group here, with Gib and Daphne and Sam. And now you, of course. Our little makeshift family gets us through the tough times. Better not to put it at risk." He stopped, panting like a thirty-year-old poodle, and bent in half to rest his hands on his thighs.

Mira felt sorry for him. However, she also felt loose for the first time in days, and wasn't nearly ready to cut the run short. "Man up, Westcott. You can't stop already."

Ben shook his head and, still bent over, threw an arm out straight ahead. She turned and fell in love. Well, not with Chicago as a whole, but with the most beautiful fountain she'd ever seen. It looked like a three-tiered pink marble wedding cake. Surrounding the enormous fountain was a moat. Four Art Deco seahorses covered in a lovely green patina sprayed water onto the fountain. "It's spectacular."

"Bowled me over the first time I saw it, too." Shuffling off the path a bit, Ben slurped at a water fountain, then waved for Gib and Mira to take a hit. "They do a light show at night you'll have to see. And if you weren't so fired up to keep running, we could hang out and catch the big spray. There's a center jet that shoots up one hundred and fifty feet, straight into the air."

"We can do it on the way back." Gib used the back of his arm to swipe his forehead. "If she liked Buckingham Fountain, she's going to love Millennium Park. Off we go," he ordered.

They fell into a loose horizontal line. Mira could've stayed and stared at the fountain all morning. But something niggled at the back of her brain. "Gib, do you really have more reasons you can't hit on me? Be gentle—my womanly pride is at stake here."

"Ah. Can't have that. The last, and least important reason, is that Sam growled at me when I commented on your alluring combination of beauty, charm and wit. I don't know what's going on there, but I do know the man's got biceps the size of Queen Elizabeth's corgis. I usually aim to not piss him off."

"What? He's got no right," she spluttered. "I take it back. What he's got is a load of nerve. How dare he? He hasn't got a leg to stand on!"

Ben took her hand and steered her over to a curlicued wrought-iron bench. "Whoa. The only thing I'm clear on is that Sam's got you twisted up in knots over something. Want to back up and clue us in?"

Without bothering to cool down or stretch, Mira plopped down. She waved her hands back and forth as if trying to pull the right words out of the air. But once Ben and Gib crouched in front of her, each holding a hand, she gave up. What did the right words matter to describe how he'd done a very wrong thing? "Sam's the one who stood me up."

"Son of a bitch." Ben's grip tightened to the point

of pain, then released. Mira resisted the urge to flex her hand. "I don't know what pisses me off more. That he went after you *after* I told him not to, or that he jacked you around."

"Easy choice." Gib's low tone soothed as much as his thumb rhythmically brushing across her knuckles. "You don't leave a lady waiting for five minutes, let alone all night. His behavior is inexcusable."

The validation was a bit of a salve to her wounded ego, but Mira needed more. "Oh, it gets worse. Want to hear his reason? Sam needed to help his mother with her bunko night." In perfect synchronization, they leaned back on their heels and stood. Ben looked at Gib. Gib looked at the ground and shrugged. Then they crossed and sat down, one on either side of her. What was going on? What happened to the righteous sympathy?

"There's…more to Sam than meets the eye," Ben said.

Gib chimed in right on top of him. "You shouldn't judge him too harshly."

"Wait. What?" They'd pulled a U-turn on their sympathy so fast she could almost smell the burning rubber. "Why? Why does he suddenly get a free pass as soon as I mention his mother? He's thirty-one, not three."

"It's a long story. I'm not even sure if it's our story to tell," Ben said.

"Well, it certainly isn't for *you* to tell. You've known Sam less than six months. Just because Ivy talks your ear off incessantly doesn't mean you know all the nuances of Sam's story and can do it justice."

Gib scooted into the corner of the bench to face Mira on an angle. "*I'll* fill her in."

They hadn't begun the story, and she'd already had enough of this pussyfooting around. Mira wanted to pout, to lick her wounds and have them soothingly agree that Sam's behavior was crappy. "This is ridiculous. Unless this tale ranks up there with Sir Gawain and the Green Knight, I'd say you two are overhyping whatever chapter of Sam's life you're about to recap."

Ben pushed sun-streaked bangs off his face. "Sorry. We're very protective of Sam and his mother. At least one of us pops in every day, and not just for the doughnuts. Kathleen's a wonderful woman. Somehow she makes us feel mothered without feeling smothered."

Mira had never experienced either end of that spectrum. Distant neglect and disapproval was a more apt description of her mom's parenting style. What would it be like to have that sort of connection? Pretty darn awesome, she assumed. So now, in addition to being miffed with Sam, a certain green-eyed monster had also shown up at the pity party.

Solemnity darkened Gib's startlingly light blue eyes. "After college, Sam worked full-time at the bakery. Then he got this notion that he wanted to make chocolate. Drove his father nuts for months and months, asking to go train with a master. Mr. Lyons didn't see the point, and didn't want to go back to the workload he had before Sam came on board. But finally, Kathleen talked him into it."

"I've recently learned it is impossible to say no to the woman you love," Ben said with a small, private smile. Mira wondered if a man would ever think about her and smile like that.

"Huh. Well, I've recently learned you are one whipped puppy," Gib retorted. "As I was saying, Sam flew off to Europe to study with the best chocolatiers in the world. He bopped from France to Belgium to Switzerland."

"You don't say." When Sam heard about her sailing in the Mediterranean, the man had shut down faster than a bar at closing time. And now she learned he had the money to roam from country to country at will? Where did he get off judging her? Sure, he'd apologized at the time, but this put a whole different spin on his reaction.

"Three months turned into six, turned into almost two years. That's when Mr. Lyons had his heart attack. Do you remember that huge storm a few years ago? The one that shut down every airport in Europe for a couple of days? Sam got stuck. He rushed right to the airport after the first frantic call when they loaded his dad into the ambulance. All through the quadruple-bypass surgery, Sam wore a hole in the linoleum of the Belgium airport."

"How awful. He must've felt so helpless." Mira's simmering resentment disappeared. What a horrible situation. If she knew one thing about Sam already, it was how much he valued his family. She couldn't imagine how hard it must've been to do nothing but wait. Mira shoved to her feet and walked down the path. It was impossible to sit still and listen. The guys flanked her as Gib continued.

"When he got the call that his dad survived the surgery, he started to hope things would be okay. Spent the night on the floor with hundreds of other stranded travelers. By noon, everyone said no flights would be able to get out for at least another day. That's right about when Sam got the next phone call. He knew from the number it was his mother, but she didn't say a word. Just sobbed into the phone for an entire half hour. Sam was out of his mind. He didn't know how to comfort his mother, and he especially didn't know how to do it from another freaking continent. It was the worst day of his life."

Mira walked faster, on the verge of jogging. She didn't want to hear any more. Experiencing his pain even through a third party was almost unbearable. Desperate for a distraction, she focused on the surroundings. On her left was a hulking marble building that must be the Art Institute. Clustered in its shadow were students carrying sketchbooks and oversized watercolor pads. Pierced and tattooed on every visible inch of skin and all about twenty pounds underweight, they looked like the epitome of modern artists.

Relentlessly, Gib pressed on. "Sam never got to say goodbye to his father. In fact, the last time they spoke, they'd had a huge fight. Yet in the hospital, Mr. Lyons wouldn't stop asking for Sam. Said he couldn't go until he'd made things right with his boy. Mrs. Lyons felt horrible. He never would've gone to Europe if it wasn't for her. She took on all this guilt about Sam and his father not being together at the end. Figured it was her fault Sam couldn't say goodbye, and that her husband couldn't be at peace when he died."

"The woman's got a heart as big as Lake Michigan. Too bad sometimes, that comes around and bites her in the ass," Ben said.

With a hand at the small of her back, Gib steered Mira across the busy intersection toward the museum. "By the time he made it back to Chicago, it was the morning of the funeral. Kathleen had locked herself in her room and hadn't spoken to anyone or eaten in two days. Sam's little sister, Diana, pulled the whole funeral together by herself. When Sam got there, they both fell apart on him. He never got to properly grieve himself, he was so busy holding the two of them together."

The heat pressed inexorably against Mira like a smothering velvet fist. Her head ached, whether from the sun or the oppressive pain of the unfolding story or the blare of car horns. This casual morning jog had taken one heck of a dark twist. She wanted to break away, run to Sam and hug him until they were both breathless. Instead, all three stood on the curb, waiting to cross again as taxi after taxi sped past. Gib raised his voice to be heard against the din.

"Diana was young and resilient, and bounced back in a few months. But Kathleen was a mess. She wouldn't eat. She wouldn't work. She wouldn't leave the house, except for the twice-weekly therapist visits Sam bullied her into. Sam had to keep the bakery going all by himself. He worked crazy hours, doing the work of three people. Some of us tried to pitch in when we could, by manning the register during the early morning rush a few times a week. After a month, Kathleen admitted herself to the hospital. Well, Sam gave her no choice. He was so worried she'd just fade away. Paying off the bills from his father's surgery, and then her hospital stay on top of it—well, money was super tight for a while."

Finally Ben took up the story, words gushing out now that he could share what he knew. "Without telling Sam, his parents had taken out a second mortgage to help finance his trip to Europe. If the payments didn't get made, his mom would lose her house—all because of him. He had to find a way to bring in more money. That's when Sam upscaled the wedding cake side of the business. Lyons Bakery was known for delicious cakes, but the works of art he turned out almost looked too good to eat. He could charge triple their going rate, and still have customers offering huge tips just to get on his books." Ben smacked his lips. "When you get the chance, take it from me and don't just stare at a Sam Lyons cake. Eat every crumb of that deliciousness."

"Watch out, mate. I know that look in your eye. If you nip over to Lyons for a slice this afternoon, I'll make you pay for it with an extra twenty sets when we hit the weight machines tomorrow," Gib warned.

Ben grabbed his ankle and twisted it behind him for a deep thigh stretch. "Why don't I just join a real gym and get a trainer who doesn't bully me?"

"Because I let you use the gym at the Cavendish for free?"

"Yeah, that's the kicker." Ben leaned behind Mira and gave him a playful punch in the arm. "I'll do the weights, as long as we finish with a stint in the pool. What was it I beat you by last time—a lap and a half? Can't wait to see if I can better that record."

Gib ignored him as they crossed the street. "Things turned around for Sam after a while. His father's life insurance finally made it through probate and fixed the cash-flow problem. Kathleen came back to work, only making outpatient therapy visits. But she was still so fragile. Sam's entire life dwindled to taking care of her and the bakery. Diana insisted on following in his footsteps and going to Europe. We insisted he come to our weekly poker games through all of this. He needed the normalcy, the chance to hang with other guys and not worry about his mother's nervous breakdown for a few hours."

Passing between a cluster of hedges, Mira was suddenly transported. Clusters of low, leafy bushes and wildflowers were on the right. To the left, deep purple flowers made up a carpet for the backdrop of the downtown skyline. It was exactly the pick-me-up her spirits needed. "I love it here," she exclaimed.

Gib turned to stare at the city. "Thought you might. Millennium Park's one of the best things to happen to downtown in a long time."

"This garden is too pretty to be spoiled by depressing reality. Is there much more to this story?" Mira asked. "If so, I might as well turn around and stare at traffic while you finish."

Ben shook his head and pulled her deeper into the garden. "Nah, we're finished bringing you down. Kathleen's much better now."

"They say that when you break a bone, it heals twice as strong." Gib paused at a trickling fountain that dripped into a slow-moving, glistening trough. "She was broken, all right, but now she's right as rain. Unfortunately, Sam's having a bit of trouble accepting that. He's too used to watching over her every second of every day. His mother's independence is hard for him to trust. She had a lot of setbacks along the way. Let's just say he's got a hair trigger when it comes to her. And you've been the unintended victim a few times now."

"I see," Mira said. Except she didn't. Not entirely. Sam dropping everything to go running the moment his mother blinked in his direction? Absolutely understandable. Now, she deeply regretted the fuss she'd made over him not picking her up at O'Hare. Given her new insight into his situation, it made perfect sense. What she couldn't see was, given all he had to juggle, why Sam wanted to go out with her. Mira knew she could be a handful, especially when her temper slipped out. She'd been batting at him like a cat with a ball of yarn since they'd met. Didn't he deserve some peace and quiet?

Gib pulled off his shirt and swiped it through the fountain. Mira tried not to stare, but it was hard. At Ben and Ivy's rooftop party, his tailored clothes hung off what looked like a lean frame. But underneath he hid a sculpted chest artists would kill to immortalize in marble. No wonder he had such a reputation as a ladies' man. Killer charm mixed with a killer body topped off with his royal accent made Gibson Moore a triple threat.

After a quick wring, he pulled the shirt back on with a shiver. "Easiest way to cool off without walking straight into Lake Michigan. Now let's get this sorted so we can finish our run. Should Sam have stood you up at all? Of course not. Sam's a decent guy. He doesn't lead women on, and I've seen him act like a proper gentleman. But when it comes to his mother, you've got to give him some leeway."

"You sure do know how to spin a compelling story." Mira didn't know quite what to say. He'd given her a lot to think over. A bit unfortunate, since the whole point of a good run was to not think about anything.

"We've lolled about in one place too long." Gib began to jog in place. "Let's at least get you to the Cloud Gate. You strike me as the type of woman who would appreciate a gigantic silver kidney bean sculpture. Then, if Ben looks like he's about to swoon like a Regency debutante, we'll take a cab back."

Ben splashed water at Gib. "Stop bitching. You missed me while I was gone. Admit it."

"You two are adorable." Mira giggled. Every Christmas until about the age of ten, she asked her parents for a baby brother. It never panned out, but it looked like now she might have finally scored a pair of older almost-brothers. "Ben, if you ever break up with Ivy, you could move straight into a relationship with Gib."

"Hardly. Putting aside the fact I could never leave my beautiful fiancée—"

"—And that I'm as straight as they come," added Gib.

"—I don't have the patience to wait in line. Half the city of Chicago wants to sleep with Gib. Of course, the other half already did. The man's legendary."

Mira appreciated the switch in topics. Their light-hearted banter gave her the chance to absorb Sam's story. It felt good to pound her heartbreak into the asphalt beneath her feet. So much despair, so much pain. Sam Lyons must have the strength of ten men. Her respect for him soared higher than the antennas blinking red and white atop the Hancock Building. His resilience after so much tragedy acted like a magnet, drawing her to him. After their boat ride, she'd wanted more of his scorching kisses. Now she wanted more of all of him. And when Mira set her sights on something, she worked and clawed single-mindedly until she got it.

SEVEN

SAM WANTED TO walk out some of his nerves by pacing back and forth at the entrance to the Chicago Botanic Garden. But his strategic hiding place behind a pillar afforded him a whopping fourteen inches of legroom. Which meant all his pent-up energy still had to go someplace.

Sure enough, his fingers tightened on the thick green stem he held until it snapped. Shit. He bobbled the hot-pink gerbera, just catching it before it hit the pavement. This is why he rarely went to the trouble of making romantic gestures, big or small. They were a pain in the ass. But after two bad starts with Mira and then canceling on her, Sam knew he needed to pull out all the stops tonight. He'd even ironed his lucky shirt.

If she ever showed up. Daphne had texted him five minutes ago they were pulling into the parking lot, and he still didn't see them. Had Daph blown the surprise? Was Mira still so pissed at him she refused to get out of the car?

This was a stupid idea. A better plan for their date, the smart way to go, would've been a reservation at Spiaggia or Gibsons. Someplace that would make his credit card whimper. Someplace snazzy with candles and snooty waiters and, hell, chairs. What made him think Mira would want to spend the evening sitting on the ground?

"I'm going to run back to the car and grab my sweater." Daphne's voice rang out loud and clear. "Wait for me, okay?" It was the signal he'd been waiting for. Sam peeked around the pillar, trying not to get jabbed in the eye by the climbing rose. Mira stood near the entrance. A sleeveless denim dress clung in all the right places, and stopped gratifyingly high on her thighs. Her white sneakers were appropriate for tromping around the gardens. Combined with the short skirt that showed off miles of leg, they lent her a sexy cheerleader air. Sam'd had great success working his way through both the jv and varsity teams in high school. He hoped his luck in that department still held true.

Sam jammed one hand into the pocket of his cargo shorts, took a deep breath and left the anonymity of the pillar. "Hi."

As she twisted around on one foot, her hair lifted and spun like a bullfighter's silken cape. "Oh, hi." Mira's eyes widened, and a cautious smile bloomed. "This is a surprise."

"That's the idea."

"Hmm, that could be good or bad. Is this a new reality show?" She made a big show of looking over both shoulders. "Am I being filmed? Have I been randomly chosen to participate in a treasure hunt through America's public gardens?"

She hadn't run away, or slapped him. Better still, she was teasing. A couple pounds of anxiety fell off Sam's shoulders. They were off to a great start. "No. I leave all the true-life videography to Ben. But if you mention that idea to him, he could probably sell it to

RealTV and get you some royalties. They'll stick any reality crap on the air at that network."

"Have you seen their new show that follows around people who work at amusement parks? There's nothing exciting about watching someone remind you to keep your hands and feet in the car a hundred times a day." Mira shook her head. "As much as I wouldn't mind augmenting my income right about now, I'll stick to the day job."

A safe topic, as innocuous as skim milk. Sam leapt on it. "How's that going?"

Mira cocked her head. "Is this the surprise? Because work-related small talk is more the norm than a surprise."

Maybe they weren't off to such a great start. "No. I'm the surprise." Belatedly, Sam thrust the hot-pink flower at her. Mira took it, then looked toward the parking lot.

"Daphne's not coming back, is she?"

"Nope. I arranged for her to bring you up here."

She pursed the generous lips he so badly wanted to kiss. "Why the cloak-and-dagger routine? Why didn't you just ask me?"

Should he admit Ben warned him how mad she was when he dropped in for his daily peach fritter? Or would that make him look worse for not figuring it out himself? "I canceled our date at the last minute. It was thoughtless, and I'm sorry. You've got every right to be upset. I just didn't want to risk you not giving me another chance." Sam refused to grovel. A man had to keep his pride. But hopefully he'd said enough to at least coax her through the turnstile. He couldn't gauge her mood. Those bright blue eyes of hers weren't sparkling or sparking. They were giving him a thorough once-over.

"Okay."

Now he understood why his friends got frustrated with his usual low word count responses. What the hell was he supposed to get out of one measly word? Did it mean she wasn't still mad? Or was still mad but accepted his apology? Men could barely understand women under the best of circumstances. The one thing Sam knew without a doubt was that if he interpreted it wrong, his window for kissing those glossy pink lips would slam shut for good. He shifted his weight from one foot to the other, stalling for time. Then he realized he'd already bluffed once. The odds of it working again were slim.

"You've got to give me a little more to go on here."

Mira bridged the distance between them and threw her arms around him. Not one to look a gift horse in the mouth, Sam pulled her into a tight embrace. She smelled like flowers and felt like heaven. It left no doubt in his mind she wanted to be with him tonight. And it also left no doubt in his mind that he wanted to skip over the entire date and go right to the good stuff at the end.

The process of dating had always been fun for Sam, sort of like working a puzzle. He genuinely enjoyed listening to people talk. Mira's combination of vulnerability, feistiness and dogged drive intrigued him. Even sparring with her was sort of fun, now that he didn't have to worry about her clocking him again.

But with her tight body burrowed against his, all thoughts of giving her the date she deserved were smothered under one hundred percent, pure animal lust. If he lowered his hands just a few inches, he could lift her up and urge her legs around his waist. Then he'd back her up against a wall and kiss his way down from her cotton-candy lips until he discovered if her nipples were the same shade of pink.

Mira rose up on tiptoe to murmur in his ear. "I'm not mad at you."

"Not even a little? I didn't have to make the grand gesture with the daisy?"

"The daisy definitely earned you points. But I'm not mad because the guys told me all about your mom."

Well. Nothing could shrink a hard-on faster than revisiting his family angst. The whole sex-against-the-wall fantasy disappeared faster than sugar stirred into boiling water. Sam dropped his arms to his sides and pulled away. "This is awkward. On the other hand, it saves me from having an even more awkward conversation with you down the road. You know the whole story?"

"I think so. I'm very sorry for your loss, and for everything you've struggled with since your father died."

Sam had spent too long mired in the darkness of grief. Grief not just for his dad, but for his mom, and for the life he'd given up. Now that he'd come out the other side, he didn't want to dip his toes back in that black pool of despair. No matter how sincere Mira might be, covering old ground would merely ensure he wouldn't pop wood for days. "Thanks. Can we agree not to talk about it anymore tonight?"

"Oh. Sure." Mira tucked the flower behind her ear. "I love daisies."

"Want to see some more?" He pulled two tickets out of his pocket and ushered her through the turnstile. "Ivy, as usual, was right. Chicago's too big to take a bite out of by yourself. So I'm going to keep introducing you to bits and pieces of it." Sam held out his hand, fingers spread wide in invitation. "If that's okay with you?"

She interlaced her fingers into his and held on tight. "I'm game."

"Figured as much. You don't turn away from any challenge, do you?"

"I try not to. I'm still walking with you, aren't I?" she sassed back. Sam interpreted the sass as a very good sign. He swung her arm in a slow arc.

"The Botanic Garden's one of Chicago's treasures. I thought I'd show you my favorite spot here. Hopefully you'll be impressed. They're no gardens at Versailles, of course," he said, not entirely teasing. Her silver-spoon background still made him twitchy. As if no matter what he did with her, it wouldn't measure up to everything else she'd seen and done in gilt-edged, diamond-encrusted circles. They passed the wide oval of the lily pond. Dragonflies dive-bombed the water bugs skating between the flat, shiny leaves.

Mira elbowed him a short jab to the ribs. "Hey, if we can't talk about your emotional baggage, mine's off-limits, too."

"Fair enough." Sam thought about it for a minute. Then he got distracted by the feel of her palm against his, and wondering what it would feel like cupped around other parts of his body. "So what will we talk about?"

"Hmm. Politics and religion are always good for a few rounds."

Hardly. Talking about his mom's stint in a mental hospital and Mira's parents' boatloads of money would be less contentious than those topics. Throw in a debate about capital punishment, and they'd have one heck of an evening.

"Perhaps I wasn't clear when I gave you the flower. This whole night isn't just a continued introduction to Chicago. It isn't part two of Ivy browbeating us into coexisting well. This is a date. I only talk politics with Ben, and I only talk religion with people I *don't* want to see again." He angled them off the brick walkway to cut across the grass toward the rose petal fountain.

Mira shot him a sidelong glance from beneath half-lowered lids. "Does this mean you're already planning on seeing me again? That's a pretty optimistic stance, considering we're only five minutes into a date you tricked me into going on in the first place."

They strolled past massive pink-and-red rose-bushes, a living wall of color and scent. Mira tugged him to a stop. They watched in silence as the water spilled unevenly off the fountain's petal-shaped ledges. Since she arrived, he'd had trouble reading her. She wore an air of mystery, almost like she knew something Sam didn't about tonight. Funny, since he was the one surprising her. Or was it that Mira thought she was the one pulling his strings? Well, he'd put a stop to that. Sam didn't need to be in charge, but he did need them to be on an even footing. Might have to step it up a notch already. He faced her and rested his hands loosely on her waist. And tried not to think how fantastic it would be to cup her rounded hips and rock her back and forth on top of him.

"I'm sure I want another date with you, Mira. Want to know why?"

She nodded.

"You're like a cannoli. They aren't chocolate, so I assume you've had one?"

She nodded again, with a mystified smile.

"Their outer layer seems both indestructible and brittle. Once you break through, the center is sweet and creamy, yet still studded with interesting surprises of nuts and dried fruit. One bite is never enough. Oh, and that dusting of powdered sugar makes them delicately beautiful. And you are the most beautiful woman I've ever seen."

Mira's eyelids drooped heavily—the personification of bedroom eyes. A faint blush that matched the nearest rosebush pinked her cheeks. Then her tongue slipped out to moisten her lips. It did him in. Sam tightened his grip, pulling her so close he felt the rapid rise and fall of her chest.

"Don't look at me like that. Like you could gobble me up whole," Mira said. Her cheeks grew darker. "I might have to take action."

Sam wondered if she was one of those ultra-feminists who got offended by an honest compliment. Damn it, was she mad or aroused? Why couldn't he figure her out? "I chose this location carefully. We're surrounded by nature, not knickknacks. There's nothing here you can use to assault me."

"Not true. There's one thing." Mira launched herself at him, throwing both arms around his neck. Instinct lowered his hands to her tight, curvy ass for a better grip. Sam barely managed to keep both of them from toppling into the fountain. He did stagger backward a few steps until the spray misted them lightly.

The heat of the late-afternoon sun on his back didn't come close to matching the heat she kindled between them. Eagerly, Sam sank into those luscious lips. She took quick nibbles, even nipping. A zing shot straight down to his dick. Yeah, if this was her taking charge, sign him up for more of that!

With a final lick around the outline of his lips, she slid her tongue inside. And Mira didn't stay still. No, she wriggled against him. He wouldn't be able to hold on to her much longer. The heavy scent of roses twined around them like something out of a fairy tale. From now on, whenever Sam smelled roses, he'd feel Mira's breasts tautly pushing against his chest. He'd remember the perfection of her kisses, and the silken glide of her legs against his. No doubt he'd go from zero to titanium-hard in two seconds.

She broke away first. "You were right. Another date is inevitable."

Being right felt great. Not quite as great as kissing her, but Sam had plans to get back to that later. "Don't jump the gun. We've barely begun the evening."

Mira shaded her eyes with her hands and twisted to look at the sun. "Isn't it almost closing time? Or did it already close?" She situated the now slightly battered daisy more firmly behind her ear. "Come to think of it, I haven't seen any other people since I got here."

Good thing, too, the way they'd gone at each other like hormonal teenagers. Sam took her hand again and guided her out of the rose garden. "I wanted you all to myself."

"I can't decide if that's sweet or creepy."

Just what every guy wanted to hear. Especially after pulling enough strings to make a skein of rope. Oh, yeah. Mira kept him on his toes. Kind of like walking over hot coals. He decided to brush right past her remark, and hope she'd lean toward romantic sooner rather than later. "The place closed early tonight. For 'maintenance,'" Sam said, making quotation marks with his fingers.

"How on earth did you manage that?"

"I know a guy."

Mira snorted. "Come on, you sound like a line from a bad movie. Wow me with how much effort it took to set this up."

"Really, I went to high school with a guy who works here. No big deal." Sam didn't want to impress her with the details. He wanted to impress *upon* her the moment. It didn't matter his supposed friend had extorted a baby shower and a birthday cake out of him in exchange for free run of the place. He didn't want Mira to feel guilty if she found out both cakes were in a week when he was already overbooked.

All Sam wanted was for her to walk past the sweetly scented lavender bushes with him. Talk about nothing as they watched the sun set. Most importantly, leave everything outside the gates and just *be* with him. No store, no arguing over the connecting door, no nosy friends. A man and a woman sharing what could be the last summer night of the season.

"Here we are." The pathway opened up onto a terrace that jutted out into the lake. A weeping willow provided ample shade over the heart-shaped blanket.

Plates and glasses sat next to an old-fashioned wicker picnic basket.

"Sam, this is wonderful. Although the kiss at the fountain alone would've been enough to catapult this onto my top ten first dates list." Mira beamed at him, an over-the-top smile that warmed him to his toes. "Wait a minute. Isn't that one of my blankets? From the store?"

"Yep. We're conducting a quality control experiment on it tonight. Before you start selling it to the general public."

"But how did you get it?"

"Your new cook, Helen, stopped by for some éclairs on her way home. She's great, by the way. Hit it off instantly with my mom."

"Wait a minute. *Helen's* already met your mom, but *I* still haven't? I'm in the store every day."

"Mom's been pulling the pre-dawn shift to do the heavy baking the last couple of weeks. We swap it off. She sometimes leaves before you even get in." Yet another pressure weighing him down. She'd scaled back her hours without any explanation. It left him frustrated. More than that, it significantly tipped the scales—the wrong way—on his looming, potentially life-changing decision about the bakery.

"Anyway, I mentioned the picnic, and Helen insisted I use the blanket." Sam thought, after that whopper of a kiss, they were finally on the same page. But he was so used to Mira being prickly, he worried at her continued silence. Could she be mad? "Don't worry, I'll pay for it. Your bottom line won't be negatively impacted by our date."

Mira sat down on the blanket. Curling her legs

beneath her, she patted the other half of the heart in invitation. He sank down and pulled his legs into a pretzel. "At our first couple of meetings, if you told me the earth was round, I would've picked a fight and argued that it's a flat plane in a curve. We let our tempers bring out the worst in each other."

"Agreed," he said cautiously. Where was she going with this?

"I'm not mad you brought the blanket. I'm touched by the detail, by your thoughtfulness in setting up this entire date. You can't spend the night worrying about pissing me off, and I can't worry about biting my tongue. We like each other. We want each other."

"Hell, yes." In that position, her skirt rode up high on her thigh. If she took a deep breath, he might be able to tell what color panties she wore. The tantalizing possibility made Sam scoot closer until their knees touched. Those few square inches of skin-to-skin contact would have to tide him over. Now he could meet her eyes, the same shimmery blue as the placid water behind her.

"So this is truly a first date, starting fresh. Let's make a pact. No more knee-jerk reflexes. All our preconceived notions about each other go out the window." She stuck out her hand, and they shook.

"What treats did you bring?" Mira asked, pointing at the basket.

"It's a surprise. To both of us," he admitted. "Gib had the head chef at the Cavendish throw it together for me."

She whistled, long and low. "The Cavendish Grand is a five-star hotel. They cook for heads of state and celebrities over there. Doesn't their chef have better things to do than put cheese and crackers in a basket?"

"Probably. But Gib owes me, and I was desperate." How much should he tell her? After all, the whole point of tonight was to get to know each other. Why not vent a little and see how it goes? "At the last minute, my mother took the afternoon off to go see some weep-fest movie with her friends." Again. With no warning. "Busy afternoon, steady stream of customers, so I got behind in my baking and prep for tomorrow. I ran out of time." Sam realized he'd clenched both of his hands, and made a conscious effort to spread his fingers flat. Also a good opportunity to slide a palm onto Mira's soft, smooth calf.

"Hmm. While it's probably good for your mom to have some girl time, it sounds like she knocked you for a loop."

"Not just today." Now that he'd begun, he didn't want to stop. It felt so good to unburden himself to someone objective. Someone who hadn't been a spectator on the last few, gut-wrenching years. "She's doing that more and more. Coming in late after yoga class. Taking off early a couple of times a week for wine night, or bunko night, or whatever other excuse her friends make to get together and drink wine."

"Doesn't it indicate she's back to normal?"

"Sure. And a big-ass sign that she's ready to retire. Plus, she flat-out told me." Hadn't that been one hell of a conversation. *Thanks for busting your butt to keep the family business open for me, but hoping to walk away soon.* Sam got that his mom had to figure out how to live life without her husband. But did it have to be without their bakery, too?

Mira brushed her hands against the fleecy softness of the blanket in a fan motion. "When she retires, would she close the bakery?"

"No." The word exploded from his mouth, loud enough to startle the swans floating by into taking flight. "It's my dad's legacy. Something to pass down from generation to generation. Closing isn't an option. The family business survives, no matter how few Lyons are manning the ovens. But I'm working on that."

"Really?" Mira quirked an eyebrow. "Am I part of your master plan? Because even if you get super lucky tonight, a baby won't pop out for at least nine months. I doubt it'd be ready to man the ovens until it mastered, oh, walking, for instance."

"Very funny." And it was. He and his mom always had long, serious conversations about the bakery. Mira's humor was a nice change of pace. "I've got a sister, Diana. We'll say she's on the reserve list. She's in Europe right now."

"Quite the commute to bake a couple dozen trays of scones."

"She'll come back when Mom finally steps down." At least, he hoped so. She'd been AWOL for a few months. If he didn't follow her Twitter account, they wouldn't know which country she'd flitted to each week. When he thought about Diana's open-ended return, it threw him into a cold sweat. Sam tried not to think about it too often. Easy during the day, but too often he'd fly awake in the middle of the night in a head-pounding panic.

With the grace of a daddy longlegs, Mira trailed

slender, pink-tipped fingers across the top of the basket. "Are you ready to peek?"

Did his face show his growing discomfort? Or had she just sensed that, while grateful to air some of his dirty laundry, he was ready to talk about, well, *anything* else? "Not yet. See those swans?" They floated placidly once more, in pairs, like wedding cake toppers. "If we take any of the food out and walk away, they'll be all over it. I have one more place to show you, and then we'll come back and eat." According to his master plan, they'd uncork the wine as the sun set. He'd just have to be sure not to get distracted by Mira's many charms and make it back in time.

"Are you sure you want to get up? I can't imagine anything more beautiful than this."

Sam ran his hand over her shiny hair, enjoying the slide of it through his fingers all the way down to her shoulder blades. Thinking about the silken torture it would be against his bare skin. Then he cupped her face between her palms. Bending down close enough to see the minuscule flecks of gray and violet in her eyes, he said, "Neither can I."

"Oh." She sucked in a ragged breath. "Oh my."

The growing pressure from the zipper of his shorts reminded him to stick to the plan. As tempting as it might be to push her back onto the blanket and kiss her senseless, Mira deserved more. Tonight was dedicated to romance. Sam intended to make one hell of a first-date impression, to offset the disastrous actual first impression he'd made on her. "Let's go."

They strolled past tall marsh grasses hugging the water, and watched a blue heron swoop down and grab a snack. Random rocks gave the illusion of a secondary path across the water, interspersed with clumps of lily pads. The ever-present buzz of cicadas warred with the throaty call of mockingbirds. "This is so peaceful," Mira said in a hushed tone.

Now was his chance. Relaxed, quiet and her guard dropped, he couldn't imagine a better time to tease an answer out of her. "I can't be at peace until you answer one question. One question that's driving me crazy."

"Here it comes. The typical first-date question out of every guy's mouth. Let me save you the trouble. Yes, I can do the splits. Front and sideways. I'm very bendy."

Sam stumbled over the lip of the wooden serpentine bridge. Only a quick arm cartwheel kept him from plunging into the water. "Are you trying to kill me? I can't be expected to walk a straight line with that kind of visual."

She grabbed his wrist and pulled him back upright. From there, it was only natural to curve his arm to rest against her waist, palm firmly anchored on her hip. "Sorry," Mira said with a giggle. "What's your question?"

"Why don't you like chocolate?"

They made it halfway across the bridge before she answered. "I used to be chubby."

If Mira was soaking wet, he could still probably bench press her with one hand. She had a dancer's build, long and lean. Now that he'd pressed up against all that toned muscle, he knew there wasn't a single extra ounce on her. In fact, she should probably add a couple meals' worth of burgers and fries to her weekly routine. A few helpings of his famous triple-cream cheesecake wouldn't hurt, either. "I don't believe it."

"I wasn't the huge girl in *Hairspray*, just a little roly-poly. Like a lot of preteen girls before they hit a growth spurt. My parents picked me up from boarding school and were shocked. Or, to be more precise, embarrassed at the thought of their friends seeing their less than perfect daughter. So instead of us enjoying a family summer vacation, they packed me off to a fat camp."

"Seems drastic." Cruel was more like it.

"No, the drastic part was feeding me chocolate for the entire weekend before I left. Nothing else. Just chocolate bars for breakfast, lunch and dinner. Oh, and snacks several times a day. By Monday morning even the smell of chocolate made me queasy. I've never touched it since."

Birdsong grew louder as they stepped onto Evening Island. The carillon with its multiple tiers of huge bells towered over them. Bushes, some flowering pastels and some a vibrant green, formed a sweeping carpet away from the water. Tall, wispy, white-frothed stalks speared into a living wall. Sam didn't see any of the natural beauty.

All he could see was a distraught girl with long brown hair choking down chocolate until it made her sick. He wanted to punch something, curse a blue streak into the growing twilight. Most of all, he wanted to scream at the Parrishes. Tell them to their face what horrible parents they were, and how they'd scarred their precious little girl.

"I…God…I don't know what to say. I'm floored." Sam thought of and immediately discarded at least half a dozen responses. None of them fit the enormity of his feelings. "I'm sorry, Mira."

She flashed a quick smile, then just as fast, glanced away again. "Don't be. That summer turned out to be amazing. It nipped in the bud any issues I might have had, and taught me healthy eating. Most of all, it taught me to respect myself. To know that I control my choices, my life. I've never forgotten what a difference Camp Ticonderoga made in my life. It's why I go back every summer for six weeks to be a counselor. So I can teach other little girls how to grow up into strong women."

Strong? Mira was a true heavyweight. She put those guys who pulled semis with their teeth to shame. "I can't think of a better role model. They're lucky to have you."

"Oh, I'm no hero. It goes both ways. Being an only child, especially with parents who barely noticed me most of the time, well, it sucked. I always wanted a sister. When I'm at camp, sharing that cabin with a dozen girls, I get to live out my childhood fantasy. Late-night talks, sharing secrets, braiding each other's hair—fun stuff."

"Pillow fights?" he teased.

"Maybe one or two. Honestly, with synthetic pillows it isn't like in the movies. You need a good down pillow that might explode into a flurry of feathers to have a real pillow fight."

Suddenly her heart-wrenching story floated straight out of his head. Same with the heartwarming story of her summertime pseudo-sisters. All he could think of was Mira, in just panties and a bra, wielding a pillow through the air thick with feathers. As though using Photoshop, he turned the matching underwear into a lacy, pale blue set. Then he pasted himself into the picture. "I've got down pillows."

"Really?"

"Five of them." Sam drew her off the path to the edge of a swath of something tall and purple and spiky. It smelled amazing. Two steps in and they were against a tree trunk. Sam twisted to put his back against the rough bark. Widening his stance, he pulled her in between his legs. Mira tucked her lower body against his, but placed her palms on his chest. She angled her head to the side and flashed him a knowing look, full of feminine wiles and guile.

"Is that an invitation?"

Did she want one of those thick, gold-edged invites Ivy liked to charge the sun and the moon for? God, she was toying with him. Could she see the base, animalistic need in his eyes? Or did she just feel it pressing against her thigh? She knew, all right. The hardworking, nose-to-the-grindstone, overachieving Mira had finally clocked out for the night. Now he was left with an armful of warm, willing, wanton Mira the seductress.

"You bet."

"If I win the pillow fight, would you promise to stay up all night, talking to me?"

"Sweetness, I'll stay up all night, no problem. But we won't be talking." A man could only withstand so much. Sam crushed her against his chest and took her mouth. He laid claim to her, using his tongue to learn every soft and sensitive crevice. Mira moaned, a low sound that vibrated through every hair on his body. Dark, spiky lashes fanned out over her pale cheeks. His hands moved over her slender back, hugging her close. Didn't matter—he wouldn't be close enough until he was inside of her.

Mira moved her palms up, over his shoulders to twine around his neck. Added bonus? She rubbed her firm, tempting breasts back and forth with every breath, every movement. He couldn't wait to get his mouth on them. Literally.

Grabbing her ass with both hands, he stepped away from the tree and urged her legs around his waist. It didn't seem to take much urging. Mira clamped on like a rodeo star. Sam looked around the garden, desperate to find something more solid than flowers. His gaze landed on a large boulder, artistically encircled with—well—something delicate and blooming. He'd follow the Garden's rules and not pick any of the flowers. But there were a few that would be the worse for wear in a few minutes.

Dropping to his knees, Sam leaned Mira back onto the boulder. To make sure her legs stayed around him, he kept his fingers kneading her ass. "I had a whole plan. Sunset. Wine. A civilized picnic."

Mira opened one eye to squint at the sky. "Sunset's still at least five minutes away. A man with your considerable talent should be able to show me a very good time in five minutes."

"Are you double dog daring me?"

"Well, since we're work neighbors, and need to maintain some element of professionalism, let's call it a request for services."

Sam almost choked on his chuckle. Good to know she still managed to find ways to parade her MBA. "Looks like we're two peas in a pod. I don't back down from a challenge, either."

He lowered his head to the side of her neck with all the fervor of a blood-starved Dracula. Pale skin as translucent as phyllo dough made it possible for him to watch her pulse beat faster and faster just beneath the surface. Using the flat of his tongue, Sam took a long, slow, meandering lick. Then he latched on, trying to suck that pulse even faster. Once the rhythm beating against his taste buds increased, he moved down.

With her wriggling nonstop, it was difficult to keep a hold on Mira. He angled nearer to the boulder, pinning her in place at her hips with his more-than-willing dick. It surged into the notch between her legs, almost bursting through his shorts. Sam tried with all his might not to process any of the sensations his nerves were processing. He ignored how fan-fucking-tastic she felt, how they fit together more snugly than puzzle pieces. Above all else, Sam refused to acknowledge how much he wanted this beautiful bundle, currently writhing in his hands. If he reveled in it for even a second, he'd give in to those base instincts, rip her clothes off with his teeth and plow into her.

Instead, he concentrated on pleasing Mira. She made it so easy, moaning and smiling and lifting to his touch like a flower to the sun. Licking across her collarbone, he nudged aside the open collar of her shirt. In this position her breasts strained the fabric to its limits. It was easy to pop the top button open with his teeth. Then one more, for good measure. Now her beautiful breasts were laid out for his enjoyment. They were as white and perfectly round as a cup of powdered sugar, framed by the pale blue satin of her bra. Sam absolutely loved it when women matched their underwear to their clothes. It was a little thing, but it drove him crazy in a very good way.

With absolute concentration, he licked across one creamy mound, then over to the other. Sam could've died a happy man doing that all day. Mira, though, apparently had other ideas. She grabbed his head with both hands and maneuvered it into position straight over her nipple.

"Want something?" he asked, his breath feathering over the satin.

"Yes. You," she panted. "Now."

"Glad we're on the same page." Sam lowered his head a quarter of an inch and just exhaled. Her nipple immediately reacted, poking through the fabric. Target acquired. He laved back and forth across the pronounced tip, the pale blue darkening from the trail of dampness he created. A few more passes, and then he sucked in, biting down with a gentle nip.

Mira practically jolted out of his grasp. "Sam," she cried, "oh, wow."

"Funny, that's just what I was thinking." It was harder to talk now, harder to think, hard to do anything but give in to the monstrous lust she roused in him. Sam switched to the other side, replicating the teasing with his tongue. But it wasn't enough. In one swift motion, he picked her up and deposited her on the ground.

He straddled her, but kept his weight off. Mira threaded her fingers through his hair and tugged him up for a thorough, drugging kiss. If his eyes were open, they would've crossed. Still, she couldn't distract him for long. He was a man with a purpose. No time to wrestle with the stupid back clasp. Why the hell didn't women have front clasp bras anymore? Oh, well. Just as easy to scoop her breasts in toward the center and sweep the cups underneath.

Now, finally, he had skin-on-skin contact. Even better, he could see her pretty nipples, the same vibrant pink as his strawberry icing. Sam drew as much of her breast as he could into his mouth, lapping circles around the nipple hardening to a sharp point under his tongue. It was so good that he eased his knees to the ground. Legs caging hers, they touched from toe to chest. The pressure of her body against his offered both relief and an immediate spiral into frustrating, driving need. Giving in, he rocked his hips back and forth, and she met his pattern, thrusting upward. As soon as a guttural moan of pleasure escaped his lips, he rolled off her to the side.

Stopping wasn't easy. Not by a long shot. But Sam forced himself to for two reasons. Mira deserved better than a literal roll in the grass. He'd screwed up enough with her already. When they had sex for the first time, it wouldn't be in a place where they ran the risk of being caught. He could only imagine what hell she'd rain down on him—rightfully so—if they got arrested, naked, for public indecency or something.

And he'd put a lot of thought into planning this date. Sex was not on the agenda. A long, romantic picnic watching the sun set over the lake was. Smarter way to go all around. Sam wasn't in this for a one-night hookup. That would be the stupidity all his friends warned him against. He wanted to keep peeling back the fascinating layers to Mira, not just her clothes. So they'd spend the rest of the night talking. Okay, maybe a few more kisses. And he'd start thinking about a plan for getting her into his bed sooner rather than later.

"Open your eyes," he ordered.

Hands curled into fists, every line of her body taut with anticipation, her eyelids sprang open. "What is it? What are you doing all the way over there?"

"Look at the sky," he ordered. The bright blue had dulled to a haze. Streaks of red and pink undulated to the west, and the sun sat almost at the horizon. "If we run, we can still make it to watch the sunset."

Mira pulled her clothes into place and clamored to her feet. It gratified him to see her knees wobble. She leaned one hip against the boulder and inhaled deeply. "You put on one heck of a first date, Mr. Lyons."

Sam grabbed her hand and took off for the bridge at an easy lope she'd be able to match. "Glad you're enjoying yourself. Wait'll you get a load of date number three. That's where I really hit my stride."

EIGHT

MIRA MADE ONE final pass with the steamer over the deep red fabric, then set down the wand. With a groan, she shook out her arms and rolled her shoulders. It didn't help much. Instead, it made her aware of sore muscles she'd worked quite hard at ignoring for the past few hours. The manual labor involved in getting the store into shape had already knocked five pounds off—or maybe stress was responsible? Perhaps the constant, nagging worry about making A Fine Romance a success from day one? Either way, she longed for a bubble bath at the end of the day. Which wouldn't come for, oh, about ten more hours.

Unable to sleep—huh, maybe stress *was* getting to her—she'd gotten to the store at least an hour before dawn began to pearlize the sky. A compulsion to decorate the windows had taken root a few days before. They'd been covered with brown paper for months now. While it hid the messy chaos of the store, it did nothing to create a buzz in the neighborhood. With the opening right around the corner, Mira couldn't ignore the potential for essentially free advertising.

Now, fabric the same rich red as the store logo hung from floor to ceiling, ending in rounded puddles that would look as elegant to shoppers inside as to window shoppers on the sidewalk. Oversized black pillows in an artistic heap were centered on each side.

Balanced atop, a long-stemmed red rose. Daphne had promised to keep her in fresh roses daily. It might be a bit much. It might even look like she was about to open a bordello. But the one thing Mira didn't doubt was that it looked sinfully romantic.

Keys clattered against the door, and a moment later Helen breezed inside. A swirl of rust-colored leaves eddied at her feet. An early autumn chill darted in, an uninvited tagalong. "Mira Parrish, you have outdone yourself," Helen declared. "I've been outside for five minutes soaking in the decadent atmosphere you've created."

While the aches in her arms and shoulders and the weird one shooting from her butt down the back of her thigh didn't disappear, Mira suddenly found them much easier to ignore. "It's not too much?"

"Of course it is. The provocative, implied sensuality is completely over the top. Which is why it works so well. Don't change a thing." She utilized the old-fashioned coat tree Mira snagged for five dollars at a salvage house, still talking a mile a minute. "If, God forbid, this store doesn't pan out for you, you'd be a shoo-in as a window dresser. So simple, yet so rich, rather like a chocolate truffle."

Great. Mira had managed to go an entire twelve minutes without thinking about Sam. Aside from sleeping, it was the longest she'd gone without thinking of him since their date. Pretty much every time she blinked, a funny memory would pop into her head, or more likely, a steamy hot one. Sam's kisses were addicting. Damn it. She'd just zoned out for five seconds or so, licking her lips and imagining the brush of his mouth over hers. Luckily, Helen kept talking, caught up in getting settled. Clad in another timeless St. John knit suit, this one a seasonal burnt orange, the older woman looked ready for an afternoon of lunching and shopping.

"Helen, I'm always glad to see you, but what are you doing here?"

"I've brought more treats for you to sample." She set a picnic basket on the counter with a quizzical smile. "You told me to come by at lunchtime, remember?"

Oh, she remembered. What had slipped her notice was the time. Something Mira kept running out of with shocking regularity. She reset the hose and wound the cord in a figure eight on the back of the steamer.

"It's noon already? No. It can't be. I've got too much to do. Three interviews are on the schedule, which will suck up a huge portion of the afternoon. I still can't get the computer inventory program to work right, and our ad has to be in to *Chicago Style* magazine by end of business. Their cutoff was last week, but Ivy just arranged the publisher's third wedding. Apparently his new bride was thrilled, and as a thank-you he gave us some extra time. Which would be enough, if the graphic designer would email me the file. It's like he's holding it hostage for some reason. I don't know why. Can you tell me, what does a nineteen-year-old computer savant want from me besides the substantial check I already sent him?"

Helen deftly tucked in the end of the plug. Then she framed Mira's face with her palms. "Honey, how much coffee have you had today?"

"None." When you can't keep your eyes shut for

more than a few hours at a time, coffee became ir-relevant.

"All right, let's try another angle. How much sleep have you gotten this week?"

"Almost none?" she said with a weak attempt at a grin.

With an arm around her waist, Helen steered her to the stool in the kitchen. "I'm going to push my luck and ask when you ate last."

Too keyed up this morning, she'd skipped break-fast. Too exhausted last night, she'd gone straight to bed without dinner. Mira did distinctly remember get-ting a bagel yesterday morning. "Things are crazy right now. I opened my calendar on Sunday night and saw the big, red circle on September 30. Can you be-lieve we open in less than two weeks? Two weeks!" Mira shook her head. She'd always known the date, but for some reason, seeing it hit her like a steel-toed boot to her diaphragm. "Whatever sleep and food I miss out on now won't kill me. I can catch up once the preview and grand opening are behind us."

"Going full tilt like this, you won't last two weeks." Helen filled a glass with water and held it out. "Hy-drate. Water cures untold evils. From now on, you'll keep a bottle within arm's reach at all times."

"Sounds easy enough. I can do that."

"Keep that positive attitude. I'm not finished lec-turing you." Wagging a finger, Helen sat down next to her. "You can't run yourself ragged. Ivy certainly doesn't expect it of you. Keep in mind that as soon as you hire an assistant, your workload will be cut in half. Look at your to-do list, and prioritize what can be delegated once that happens."

The no-nonsense tone was tempered by Helen's firm grip on her hand. Mira had very little experience with the sensation, but she sensed she was being mothered. Funny, she found she liked it. A little bit of her stress melted away. She could tell because her shoulders literally relaxed downward a quarter inch. And Mira knew she'd gone overboard. Sometimes the fear of failure pushed her to a crazy place. "You're right. I can't take all the fun away from whoever I hire. I've got to leave them some scanning and dusting and, best of all, the inventory triple checks."

"That's the spirit. Now we're going to sit here for a bit and chat. Yes, that's another thing I'm going to insist on—you need to start taking breaks."

Mira hooked her feet on the rungs of the stool and pretended to scowl. It probably wasn't convincing. She was getting too big a kick out of Helen's concern. "Who's in charge here?"

"Interesting question." Helen tapped on the glass until Mira raised it to her lips. "Hypothetically, let's say that you're in charge of, well, you. If store manager Mira discovered an employee who shall remain nameless who worked sunup to sundown without eating, without taking breaks, and had dark circles under her eyes deep enough to be potholes, what would you do?"

Ooh, the woman played dirty. She'd driven her point home with a jackhammer. "Tell them to go home and sleep for a day."

"Exactly. But I'm well aware you wouldn't consent to that suggestion. As a compromise, you can take ten minutes to tell me how your date went."

Sure, she'd poured her heart out to Helen when

Sam stood her up. The woman was a font of sympathy and cheesy jokes about men. But she hadn't even
seen her since the surprise date at the Botanic Garden. "How did you know I had a date?"

"We had book club last night. *Snow Flower and the
Secret Fan*. A wonderful book, but a bit of a downer."
Helen waggled her hand back and forth in a so-so
gesture. "Sam made me a divine cake, green tea flavored and lychee icing, with the most beautiful Asian
fan on top, half folded. Covered with intricate characters, pictures of two women in gorgeous robes and
a tall mountain in the background. All edible. The
girls went wild for it."

"You pulled out all the stops. I always envisioned
book clubs as a place where you sat in a quiet circle,
speaking in iambic pentameter of literary things."

"We drink copious amounts of wine and stuff ourselves like pigs. On a good month, we'll talk about
the book for ten minutes. It's more of a chance to get
together and talk about men. Often sex. Sometimes
books. You should come to the next one."

Although it sounded like oodles of fun, Mira
couldn't. "You're my employee. It wouldn't feel right."

"You know all of six people in this city of eight
million. Expand your horizons. Come to one, and if
you don't like it, at least you will have met ten more
women."

A solid compromise. Mira rolled the idea around
like a mental butterscotch, letting the sweetness in-
fuse her. She yearned to belong. To be a part of a
group. Too many moves in childhood, and since college, left her aching to be folded into a social circle
and accepted. The chance to finally sink down roots

was a big reason why she'd come to Chicago. Mira resolved right then to try, at least once, every opportunity that came her way. "Count me in."

"Wonderful! But you can't veer me off topic so easily."

"What do you mean?" Mira tried to play innocent. But her heart was too full of Sam to not want to rewind and dissect every second of their date. On the other hand, doing it with someone old enough to be her mother seemed odd.

"When I picked up my absurdly beautiful cake, the usually impassive Mr. Lyons looked like the cat who ate the canary. It didn't take my vast knowledge of the opposite sex to figure out a woman put that smile on his face. I pried it out of him before he swiped my credit card. But the man barely spits out ten words at a time, so I need you to provide the details."

"Everyone keeps saying that…" Mira let her voice trail off.

"What?"

"That Sam doesn't talk much. Except, well, he does. When we first met, he wouldn't stop bickering with me. Now we talk about everything. And still bicker. A little."

"An oyster doesn't yield to every knife. Only the true wielder will pry it open and discover the pearl."

What on earth? How did her brand-new, oh-so-wise friend suddenly turn into a talking fortune cookie? "Are you serious?"

Helen dissolved into peals of laughter. "Sorry. We finished book club by trying to talk only in Chinese proverbs. I couldn't help myself."

Another layer of stress lifted off her shoulders as

Mira laughed, too. "Okay. For that, I'll tell you one thing about our romantic sunset picnic." Helen sighed and put a hand to her heart. "Then, when you force me to take another break, I'll dole out another detail."

"You drive a hard bargain."

Dust motes danced in a shaft of sunlight. Could she really say this in the light of day? In the middle of her still-scented-with-fresh-paint store? Mira reminded herself Ivy and Daphne had a packed week with some evening bridal showers, and wouldn't be available for a gossip session for days. Chances were good she'd burst like a water balloon on a sidewalk if she tried to hold it in that long.

"Sam kisses with his eyes open. He says it's because I'm so pretty, he can't stop looking at me." Her cheeks were on fire as she repeated his words. It might very well be the sweetest thing any man had ever said to her. And when Sam said it, his eyes burning like blue flame, Mira's heart tumbled straight down to her knees.

"Oh, my." Helen whipped a handkerchief out of her sleeve and fanned herself. "Talk about hidden depths. He is certifiably dreamy."

Mira couldn't agree more. "Hope that will tide you over. It's time for me to get back to work."

"Stay right there." Helen tapped her wristwatch. "I've been clocking you. Your break has six minutes to go. So tell me all about the progress you've made since I was here last week. Start with the obvious. The door looks new." She pointed at the connecting door to the bakery, now covered in black and red diagonal stripes.

"It got a makeover. For security and health code

reasons, we decided not to leave the door open all the time. Our compromise is a Dutch door."

The idea came to Sam on their picnic. After the sun set and they'd snacked their way through the enormous basket, it didn't take too much effort to divest him of his shirt. Since the first time they met, Mira couldn't get enough of his broad chest with its sexy cover of dark hair. She could happily spend days running her fingers across his pecs and down to that even sexier line of dark hair that disappeared into his shorts. It was when he tucked his shirt back in the idea for a two-part door hit him.

"Look at how clever!" Helen popped up and ran her fingers along the seam separating the two halves of the door. "Why isn't it open?"

"The store's a shambles." Mira looked around at the organized chaos of boxes and shelves, packing paper and cleaning products littering the floor. "Nobody should be forced to look at this mess." Absolutely, one hundred percent true. More important, with the door closed she wouldn't be tempted to stare at Sam with her tongue lolling out all day long. Plus, she wasn't in any sort of a hurry to meet Sam's mom. Usually when people started dating, they weren't forced to meet the parents until the relationship had gelled, months down the road. The whole situation was awkward times ten.

"Nonsense. It builds excitement. People love thinking they're getting glimpses behind the scenes." Before she could stop her, Helen slid back the latch and opened the top half of the door. "You're going to get a good buzz going in the neighborhood if you leave this open."

"You'll need to set up a tiered display in the kitchen area. It's the first thing they'll see when they peek in," Mira warned.

"Consider it done. Actually, while you're sitting here, why don't you try some of today's tasting menu? I brought eight different kinds of cheese."

Now that she'd sat idle for a few minutes, the adrenaline that had kept Mira going all morning drained away. Her stomach rumbled. As Helen pulled out hunks of cheese and a container of pepperoncini stuffed with salami and provolone, her mouth watered. "I think I would crawl across broken glass for some of your cheese at this moment."

"Why don't we invite your dreamsicle of a neighbor over? He deserves a tasty lunch, too. Especially after how he slaved over my cake yesterday."

"Oh, I don't think we should bother him." Eating with Sam the other night had been wholly sensual. He'd fed her, using the excuse to run his fingers over her lips until she almost forgot to chew. No way could she sit across from him—and Helen—and watch those blunt-tipped fingers stacking cheese and crackers. What if she lost all control, lunged across the counter and kissed him? No, they needed to stick to their plan to stay in their own stores during working hours.

"Why not? It'll be good to get a man's opinion in the mix."

"A man, yes. But not Sam." She grasped at the first reason, well, besides the real one, that sprang to mind. "I doubt he has a sophisticated enough palate to be useful. After all, he's spent his whole life rolling out cookies. If you needed an opinion on doughnuts, he'd be your guy."

"So that's how it is? You think I'm nothing more than a blue-collar hick with flour for brains?" Sam's forearms were braced on the bottom half of the door. He had a white towel thrown over his shoulder, and smears of chocolate like a Rorschach test across his plain blue tee. Blue flame burned in his eyes. This time it burned ice cold, and lust had nothing to do with it. Mira recoiled from his anger. Or was it hurt? Whatever the emotion, she regretted being the cause.

"I'm sorry. I didn't know you were standing there."

His full lips twisted downward. "So you're okay saying those things, just not to my face?"

"Well, no, of course not." Why did he have to turn what she said into something hurtful and ugly? "You're obviously smart. You run your own business."

"Remember when we were on the boat? You accused me of being too quick to judge you by your parents' money? Aren't you just as guilty of judging me by my appearance?" He whipped the towel off his shoulder and wiped off his hands. She didn't think the cloud of flour that arose was anything but deliberate.

Backed into a corner, and embarrassed at how his words hit home, she went on full defense. If he wanted to be a jerk, then she'd toss more proof in his face. Something she should've already brought up to him as an issue. "Clichés exist for a reason, Sam. You know what? Sometimes you *can* judge a book by its cover."

"Is that so?"

"I think I left the crackers in my trunk. I'm just going to nip out and get them," Helen murmured as she eased off her stool.

Mira whirled around. She'd completely forgotten they had an audience. Humiliation stung like lemon juice on a paper cut. "No. Sam chose to pick this fight in front of you, so you should stay to see how it ends. What I'm about to say affects you, too."

"You want to spread your gospel of judging people to the whole world?" Sam slammed through the door to glower at Mira up close. Like her own personal storm cloud about to crack open and pelt her with icy pellets of anger. "Be my guest."

"Okay, I've got an iron-clad example for you. There's a group—maybe even a gang—of teenage hooligans who hang out in the alley. Jeans halfway down their butts, hoodies, chains, your typical thug wardrobe. As a matter of fact, I planned to warn Helen about them today. They scavenge your leftover cookies out of the Dumpster." She shivered at the memory. Whether she was being overly judgmental or reasonably paranoid, Mira wasn't sure. She just knew that they'd scared her. Now she didn't go out in the alley without first cracking the door and peeking to be sure the coast was clear.

A loud, dismissive raspberry burst from Sam's lips. He backed off a few steps to lean against the refrigerator. "Those boys are harmless. Don't get your panties in a knot because they're eating cookies."

Mira snapped. Ripped the muzzle and leash off her temper and let fly. "Are you siding with them? Is this a stick up for the entire male race sort of thing?" She knew she was loud, and how had her fists crept onto her hips? But she couldn't stop the tirade. "Any chance you encourage gang activity by leaving them sweets on *top* of the Dumpster? Tell me, how is that good for customer relations? When one of our customers gets mugged by them, or worse, are you going to explain to Ivy how you turned a blind eye?"

"For Christ's sake." Sam rolled his eyes. "Can't you accept that they're decent kids with a bad fashion sense and leave it alone?"

Why did he insist on being so lackadaisical about a genuine safety issue? Would it take an actual attack for him to take her seriously? "No, I won't. They've already scared me once. I'm not going to stand by and let them scare someone else."

Sam lurched forward and gripped her by the elbows. "Explain how they scared you. Did they threaten you? Call you names? Did they touch you?"

"I...I don't know. I didn't hear." His fingers dug into the soft flesh of her inner arms. The fierceness in his gaze made it hard to think. "They pointed at me and laughed and whispered to each other. I didn't want to stick around to find out the specifics of the conversation. Why are you interrogating me all of a sudden?"

"Sorry." His fingers gentled, then stroked her arms in a quick caress. "You had me worried there for a minute. If those boys had truly hurt you, I would've pounded them into next week. With a lot of help from their probation officer."

Their what? The perceived danger ratcheted up into a whole different level. "They're criminals?"

"Not anymore." Sam gestured for the ladies to take a seat. He walked around the counter to lean his palms on the sink. "They're part of a work-release program with a juvenile halfway house. None of them are violent offenders. Just good kids who took an extra dose of stupid one day, and got caught."

"So you know them?" asked Helen. Interest lit her face, and she looked far more intrigued than scared. Mira, however, wasn't there yet. She needed to hear more.

"They work for me. Well, for Lyons Bakery. We keep it a secret because we don't want other retailers in the neighborhood to fly into a panic over nothing. Technically, they're ex-cons."

Mira cleared her throat. "Sounds like a reason for concern to me." A prison record didn't exactly make these kids sound like model citizens.

"But in reality, they're turning their lives around." Sam paced the narrow length of the kitchen. "Only a select few get invited to live at the halfway house, and even fewer get recommended for the work program. Social workers, probation officers, judges—they've all said these kids screwed up once, but probably won't ever again. They just need someone to believe in them."

"Is this a redeem-your-past sort of thing? Were you a bit of a hellion, Sam?" Helen propped her chin on her fists.

"Nothing out of the ordinary. Shoplifted gum when I was eight. Dad put the fear of God into me over that one. Had a motorcycle in high school."

A sigh slipped out. It was so easy for Mira to picture dark, brooding Sam. Under a black leather jacket he'd wear a tight white tee that strained across his pecs. Even though they were from the wrong decade, she topped him off with a pair of mirrored aviator shades. His legs were wide spread astride a Harley. Mira couldn't pick a Harley out of a lineup of bikes, but for her daydream, it seemed the way to go. Then she realized she'd sighed out loud. Helen and Sam both stared at her. In a less than convincing attempt to cover her sigh, she sniffled several times.

"Sorry. Fall allergies must be kicking in."

Coming to their side of the counter, Sam hitched out a stool with his foot and sat. "I've worked with six of these kids for almost a year now. Every single one shows real promise, and a strong work ethic. They have to stay in school and keep their grades up before they're allowed to come help me. Two of them are finishing their GEDs, at night. And they've been a huge help. I don't think I could've kept the bakery afloat without them."

Wow. Talk about a ringing endorsement. And aside from bad clothes, the boys hadn't really done anything in the alley to alarm her. In a new city, not yet able to feel out the danger vibes of Chicago, she'd jumped to conclusions. The wrong ones. "Your mother knows about this?"

He gave a short, sharp nod. "You bet. We're proud to be a force for change."

"I'm proud of you, too." Helen gave his forearm a squeeze.

Tears welled up at the corners of her eyes, but Mira blinked them back. It was too important to get her point out without it being choked off by stupid, emotional waterworks. She'd already cried once in front of Sam. If she did it again, he might wonder if she was actually stable. "When you think about it, my commitment to Camp Ticonderoga and teaching the girls to respect themselves is similar to you teaching the boys a trade, to respect themselves enough to better themselves."

"Maybe you two have more in common than you thought," Helen murmured.

Sam pushed off his stool and jammed his hands into his front pockets. "Speaking of things in common, did you pick up any other languages on all your trips through Europe?"

"I speak French." Poorly. She'd never learned to properly conjugate verbs, but did know how to order ice cream in five languages.

"Comment osez-vous me juger pour la cuisson des biscuits? Vous pensez qu'il y a pas d'art à la cuisson des cookies?"

Oh. My. God. Sam just standing in front of her was the epitome of sexy. But Sam spitting out a barrage of perfectly accented French she didn't begin to understand took her breath away. "I'm a little rusty."

"He asked how dare you judge him for baking cookies. Do you think there's no art to baking cookies?" Helen met her astonished gaze and shrugged. "I helped my kids with their homework. A lot. At a certain point, it became easier to just break down and learn the language. I'm also a whiz at history. I'll bore you silly one day by listing all the Plantaganets and Yorks involved in the War of the Roses."

Sam stalked forward, bristling with offended aggression again. "Baking is a profession people spend their entire lives mastering. You think all I do is pop open a tube of Pillsbury slice-'n'-bake and upcharge the hell out of my customers?"

"No." Mira thought they'd talked it out, reached a truce. And yet waves of some murky emotion still radiated from him. She couldn't one hundred percent classify it, but the top contenders were fury or annoyance. Either way, he might as well have picked up a Sharpie and written *I'm still mad at Mira* across his shirt.

"Gib and Ben filled you in on my life story, right? They tell you I went to college?"

"Yes." Had she somehow disparaged his college? Unwittingly made fun of his unknown mascot?

"I got my degree from the Culinary Institute of America. A bachelor's in baking and pastry arts management, to be specific. That's where I learned to speak French."

A long, low whistle from Helen stopped his monologue. "Your credentials are quite impressive. The CIA's renowned the world over."

Once again he paced, this time the width of the store. "It was a terrific school, but it wasn't enough for me. After working with my parents for a few years, I still had the urge to learn more about chocolate. So I went to Europe and studied with French, Belgian and Swiss masters." The pace of his pacing picked up. Sam stared at the floor as his words came out in a torrent.

"I learned to make truffles, and sculpt sugar art and distill flavor essences. I'd spend three months at a bakery, then a month at a restaurant in another city apprenticing to a dessert chef. But when Dad died, I came home early. All of that experience and drive got back-burnered while my hands were full keeping the bakery and my family afloat."

Hearing the story again, with more detail, put a lump right back in Mira's throat. Sam tossed aside his dreams. Declared them to be less important than his family. The man had a spine of steel and a heart of pure gold. "Sam, I'm so sorry for what you went through. It isn't fair."

He finally stood still, leaning against the wall, his tan ankles crossed. "Yeah, I've tried that argument on my mom. Ever since she's been back on her feet, I've begged her to let me do a line of gourmet truffles. I tried to keep everything as normal as possible for her once she came back full-time. Which means Mom's back in charge. The final decision-maker. Kind of screwed myself with that step back."

It didn't make any sense. "But you do that already. Ivy told me she's used your chocolate as wedding favors, and we're going to be selling them here in the store."

"Side jobs only. I do that for fun. In my spare time. What I really want is to devote myself to just specialty chocolates and designer cakes."

Helen beamed at him. "You want to be an artist. What am I saying? You *are* one. Everything I've had from your bakery, whether my lovely cake or your famous cherry fritters, has been a work of art."

"Thanks."

She turned to Mira, laying an index finger alongside her nose. "Have *you* ever tried one of his creations?"

"Um, no. Not yet. But the smells that waft over are amazing." Shame filled Mira. After she pushed his éclair back in his face her first day in the store, an apology wasn't enough. The right thing to do would've been to march right over and buy a non-chocolate pastry. If she dated a painter, she'd ask to see his work. Or listen to the band of a guitar player. Being a groupie in a smoke-filled club at 2:00 a.m. was a lot harder than strolling next door to try a doughnut. How could she have been so thoughtless?

"Well, until my sister comes back from her no-end-in-sight trip across Europe, I can't fully expand. There simply isn't enough time to carve out of the regular daily schedule of baking. And if she doesn't come back before Mom retires, I'll have to give it up entirely to handle the bakery by myself." The passion dimmed, both from his voice and his face. "It isn't fair that Diana's off having the time of her life while I churn out those cookies you mentioned. But since we were old enough to speak, Mom's told me life isn't fair. Funny how she hasn't mentioned that to Diana recently and dragged her butt back home."

She couldn't listen to any more. His melancholy story made Mira want to tuck him tightly into bed, bring him a glass of warm milk, stroke his head and promise him everything would be better when he woke up. While she couldn't fix his bakery and family woes, she could fix the pain she'd caused him. Mira walked over, tugged his hands out of his pockets and held on tight.

"Sam, I'm sorry. I guess I'm more my mother's daughter than I care to admit." *That* was a bitter pill to swallow. Turning her back on her family might've distanced Mira from their money, but apparently not from the skin-deep snobbery. "I was wrong."

Helen clapped her hands together. "Three little words everyone longs to hear after a fight. Can't ask for more than that in an apology. Let's move on to the food sampling. Once you've both eaten, you'll be in much better moods."

She gave Helen kudos for trying to sweep the unpleasantness under the carpet. But Mira had to keep going. Apologizing wasn't enough this time. She needed to make amends. "No, more than that, I was a judgmental idiot. Every time I eat a cookie or a slice of cake, it puts a smile on my face. Sam, you create instant happiness. That makes baking a pretty noble profession, in my book."

A smile spread across his features that warmed her to her toes as fast and strong as a double shot of bourbon. "You've summed up what I love about baking in a nutshell. You get it. Thank you."

Helen scooted her stool back and stood. "If I hadn't seen it with my own eyes, I wouldn't have believed it. You were right, Mira. He certainly does talk a lot more around you." Grabbing her coat, she headed for the door. "I'm going to check my car for those crackers. In case you two need a little time to, oh, I don't know, kiss and make up?"

Her pumps clattered on the hardwood floor. Mirroring Sam, Mira stood stock-still until the tinkle of the bell on the doorknob signaled they were alone.

"How do you feel about her suggestion?" He laced his fingers between hers. Gone from his eyes was the icy blue flame. Now they smoldered beneath half-closed lids. Bedroom eyes, indeed. Mira wished they were within five minutes of a bedroom, because she'd sprint there with him.

"I think my new employee, in addition to being a talented cook, is a very wise woman."

Sam drew her closer, until she had to tilt her head back to look at him. He waited a beat, and Mira's breathing hitched. But as he lowered his mouth, she leaned back and put a finger to his lips.

"I want to learn more about what you do."

"Sweetness, I'm about to demonstrate what I can do to you."

"No, I mean your baking. I know you don't just roll out cookies all day, but I don't know the extent of what you do."

"I bake cakes, too. Consider yourself informed." He captured her finger between his lips and sucked on it, his tongue swirling up and down and around in a pattern that sent a corresponding pattern of prickling awareness through the center of her body.

"I want to give your career the respect it deserves. Show me what you do."

"You're serious?" An astonished grin tugged up the corners of those firm, talented lips.

"Yes. Start by telling me which one of your amazing pastries I should buy for my midafternoon snack."

"All right. A piña colada cheesecake bar. Chocolate-free and delicious. But if you really want to learn about what I do, we'll have to start with the basics." Sam flipped them around so Mira was caged against the wall by his body. "Whether it's cookies or cake or truffles, the one thing you always start with is plenty of sugar."

This time when he lowered his mouth, she didn't stop him. And when his lips parted hers, she didn't feel sweet at all. Spicy and sinful, those were the flavors she thought of until his hands slid down to grab her ass. Then she stopped thinking altogether.

NINE

"TODAY'S FIELD TRIP is two-pronged." Sam slammed the door on his delivery van. With a jerk of his head, he indicated Mira should start walking. Easier said than done, when helping carry a seventy-five-pound cake. The current version rose four tiers high, with a basket weave design on the sides, and marzipan fruits in deep rust, burgundy and gold spilling along the bottom of each layer.

Sam didn't normally like to roll out the fall colors as decoration in September, but the client insisted. With her mind set on wanting to use cornucopias as table centerpieces, she went with a whole autumn theme. That was a battle for her wedding planner to fight. All he had to do was hand-paint a hundred or so pieces of sugared fruit. His fingers might've cramped and he had a wicked crick in his neck, but he far preferred that to the massive pain in the ass of dealing with a bride on a daily basis. He didn't know how Ivy managed not to stuff a balled-up sock in their mouths half the time.

Brides didn't have an off switch when it came to their weddings. Ever. Sam got a kick out of being a tiny cog in the happiest day of their lives. He just didn't need to hear them ramble on about it. His favorite parts of the day were when he holed up in the back kitchen. Hours would go by with only the flour and sugar for company. He loved the peace and quiet. And yet he didn't mind a bit that Mira hadn't stopped talking since she got in the van. Funny.

"Really?" Mira panted, but kept on a straight line through the loading dock and into the dim back hallways of the InterContinental Hotel. "Looks like you've got exactly one purpose for bringing me along. Free labor."

What was she complaining about? He was the one walking backward. "That part doesn't hurt. Of course, if you weren't here, I'd draft one of the assistant pastry chefs to help me lug this inside."

"What?" She stopped walking all of a sudden, mouth hanging open.

Sam executed an emergency two-step forward to keep from dropping his half. "Careful. What did I tell you before we started?"

She rolled her eyes. Then she lifted a knee to support the base while readjusting her grip. "We've got to work as a single pair of legs."

"That's right. Or else this five-thousand-dollar cake ends up a very expensive pile of crumbs on the floor. You know how they say the landing is the most dangerous part of an airplane flight? Transporting a cake from the van to an event site is the most dangerous part. Lots of people think driving is the scary part. Not true. More cakes are dropped than ever slide into the sidewall of a van."

Her second eye roll made him wonder if she'd ever sat through detention as a kid. Mira sure had the spunk to land herself there on a regular basis. "With all due respect, oh master baker—"

Sam cut her off. "Gotta say, I like that title. Maybe

you can use it again soon. You know, when I show you what else I do masterfully." Ah, there it was. The tell-tale rush of pink to her pale cheeks. He knew by now, after a week of stolen daytime kisses and late nights spent hanging out on her couch, that it didn't signal embarrassment, but desire. Good. Because beneath the brown Lyons Bakery half apron he wore for all setups, he'd been half hard since she walked into his store today. She'd followed his instructions and worn brown pants. But the pants cradled her ass the way his hands longed to, showcasing the peach-shaped glory of it. And her cream Henley clung to all the curves on her front as close as the icing on this cake.

Thankfully, the full bakery apron he'd tossed at her hung shapelessly almost to the floor. Hiding her breasts merely enabled him to walk without a hitch. It didn't stop the visual from popping into his head every damn time he looked at her. God, he needed to get her under him again, as soon as possible. Judging by her rosy cheeks, she felt the same way.

"Don't get ahead of yourself. Maybe you'll be the one screaming my name in praise."

She could flip so quickly from all business to all sass. Sam loved it. "I'm a liberated, twenty-first-century guy. I've got no problem with that. Now start walking."

Mira resumed their measured pace. "As I was saying, this cake, while a work of art, is not a thin metal shell defying all laws of gravity around hundreds of people. You can't compare it to the potentially fatal danger of crashing a plane."

"You've never dealt with weddings before, have you?" As she shook her head no, he guided them around the corner and onto the elevator. "For a year, give or take, the wedding day is a bride's entire world. When something goes wrong during the planning, and something always does, holy hell breaks loose. From the caterwauling, you'd swear an entire family had been wiped out. When something goes wrong on the actual wedding day—"

Mira sniggered as she interrupted. "Like the cake in a heap on the floor?"

The elevator doors swooshed open, and he eased out toward the ballroom. "You laugh, but it can ruin the whole damn day. I've heard of brides holing up in their dressing room and not coming out because of a drop of red wine on their dress. Or leaving the reception before the food's even served because the best man said something mean in his toast. Brides are as volatile as a grenade with the pin already pulled. So keep walking, nice and smooth."

"Great pep talk."

"You said you wanted to know more about what I do. I don't just make cakes. My cakes make a memory for people. This cake is part of the ritual of their special day. Guests will talk about it for years to come."

"Pretty sure of yourself, aren't you?"

"I'm sure this cake is exactly what the client wants. I'm sure everyone here will think it is delicious. And I'm sure the bride and groom will never forget their symbolic first meal together when they share a bite of this cake."

"That is downright eloquent. Helen has this crazy idea you don't talk very much."

"I can talk for days about chocolate, pastry cream, experimenting with fruit to come up with fondant dye.

Most people just don't want to hear it. When I'm passionate about something, I talk. Want to hear what I think about your breasts?"

"Not while I'm lugging around someone's precious memories. I'm quite sure you'd make my knees go weak, and then we'd be faced with the cake on the floor scenario."

"You're right. We'll stick to our plan. No flirting during the workday. But, for the record, would you rather hear an ode to your breasts, or a really raunchy limerick about them?"

"Surprise me."

"I intend to." They rounded another corner, and Mira angled toward the baby grand piano in an alcove. "Need a break?"

"Just a quick one. My arms are about to fall off. Now I know why your biceps are so massive." They eased the cake onto the lid of the piano. Sam still held most of its weight while Mira shook out her fingers.

"Have you been to the Casino de Monte-Carlo in Monaco?"

"Yes. For my eighteenth birthday. I lost all my money in half an hour and spent the night flirting with the bartender. It was a terrific night."

Sam noticed she dispensed the memory from her globetrotting, wealthy past with the ease of a well-oiled vending machine. It wasn't a hot-button issue between them anymore. Mira had let down her guard one hundred percent. He called that progress. "In that case, you've got the experience to be able to appreciate where I'm taking you. Let's go."

"Sam, we're in a downtown Chicago hotel. Do you really think you should be comparing it to a place where royalty hangs out on a nightly basis?" Mira hefted the cake and, on Sam's nod, resumed walking.

"You tell me."

"Oh my." Mira stopped in the doorway and goggled at the enormous oval room. Dozens of tables covered in burgundy taffeta were encircled with gold, laddered chairs. The centerpieces overflowed with autumn leaves and fruit that matched his cake perfectly. "Are those green marble columns real?"

"Yep. And that gold-leaf dome has a six-ton Baccarat crystal chandelier hanging from it. The largest one in North America. See the balcony all around the second floor?"

"It's big enough to be another entire room."

"It gives it that feeling. But that's where the cocktail hour will be." They started walking again, to the table in the center of the room. "I've pestered the staff here over the years to fill me in on all the details. This is my favorite ballroom in the city—and I've seen all of them."

"What makes it your favorite?"

That interested glint in her eyes coupled with the half smile worked on him like truth serum. She made him feel like the most fascinating man in the world. It made him uncomfortable, but in a nice way. "Well, it's almost as gorgeous as you are, for one."

"Compliment duly appreciated."

"My dad brought me here on a delivery for the first time when I was nine. My sister was watching *Cinderella* about ten times a day at that point. I was little enough I thought this was the ballroom from the movie." Sam remembered every second of that first, grown-up "work trip" with his father. It made him smile every time. "Even hoped I'd marry my princess here someday. Which is stupid, now, I know. I'm not this fancy."

"Oh my gosh."

"What?" he asked, only half listening. This was the crucial moment. Gingerly, they slid the cake onto the table draped with gold taffeta. Sam stepped back to eyeball his creation. He'd brought some extra marzipan fruits, just in case anything needed touching up.

"You are the most adorable thing ever. I can just picture you as a little kid, taking this all in. Your dad must've been so proud to bring you along and show you off to everyone." Mira rushed forward, leapt up and into his arms.

Sam didn't need any urging. He held her close, crushing those pert breasts against his chest and cursing the thick apron that kept him from feeling her nipples. She wrapped her legs around his waist and clung while kissing him deeply. He could hardly believe his luck. One finished, kick-ass cake, his favorite event site, and a hot girl all over him—this was the kind of stupid fantasy they'd make up after a ten-hour day at the CIA. He felt like a celebrity chef, and the luckiest guy in the world, rolled into one. Mira Parrish was turning out to be the handful he'd predicted, but in a good way.

"And unless you offer me a significant bribe, I'm telling Ivy that you've been dreaming about your wedding day as long as she has." She slid back down his body with an evil twinkle in her eye. "I hear you guys all gave her grief about the wedding scrapbook she started back in high school. She'd love to know you pictured yourself as Prince Charming."

Damn. She loosened the gates on his memories as easily as he'd opened hers. He never, ever told that story. To anyone. It was hard enough to maintain a manly image making desserts for a living. If Gib and Ben found out he'd had this stupid, recurring dream of his wedding day, they'd start keeping handfuls of rice in their pockets to toss at him. Tie tin cans to the back of his delivery van. Other horrible, embarrassing pranks that wouldn't end for months. Mira had to be stopped.

"How about I get you in to the most exclusive, swankiest party in town? Open bar, great food and hot guys." With a final look at the cake, Sam grabbed her hand and led her out of the room. If he stayed, he'd be tempted to tweak it, add one more row of piping or a few extra decorations. He knew in his gut when a cake was finished, but the hardest thing was walking away and leaving it to be eaten.

"Really?"

"Well, only one hot guy that matters. You'd be my date." He took her a different away, out the front door right into the hustle and bustle of Michigan Avenue. "To be clear, the bribe isn't the party."

"I'm listening."

"The bribe is that it's the chance to see me in a tuxedo. I'm pretty damn hot. Might even melt your panties right off at the sight of me."

Mira started to giggle, then caught her breath. She caught her bottom lip with her two front teeth, obviously considering the merits of his offer. "There is every chance you're right. I look forward to testing your theory."

God. Not half as much as he did. "Great. Party's

in two days." A little fun, some booze, some laughs would melt away that crease between her eyebrows which started out renting space, but looked to be moving in permanently. And it would give him a night off from worrying about his own future.

"What are we doing out here? Aren't we going to have to walk all the way around the block to get back to the van?"

"I told you this trip was two-pronged. You've seen me wear my baker's hat. Now, I'm slipping back into my tour guide hat."

"Crap. Did Ivy order you to show me the city again? You don't have to jump every time she snaps her fingers."

Look at how adorable she was as she leapt to his defense. Her nose crinkled, and color bloomed in her cheeks. "Mira, Chicago's your home now. I want you to like it here." He waited for a lull in the traffic, then grabbed her hand and crossed the street at an easy lope along with dozens of suited-up office workers. "Ivy has nothing to do with this. I know how hard you've been working. Helen told me you've been skipping meals."

"My employee's been snitching to you?"

Whoa. He'd let that slip, and now needed to back away with the caution of a soldier's untended swerve into a minefield. "She's worried. Helen's got that whole maternal vibe she just can't turn off. She wanted me to take you out to dinner, that's all. Make sure you got one square meal under your belt." Sam slid a finger in the noticeable gap between her pants and her waist. "After all, I thought you said your eating problems were a thing of the past?"

She slapped his hand away, but then intertwined her fingers with his. "They are. I'm just stressed. There aren't enough hours in the day."

"Well, I'll have you back within the hour. I just want to show you the Tribune Tower while we're here."

"Didn't we just take an architecture cruise down the river a few weeks ago? It was fun, but a girl can only take so many hours of staring at buildings."

"This one's different. It's got rocks and bricks from a whole bunch of historic sites. The Parthenon, Lincoln's tomb, the Taj Mahal, Notre-Dame. Very cool. A trip around the world without leaving the city limits."

"Tribune Tower. You mean like the newspaper?"

He pointed at the tall stone turrets in front of them. "Yep."

"This is great. The store's supposed to be featured in the paper today. Well, not featured. More like a mention. A teaser about the opening." Mira darted ahead to the line of newspaper vending machines. "Spot me a dollar."

Sam fed in his quarters and yanked open the door. "Is this going in a scrapbook, or right into a frame?" he teased.

"Depends on how much they like the idea of our store. This article, if it's good, could generate a lot of foot traffic. That leads to word of mouth, and suddenly," she clapped her hands, "we're a success." Mira snatched the paper out of his hands. "Where would it be? Which section?"

"Try the second section. Although, if they really want to start a buzz for you…" Sam broke off. Her face had gone whiter than a sheet of parchment paper. "What's wrong? Are you sick?"

"I made the headline."

"Congratulations."

"No, not the store. *I* made the headline."

Sam followed her finger to the bold writing next to a picture of a younger Mira, with shorter hair. Store Manager Could Add Chicago Boutique to Her String of Failures. "I don't understand."

"God, I knew this would happen. I warned Ivy. She said everyone deserves a fresh start. That she couldn't do it without me. She told me not to worry. That's a laugh, isn't it? Me, not worry? Might as well ask a waterfall to reverse direction. Or maybe have a couple of planets swap places in their rotation around the sun!" Mira's breath came in short, jerky gasps. The newspaper fell from her hands and spilled onto the pavement. Sam could tell a full meltdown was imminent.

"Come with me." He scooped up the pile of paper and pulled her with him to the park on the side of the building. She flopped onto an iron bench. Sam pushed her head between her legs. "Breathe," he ordered. "Don't freak out. Just breathe while I skim this and see how bad it is."

"Read it to me." She shot one hand up in the air, stopping him. "No, just tell me the high points. Or the low points."

There weren't any high points. As he scanned the article, one thing became clear. It was a hatchet job. "They've got the store name, and yours and Ivy's. Everything's spelled right."

"The high point is the spelling?"

Yeah. "It's a short article. Like you said, a teaser.

Just a long paragraph, really. Most of it is the address and the date of the opening."

"You're stalling."

"Okay. It mentions—briefly—how the last two stores you managed failed. Spectacularly."

"Is that it?"

He wanted to say yes. But if he lied, she'd just find out eventually. "It finishes with a prediction that you'll run the store into the ground and 'tarnish Ivy's crown as Chicago's premiere wedding planner.' That's all."

"That's all? My phone interview lasted twenty minutes, and that was the reporter's take away? No mention of our wonderful products, our delicious and convenient picnic selections?"

"Nope." Sam eased down beside her. In long, slow circles he ran his hand over her back.

"I am a failure. He's right. If this is indicative of the press coverage we'll get, the store is doomed."

"You're not a failure."

"Oh, but I am. You don't know." She sat up and lifted her red, swollen eyes to meet his. "I'm mad because the writer didn't give the store a fair shake. You'll notice I'm not saying he's wrong."

He couldn't bear to see her so upset. Sam drew her to lie across his lap. After a few minutes of stroking her hair, her eyes fluttered shut. Her breathing slowed.

"I never fall apart like this. As a matter of fact, I pride myself on how well I can hold it together, stay in control. Except around you." Mira leaned her cheek into his palm. "You're a dangerous man, Sam Lyons. You're emotional truth serum wrapped up in big muscles and a devastating smile. How do you do it?"

Did she realize what a compliment she'd given him? That she trusted him enough to lay herself bare? Her admission humbled him. They'd come so far, so fast. "Maybe I make you feel safe?" Sam offered. Over the steady blare of traffic, a few birds twittered in the trees. This probably wasn't the right place to get all sappy. Even though he wanted to tell her he felt the same way. "Or maybe you're trying the whole gamut of feminine wiles to get me to take off my shirt."

Mira gave a weak chuckle. "You see right through me. Is it working?" She tried to slide her fingers beneath his shirt, but the apron strings stopped her. Still, it showed her sass reserves were filling back up. Might as well dig up the rest of it now, while she was already upset. Get it over with, like ripping off a bandage.

He feathered a kiss to the middle of her forehead. "Want to tell me the real story?"

"You know what? I do."

"Okay. As a reward for being brave, I'll take my shirt off for the ride home."

"Deal. I'm definitely getting the better half of the bargain." Mira closed her eyes again. "I managed a mall store after grad school. Nothing big, but we carried good merchandise, and had a solid clientele. I loved it. I loved the thrill of finding just the right pieces for our customers. I loved seeing people leave the store with a smile on their faces, and I loved seeing them come back even more. Then a blizzard dumped three feet of snow, the skylight collapsed under the weight, and everything was ruined. The whole mall shut down."

"You didn't fail. I think insurance companies call

that an Act of God, not a lack of action by Mira." Sam called it bad fucking luck.

"I agree. But the bottom line is that the store I managed folded. The whole snow thing got to me. So I took a job managing a boutique down in Palm Beach."

Mira had a spine of titanium. Sure, she cried on his shoulder weirdly often. But deep inside, she was as strong as they came. "Way to regroup."

"Two lovely couples opened it as an investment. Honestly, it was a place for all their friends to shop. But their friends came in religiously and spent lots of money, so it worked out. For a couple of years."

"That sounds ominous." He slid his hand down to make soothing circles around her shoulder. Sam didn't like the odds of this story having a happy ending.

"I'll give you a clue: Palm Beach." She paused. When he shrugged, she continued. "Tight-knit group of clients—you can't guess what went wrong?"

What did she expect him to know about Florida socialites? "Somebody drove a golf ball through your front window?"

"Nope. Bernie Madoff."

"Oh, no." Sam winced. Quite the knack for being in the wrong place at the wrong time, Mira had.

"The owners, and all their friends, were wiped out by his investment scandal. I guess I was lucky. They lost their savings, their houses, everything. All I lost was my job."

"Okay, technically strike two, but still not your fault."

Mira reached up to cover his hand with hers. "Palm Beach didn't fit me, anyway. Nice people, but the overall vibe was too snobby, too much like the life I ran away from with my parents. So I moved up the coast to Myrtle Beach."

God, he knew where this was going. If he believed in that sort of thing, he'd swear she was cursed. Jinxed. A reincarnation of Attila the Hun. "Last year? So you were there for Hurricane Beryl?"

"Uh-huh. Second storm of the season, and it caused the most damage of any hurricane in the last twenty years."

As a news junkie, Sam had been glued to pictures of the devastation for days. So many heartbreaking stories emerged, along with touching examples of heroism. He couldn't imagine going through a natural disaster. God, no matter how often she got knocked down, Mira kept going. What an amazing woman. "Were you hurt?"

"No. We all evacuated in time. But my store was a victim. I lost a lot of my belongings to water damage. It only took me a few hours to pack what was left and hit the road. I got to Camp Ticonderoga a few weeks early, but I didn't know where else to go. I didn't have anywhere else. And then Ivy called, and offered me this amazing job. She's like my fairy godmother."

"I can see that. She does wear a lot of pink."

Mira crinkled her nose, frowning at him. "Ivy entrusted me with her dream. Look at how I'm repaying her." She kicked at the stack of newspapers with her foot, startling the ever-present circle of pigeons. "What am I supposed to do now? This bad publicity is a nightmare."

He didn't disagree. "Well, I promised I'd have you back in an hour. So we take five more minutes to chill, and then you go back to work."

"No, I mean should I leave?"

"Yeah. I just said I'd take you back in five minutes."

"Sam, should I leave Chicago?" She clutched his arm, nails digging into his flesh. Of course, if they were naked and her nails dug trails into his back, he wouldn't complain. So Sam kept his mouth shut.

"Before my reputation spreads, and completely ruins Ivy's chance to fulfill her dream of a romance store? It's not even the money. Obviously, the money matters. Ivy's thrown every cent she's got into this store, and quite a few she hasn't earned yet. But more than the money, I can't bear to let down my friend."

He could make a light-as-air sponge cake. Tiramisu so good it brought tears to the eyes. Sam knew how to handle the complex chemistry of baking with his eyes shut. Handling messed-up lives? Not his thing. Whenever one of his friends had a personal problem, well, Ivy handled it. Occasionally his mother doled out good advice along with the morning scones. Too bad she wasn't here to take over.

Mira had a couple of different issues to solve. Sam flipped a mental coin for which to tackle first. "How many days ago was it that you gave me crap about not opening up to you? About the whole Diana off in Europe leaving me hanging mess?"

"Less than a week."

"Interesting."

"What does this have to do with my problem? My secret string of abysmal failures?"

"Looks like we were both keeping secrets from each other. So I'm going to share a secret with you right now." He looked over both shoulders, then bent down to whisper in her ear. "We're not spies."

"No kidding. And here I've been wondering if your whisk was a secret recording device."

Smart-ass. Yeah, he was crazy about this woman. Sam pushed her back upright. "A relationship can't be built on a need-to-know basis. We've got to put it all out there."

Those beautiful blue eyes of hers widened to the size of his white-chocolate tartlets. "I just told you what a jinxed, pathetic mess I am. I blubbered like a baby in front of you. And my job is quite possibly hanging by a thread. After all that, are you offering me a relationship?"

"You're not a mess. Your story proves how resilient you are. The bad publicity's going to go away. Once the store opens to brilliant reviews, you'll stop worrying and Ivy will thank you every day for bringing her dream to life."

"Wow. If you ever give up baking, you could have a career as a spin doctor."

"I'm addicted to political shows. Probably picked up a trick or two." Sam took her small, soft hands in his. The timing and location kind of sucked. A homeless guy on the bench behind them gave off a ripe odor. Two pigeons kept pecking at the flecks of buttercream frosting on his shoe. And Mira had just staggered off an emotional roller coaster. But he decided to plow ahead anyway.

"I'm not Gib. I don't get a kick out of sleeping with a different woman every time the second hand moves. We've each got shit to deal with, but it feels kind of good dealing with it together. At least to me."

"Me, too."

Good. Staking his claim to Mira felt right. Calming and exciting at the same time. Like the smooth, warm burn of a twenty-year-old scotch. "To be clear, I do want to sleep with you."

Her laughter pealed across the park. "Me, too, with you."

"So forget you even thought about leaving town. You're not a quitter. You've got a great job, friends, a roommate who I happen to know keeps the freezer stocked with a minimum of three ice cream flavors at all times, and me. Are you going to let one newspaper hack drive you away?"

"No. Good pep talk. Would've made a bigger impact if you weren't wearing a shirt, though."

Yep. Just that fast, Mira had bounced back. He pulled her up from the bench, then swatted her ass. If his hand lingered a bit, Sam figured he'd earned it. "I don't know about you, but I've got to get back to work. Somebody turned this into the longest, most complicated delivery on record."

"Does this mean I don't get a tip?"

"I'll give you a tip. Don't give up your day job. Seriously."

Mira doubled over with laughter.

TEN

Sam opened the limo door and helped Mira out. A barrage of flash bulbs went off. She paused, one crazy-high stiletto planted on the strawberry-red carpet. The slit in her blue satin gown that flowed over her like water exposed enough thigh to make him want to throw his coat over her. Or push her back onto the leather seats and climb on top of her.

"Are those paparazzi?" she asked in a stage whisper.

"Not real ones. Gib hired some actor friends for the night. To give us the total red carpet experience for the premiere. Have fun with it." She considered for a moment, then threw her shoulders back and strutted down the carpet with a sassy sway. He got so caught up in watching the twitch of her hips that he had to scramble to catch up. It was kind of a kick seeing her wave and smile. They were so late, he'd been worried they would've missed out on all the hoopla.

Sam pushed them through the revolving doors into the refined gray-and-black elegance of the Cavendish Grand lobby. A soaring atrium rose three stories, with one entire wall of windows overlooking the hustle and bustle of Michigan Avenue. The walls were covered in dove-gray satin echoed in the chairs and sofas grouped around a cascade of water streaming from the ceiling into a mound of shiny black river stones.

Sheets of glass formed the check-in desk, supported by columns of dark granite.

Mira took his hand as she looked around. "Out of all of us, I think Gib wins the award for prettiest workplace."

"Nope. I win, hands down."

"Sam, your bakery is cute, and it does smell great, but you can't convince me it comes close to the beautiful elegance of the Cavendish."

"At my workplace, I get to stare through the doorway at you all day. Nothing's more beautiful." Helen had insisted they leave the top half of the connecting door open. He and Mira still stuck to their guns and didn't speak to each other during work. But that whole *picture is worth a thousand words* thing rang true. Catching intermittent glimpses of her sure kept a perma-grin on his face. Sam pressed the call button for the elevator.

"Oh. Oh my. You do know how to pour the sugar on, don't you?"

"You look like you've been drizzled in melted blueberry sugar. Did this," he stroked a finger along the satiny length of her ribs, "really survive the hurricane?"

Mira looked down at the dress with a rueful laugh. "God, no. I don't have a lifestyle that requires formalwear anymore. Apparently neither does Daphne. So Ivy hooked us up with a bridal salon she uses. The three of us are all wearing samples of bridesmaid dresses."

It might make him a selfish bastard, but Sam liked hearing that she didn't nip out to formal parties anymore. It helped level their social playing field. "We're in the same boat. I borrowed this penguin suit from Ben. Guy's got a closet full, since he wears them on the job. Weird, shifting from apron strings around my neck to a bow tie." It didn't completely fit. He was wearing his own black pants beneath the jacket, which he hoped to ditch the moment they got inside. With a hand at the small of her back, he ushered Mira into the empty elevator car.

"I feel very Cinderella-esque. They have to be returned tomorrow. In good condition, too, so curtail any plans you had for ripping it off of me."

"You really know how to spoil a guy's fun." That image would stay planted in his head all night, take root and guarantee a solid eight hours of no sleep.

"Or, you could realize I'm presenting you with an opportunity to be creative." Mira pushed him against the wall, lifted her leg all the way to her shoulder, then hooked her foot through the waist-high railing. Her dress rode up almost to her panty line—if she was wearing any. Sam hadn't been able to definitively rule one way or the other on that, yet. But he damn well wanted to find out.

Caged on one side by her leg and the other by her hand, Sam had no choice but to stand there and enjoy as she began to sinuously writhe against him. Her reflection in the shiny elevator doors gave him the one-two punch of feeling her curves while watching the perfection of her sweet, tight ass. Mira licked delicately along the edge of his ear. It sent chills through him faster than the first, icy dip of the Polar Bear Plunge in Lake Michigan on New Year's Day.

Sam knew enough about women not to give in to the temptation to plunge his hands into the complicated mass of curls that left her neck tantalizingly bare. Instead, he anchored them low on her hips. The slick fabric gave him an excuse to dig his fingers into her roundness. She bit down on his lobe.

Was it a challenge or a come-on? Hard to tell with this strong-willed woman. Either approach worked for him. Oh, game on. Sam shifted his right hand to stroke all the way from her ankle up, lingering behind her knee with a feathery touch that teased a giggle out of her, up the back of her thigh. At every inch he gained, her dress obligingly streamed out of his way. Her pale skin contrasted with the cobalt gown pooling at the crook of her hip. The visual fired his blood.

Suddenly his tie choked him, and his shirt cut off his circulation and his pants were definitely three sizes too tight. Sam couldn't breathe for needing her. For the need to strip away everything between them, until only skin pressed against skin, heat against heat. Holding her waist tight, he lunged forward to press the emergency stop button. He needed this ride to last longer than a five-floor ascent. But then a pinhole red light caught his eye, high up in the corner.

"Shit." Sam slid out and reversed positions, sandwiching Mira to the wall. The press of her ass on his already throbbing dick grew to exquisite torture in about half a second.

"What happened?"

He unhooked her leg and stood her on both feet. "Security camera." She shimmied her dress into place. "Sorry. I don't want to share you."

"Don't apologize. You've got a whole knight-protecting-his-lady's-honor thing going on now." Mira spun around to kiss his cheek. "It's equal parts sweet and hot."

The elevator doors swooshed open to a party already spilling into the hallway. Women in bright, tight dresses tottered masterfully on matchstick heels. Tuxedoed men mixed in with the waiters circulating trays full of pink drinks that looked sweeter than his raspberry linzer bars. Sinatra's smooth tenor lent a swinging, classy vibe. On pedestals flanking the doorway, sprays of something tall and hot-pink sprouted out of pastel pink vases.

Gib, in full white tie and tails, leaned against the doorjamb, tapping his fingers on his watch and laying one hell of a stink-eye on Sam. It turned to wide-eyed appreciation as he slid his gaze to Mira. Maybe too much appreciation. Maybe a little kid-in-a-candy-store gleam in his eye as he bent forward to kiss her hand. The bending gave Gib an up-close-and-personal eyeful of her barely covered breasts. Sam restrained the urge to elbow one of his best friends right in the teeth.

"Mira, you are like ocean-clad Aphrodite in that dress. Beautiful, alluring, irresistible."

Damn it, Gib always knew the perfect thing to say. Sam knew he should've told Mira all those things—minus the smarmy accent, of course. He took comfort in the fact that actions spoke louder than words, and they'd just gotten plenty of action in the elevator. Gib would never break the man code and try to steal Mira from him. But to err on the side of caution, Sam didn't intend to give the guy the slightest opening, either. He slung an arm low around her waist.

"And you look like you're ready for a royal wedding. I especially like the pocket handkerchief. So few men wear them anymore."

"I don't believe in doing things halfway. Go full out, or not at all, I always say."

"No wonder you break the hearts of so many women. Your charm at full force must be quite something to behold."

Gib backed away, palms up. "Are you seeing this, Sam? Your lady's flirting with me. I swear I did nothing to encourage it."

The guy walked around with the looks of a model in one of those black-and-white perfume ads. Not only could he talk like a freaking poet, but he layered those pretty words with a rich icing of hoity-toity Brit-speak. If Gib so much as recited from the phone book with that accent, women lined up and spread their legs for him. Removal from his vicinity was the only way to protect Mira. "What's the matter—couldn't you find your own date?"

"Oh, I'll have one by the end of the evening. I'm currently in the selection process." He crossed his arms, and leaned in closer. "See that blonde by the bar? She's a contender, but might be edged out by that brunette talking to Milo."

"You're trolling your own party for a date? Didn't you invite all these people?" Mira sounded shocked. Sam relaxed a bit. Gib's bed-hopping ways might just be enough of a repellant to keep him from worrying.

Gib frowned. "Goodness, no. Then I wouldn't have any fresh water in which to fish. This is Ivy and Ben's party—I just threw it together for them."

"Such a sweet gesture. I can't believe you're throwing them a formal party to watch the premiere episode of *Planning for Love*."

"The first time they were on television—*Wild Wedding Smackdown*, did you catch it?"

"No."

"Ghastly show. The only good thing about that night was Ivy throwing a pajama party. But this is the start of an entire series based around our friend. How could I not up the lavish stakes accordingly?"

Gib might run through women faster than water vaporized on a cold January night, but he was true blue to his friends. Sam gave him the double half hug, half back slap. "You did pull out all the stops, buddy. Job well done."

"Oh, I'm not completely selfless. It's not as if I'm walking away empty-handed. There will be a party favor at the end of the night. About this big." He traced the shape of a woman's profile in the air. Well, if that woman were Jessica Rabbit. "Merely a question of deciding which one. I haven't yet acquainted myself with all of Ivy's lovely friends. Although I did already remove a few women from the running. Sam, if you'd been on time, you could've weighed in on the first round of cuts."

"You're really judging Ivy's friends? To see who goes home with you tonight?" Mira unsuccessfully tried to stifle a giggle. "That's horrible, Gib—but you're so up front about it, I can't help but laugh. Which makes me horrible, too."

On behalf of his entire gender, Sam had to step up and defend his friend. "I hear Gib shows his women a good time. And there isn't a single woman in Chicago who hasn't heard of him. Last fall, he won a write-in poll in the *CityPaper* as one of their top ten bachelors. Anyone who gets involved with him knows the score."

"Thank you." Gib dipped his head. "For that staunch defense, I'll let you be the tiebreaker tonight—if it comes to that."

He'd weighed in many times on Gib's flavor of the day. It felt, well, dirtier doing it with Mira by his side. Still, Sam couldn't leave Gib hanging. "Always happy to help a friend in need."

"You both require drinks immediately. The viewing will start in just half an hour." Another stern glare with an accompanying watch tap.

Sam took the cue for his apology. "Sorry we're late."

"I suppose you're going to hand me some trumped-up excuse about a cake emergency, or a cookie catastrophe."

"Shut it," he warned. "Pastry can be a high-tension business. But tonight I had to drop my mother off at bingo. She's trolling all the denominations this week to find the best game—then she'll bring in her friends. The Catholics put on a good show last night, but she's got high hopes the Lutherans may give them a run for their money."

"Your mother, again?" Gib tsked and shot his cuffs. "I understand when you drop everything to drive her to the doctor. But bingo is not an important enough event to make you late. Not to Ivy and Ben's big premiere."

Didn't matter if Gib thought bingo was stupid. Hell, it didn't matter that Sam agreed with him. Whatever made Kathleen Lyons happy and kept her safe zoomed straight to the top of his to-do list. She'd tried to wave him off, insist a friend could take her. Sam wouldn't hear of it. Driving her places gave him the chance to interact with his mother outside the bakery. It was a way for him to check that she was still firing on all four cylinders. That the professional cheerfulness she wore all day wasn't just a mask that dropped away to reveal another episode of soul-crushing depression. Twenty minutes in the car listening to her happy chatter assured him—for at least a few days—that happy really was her new normal. But he couldn't let her or his friends know that. So he simply said, "It's important to her."

Silence hung, as heavy in the air as a crappy gluten-free cake sat in a stomach. A waiter paused, hovering on the edge of the circle with a tray full of God knows what. Mira seized the chance to change the topic. "Is this the signature cocktail for the evening? I know Ivy adores a themed cocktail."

"Right you are. Do try one." Gib took two off the tray, but Sam held up a restraining hand. Any drink that pink would probably corrode the enamel off his teeth with one sugary sip.

"What the hell is that?"

"A Love martini—coconut rum, peach schnapps and cranberry juice."

Mira took a sip. "Delicious." She looked at the abject horror on Sam's face and laughed. "A tad on the sweet side, possibly, for the men."

"Possibly? Like you could *possibly* get a nice tan on the surface of the sun?" Sam spluttered.

Gib clapped him on the arm. "Don't panic—we've got a fully stocked bar, too. Made sure to load up on your favorite Goose Island beers."

Relief slowly filled him, like foam rising on a freshly built Guinness. "You're a good man. And a great host."

"Just do me a favor and say hello to Ivy and Ben on your way to the bar. Our girl was in a bit of a panic about this premiere. I think she downed a few cocktails before arriving, and quite a few more since. Her chances of being vertical by the time it begins are slim, at best."

"I'll take her some water," Mira promised. A worry line formed between her eyebrows. "Ivy doesn't have much of a tolerance. In grad school, after half a bottle of wine she'd dance down the hallway in just her underwear. And I don't just mean our dorm—I mean any hallway—bar, restaurant, football stadium. Her chances of being conscious for much longer are less than slim, if she's had as much as you say."

Sam wanted to lend a hand, too. Gib had pulled everyone together for this party, getting their industry friends to donate all their services, from the band to florists to their poker buddy Brian, making his limo fleet available to all the guests. He couldn't imagine how many phone calls, wheedling and time it must've taken. Of course, it was a typically perfect Cavendish event. Sam couldn't offer much at this point. "We'll save you a front row seat, too."

"Much appreciated, mate." Gib straight-arrowed for the blonde at the bar.

Mira tugged at his arm. "We'd really better go check on Ivy. She doesn't go on a tear like this often. Ben's only known her for six months. He probably doesn't realize she can go from life of the party to body on the floor in the blink of an eye."

This was sounding less like a party and more like babysitting every second. Still, if he got to stare at Mira in that dress that left nothing to the imagination, Sam would bring water and coffee to Ivy all night long. He led Mira past the DJ's table to the burst of pink he knew had to be Ivy. Who else would wear a big pink flower tucked into a complicated-looking up-do? And God, he hated that enough of his friends worked in the wedding industry that he even *knew* the word *up-do*.

Ivy did look like a star tonight, in a cotton-candy-pink satin corset that smushed her breasts together and up into a shelf of creamy perfection. Sam tore his eyes away, not wanting to ogle one of his closest friends. Hell, not wanting to ogle anyone with Mira next to him. Below a wide black sash, her taffeta skirt poofed just below her knees, like a dress from the fifties. Classy and beautiful, her dress matched her personality. Sam walked right past her to Ben, and gave him the double shoulder pat that served as the male version of a hug.

"I will never figure out how someone like you managed to snare this beautiful woman." Ben shook his head and laughed.

"I could say the same to you. We must've been really pathetic in a former life to deserve these gorgeous ladies. Maybe we were salamanders?"

"Oh, that explains why you've got such great tongue action." Ivy leered at her fiancé then stood on tiptoe to nibble along his jaw.

Wow. That answered the question of whether or not Ivy was plastered. Sam shot a look at Mira, who flagged down the nearest waiter. She took a few steps away to murmur in his ear. Hopefully she'd cut off the steady stream of Love martinis to the guests of honor. When she kept whispering, Sam assumed she'd also ordered a vat of coffee for her friend.

He pressed a kiss to her cheek. "Ivy, you look like a million dollars."

"Not me. That would be Mira. Mira the millionaire, or Mira the married," she said in a singsong voice. "Pick one, because she sure can't!"

What came after wasted? Mira told him Ivy never divulged the secret about her family's wealth. And there were too many people in the vicinity to hear her blurt it out for Sam's comfort. He had to stop her before she said anything else she'd regret in the morning. "I think you've had a couple too many drinks. Mira's not a millionaire. Unless you're offering to give her a raise, of course. Now that you're about to be a huge television star."

Ivy shook her finger in his face. "I don't need to give her a raise. If she wants millions of dollars, all she needs is her marriage."

"Mira's not married." Sam held out his hands to Ben, asking for help. The big idiot was laughing silently, one arm around his stomach. Guess he'd never seen his wife-to-be this shitfaced.

Her skirt rustled as she twisted side to side, a knowing smile on her face. "She might be soon. You'd better kiss her quick, before her parents marry her off and you miss your chance." Ivy planted another huge, wet kiss near the vicinity of Ben's mouth, for emphasis.

To keep his jaw from falling open, Sam bit the inside of his cheek. It couldn't be true. She wouldn't keep a marriage in the works a secret. Mira wouldn't let him make a fool of himself like that, would she? But why would Ivy lie? Sloshed to the gills on those stupid sugary cocktails, could she?

Mira all but shoved a steaming china cup at Ivy. "Drink this." She handed a second, reserve cup to Ben. "Now go sit down. Your show's about to start. We don't need you to provide a floor show on top of the premiere. There's only so much excitement we can handle in one night."

Ben, finally cluing in to just how far gone Ivy was, put an arm behind her knees and picked her up. "Come on, sweetheart. This will all be over soon. Then you can go back to ordering everyone else's lives."

Wishing fervently for that beer Gib mentioned, Sam stood, glued to the spot. How much of Ivy's loose-lipped speech had Mira heard? And could she explain any of it? "Got anything to say?"

Mira opened her mouth, obviously thought better of it, then took his hand and led him to the far corner of the room. The rest of the crowd were clustered by the bar and the swinging doors where the appetizers appeared. Aside from another big pink flower display, they were alone. And that suited Sam just fine. Before Mira could respond, he held up his hand, palm out, to stop her.

"Do you remember two days ago, when I invited you to this party?"

"You mean my epic meltdown in the park? Of course I remember."

These questions were a formality. Sam knew deep in his sinking heart what she'd say. "So you remember us talking about not keeping secrets from each other anymore. Putting it all out there."

She worried her bottom lip with her teeth. "Yes."

"I know we didn't sign a blood oath, but didn't you agree? No more secrets?"

"Yes."

That one syllable, delivered in a near whisper, unlocked the floodgates on his anger and confusion. "Then do you mind explaining why Ivy, who is clearly incapable of lying right now, just told me that your parents are marrying you off? Oh, and while you're at it, why don't you let me know if you were going to clue me in on this before or after I took you to bed?"

"Sam, I'm sorry." Mira put a hand on his upper arm, but he twisted away. Did she think a soothing pat would smooth this over?

"Sorry for what? For leading me on? For wasting my time? For lying to me?" He raked his hand through his hair. Never would he have pegged Mira as a game player.

"I didn't lie to you."

No way would he let her split hairs over the wording. What struck him was that she didn't immediately say that Ivy had lied. Really, wasn't that the bottom line? "You know, if all you wanted all along was a quick fuck, why'd you bother with the whole tears and heartfelt talks routine?" Sam deliberately grabbed her ass to drag her closer, digging his fingers into the tight curve. "I would've serviced you that first day in the store. Hell, this place is full of bedrooms. Want to go upstairs and scratch that itch right now?"

"Don't be cruel." She made no move to shift out of his embrace, though.

Sam pulled her flush against the rock-hard cock that responded to her nearness, no matter how pissed he might be. God, she slid onto him like icing on a hot cake. "Weren't you? Or don't you think that men have feelings, too?"

Bracing both her palms against his chest, Mira arched back to meet his eyes. "I didn't intentionally keep any secrets. This is all so new, and I'm used to keeping everything under wraps. I wanted a fresh, open start with you. But were we really supposed to air all our dirty laundry at once? Wouldn't that have sent you screaming into the street? I thought as things came up, we'd talk. Organically."

Turning back his anger would be about as easy as halting a lava flow. That's pretty much how the burning in his throat felt. Why should he listen to her excuses, when she still didn't deny the one simple fact at the center of this fight? But she also hadn't turned tail and run away. Mira met his anger head-on, bravely. It was enough to make him listen.

Sam glanced around the room. So far, nobody seemed to notice their heated exchange. The last thing he wanted to do was ruin Ivy's party. "How can you rationalize away Ivy's claim? Are you, or are you not on the ropes for a marriage?"

Her gaze skittered sideways. "Yes and no. Maybe."

"Mira, I swear to God, I can only take so much. Tell me the truth, right now."

A big sigh, then another. She squeezed her eyes shut, then sighed once more before looking at him. "The truth is I didn't intend to hurt you, or mislead you. Or make you so mad. Sorry doesn't begin to cover how I feel." A faint blush pinked her cheeks to match the same color he remembered on her nipples. Guess his anger must've dialed back a few notches if he could think about sex. "Sam, you're really terrific. I don't want to screw up what we've started."

Good to hear, but hard to piece together with Ivy's comments. "Really? How are you going to explain me to your husband-to-be?"

"Will you calm down for two minutes and let me explain?"

"This better be good," he warned. But Sam let her go, and led her to the bench covered in two-tone gray stripes against the wall. At least she was making an effort. He'd hear her out. And then probably station himself right by the beer for the rest of the night. Maybe wake up tomorrow with a hangover to match the guest of honor's. The music switched from Sinatra to Tony Bennett. A few couples began to dance in the wide-open space in front of the giant plasma screen.

"You know my family's wealthy."

"Yeah." Why revisit what he already knew? Besides, Sam thought the Parrish moneybags were permanently off the conversational menu.

"They had a problem with fortune hunters a while back. A long while back, actually. Pre-Civil War. My ancestors got sick of people trying to marry in and gain control of the money, or worse, fritter it away. So a very specific clause got added to the family trust to prevent us from being taken advantage of ever again."

This sounded ominous. And not at all like something that would suit the highly independent Mira. "Lay it on me."

"The rule is that each family member must either

make their first million—proving that they can continue to contribute to the growth of the coffers—or marry appropriately."

Sam couldn't imagine the pressure of attaining the millionaire label, just to keep your family off your back. He ran what they'd always considered to be a successful family business, and never come close to achieving that status. Marrying some random schmuck didn't strike him as a great prize, either. "Appropriately meaning…"

"Meaning someone the parents or grandparents chose. An upstanding person who would most likely enhance the family fortune, but definitely be an asset in terms of connections or pedigree or sometimes, just stunning good looks. My great-great-grandma Lillian was quite the looker. She perked up the genetic mix." She looked down at her fisted hands. "But there's a catch."

"Of course." Like the clause didn't suck enough already.

"The marriage or the million has to happen by the thirtieth birthday, or you're completely cut off from the family trust. Forever."

Sam leaned back, rubbing his hands up and down his thighs. Yeah, it was a lot to take in, and too much to digest in a single gulp. It made sense that Mira hadn't blurted it all out in the park. Small doses kept a guy from banging his head against a wall. As he well knew, family had a way of complicating things. The anger drained out of him, leaving behind a well of calm frustration. "And let me take a wild guess. Your birthday is right around the corner?"

"Not quite." One side of her mouth lifted into

something about ten shades below a smile. "I've got almost a year left."

Unless she started buying lottery tickets by the truckload, her chances looked about as good as those of the Cubs winning the World Series anytime this century. "How close are you to packing that first million into the bank?"

Mira crinkled her nose. "Not very."

"Well, that sucks." Sam scooched closer, needing to touch her. He laced his fingers with hers and stared down at their entwined hands. "You want to know why I lost my cool at the thought of you marrying someone else? Because I happen to be falling pretty damn hard for you. And there's no way your family would look at my pedigree and call it appropriate. My great-grandfather? A soybean farmer. My grandfather? An auto mechanic."

"You're falling for me?"

How could he make it more obvious? Hire a skywriter to put a giant heart with their initials over downtown? Sit through a chick flick marathon with her—without complaining? Sam wasn't a big, romantic gesture type of guy. But they'd already covered a lot of ground in a few weeks. Didn't she know how he felt? Hell, why did it even matter? He wasn't exactly a prize. Not one big enough to make her permanently turn her back on everything her family offered. Just because she'd said no to a few family yacht trips and ski vacations didn't mean Mira would say no to her slice of the family pie.

"What difference does it make?"

Mira used her fingertips to tilt up his chin. "Well, it makes a big difference because I'm crazy about you."

"Right. Like you're crazy enough to give up—what—millions of dollars? Based solely on a couple of good make-out sessions?"

"Don't sell yourself short." She trailed butterfly-light kisses along his jawline. "You're the best kisser with whom I've ever locked lips. Makes me wonder what else you do extraordinarily well in that same vein. Using other body parts…"

He blinked, astonished at her shift in mood. "Now? Now is when you decide to flirt with me? Have you been drinking as much as Ivy?"

"Sam, I've been turning my back on my family and their money for years. Do you really think store manager is a job they'd deem appropriate for their sole heir? When the only reason they paid for my grad school was so I could then join the family firm? To fill the figurehead gap left for a decade because they were too busy partying to step in once my grandfather died, by the way. My parents ignored me when I was a child, and only pretended to scrape together interest once I could be useful. I haven't touched a penny of my inheritance since the day I graduated. And not just because I'd go stark raving mad if I worked for the company."

Somewhat reassuring. Although Sam still didn't think his kisses were worth giving up life on easy street. "Okay, I've gotta ask. Where did all this money come from? What does your company do?"

"Cement." Mira spat the word out like it was week-old sushi.

"That's it?"

"Not *just* cement. Edgewater Aggregate is one of the world's leading suppliers of cement, concrete, asphalt, gravel, sand and crushed stone." She ticked each of the items off on her long, slender fingers.

Sam still couldn't wrap his head around it. Not that he had any idea what he'd expected her to say. "You make millions of dollars selling cement?"

"More like billions. We're a leader in the industry, both manufacturing and distribution. We have locations in more than sixty countries. Is that enough for you? I'd really like to stop quoting the company brochure. If you're interested, I can send you to our website."

"No thanks. Wow. That could easily be one of the top ten most boring companies on the planet. No wonder you don't want to work there." He tried to choke back a laugh. It didn't work. It turned into a full-fledged belly laugh that wouldn't stop. Mira giggled. He leaned into her for support, one hand holding his stomach as she dissolved into more giggles. They sat like that, wrapped around each other until their laughter fizzled out.

"Do you forgive me?"

"For putting me through the ringer? Yeah. You had good reason not to dump on me." Sam straightened up. He wouldn't be able to sleep tonight if he didn't press her one last time. "Tell me—is there any chance your parents will show up on your doorstep with a husband candidate?"

"The honest truth is that I don't know. I haven't laid eyes on them in three years, and we don't talk on a regular basis. They've sort of written me off as a disappointment, and repeat failure. So I can't promise you anything where they're concerned." She shifted onto his lap, legs dangling off to one side. "I can promise you that I currently have no marital intentions. I do, however, have some lecherous intentions toward you." She walked her fingers down the path of his shirt studs, then traced back and forth along the line of his cummerbund.

Sam liked where her mind and her fingers were headed. "I *am* friends with the manager."

"Oh, so you're a well-connected big shot, after all?"

"Very. He could hook us up with a room." He wrapped himself around her to growl in her ear. "God knows I don't want to wait to drive back to my apartment. The moment this premiere is over, we're hitting the elevator."

"Mira?" Ben's shout rose over the music and laughter. "Mira, where are you?"

They both popped to their feet, and hustled toward Ben, hands linked. Ivy sat next to him where they'd left her, listing to one side. "What's wrong?" asked Mira.

Ben's usually carefree smile was upside down in a worried grimace. "That coffee was a good idea in theory. In reality, it doesn't go well with Love martinis. Ivy's found the ultimate way to get out of watching herself on television. I'm pretty sure she's about to hurl."

"So you called us over to watch?" Ivy looked like she was channeling a chameleon, turning about eight shades of green.

"Ivy won't let me help her. Says she doesn't want all the mystery between us to disappear before the wedding. Daphne's over in a corner flirting with some guy. I don't want to cock block her. Besides, Ivy asked for Mira."

"We've done this before. In grad school we had a quarters tournament every semester. Each floor worked their way through elimination rounds. Ivy hung in there one year all the way to the finals. The drink that took her down was about a pitcher of screwdrivers. I took care of her, and she returned the favor the next semester when I didn't survive a round of tequila bombs."

"Walk us down memory lane some other time. Look at her. She's going to lose it any second." Ben pressed a key card into her hand. "Gib set aside a room for her on the eighth floor. Will you help her up there, and stay with her?"

"Of course."

"Don't let her sleep on the bathroom floor. Give her water, and aspirin, and remember to put a trash can by the bed—"

"Ben, quit hovering. I'll take care of your girl." Mira helped Ivy to her feet and shot Sam a look full of regret. "Well, on the bright side, I will get to see the inside of one of these rooms tonight."

Sam crossed his arms and huffed out a breath. "Yeah. But I wouldn't trade places with you for anything."

ELEVEN

"GOOD MORNING." Daphne waved through the open half of the connecting door from the bakery. Her motion wafted in some of the mouthwatering aromas Mira had been trying to ignore for the past two hours. Lyons Bakery tempted her constantly. Despite keeping both halves shut—at least whenever Helen wasn't around— the scents often crept in under the door. She'd been able to hold firm against indulging until Sam finally hand-fed her a piña colada cheesecake bar. The creamy swirl of pineapple and coconut transported her in one bite to a Caribbean beach.

Last week, Ben made her try a bite of his current favorite bourbon pecan pie. Apparently he changed favorites as often as Lyons changed their monthly specials board. She'd plowed through the entire slice. Mira had to admit it. Lyons was not one of those run-of-the-mill bakeries, churning out dry cookies and sheet cakes. Sam and his mom were artists. The smells from that bakery utterly destroyed her willpower. Mira planned to have gardenia-scented candles burning once the store opened. In order to strengthen her resolve against tasting the entire bakery on a daily basis, she should probably start burning them immediately.

"Hi, roomie." Mira leaned her broom against the wall. Daphne wore a lavender Aisle Bound apron over her jeans and long-sleeved tee, which meant she'd been deep in flower prep. "What brings you to our little corner of the Windy City?"

"Don't call it that. You sound like a tourist." Daphne lifted a white paper bag. "Two fritters to tide me over till lunch, and an éclair for a midafternoon boost. Today's going to be a nightmare. Delivery at dawn, stripped roses for two hours, then finished banging out these super-bright fuchsia-and-orange quinceañera centerpieces." She slipped through the doorway and gave Mira a quick hug. "They're so bright only the fifteen-year-olds at the party will be able to look directly at them. Funky and fun, if I do say so myself. Still have to do three cake toppers, process another delivery in a couple of hours, and do twelve bridesmaid bouquets."

"Twelve?" Add that to twelve groomsmen, both sets of parents, bride, groom, flower girl and ring bearer... Mira shook her head. "So, a bridal party of more than thirty people?"

Daphne perched on a stool at the gleaming granite counter. "Crazy, huh?"

"If I got married tomorrow, I'd barely be able to scrape together thirty people total to invite." She hadn't stayed in one place long enough since grad school to cultivate any lasting relationships. Had lost touch with most of her school friends. In fact, the group of amazing people here she'd gained access to through Ivy were already closer to her than just about anyone else.

It took less than a week of running with Gib and Ben every other day before they started treating her like a favorite sister. And Daphne cracked her up on a regular basis. The woman dealt with delicate, exquisite flowers, but had a down-to-earth, raunchy streak. Plus, she always kept their freezer well-stocked with ice cream and shared Mira's idiotic obsession with reality dating shows. Mira ran her hands across the cool counter that signified Helen's domain. She'd wanted a cook. In Helen, she'd gotten an amazing chef, a sounding board and a surrogate mother. For a woman with the lowest bank balance of her life, Mira felt richer than ever before.

"I can't explain it. Big family, sorority sisters, who knows? Well, Ivy knows, because she knows all. They're contributing to a pretty sweet profit margin for us this month, so I don't question." Daphne opened the bag and dug into one of the fritters with a satisfied moan. It made Mira bitterly regret the sensible container of plain yogurt she'd scarfed down four hours ago. "Today's a marathon, not a sprint. I'm trying to pace myself. This is my half hour to take a breather and talk about anything besides flowers."

Sounded good. The utter quiet of working alone was getting on her nerves. Mira welcomed the company. Otherwise she'd have to start talking to herself. Then Sam might hear her, decide she was halfway to crazy and wash his hands of her. A quick break was a better plan. "What do you want to talk about?"

Daphne licked her fingers, scowling. "I'd like to not be talking at all. I'd like this half hour to consist of hot, sweaty, mindless sex."

"You and me both," Mira muttered. Ivy's inability to hold her liquor—well, to be fair, enough liquor for three people—kept Mira by her side in one of the Cavendish's romantic rooms the night of the party.

Not a lot of romance to be had holding back the hair of her best friend, though.

For the last two days, Sam had kept busy shuttling his mom to every bingo game in the city. Mira didn't begrudge the poor, widowed woman a hobby. But why wasn't Sam going as stark, raving mad with desire as she was? Why hadn't he found a way to ditch his mom for just one night? Heck, at this point, she'd take quick, predawn nooky. Sam and his magical fingers and talented tongue had set all sorts of needs and lust in motion. And Mira was strung as tightly as piano wire, waiting for him to finish what he'd started.

"I'm in an epic dry spell. It's like all the eligible men in Chicago hooked up this summer and were tagged out of the dating pool. The situation is so bad, I'm actually contemplating online dating." Daphne shuddered. Then propped her elbows on the counter and leaned forward with a gleam in her eyes. "But you shouldn't be equally hamstrung. Is the lickably luscious Mr. Lyons not seeing to your needs?"

"You two are pretty close friends. Doesn't that make discussing his sex life off-limits—like a brother would be?"

"Nope. Makes it all the more interesting when two of my favorite people are involved."

Mira almost welled up. Instead, she blinked back the damp tickle at the corners of her eyes. God, did the Chicago River pump out extra estrogen into the air? She'd been an emotional basket case since moving here. Or was it just that she wasn't keeping herself closed off for the first time in years? It'd be nice to pick up a mental allergy pill against it—something to pull her tear ducts out of overdrive. "I'm one of your favorite people?"

"Of course." Daphne reached out and gave a gentle tug to Mira's ponytail. "It doesn't matter how long you know someone—it's how you connect. We've cobbled together a little clan here, and you fit in as though you'd known us all for years. You've got sass and spunk, you're just as driven and Type A as me and Ivy, and you don't hog the remote. Easily puts you at favorite friend status."

Mira gave an answering tug to Daphne's long, blond ponytail. "Right back at you."

"Don't think you're ducking the subject, though. If you want to keep your BFF status, you've got to dish. Have you and Sam really not gotten horizontal yet?"

She sat down with a sigh. "If I tell you, do you promise not to hassle him?"

A big eye roll made Daphne's feelings clear. "So that's a no, then?"

"I think it would've happened the night of the party—"

"Except you played nursemaid to Ivy, instead." Daphne finished her fritter and dusted off her hands of the excess sugar. "But that was a couple of days ago. Why aren't you two burning up the sheets?"

That's exactly what Mira wanted to know. From her point of view, they'd resolved the spat at the party. He hadn't been shy about showing his desire. Why hadn't he banged down her door the very next night and, well, banged her? "Sam's been busy with his mother."

"Honey, he's *always* busy with his mother. Sam's

the ultimate Too-Mr.-Nice-Guy. You're going to have to jump him."

No way. Not in a million years. Not if they were the last two people on the planet, and the future of the human race depended on them. To Mira, the chance, no matter how minuscule, of rejection had always ruled out making the first move. "Not really my style," she said, trying to play it cool.

Daphne shrugged. "Then you'd better tell me what toppings you want on the pizza tonight, because I predict many more nights of hanging out on the couch with me."

"Not exactly the worst fate in the world," Mira teased. "Besides, I've been working so hard that a relaxing night sounds blissful."

"Uh-huh. Blissful, maybe, but not orgasmic."

"Well, no."

"Your exhaustion will soon be a thing of the past. Besides the sugar fix and the mental health break, that's why I'm here." Daphne glanced at her watch, then pushed Mira off the stool with a gentle nudge. "I came for the show."

"What show?"

"Thanks to Ivy's over-the-top insistence on punctuality, I'd say you're going to find out in one minute or less. Go pretend you're working, 'cause the boss is on her way."

Mira didn't worry about Ivy discovering her on a break. Not when she'd managed to pull the store together from nothing. Now it sparkled like a romantic version of Ali Baba's treasure cave, full of pretty temptations. She had no doubt they'd be ready for the soft opening to begin on Monday. But to pacify

Daphne, she retrieved the broom and headed to the front of the store.

"You want to tell me why I'm pulling the Cinderella routine on a floor that's already spotless?"

The wind chimes tied to the knob tinkled as Ivy burst through the front door. Dressed to impress clients in a burnt-orange sweater dress and boots that made Mira drool with envy. Ivy's look also made her self-conscious yet again of her yoga pants and faded pullover. She could hardly wait for the insurance check to cover all the clothes she'd lost in the hurricane. Between not having renter's insurance but the government insisting companies paid out to all renters, as well as federal funds being slowly diverted to everyone who'd suffered, the process was full of red tape and glitches. As soon as it came in, she'd have Ivy show her all the best places to shop. Even though she'd planned to just spend the day cleaning, Mira hated feeling like a slob.

Right behind Ivy trailed a very attractive man. He skated the thin line between almost pretty and classically handsome. A super-tight black tee bulged across muscles so defined Mira knew they reflected a dedicated gym rat. Gelled blond hair lay in a careful sweep, curling up like a crashing wave at the side. Aquiline nose, melted chocolate eyes and lashes so long Mira suspected mascara added up to a face that could sell anything from cologne to condoms to a luxury cruise. He did not, however, look like he belonged with her best friend. Mira's radar went on high alert. She slapped on a full-blown anyone-could-be-a-client smile and aimed it at the suspiciously hot guy.

"Ivy, I'm surprised to see you. It's the middle of

the morning. Shouldn't you be calming nervous brides and refereeing overzealous mothers?"

"Yes. I have four more consults today, plus three site walk-throughs. So you should be able to tell how very important this visit is." Ivy winked. Well, squinted with one eye. Then dissolved into giggles. "Sorry. I'm trying to perfect a wink to surprise Ben. He does it to me all the time. Harder than it looks, though."

"Well, a bus ticket to New York and twenty years of practice can get you to Carnegie Hall." She propped the broom against the counter.

"Funny. You'll regret that remark when I tell you that I brought you a present."

"Ooh, is it the tiara you promised me?"

"Nope. I'm dangling that shiny carrot for opening day, remember? But speaking of your grand opening, this present will help get you there." Ivy pushed forward the silent man. "Mira Parrish, meet Hays Dellimore. Your new store assistant."

"It is my genuine pleasure to meet you, Mira." Hays bent over her hand in a shallow bow. When he rose, he trailed the pad of his thumb down the length of her hand before releasing it. The touch straddled the fence between flirtation and appreciation. It took practice to be able to pull off a move so subtle. Impressive.

"Nice to meet you, too."

Daphne appeared at her side, hand outstretched and flirt switch turned to on. "Daphne Lovell. So glad you're joining the team as an accessory. I mean, an associate."

"Ivy? May I have a word?" Mira jerked her head

to indicate the back of the store. "We'll be right back, Hays. Daph, would you keep him company?"

"It's why I'm here," she said, throwing her shoulders back and tossing her long, blond ponytail.

Ivy's heels beat a staccato rhythm against the hardwood floor. "What's going on?"

"Funny, I was about to ask you the same thing." Mira stopped in the hallway outside the bathroom. He shouldn't be able to overhear their conversation, this far back. "I've been interviewing candidates for a few weeks now. Have we been duplicating our efforts? You didn't mention you planned to search for my assistant."

"I didn't. Honestly. But you haven't found anyone yet, right?"

For a workforce supposedly in the grips of a recession, the candidates had been few and far between. So far, none had displayed the necessary mix of experience and personality. Frankly, nobody that she'd be willing to share space with for eight hours a day. "No."

"Hays practically dropped into my lap. You remember Milo, my office manager? He's friends with Hays, and heard the lingerie store he worked at recently closed. Which is a shame, because I wanted to go crazy in there to prep for my honeymoon. They carried a great line of lace tap pants and matching camis."

"Ivy, focus."

"Sorry." Ivy flashed a guilty grin, reminiscent of someone caught licking the icing off a newly frosted cake. "I'm trying not to turn into one of those brides whose entire life narrows down to her wedding. Hard, though."

"Daphne and I won't let you turn into bridezilla. And I promise to give your honeymoon underwear all the serious attention it deserves. But for now, could we get back to my potential employee?"

"He's a struggling actor." Ivy lowered her voice to a whisper. "According to Milo, Hays is talented, but keeps getting cast in bad productions. He can't break out of the community theater circuit. Which is a plus for us, because it diminishes the chance he'll make it big and leave you in the lurch."

That explained the leading-man good looks. Given his connection to Milo, it also made her briefly wonder which side of the sexual fence he grazed on. "Not really a big enough reason to hire him."

Ivy rolled her head around, cracking her neck. "I'm coming at this backward. As a struggling actor, he's worked for years in retail. Has experience with all sorts of customers. The acting experience helps him pour on the charm. He'll be able to flirt with the women and help the out-of-their-element men feel comfortable. We're lucky to be able to scoop him up."

He sounded good in theory. But so did Communism, before anyone put it into effect and discovered what a disservice it did to most of the population of a once-happy empire. "What about references? I need more than Milo's seal of approval."

"Forwarded to you before I left the office. I thought you'd prefer to speak with them. Look, I'm not trying to step on your toes. On paper, he adds up to a perfect fit. Why not give him a one-week trial run, through the preview? You can even keep interviewing people. But you need help lined up before we open."

The idea of a probationary period worked for her as a compromise. "Okay."

"Great."

"As long as you promise to stop with the winking. My job as your best friend is to let you know the cold, hard truth. It isn't cute. Looks like you have Tourette's. Stick to flashing Ben your bedroom eyes."

Ivy fluttered her eyelashes. "They do work well." She bustled to the front door. "I'll leave you two alone to get acquainted. Daph, are you coming back with me? We have the Clough-Nakano consult in less than half an hour."

After nipping back to grab her bakery bag, Daphne waggled her fingers in a goodbye. "Slave driver," she muttered, following Ivy out the door.

Mira eyed the almost too-handsome man lounging against a display case. It could be a brilliant fit, or it could be Milo hooking up an unsuitable friend. Time would tell. "Hays Dellimore. Tell me, is that your real name?"

"Nah. Stage name. Lewis Keller just doesn't have that theatrical ring to it. Don't worry—I'll fill out the W-2 with my legal name, so it'll all be on the up-and-up."

"I hear you've worked in stores—"

Hays cut in and corrected her, raising one eyebrow. "Boutiques."

"My apologies. You have years of experience selling in boutiques. Generally populated by high-class customers, sometimes difficult to please. Do you enjoy it?"

He flashed a wide, disarming smile. "Immensely."

"Why?"

"When people come to see one of my plays, they get a reprieve from life for two hours. They're happy, even get a little serotonin buzz that lingers, like the endorphin rush after working out. When I help people shop, the same thing happens. They derive pleasure from the treasure hunt, from the thrill of victory. I help make them happy. What could be better?"

"What could be better, indeed?" Mira had to hand it to him. It was the perfect answer. It mirrored her own feeling. A thin layer of stress flaked off as if Hays were an emotional loofah. "All right, I'll offer you a trial run for a week, through preview. If we're both still happy after that, the job is yours. Of course you'll be compensated for your time either way. I may run you ragged, since we're up against a time crunch," she warned. Better to set out her expectations right from the start.

"I'm not afraid of hard work."

A man after her own heart. Almost starting to sound too good to be true. But she'd take her chances. "Can you start right away?"

"I'd like that." He pushed off the display case full of heart-shaped lockets. "I took a quick peek around while you two debated my merits." A self-deprecating smile, this time. "This store is full of beautiful things. None more so than the manager."

Mira appreciated compliments as much as any woman. However, she also knew how less-than-impressive she looked at the moment, after spending the morning sweeping, dusting and sanding the edge of a kitchen cabinet that didn't close quite flush.

Most men tossing out a line that cheesy and obvious would be feeling her coldest, withering stare already. Yet Hays's assertion had the crystal clear peal of sincerity to it. And his eyes were full of nothing but appreciation. He made her feel pretty. Then it hit her.

"You're auditioning for me, aren't you? Showing me how nicely you can turn on the charm and treat our customers?"

He shrugged, the movement rippling his pecs and abs in a cascade of muscle. "You caught me. How'd I do?"

Mira laughed, more and more delighted every second with her new addition. "You get extra points for thinking to impress me, unasked, as well as a big thumbs-up for your performance."

"I like to flirt. Why not use my talent to make women feel good about themselves?"

"As long as you don't overstep," she cautioned.

"Don't worry. I have a strict policy against dating the customers. And coworkers," he hastened to add. "But, to be clear, you *are* a beautiful woman. You have luminous skin."

What red-blooded man ever complimented a woman on her skin? Only the ones who weren't interested in women. With that one comment, Hays made it clear he pledged his allegiance to the rainbow flag. She'd have to warn Sam that she wouldn't be the only one throwing lustful looks his way anymore.

"I think you'll definitely be an asset when it comes to moving merchandise." Mira shook his hand. "Welcome to A Fine Romance. And in the spirit of reciprocity, I should mention you're not too hard on the eyes, either."

"I do a little modeling on the side. Just local catalogs and stores. Great place to pick up dates, walking the catwalk." He picked up the broom like a knight hoisting a lance. "Do you mind if I look around and acquaint myself with the layout for five minutes? Then you can ask me to do, well, anything, boss." Hays winked, and pulled it off with all the smooth aplomb Ivy had miserably lacked.

Mira patted him on the arm. "Take your time. Get comfortable."

"Like hell he will," Sam bellowed from the doorway. He'd bent at the waist, leaning so far out she was amazed he hadn't toppled over. And if this was a cartoon, he'd have twin plumes of steam curling from his temples, along with angry red darts shooting from his eyes. Damn it. She knew having the top of that door open would lead to trouble.

TWELVE

BOTH HALVES OF the Dutch door slammed shut behind Mira. She glanced at the mother and two toddlers seated at a café table, all slurping hot chocolate. "Is there someplace we can talk?"

He'd talk with her anywhere, as long as it got her away from the smooth-talking muscle boy in her store. With a gentle palm against the soft nape of her neck, Sam steered her down the hallway, stopping just short of the entrance to his cooler. "I've got to stay visible in case Marla and her daughters need a refill. This is as private as we get."

"Understood." Mira crossed her arms over her chest, to his disappointment. "We agreed to not talk to each other during the workday, not to indulge in our relationship. But evidently I should've added that you have no say on how I conduct my business. Care to explain yourself?"

"Me? You're the one hanging all over Mr. Muscles."

She huffed out a breath hard enough to lift her bangs off her forehead. "Exaggerate much? For crying out loud, I touched his arm. Let's see, I also ran by the pharmacy this morning. Pretty sure the pharmacist and I touched fingers when he handed over my bag. Oh, and a guy running for a taxi slammed right into me. Full contact. Got a problem with all of that touching, too?"

"Only if they also mentioned your 'luminous skin.'" On the last two words he made air quotes with his fingers. What the hell kind of a compliment was that, anyway? Had to be one of the worst lines he'd ever heard. Worse still, Mira seemed to have liked it.

"You were eavesdropping on me?"

Nice try, but he refused to let her turn the tables. Daphne's the one who left the door open. Why should he take the blame? "Not on purpose. I delivered the hot chocolates, and as I came back around I heard you two obnoxiously flirting the day away."

"I can't take credit for this oldie but goodie." She spread her arms wide, palms up in exasperation. "Don't listen to other people's conversations. You might not like what you hear."

Yeah, he knew that now. "Not the point."

"You're right. The point is that you can't holler at people in my store."

Sam crossed his arms, mirroring her. "I can when they're making a move on my woman."

"Oh. Ohhhhh."

"What?"

Rising onto her tiptoes, Mira kissed him on the cheek. Her lips were as soft and luscious as crème brûlée. "You're adorable when you're jealous."

Torn between enjoying the kiss and annoyance, Sam gave in to his aggravation and stepped away. "Men aren't adorable. We're rugged, or sexy. Sea otters are adorable."

"I notice you're not disputing your obvious jealousy."

How was that a bad thing? Didn't it prove how much Sam liked her? Damn it, he wanted her all to himself. "So what if I am jealous? How am I supposed to work when ten feet away someone's trying to get in your pants?"

Mira wound her arms around his neck. "I hear healthy competition is a motivator for men. Maybe this will give you the encouragement necessary to get into my pants first."

First? Was there a line Sam didn't know about? Should he have taken a number? Then sheer gratitude for his apron washed through his brain. With Mira rubbing against him like that, there was about to be a big-ass bulge in his jeans that none of his customers should see. "Mira, there's kids in here."

"I know. Just one minute…" She licked the edge of his jawline, then again on the side of his neck where he knew his pulse had to be jackhammering. Easing back, she drew her index finger along the hollow at his collarbone and held it up on display. The end of her finger was now covered in lime-green frosting. "I was cleaning up the splatters." With a wide-eyed innocence that belied the porn-star suction of her lips, she licked it off. "Tasty. Citrus?"

"Mostly." Sam pointed at the multilayer cake he'd walked away from when he'd glimpsed ridiculously handsome guy flirting with her. "Margarita flavored. The bride and groom got engaged in Mexico, so they're shoving the whole sombrero and mariachi thing down their guests' throats."

"Oh, no shoving required. It's delicious. Like everything in this bakery." Mira popped off a flirty grin. "Including the handsome baker."

He'd take a wild guess that she wasn't bothered anymore by his interruption. But the reason behind it still didn't sit well with Sam. "We didn't set many ground rules as things have progressed. You should know that my eye doesn't wander when I've got a girl locked in my sights. Kind of assumed it was the same way for you. If not," he rolled his shoulders, trying to work past the tightness that suddenly seized all his muscles, "then just be up front. If I don't have a claim on you, I deserve to know."

"Don't you get it, Sam?" Mira headed for the doorway, a mysterious smile tilting upward. "I'm waiting for *you* to stake your claim. Plant your flagpole on top of the mountain. And I don't mean theoretically. Figure it out. Fast. I'm tired of waiting." She crossed into her store and paused, one hand on the frame. "Get used to seeing Hays over here, by the way. He just joined the team. But don't worry about him. I've got, hmm, two too many breasts for him to ever be interested in me." She slammed the door shut, bolting top and bottom.

It took Sam a second to catch up. The too-handsome-for-his-own-good guy must be gay. Which meant there weren't any others making a play for Mira. She'd been egging him on because... God, he was an idiot. If she'd whipped off her pants and twirled them above her head, she couldn't have made her intentions any clearer.

The past couple of days had been torture, not being able to get his hands back on her. He'd almost told his poor, widowed mother to get one of her friends to drive her on the great bingo face-off. Of course, guilt poked the soft, fleshy underside of his heart a moment later with all the subtlety of the stingray barb that caught that crocodile-hunting guy right in his ventricles. What kind of a son chose sex—no matter how earth-shattering it promised to be—over his mom?

Luckily, Mom had plans tonight with a friend. He'd been planning to call Mira to see if she had the energy to go out. Sam knew she'd been working like a dog to get the store ready. Now, though, he didn't need to check. Although the actual door between them was firmly closed, she'd pretty much opened the metaphorical door, stuck out a welcome mat, lit candles and baked him a cake. Good thing he had all day ahead of him to plan the next step, with Javon and Isaiah coming in to work a shift. He'd give Mira until exactly five o'clock. With the amount of need pooling in his pants right now, it'd be a miracle if she still had any clothes on ten minutes later.

The bakery was dim, lit only by the soft glow in the display cases. Sam had turned everything else off an hour ago. Mixer cleaned, dishes washed and dough prepped for his mother to start the early baking predawn. After buckling to his nerves—the good kind—he'd closed the shop early and ran around making preparations.

While Sam had enjoyed the hell out of their makeout session in the elevator at the Cavendish, Mira deserved more than a quick screw against the wall. She deserved romance by the bucketload. This wasn't just sex with his hot and convenient neighbor. They were building something here. So he'd scrambled around getting things ready. Even shaved off his heavy-by-three-o'clock shadow.

When he got back to the bakery, he'd eased open the connecting door a crack. Not to intrude. Just to know the moment she turned the key behind the back of her new employee. No such luck. Quitting time came and went. He'd mopped the floor, practically scrubbing divots in the aged linoleum in an attempt to take the edge off his feverish desire. Yet still the two of them worked and chatted and laughed, the sound like nails down a chalkboard to him.

The freaking sun had set half an hour ago. Sam knew he'd already crossed a line once today, intruding on her business. No way could he give in to instinct, pull a caveman routine and go over there and drag her back to his lair. Patience was his only option. It was killing him.

"Good night, Hays. Thanks so much for all your hard work today." Mira's voice set him off like a starting gun at a racetrack. He shot through the door, leading with his shoulder to push it open.

"Sam?" Surprise colored her tone as she finished locking the front door. "Isn't it late for you to be at work?"

"Yes." He couldn't manage more than that one word. His mouth dried up just looking at her, knowing what he hoped like hell they were about to do.

"You look so nice."

Self-conscious, he smoothed the front of his midnight-blue shirt. Gib called it The Closer. Sam just knew that, paired with his black slacks, it worked in any romantic situation from casual date to fancy restaurant. In other words, nice enough to hopefully entice Mira back through the door. "As you pointed out, the green frosting left its mark all over me. The Kermit look isn't really in right now."

"What are you doing tonight?"

"You."

Mira dropped her keys to the floor. "Excuse me?"

Shit. For two seconds, his dick had taken over the speech center of his brain. He scrambled to fix it. "I, uh, hope you're not too worn out. It's late for you to be here, too."

She turned off the bank of lights that covered the front half of the store. "Are you kidding? Today was easy. Amazing what a difference having another person makes. Hays is tireless and motivated and enthusiastic."

Sam could be all those things. Hell, he was all those things. Just not about her store. But the minute he got Mira into his bed, he'd show her just how tireless he could be. "I'm glad you finally have some help."

She disappeared into the back office for a minute, then reappeared carrying a lavender windbreaker, folded to show the Aisle Bound logo. "Me, too. At first, it bothered me that Ivy hired him without consulting me. I mean, I know it's *her* store on paper, but at this point, it's really *my* store. The problem is that I took it personally." Mira closed her eyes and shook her head. "Entirely the wrong reaction. Hiring Hays was just good business. Ivy had the best interest of the store at heart. We both do. Silly of me to get so possessive. After spending the day with him, I can tell Hays is going to work out great."

He had to stop her. When Mira started talking about the store, she tended to keep going indefinitely.

On a normal night, Sam didn't mind. Full of passion, Mira could make reciting the multiplication tables interesting. Tonight, however, he would not be swayed from his mission.

"Mira."

She paused in shoveling the entire contents of the countertop into her purse. "Yes?"

How to begin without just jumping her? "You're very smart."

"Thank you. Any particular reason you're dispensing that compliment? I don't remember saying anything brilliant since you walked in."

"You gave me some sage advice this morning."

"Really?" She looked pleased, then slid her purse strap onto her arm. "The day's been crazy. Refresh my memory. How brilliant was I?"

"Very." Sam batted at the rest of the light switches with his elbow. Now they were both backlit by only the dim light filtering over from the bakery. He strode forward, full of purpose and hoping like hell he'd read all her earlier signals right. "You told me to stake my claim. I'd have to be dead ten years and brainless not to act on that invitation." Framing her tiny waist with his hands, Sam bent over her, his mouth a breath away from her. "I know you've had a long day, and a longer week, and a draining six months. But do you think I can entice you to stay up with me tonight? Just the two of us? Nobody else, no interruptions, and no clothes?"

Mira's breath caught. "Trust me. *I'd* be the brainless idiot if I turned down an offer that good."

"Glad we're on the same page. Now put your legs around me," he ordered. It took no effort to lift her to meet his kiss. He'd spent the entire afternoon telling himself to take it slow. Yet the moment their lips met, even the possibility of going slow went right out the window. Especially with her legs hugging his waist and her breasts tight against his chest. Heat flashed between them, a spark almost visible in the darkness. They were through the door in two steps. Sam kicked it shut with his foot.

In the cooler he had already plated chicken salad, broccoli in a lemon vinaigrette and a raspberry mousse pie. Sam readjusted his plan for the night. All the food would be there when they finished. Unless she called a hunger time-out, Mira's dinner would have to wait. Because he sure as hell couldn't any longer.

"Did I mention how nice you look?"

"You did."

"I mention it again, because I've simply got to touch you. If you don't take that very nice shirt off right this second, I'm going to rip it off you with my teeth."

"Thanks for the warning." Sam turned sideways to slide into the work area, then adjusted his grip on Mira to one hand supporting her ass. With the other he pulled open the door to the cold room. In most restaurants they called a closet-sized refrigerator a walk-in. But at Lyons Bakery, the entire back of the store had been turned into a refrigerated room. It was impossible to bake a four-tier wedding cake from scratch, frost and decorate it the same day and deliver it. On any given week there might be five or six cakes in various stages of decoration on the glassed-in refrigerated shelves, along with an entire rack of cake layers. He'd also carved out a small section for his chocolate truffles. In the middle of the room sat his white marble island, where all the magic happened. Why break tradition?

Candles burned in the sink, giving off a flickering light that danced shadows across the walls. He set her on the end of the island, leaving her legs dangling. Then, ever respectful of her needs, Sam quickly unbuttoned his shirt and tossed it into a corner. "Happy now?"

Mira placed her palms on his chest and started rubbing in slow, teasing circles. "Very."

"Uh-huh. I demand equity and fair play in this relationship. Yours, too."

In a flash, Mira tugged her shirt over her head, revealing a lacy cream bra. "Satisfied?"

"No. That's not going to work at all for what I have planned."

She looked down at her chest. "What's wrong with my bra? Remember, I didn't know we were having a date tonight, or I would've pulled out the really good undies."

God, if only she knew the effect she had on him, no matter what clothes she wore. Already his dick pressed against the fly of his pants with the insistence of a battering ram. "Your bra is sexy. Every perfect inch of you is beautiful. But we're about to get messy, and you're wearing white." Before she could ask questions, he'd flicked open the clasp and slipped the straps down her arms. Then he leaned her back, her head landing on the soft stack of towels he'd placed there as a pillow.

"What are you up to, Sam?"

"Close your eyes and you'll find out." The minute

she obeyed, he pulled a squirt bottle out of the pan of warm water on the stove. He soooo wanted to stand out from any other guy who'd been lucky enough to see her naked. For their first time, by-the-numbers sex wouldn't be enough. Sam intended to give her an experience she'd never forget.

With the same careful precision he used to create the intricate basket weave designs on wedding cakes, he squeezed the warm, melted chocolate onto her breast in a heart shape. Then he opened his mouth around that creamy mound and began to lick. The thick stickiness of the chocolate made him rasp his tongue a little harder as he swirled up, down and around. Every stroke lashed against her nipple, which instantly hardened to a delicate point. Mira locked her legs back around his waist.

"That's…oh my…you know how to get me from zero to sixty in about one heartbeat," she said breathlessly. "God, Sam, I feel it everywhere. Like you crawled into my bloodstream and are licking every inch of my body at once."

"Good." He was reduced, yet again, to monosyllables. With his concentration split equally between pleasuring Mira and not exploding like a virgin from the sheer sweetness of her, Sam couldn't spare any brain power to talk. He squeezed out another fat drop of chocolate sauce, this time right on the pale pink tip of her other nipple. Sensitized at this point, she squirmed against him. Enjoying the view, he waited, and squeezed out another drop.

"Please, Sam," she begged.

The flat of his tongue worked the nipple, back and forth. It only lasted a few seconds before she fisted her hands in his hair and yanked him up for a kiss. Her tongue darted into his mouth, seeking and swirling. Then Mira gasped. Her eyelids flew open.

"What is that?"

Crap. She was tasting the chocolate. He'd thought about using honey, but it was twenty times stickier and frankly, less fun. Sam had figured since he would be the only one licking the viscous sauce, Mira wouldn't have to know he'd used the chocolate she'd loathed for so long.

"Sorry."

"Don't be. It's the most exquisite thing I've ever tasted."

"Really?" Ridiculously pleased, he picked up the bottle. "I make it myself. A special blend with extra vanilla and a kick of cinnamon."

"Skip the ingredient list. Just tell me what it is?"

Had it been so many years she really didn't recognize the flavor? Once he told her, would she be mad? "Melted chocolate sauce."

"No. Seriously?"

Sam waggled the bottle in front of her nose. "I never joke about chocolate."

She nipped it right out of his fingers. Then she tilted her head back and squeezed a long, steady stream right into her mouth. It could very well be the most erotic thing he'd ever seen. A throaty purr came from deep in her throat. "I hope you didn't have plans for the rest of this bottle. There won't be any left by the end of the night." Mira captured his mouth. The sweet, dark aftertaste of his chocolate mingled with her own sweet flavor. It pushed Sam straight over the edge.

It only took one good yank to strip off her yoga pants. She toed off her sneakers while he stepped out of his slacks and ripped open the condom he'd strategically left at one corner of the island. As he slid it on, he planted his feet wide. "Mira, I don't want to rush you."

"Impossible. You primed me on our date at the Botanic Garden. You pushed me about twenty steps past ready in the elevator at the Cavendish. All I've done for days is think about getting you naked. I appreciate the thought, and the way you've reopened my eyes to the delights of the cacao bean. But what I would appreciate more than any tender foreplay or sweet nothings whispered in my ear is you driving yourself into me. Now."

No wonder he'd fallen so hard for this woman. Sam anchored his hands on her hips, tugging her a little closer to the edge of the island. Locking eyes with her, he entered in one smooth, slow stroke. Mira bowed off the marble with a long moan. He drew back, practically seeing stars from the soft tightness she squeezed around his dick in warm pulses. Again he drove into her, sinking into her welcoming, perfect fit.

This time when she arched up, she stayed, planting her hands flat on the marble to steady herself. The position allowed Sam to latch on to her breast and suck in rhythm to his strokes. The combination of seeing her luscious breasts, tasting them and losing himself inside her stoked the fire inside him past all control. Faster and faster he pumped. Mira answered him with breathy little cries and pants, locking her ankles together on his back and meeting every thrust.

"Sam, oh, you're amazing. It feels so… I can't

wait…" Her head dropped back and she let out a satisfied scream as he exploded inside her, waves of rippling pleasure washing over him. Before the last inner pulse subsided, Sam gathered her close and kissed her the rest of the way to senseless.

"Wow. I mean, wow!"

Sam agreed one hundred percent. "And that was just my chocolate sauce. Wait till you see what happens when you taste my whiskey caramel sauce."

She threw back her head and laughed. "Looks like I'd be smart to test every flavor."

"Fine by me." Sam loved it when laughter and fun could be a part of sex. With one last kiss, he disentangled himself. Walking over to the sink, he disposed of the condom in the trash can and blew out the candles. "If you want something a little more substantial, though, I've got dinner ready for us."

Mira gave a dramatic gasp and made an exaggerated show of covering her mouth with her hands. "You mean even though you've had your way with me, you still want me around the rest of the night?" she teased.

Beginning to root in his belly was the certainty he'd want Mira around a lot longer than just one night. "You bet. Except, I've left you super sticky. How about we go to my place and we can take a shower? You'd be amazed at how good I can be with a bar of soap."

"Talk about the ultimate walk of shame. What am I supposed to do—walk through the city topless?"

Other men ogling the beauty of all her parts? Especially the ones he'd just paid tribute to so lovingly with his hands and mouth? Sam hated the thought.

"I've got a short commute. Down the hall and up the stairs."

"You live over the bakery?"

"Yeah. So I hope my new neighbor doesn't plan on throwing any all-night raves."

"No promises. But if I do, you'll at least get an invitation."

Sam decided to come back for the dinner plates after their shower. He had high hopes it would be a long one. "Leave your clothes for now. I've got a robe you can wear." After helping Mira off the island, he guided her up the narrow wooden stairs. He paused at his front door. "Remember, you told me to stake my claim. I just followed directions." Either she'd go nuts for it, or think he was the cheesiest idiot ever born. In which case she'd probably make a nervous excuse and avoid him like the plague from here on out. Sam held his breath and pushed open the door.

Candles flickered on every surface. On the low coffee table, he'd created a heart out of his white meringue cookies. In the middle, the cookies spelled out M + S. At least, he remembered doing it. Sam couldn't take his eyes off Mira, naked next to him. How did he get so lucky?

"I guess, to prevent any misunderstanding, you had to spell it out for me?" She shot him a sly, sassy look from beneath her lashes.

He barked out a laugh. "Yep."

"Message received."

THIRTEEN

"WHEN DO I get to meet the sexiest man alive?" Helen asked, clattering a whisk against the glass mixing bowl at a steady rhythm.

Mira lifted her head, grateful for the excuse to look away from her laptop. She still hadn't unlocked all the quirks in the new inventory system. Two solid hours of staring at spreadsheet gridlines had a killer headache cued up and waiting to attack. Even her fabulous new high-backed stool didn't cheer her any longer. "Um, I don't know. Is this a trick question? Is your book group taking a field trip to a strip club?"

"My book club?" Helen hooted. "I'd bet most of them don't even watch their husbands strip anymore. The mere sight of man flesh might set them off into a hot flash cycle." As usual, she wore an impeccably tailored St. John suit—today's was burnt orange—and never splashed so much as a flake of flour on it.

"Not you, though. I bet you'd sit in the front row waving a fistful of dollar bills."

"Why be stingy? For a good set of abs, I'd stuff a fiver down their G-string."

Mira thought, for about the millionth time, how she'd lucked out with Helen. Here it was, Sunday morning, and she'd come in to create one last test batch of focaccia to kick off the preview week. Mira didn't have to wrestle her spreadsheets in sullen silence, and now they were talking about rock-hard abs? They might not have any customers yet, or earned a single dollar, but already A Fine Romance had eclipsed every other job to be her best managerial experience. She sure hoped the store survived the possibly slow first few weeks to give her a taste of the real thing. Of course Mira wanted the store to succeed for Ivy's sake, and because she believed in it. But at this point, she also really wanted it to take off because it was flat-out so darn much fun.

"It's never too early for Daphne and me to start planning Ivy's bachelorette party. If you'd like to sample some high-class male, uh, entertainment, you're welcome to help us."

Helen threw a towel over the top of the bowl and set it near the heat vent to rise. "Thank you for the lovely invitation. But I was asking about my new fellow employee, Hays. I hear he's hotter than a stack of fresh pancakes."

Imagery she abso-freaking-lutely did not need. Pancakes made Mira think of syrup, and that led her thoughts straight to Sam. Sam's tongue. Sam's fingers smearing things on her for his tongue to lick off. Best to derail that train of thought before her eyes crossed in joy at reliving those moments.

"I won't bother to ask where you heard that little nugget. I've accepted the fact you know everyone and everything." Mira switched over to email. A steady stream of responses to their grand opening party came in every day. It both soothed and excited her to add names to the RSVP list. Sort of the same reaction she got trying out a new hairdresser. Or trying to cool her tongue with too big a margarita gulp after accidentally chomping on a jalapeño. "Hays is undeniable eye candy. Also as charming as a gigolo and better at upselling than a used car salesman. He's the total package."

Helen slid open the doors to the display case, fussing with things for the fifteenth time. She'd moved a cluster of grapes down a shelf, then switched the order of the camembert, Brie and smoked Gouda. Mira figured the constant rearranging wouldn't stop until the first customer asked for a chunk of cheese. "I hate that I keep missing him. Good thing he's coming on full-time soon. But I can absolutely tell the difference he's made in the store already."

"Oh, you noticed he rearranged the fragrance display?" The shelf of mix-your-own perfume scents now sat on the wall between two windows, protected from the damaging heat of the sun by a wide column of bricks. Blown-glass flowers balanced near their namesake bottles. Mira didn't know if the flowers or perfume would sell out faster, but she anticipated barely being able to keep both in stock.

"No, I noticed you look like you caught up on your sleep. The complete set of luggage that shadowed your eyes for the past few weeks is finally gone."

Mira bit her cheek to keep from laughing. Definitely a case of quality over quantity. She and Sam had averaged a total of maybe three hours a night of sleep in the past week. They'd been in bed. Well, in the bathtub, shower, on the couch, back to his pastry island to sample two more of his dessert sauces, and then back to bed. At the end of each workday, Sam acted as desperate to get his hands on Mira as if she'd been stationed in Antarctica for eight months, instead of on the other side of the door for eight hours.

Not that she minded. Sam excited her more than any other man she'd been with, and she could not get enough of him. So the immediate, gotta-have-it-now hunger sex happened fast and hot. Once they hadn't even made it up the stairs to his apartment. Then they'd have dinner. Talk, laugh, catch up on all the little things about each other's lives they'd missed in the past three decades. It cracked her up to learn that Sam refused to let his father take the training wheels off his bike until his tenth birthday. He made up for the lost time, using a secondhand bike to explore the countryside mile after mile during his time in Europe. She loved picturing the stubborn, scared little boy who'd turned into such a secure, strong man.

Sooner rather than later, Helen would probably figure out Mira and Sam's relationship had progressed to the sleepover stage. But for now, Mira wanted to play it cool. Otherwise, she'd end up gushing about Sam all day, and the damn spreadsheets would never get straightened out. "I feel much better. Relaxed. Rejuvenated. Like a walking ad for a day at the spa."

"Glad to hear it. I was worried about you."

"Thank you. Truly, I appreciate the concern. But I've been taking care of myself for a long time now. I'm all good." The words rang so true to her. Her dream job (well, her third try at a dream job) had turned out to be better than she'd hoped. A man she couldn't in her wildest dreams have hoped for delighted her on a nightly basis. Life was so good for Mira, she had no choice but to worry about when the other shoe would drop. That worry scratched at the back of her subconscious like a pimple lurking just under the surface, about to erupt in all its oozing, painful protuberance.

Helen came around to eye the display case from the front. Also for the fifteenth time. "So when will you trot out Hays to amaze and astound me? I need to give my daughter incentive to come home over her Thanksgiving break. He sounds just delicious enough to be the perfect bribe."

"Hays wanted to be here this morning, but I ordered him to stay home. Next week will be busy and stressful as we tweak things during the soft opening. He started work here about two seconds after I hired him, without any advance notice. I knew he needed a day to deal with the rest of his life before I lay claim to him twenty-four-seven."

"Do you plan to take your own advice?"

"When we wrap it up here in a few hours, I have nothing more on my schedule than to go home and soak in a bubble bath. Maybe see if I can prop my eyes open long enough to crack a book." All true, but only because Sam was off to his regular poker night. Clearly the women needed their answer to poker night. Next time it rolled around, Mira vowed to rally everyone to go out, wear stupidly high heels and sip fruity vodka drinks at a trendy bar. Or possibly just go for sushi. She didn't want to turn into one of those women who pined for her man. Even though she was doing exactly that, staring blankly through the crystal vase display case.

Annoyed with herself, Mira clicked on the next email. She skimmed it in two seconds, then went back and read it a second time. The third time around, to her utter shock, the two-sentence message still read the same. Funny thing about waiting for the other shoe to drop—she never had to wait very long.

"Helen, did I miss a news report? Did Hell freeze over recently?"

"Oh, you mean the draft creeping under the front door?" Helen walked to the front of the store and ran her hands against the floorboard. "Some good weather stripping should fix it. I can ask Dan to rummage through the basement and find some for us."

"Probably a good idea." Mira knew she should make a note on her seemingly endless to-do list. Anything to do with her list always calmed her—reviewing, adding, crossing off items. Instead, she got up and paced the width of the store. Her hands clenched and unclenched around the hem of her faded purple Northwestern sweatshirt.

On the turn, her sneakers squeaked against the hardwood floor. The harsh sound jolted Mira to continue speaking. "But I meant in the actual sense, not just today's cold spell. Hell freezing over, earth turning backward on its axis. Somebody went back in time, stepped on a fire ant and now everyone has an aardvark for a pet and the Tooth Fairy stars in an action movie series."

"Not last I checked," Helen said slowly. "Of course, I don't get out to the movies much. Dan hates listening to an entire theater of people chewing on popcorn."

Damn. Any one of those possibilities would've been better than the reality sitting on her computer screen. Mira squeak-turned again. "What about that Mayan apocalypse thing? Did it happen already? Is it coming up? That could explain it."

"Explain what? Oh my goodness, will you sit down and tell me what has you so lathered up?" Helen grabbed her shoulders. After a quick squeeze, she steered Mira back to the stool at the checkout counter.

"This email." Mira tapped her fingernail against the screen. "It makes no sense. Listen to this: 'Coming for your store's grand opening. Can't wait!'" She tapped her fingers again, rolling into a nervous drumbeat. "What is that supposed to mean?"

"Weren't the RSVPs at fifty yesterday? I'll go out on a limb and assume that means we've got at least fifty-one now."

"Fifty-two," Mira corrected with a slow shake of her head. "It's from my parents."

"Oh. Oh! How wonderful."

"No. Unless you mean, how wonderfully crappy."

"Mira, they're your parents. They love you."

"They love the idea of the continuation of the grand tradition of the Parrish name. That's a direct quote, by the way, from a card they sent me for my high school graduation."

Helen grabbed her still-drumming fingers with both hands and gave her a look overflowing with sympathy. "Some people aren't great at showing their feelings. It doesn't mean they don't have them. So your parents aren't huggers. And yes, it hurts when they never call, and forget to email. It doesn't diminish the fact that they're proud of you. How could they not be full to bursting with such an amazing daughter?"

"I used to ask myself that on a daily basis." Mira knew she sounded as bitter as the peel on a grapefruit. The kindness in Helen's brown eyes only made her yearn all the more for parents who'd treat her like family, and not like a piece of stock to be framed and handed down. She pulled her hands away.

"You've got to give them a chance to make up for all the times they let you down in the past."

"No. That can't be the reason why they're coming. There has to be a reason that involves the Parrishes. Some way they profit from this visit." Mira twisted the store key chain around her finger like a ring. And it hit her. "It's because of my birthday. Their lawyer probably reminded them I'll turn thirty in less than a year. God knows I'm nowhere close to becoming a millionaire. What if they're bringing a prospective husband for me?"

"Then our guest list goes to fifty-three, and I consider ordering another case of champagne. Mira, stop panicking. I know you told me about that ridiculous caveat in your family trust, but times have changed. No one is going to shove a husband down your throat. This isn't medieval Europe."

Shoving back the stool, Mira paced again, this time going the length of the store instead of across. It meant dodging a few display cases, but being able to take long strides worked off more of her tension. "How did they even find out? I didn't tell them. I thought we were only getting local coverage with the papers. Even if we got a bump in recognition because of Ivy's appearance on *Planning for Love*, the news wouldn't be big enough to catch their attention overseas."

"I did it."

"Did what?"

Helen stepped directly into her path. "I emailed your parents an invitation to the grand opening."

Her brain couldn't begin to process the logistics of

such a thing, let alone the ramifications. "How? Most of the time, I'm not even sure what time zone my parents are in, let alone which continent."

"You don't fly that far under the radar. Knowing your last name, it didn't take very long for me to match you with Edgewater Aggregate. I sent the invitation to your parents via the main company email. I suppose an accommodating flunky somewhere along the line passed it on to them."

She'd never thought of that. Of course, Mira rarely felt the urge to contact her parents. Anymore, that is. Years of unanswered letters, calls and emails had finally impressed the message they didn't want to touch base with their only daughter into her psyche, like thermal embossing on the finest invitations. "But, why? Why did you do it? Why breach my privacy?"

"You need them."

"Hardly." Mira needed a tetanus booster. She also needed the entire city of Chicago to ignore the snarky story the paper did on her and still come check out the store. She needed to figure out how to keep from falling head over heels for the strong, silent and smokin'-hot boy next door. What she didn't need popping back into her life were two people who cared more for money and status than for their own flesh and blood.

Helen cleared her throat. "Mira, I'm serious."

"So am I. You think this is a coincidence? That out of the blue, less than a year before I'm supposed to finally prove my worth as a member of this family, they decide to come visit my store? To judge me? And undoubtedly to find both it and me lacking?"

"If they do, then they would be the ones who are

lacking. Perhaps I overstepped. It's always been easier for me to act first and ask forgiveness later."

Surprise and confusion vied for first place in her emotional horse race, but anger tinged with betrayal was coming neck and neck around the turn. Whether as an employee or a friend, Helen had one hundred percent overstepped. No perhaps about it. "You interfered in my private life."

"Absolutely true. But I didn't lie, or manipulate. What I did was care for you." Helen laid a cautious hand on Mira's forearm. "Mira, you're a sponge, so thirsty for love and acceptance, and yet completely unaware. This store will be a hit. I feel it in my bones. You've poured yourself into it, heart and soul. But no matter how many people walk through this door, no matter how many thousands of dollars they drop during our first week, it won't be enough for you. Not unless you get the validation from your parents that you so richly deserve."

Fat chance. "I don't need anything from them."

"Okay, you don't *need* it." Helen punctuated the sentence with an exasperated groan. "You've got a solid titanium spine, more energy than a quasar, and if you were a man, I'd say you had brass *cojones*, too. But you want their validation. You want them to notice what an amazing woman you are. So instead of you swallowing your pride and reaching out, I did it for you. Consider it my grand opening present. If it backfires, I'll owe you big-time. I just want you to be happy. I want your parents to see the remarkable woman that I've gotten to know and admire. The one who's not only following her own dream, but helping me to live mine."

All the other emotions dropped out of the race, because gratitude surged into the lead. Tears tingled at the corners of her eyes. "Damn it. I told Sam I'd try not to cry so much. Since I moved to Chicago I've turned into a regular tear spigot."

"Maybe it's because you're finally comfortable enough here, with all of us, to let down those rigid emotional walls. After everything you've told me about your family, I understand why you erected emotional battlements. But you've made a new family here. We've already crossed the drawbridge and stormed your heart."

Laughter dried up the tears. "Wow. I didn't think you'd stick with the medieval Europe reference. When you pick a theme, you really grind it into the ground."

Helen drew her into a long, tight hug. "I'm told a person has to hear something three times before it sinks in—or maybe it's nine times. Either way, you're rather stubborn. I figured the repetition couldn't hurt."

"There's no guarantee they'll show."

"Then we'll get to finish off their champagne ourselves."

"Good point."

Sam ran his hands over the car's pale gray leather seats, softer than double-cream Brie. A guy with basic tastes, he didn't care about season tickets to the Bears, or designer sunglasses. He would, however, give his left nut to own a car this sweet. "How many paychecks did this set you back, Gib?"

"Doesn't matter. This beauty has paid for herself twice over with all the females she attracts." Gib slammed the door of the sporty silver convertible.

"Hope you don't mind if the top's down. I can't bear to put it up until the first snow."

"That's how we roll here in Chicago. Turn up the tunes and let's cruise." Sam rolled a drum riff against the dashboard with his palms.

Gib shot him a look before fiddling with the radio. "So says RapMaster Lyons. What's with the hip-hop 'tude?"

"Dunno. Good mood, I guess. It is poker night, so I plan to give most of your money a new home in my back pocket."

"You hold on to the optimistic spirit. It'll get you through the blinding depression that'll set in right about midnight. When I upgrade your crumpled cash into their new, luxury digs of my Burberry trousers."

Trash talk was sometimes the best part of poker night. Team sports, like soccer and baseball, demanded good sportsmanship. Poker demanded that you psych the other players out using any underhanded, devious, ass-hattery that came to mind. Sam couldn't think of a better way to blow off tension. Well, aside from the mind-blowing sex he and Mira racked up every night. "I'll bet you twenty dollars I come out ahead of you tonight."

"I'll take that action."

"Hey, guys. What action? I want in." Ben used one hand on the side of the car to boost himself into the backseat.

"Too late, all around." Gib gunned the engine and jetted into traffic. "Why are you late, Westcott? Doesn't Ivy understand that poker night is sacred? She didn't use her considerable feminine wiles to try to lure you into staying home, did she?"

"Hey, that's my future wife," Ben protested. "Try to notice her wiles a little less, okay?"

"No promises. That's like asking Monet not to admire a haystack."

"Or asking Picasso not to turn and stare at a Cyclops woman with three boobs," Sam added.

Ben leaned between the front seats, yelling to be heard over the wind noise. "To answer your question, Gib, I was wrapping up work. You know, that thing Sam and I do for a paycheck, and you use as a way to pick up women?"

"It's called multitasking." Gib nipped across two lanes of traffic with barely a glance in his mirrors. Every time Sam rode with him, the fear that Gib would revert to his British roots, driving on the left side of the road, kept him white-knuckling the edges of his seat. "I consider the women who stream through the Cavendish Grand to be a buffet which continually refreshes itself."

Sam shook his head. "One of these days, you're going to meet a woman who objects to being lumped into the generic mass of legs and breasts who check in and out of your bed faster than you can change the sheets. You won't have any clue how to handle her."

"Just because you've fallen ass over teakettle for your new neighbor doesn't mean you have to pair up the rest of the world. With my stellar good looks—"

Ben and Sam both groaned. It didn't slow Gib down for a second. "—and charming, almost-royal accent, I couldn't turn women away if I tried. They sneak in my office. They leave their panties hanging from my doorknob. It's a burden I'm forced to shoulder, and I try to do it with aplomb."

Sam refused to spend the rest of the night dealing with Gib in this mood. "Jesus, but you're on a high and mighty throne tonight. What shot helium up your ass?"

"If I tell you now, you won't be surprised when the January issue of *Windy City Magazine* hits your mailbox. With none other than the Right Honorable Viscount Gibson Moore on the cover."

"What?" Ben fell back onto the seat. "You mean I should've been bowing and scraping in front of you all these months? You're a freaking member of the British peerage?"

Great. Gib only trotted out his title to be particularly insufferable. Sam knew the next three months until the magazine came out would be endless if he didn't stick a pin in Gib's triple-inflated ego immediately. "He doesn't do tea with the queen. He doesn't have a castle. In fact, he rarely springs for so much as dinner. Don't think the title makes him special."

"No, what makes me special is getting featured as one of Chicago's top twenty most eligible bachelors. It was cute when *CityPaper* said it. But it's a huge honor to be awarded that particular accolade by *Windy City*."

Gib was one of his closest friends. Sam knew how smart the brains were rattling around under that overpriced and over-gelled haircut, not to mention the work ethic that kept him at the Cavendish for an ungodly number of hours each week. He couldn't think of anyone who deserved this shout-out more. The bro code demanded, however, that he not admit any of that to Gib.

"You conned a magazine into basically advertising that you've got a big Open for Business sign strapped to your crotch? Nice going. Your mom must be so proud."

The corner of Gib's mouth took an ugly twist downward. "My mother wouldn't be proud of me if I nabbed a commendation from the queen for shagging the Princess Royal."

Ben leaned forward again, the journalist in him prepping to ask the obvious—what deep, dark dirt accounted for Gib's sardonic tone. But Sam's recent experiences with Mira had taught him that sharing family angst wasn't exactly a mood lifter. He refused to let Ben's unquenchable curiosity ruin poker night for Gib. Using one finger, he drew a line across his neck, hoping Ben got the universal signal to zip it. Then he frantically cast about for a new topic to fill the awkward chasm of silence.

They were now slowed by late rush hour to a near idle past the more upscale restaurant and boutique section of Halsted Street. A late-season biker hugged the curb next to them, crunching through crispy leaf piles. "I thought we were going on a beer run. We've already passed four liquor stores. Are you heading all the way down to farmland to harvest your own hops?"

Gib shook his head, and apparently his dark mood with it. "Keep it up, Lyons. The more you yank my chain directly correlates to how little beer I'll pour for you."

"Sam's got a point." Ben jammed his feet through onto the center console, nudging Sam's elbow out of the way. "I can't believe you're using the car on something as basic as a beer run."

Gib stroked the steering wheel with both hands in a lazy arc. "Her name is Moll Davis. After one of the very famous mistresses of King Charles II. Samuel Pepys's wife called her the most impertinent slut in the world. Perfect for an auto with 100 horsepower under the hood."

"But this is your guaranteed booty-mobile. You do know that neither of us is going to sleep with you later, right? My heart—and my dick—belong to Ivy now. I'm not tossing my chastity into the pot as an ante."

"If you did, I'd fold that hand without even peeking at my cards. And don't make such a big deal about my driving. We're going to Goose Island. Thought I'd pick up a few growlers of Honker's Ale and Green Line."

"Nice plan, Moore. Be sure to get some Dublin Stout, too. You know, for those of us manly men who like a beer you can't see through." Ben kicked Sam's knee with the toe of his boot. "Speaking of being all man, I heard a rumor you finally made it to home base with the girl next door."

For about a second it surprised him that Mira would've spilled the details to anyone. Women, unlike men, didn't usually mark one up on the scoreboard, or take a victory lap. Then he did the math and realized Mira had slept at his place the last three nights running. Daphne must've figured out that her roommate, no matter how much of a workaholic, wasn't pulling a string of all-nighters at the store. But he wasn't going to sit here and give Gib and Ben a play-by-play recap. "We've…uh…gotten closer."

"How much closer?" asked Gib.

"You want me to draw you a picture?"

"Sorry, that came out wrong. Here's the thing. We really like Mira."

"Me, too." Sam had his suspicions about just how much Gib liked Mira. Running along the lines that if Sam got run over by a bus tonight, Gib would be on her doorstep by dawn to stake his claim.

Ben interlaced his fingers into a fist and rolled his wrists. "She's got a groove that works with our little group. Gib and I talked about it, and we decided to just come out and tell you that you'd better treat her right. Or else."

"Or else what?" Were they really threatening him? On poker night?

"Not sure. We're still fine-tuning the details of the threat. Just be assured the consequences would be dire should you break her heart."

Because he did care for Mira, he appreciated where they were coming from. It was all that kept him from slapping them both silly. "I'm not Gib. I can keep a woman around longer than it takes to change a pair of socks."

"So this is serious? Girlfriend material, not grab-and-go?"

"Mira's great. But, well, it's complicated."

Gib unleashed a deep, long chortle. "Sam, you are the least complex man I've ever met. Your entire life can be summed up in two bullet points: your mom first, and the bakery second."

Sam stewed a minute. He didn't know what to say, or how much to tell them without sounding like a whiny teenage girl.

"Have you been keeping a deep, dark secret from us?" Ben thumped the back of Sam's seat. "Are there a few more layers in your cake than we realize?"

"Secret agent? Superhero?" Gib suggested.

Ben snorted. "Right. What would his superpower be? Covering villains in icing? Getting people so hyped up on sugar they spin around like a Tasmanian devil?"

Hey. After all, with a little training and a lot of money, anyone could do the Batman gig. "Look, there's a lot going down right now. Money stuff and career and family—it's all up in the air. And it could all come crashing down on me in the next week. I don't want to talk about it. But with everything that could go to shit, Mira is the one bright spot. And even she's complicated. You guys know about the slam piece the *newspaper* ran on her, right?"

"We got the highlights." Gib draped his wrists over the steering wheel, the picture of nonchalance. "It was one stupid article. It won't keep anyone from coming to the grand opening."

"Maybe. No guarantees." And Sam desperately wanted to be able to provide her with a guarantee. Anything that could help erase the shadows of worry from her beautiful blue eyes. "Do either of you have any contacts with local media? Someone who could run something with a positive spin about the store?"

Ben huffed out a breath, spiking his fingers through his hair. "You know all my bridges were burned years ago. If I lit myself on fire, I couldn't get a journalist to so much as snap a picture. But more important, I don't think that's the way to go. I know Mira pretty well at this point. Not as well as you, obviously, but enough to know she wouldn't want anything she hasn't earned."

"True. But if the store folds, she'll leave town. Chicago's an expensive place to hang out without a paycheck coming in the door. She'll have to move to wherever she can chase down another job."

"Chicago's also a pretty big city," Gib noted. "What makes you think she couldn't find another job here?"

Ben slapped his palm against his heart. "You could also have a little faith. Ivy and Mira know what they're doing. That store is one classy operation. What makes you think it won't be a huge success, even with a bit of bad publicity?"

Because his mother had beaten into him that life wasn't always fair. "I can't risk it. Right now, she's like a tractor beam of sunshine holding my head above water."

A long, low whistle from Ben was loud enough to compete with the squawk of a passing flock of pigeons while they idled at a light. "Enough mixed metaphors there to push an English teacher into a nervous breakdown. You need to get ahold of yourself."

"Guess you really are serious about her." Gib chuckled, then smoothly shifted as the light turned. "Maybe we should be worried about Mira breaking your heart."

Like he didn't worry about that every damn day already. Mira Parrish was a million times too good for him. "Now who doesn't have any faith? I'm crazy about her. All indications are that she feels the same way about me. As long as A Fine Romance has a smooth opening and racks up some good word of mouth, she'll stay put. I'll get to keep her."

Ben whapped the back of Sam's head. "She's not a hamster, Sam. You can't sew your name into her underwear and declare ownership."

"Yeah—you're going a little too *Of Mice and Men* on us."

Trust the Brit to channel his boarding school style and drop a literary reference into a stupid argument about love. "You're right. I'll have at least a shot of keeping her—how's that?"

Gib swung into the parking lot of what, to the un-initiated, would look like a common strip mall. In fact, it held one of the best brew pubs in the country. He yanked up the parking brake and unclipped his seat belt to turn and face Sam. "I understand your motivation. But getting this store off the ground is something Mira needs to do all by herself. It'll be hard, but you can't do anything besides stand back and watch."

Ben waggled his hand back and forth. "Well, a little motivational nightly sex might help."

For Christ's sake. Didn't they think he knew how to treat a woman? "I've got that angle covered." Did he ever. They were both walking bowlegged after the past few days. Mira wore him out, in the best possible way. He needed to bet hard and heavy tonight, to wrap the game up early so he could get back to her.

Still, Ben pushed at him. "Sure you don't want to tell us what else is wrong? Your mom's not sick again, is she?"

"No."

"Business seems steady." Gib locked that glacial blue stare on him. "I hear you're booked almost a year in advance for wedding cakes. What's with the money trouble? Did you hit the tables too hard at that casino out by the airport?"

"No. When would I have time to do that? Wedding season's still in full swing for another month, at least."

"Quit dancing around like a ballerina and tell us what the fuck is wrong." Ben pulled his feet back and hung his elbows on the front seats. His leather jacket made a farting noise as it skated across the leather as he moved into position. "We might be able to help. Especially Viscount Moneybags over there."

"No. I shouldn't have opened my big mouth. I'm telling you, in a week, this conversation won't matter. Everything will shake out, one way or the other."

Sam threw open his door and pushed out of the low-slung car. It reassured him to know Gib and Ben were there, even if he didn't accept their help. Kind of like the security-blanket twenty he hid behind his driver's license. Never used it, but liked to know it was there. "Are you two going to Sigmund Freud me all night? Because I'm starting to think you're stalling. Doesn't matter how late we start, I'm still going to end up with your cash."

FOURTEEN

MIRA STOOD ON the raised platform of A Fine Romance's window display. A hand-painted kimono dangled from her fingertips. The delicate ivory fabric became see-through in the shaft of weak sunlight piercing a sliver of blue sky between the heavy clouds. Dainty cherry blossoms wrapped around one breast, trailed a tendril at the waist and then twined all the way down to the hem. The artist also did heavy silk kimonos in jewel tones for men covered in thick trees and fire-breathing dragons. All unique, incredible pieces of wearable art. Mira intended to charge *two* arms and a leg for them, and only take orders, not sell any off the rack. She'd lay money on there being a waiting list by week two.

But for now, she was trying to decide if the sheer fabric was too overt to be part of the display. Hinting at romance was fine. Selling sex crossed the line and sent the wrong message. Maybe draped across the edge of a chair, the transparency wouldn't be so obvious. Although she knew the diaphanous quality to the fabric to be its best-selling feature. Mira held it up one more time. Wavering over a decision like this was definitely considered a first-world problem. It brought home the sheer fun of her job, picking out and playing with pretty things. Passing them on to others and sharing the joy just intensified the fun.

But with the soft opening already under way, she needed to stop dithering about the display. How could she tease Helen about rearranging the cheese every five minutes if she did the same thing with the displays? A tallish, too-skinny brunette fiddling in the window certainly wouldn't help move merchandise. Mira stepped down and made her way back to the cash register. The bell on the door jingled its alert that her fourteenth customer had just arrived. She vowed to stop counting once they officially opened.

"Good morning. Welcome to A Fine Romance. Let me know if you need any help."

A man of average height strode straight to her, not bothering to browse on his way to the counter. "I'm on a coffee break, so I don't have a lot of time to waste. Can you point me to the good stuff?"

"Of course. But I need a little more information. Are you shopping for someone in particular? A special occasion?" His appearance didn't give her much to go on. Laptop case slung across his chest, Bluetooth attached to his ear and a sport coat with just enough of a pattern to either make him the edgiest person in the office, or a full-fledged hipster. Glasses and an unremarkable haircut widened his age window from anywhere between twenty-five and forty. Engagement, birthday, anniversary? Mira just couldn't tell. But she did so enjoy guessing.

"Any occasion's special if you do it right." He spun in a circle, palms up and arms out wide. "Come on, I know the really high-quality goods wouldn't be out here on display. I want what you hold back for the special customers."

"We like to think all our customers are special."

Did he think she had a safe with black-market diamonds in the back? Mira bobbled between flattered, intrigued and annoyed. Then, remembering that he was only her fourteenth customer, she immediately struck annoyed from the list.

After a quick glance at his watch, he scrubbed his palm across his forehead. "Don't put me through a whole song and dance, lady." With a shake of his head, he marched the length of the store. "Do you hide everything away on the second floor? Or is there a special room behind this closed door?" he asked, rapping his knuckles hard against the wood.

"There is, but we don't generally sell anything from the bathroom. The paper towels and toilet paper are provided free of charge." Mira kept a pleasant smile on her lips, but knew it no longer brightened her eyes. Experience told her that something was off about this shopper.

"For God's sake, I promise I'll spend a wad of cash. No need to make me jump through hoops." Irritation both roughened and raised his voice.

The top half of the connecting door to the bakery hung wide open. The last thing she needed was this guy losing his temper in front of a crowd of pint-sized cookie addicts and their moms. Mira hurried down the hallway to close the gap between them. "Sir, I'm perfectly willing to help you spend as much money here as you'd like. I'm just not clear on what it is you want to purchase."

"You're a romance store, right?"

"Yes, indeed. First of its kind here in Chicago." To resist the urge to fist-pump the air in glee, she tugged at the hem of her bright red sweater set.

A snort rumbled up from the back of his throat. "Hardly."

"Oh, I'm quite sure. And I'm certain we carry items you won't find anywhere else in the city."

"Now you're talking." He jerked his chin toward the front of the store. "That thing you were holding up in the window."

Aha. The reason behind his odd behavior came clear. The sheer peignoir leaned more toward lingerie than lounging attire. Lots of men were uncomfortable shopping for unmentionables for the opposite sex. Especially with a female salesperson. "Now I understand. You'd like me to show you the robe?"

His eyebrows shot up above his glasses frames. "Hell, yeah."

"I can show it to you in periwinkle and apricot as well. They're in my office." Mira made it all of one step before a strong arm reached out and encircled her waist.

"A nice set of handcuffs and a strong paddle were all I was looking for. Didn't realize you were the kind of place to model stuff and put on a show for me. I don't care how much extra it costs—I'll take the full package." Sliding lower, his hand cupped her ass and squeezed. Hard.

Mira whirled around, out of his grip. Fear didn't have time to take hold because her self-defense training kicked in. But as she lifted her knee, the man flew backward. Sam had one hand tight on his belt, and the other around his throat. Her own avenging angel. Who smelled quite strongly of cinnamon sugar.

"Keep your fucking hands off of her," Sam

growled, dragging the frightened man to the front of the store.

"Don't hurt him," Mira pleaded. Now that the danger had passed, she couldn't help it. What kind of a store manager let her fourteenth customer be thrown out or, worse, beaten up?

"I heard—and saw—enough to know this guy didn't walk in here looking to buy a heart-shaped blanket. The man's pond scum." None too gently, Sam spun around to slam the customer's back against the wall. "How dare you take advantage of a woman like that?"

Gasping and shaking his head, the man held up his hands. "I'm sorry. There's been a misunderstanding."

Sam actually growled. Like a wolf. "Obviously. Maybe things will be more clear once I put my fist through your jaw. That'll teach you not to touch what doesn't belong to you."

"Wait. I asked, just to be sure." With a shaking hand, he pushed his glasses back up his nose. Then he pointed at Mira. "She said this was a romance store. I figured that was a classy name for a sex store. All I wanted was some toys. Light bondage, you know. Then I thought she was offering me a peep show, too. I was going to pay, I swear. Even planned to tip the hot chick."

Guilt swamped Mira. She couldn't let Sam keep intimidating this poor man. Not when the mix-up was her fault. No matter how much her genetic imprinting of a medieval maiden thrilled at his knight-in-shining-armor routine. "Sam, back off." She laid a hand on his arm to soften the request.

He complied by taking two steps back, spreading

his feet wide and crossing his arms over his chest. Even wearing an apron and with flour dusting his hair, Sam still looked mean and dangerous. The position drew his tan thermal shirt tight across his pecs, and bulged out his biceps. Mira hadn't realized how intrinsically sexy it was to have someone ready to fight on her behalf.

"I'm really, really sorry," the man babbled at something close to the speed of light. "I didn't mean to scare you."

"I believe you. You see, this really is a romance store. Look around," she said, waving her arm at the sparkling display cases. "Everything we sell makes people think of hearts and flowers and happily ever afters. What we do not sell are the ingredients for the kind of *happy ending* you had in mind."

Sam huffed out a breath. "Dude, didn't you see the refrigerator case full of salads and snacks? What kind of weird sex toy store do you normally shop in?"

"All I can say is that I'm sorry. No disrespect intended." The man hunched around his briefcase, using it as a shield. Clearly he still regarded Sam as volatile as a grenade with its pin pulled.

"At least your visit helped me make up my mind about the window display." Mira reached over and snatched the robe off the chair. "I'm going to be much more careful from now on about the message I'm sending out to passersby."

"Let me make it up to you. Do you have some cards? I work at a web design firm of about fifty people. I'd be happy to spread the word about what you really do sell."

Delighted by his offer, she scooped a handful off

the counter. "If you ever have more time, you should come back and shop for real."

With a nod, and a final wary glance at Sam, the man edged sideways out the door. Sam immediately threw the lock and flipped over the Closed sign. "Are you okay?" He folded her into his arms, stroking her hair.

Mira dropped her cheek against his chest. Then she let her adrenaline drop back to normal. Shock and shaky knees took its place. Being held by Sam helped. A lot. It also gratified her to hear his heart pounding as though he'd just sprinted all the way from Lake Michigan, instead of just next door. Guess she wasn't the only one who'd been freaked out by the situation. "I'm fine." Then she took a deep breath and flattened her palms against his back. "I'm fine, now," she amended.

Sam pressed a kiss to the top of her head. "Why didn't you scream for help? I would've been over here sooner. Before he ever laid a hand on you."

"Because I had everything under control."

Hands on her shoulders, he thrust her out to glare at her with eyes the color of midnight. "Like hell you did. You need a panic button. And mace. Pepper spray, or maybe a Taser."

"A Taser? Do you even hear yourself? What kind of word of mouth do you think we'd build up if I went around Tasing everyone who gave me the hairy eyeball?" But right before she completely lost her temper, Mira caught herself. Sam must be coming down from his adrenaline high, too. And he must've been pretty scared to abandon his shop and leap into protector mode. "I don't need any of those things, silly. I've got you."

"Damn straight." His hands tightened, pulling her up to her tiptoes to meet his lips. They came together in a frenzy, with searing-hot, wet, deep kisses. Sam staked his claim, branding her as his own. With her eyes closed, Mira swore she felt the earth spin a little in a slow circle.

A loud knock popped them apart with the approximate velocity of a champagne cork leaving its bottle. "Everything okay over here?" A woman with white hair smoothed into a pixie cut poked her head through the bakery doorway.

"She's fine, Mom. I scared off the creep before he overstepped too far."

Mom? After all these weeks of working a few sheets of drywall apart, *this* was when she had to meet Sam's mother? Mira's mortification, like an infectious amoeba, immediately split into two distinct layers. Bad enough that Sam thought she couldn't take care of herself. Now his mother would always know her as the frail, scaredy-cat of a woman who'd needed to be rescued. Especially galling, considering she'd done so well in her self-defense class that she accidentally broke her instructor's nose. While Mira appreciated Sam's actions, she'd never doubted being able to handle her hands-ily inappropriate customer all by herself. It stung her feminist pride with the small but shooting pain akin to a paper cut.

Worse yet was Mrs. Lyons catching an eyeful of Mira actively thrusting her tongue into Sam's mouth. In the vast panoply of possible first impressions, sucking face never went over well. Had Mrs. Lyons been nothing more than a neighbor and fellow professional, Mira still would've felt smacked with eighty pounds of embarrassment. But Mrs. Lyons also happened to be her boyfriend's mother. That fact turned the embarrassment from manageable to crushing, her face from sheet-white shock to ablaze with awkwardness.

"Sam, why don't you come back over here and finish bagging up these cappuccino biscotti for me? I think the secretary from that law firm is going to come pick them up in about an hour. You can't expect a roomful of lawyers to stay awake all afternoon without a hit of espresso and sugar from our biscotti, can you?"

"Actually, I could."

Kathleen clomped into the store in bright green clogs. Faded jeans peeked out below a brown Lyons Bakery apron, and on top she wore a bright yellow sweater. "Please don't say that when you hand over the box to Lydia. Their daily biscotti addiction is a steady bump to our bottom line."

"The biscotti can wait. I'm taking care of Mira."

Her lips, outlined in a sassy coral, pressed tight into a thin line. "Mira can no doubt take care of herself. You do her a disservice to think otherwise."

Took the words right out of her mouth. Sam didn't need to stay and hold her hand. In fact, Mira was already itching to go and unlock the front door. The thought of prospective customers walking past instead of walking in made her spine twitch. Even though Mira wasn't anywhere close to ready for the kissing to stop. She and Sam had stuck to their resolve not to interact during work. These unexpected daytime kisses were both a treat and a pick-me-up. The sexual equivalent of a caramel mocha frappuccino. "You sound busy. Why don't you get back to work? We'll call the whole incident a false alarm."

"I won't let you downplay this, Mira." Sam jabbed his finger at her, as if she didn't take his thunderous scowl with enough gravity. "If I have to tell Ivy about it for you to take it seriously, I will. Your safety is everything."

Clearly he wouldn't leave until she threw him a bone. "Hays should be walking in the door any minute. Does that put your mind to rest?"

"Then I'll stay until he gets here."

Kathleen took the dishtowel from over her shoulder and shooed her son away. "Go on. My hands are tired from piping buttercream rosettes. I could use a break. I'll stay with her and have a chat."

Outnumbered, Sam gave Mira's hand a final squeeze and went back to the bakery. His mother carefully closed both halves of the door behind him. Mira's blood pressure shot straight back up. Why would she do that? What on earth did she need to say that Sam couldn't hear? Would she flat-out call Mira a…um…hussy? Because the whole kissing thing two minutes ago, well, the blame rested squarely with Sam. He started it. If Mira had known his mom might pop in at any second, she would have kept her lips to herself.

"Mira, it's lovely to finally meet you. I'm sorry it took me so long. I get to the bakery at three in the morning to start the bread rising, so my day is almost over when yours begins."

"You sure drew the short straw with that shift," Mira said cautiously. Should she apologize back?

Frankly, she'd been too overwhelmed to meet Mrs. Lyons at first, and then too scared to meet her once she and Sam cranked up the heat. Avoiding her had turned into a complicated, secret-agent-worthy task since they'd begun leaving the connecting door open yesterday.

"I'm used to it now. For years my husband did the early baking. I'd make fun of him banging around in the dark from the warm nest of our bed. But once it fell on my shoulders, I discovered how peaceful that time of day can be." Her eyes, a paler version of her son's, twinkled. "I can catch up on all my soap operas without Sam muttering about how stupid they are. I've even started streaming old shows on the computer while I bake. *Murder, She Wrote* inspires me. That poor woman lived in a town the size of a sneeze and had to deal with a different murderer every week. Makes the Chicago crime stats look much more reasonable."

Ready to pounce into damage-control mode the moment Mrs. Lyons let her get a word in edgewise, Mira smiled. She refused to let the taint of a bad first impression stick. "I've heard so much about you. Every time we run together, Gib mentions your scones. He says the memory of their deliciousness and the urge to eat a hundred more is all the motivation he needs to pound the pavement."

"He's a sweet boy. A liar, but sweet. Gibson could eat ten in an hour and not gain an ounce, what with the amount of calories that man burns chasing women."

Shaky ground here. Did Mrs. L disapprove of his womanizing ways? Or was it a test, to see if Mira would stick up for her new friend? When in doubt, steer around an obstacle. "I've become quite a fan of your cookies. The smell alone makes me want to burst through that door at least a dozen times a day."

Kathleen cocked her head to the side. "Is it truly the magical aroma of my banana oatmeal cookies that lures you? I thought for sure it was the obvious attraction between you and my son. From what I just witnessed, it certainly looks as though you can't keep your hands—and various other body parts—off each other."

Oh. So the pleasantries were over, just that fast. Mira flung out one last, desperate compliment as a shield. "Sam's a wonderful man."

"There we agree. You might not be aware that you're the first woman he's been serious about since he got back from Europe." She waved her hand as though erasing a chalkboard. "Don't get me wrong. He's no monk. I've seen more than one woman tip-toeing down the stairs as I'm rolling the cinnamon buns at dawn. But none of them stuck. None of them erased the clouds from his eyes. You did that, Mira, and I'm very grateful."

The compliment was as unexpected as the brisk hug that followed. "Thank you."

"Of course, I never expected my son to fall for a woman who runs a sex store." The stern, periwinkle glare held only for a second before softening. A surprisingly high-pitched giggle accompanied the laugh crinkles around her eyes.

Mira couldn't resist joining in. After all the hard work she and Ivy had put in selecting high-quality merchandise, the thought that someone actually expected dildos and vibrators on the shelves dissolved her into guffaws. Kathleen put a supporting arm around her shoulder. The two stood there, hunched over and laughing for almost a minute. It felt great. Talk about a great way to break the ice. When Mira finally straightened, she crossed to the refrigerator, pulled out two bottles of water and offered one to Kathleen.

"Thank you. I needed to laugh about this whole mess. And I don't think Ivy will be in a laughing mood when I tell her the story." She snuck a glance at her watch. The fact the front door was locked, barring potential customers, still prickled at the back of her neck. But Mira knew she needed to take this time to get to know Kathleen. An extra five minutes wouldn't hurt anything but her overdeveloped drive to sell.

Kathleen took a sip. "I'm actually a bit disappointed. It would've been nice to pick up a cute set of trick handcuffs, maybe lined in red fake fur. They'd make my John's eyes pop right out of his skull at dinner tonight."

Wait. Hold everything. Put aside the creepy factor of her boyfriend's mother talking about sex toys. Poor, traumatized, widowed, depressed, frail, helpless Kathleen was dating? Mira couldn't believe it. After everything Gib, Ben and Sam had told her, this didn't add up. "John? A friend of yours?"

"Oh my, yes. A very good friend."

No way could Mira let that comment slide. Normally, she wouldn't press someone she'd just met to share the dirt on their sex life. Especially not someone almost twice her age. But this was potentially huge. It could turn so much of what she knew about Sam and his motivations inside out. Mira threw all restraint to the wind and forged ahead. "Is John a friend who appreciates gag gifts, or a friend who would actually appreciate sharing the gift with you?"

"Do you really expect me to kiss and tell?"

Mira goggled at Kathleen. That sealed it. "You're dating? You're in a relationship with a man?"

"Yes. So are you," she said blandly.

"Yes, but I'm not...I wasn't..."

"Married?" Kathleen shook her head. "I loved Patrick with all my heart, but the marriage contract ended when he died. It's been two years, so dating's not illegal, you know."

"No. I mean, I'm thrilled you're dating. If you're truly ready, this is a normal, healthy thing. It isn't good for people to go through life alone."

"Exactly. Now, if I bribed you with muffins every day for the rest of your life, would you be willing to tell Sam that for me?"

"He doesn't know?" But as the words came out of her mouth, the answer was obvious. Of course he didn't know. Mira drained her water bottle in a slow and steady gulp. It didn't buy her the time she needed to figure out what to say next. If she mulled and strategized for a week, she still probably wouldn't be able to come up with a good response. So instead, she spoke straight from her heart. "He's going to go ballistic when he finds out."

Kathleen wrinkled her nose and scrunched her eyes together. "Probably. Which is why I haven't told him." She switched off the pained look and smiled. "John and I have been seeing each other for almost three months. At our age, you start measuring relationships in dog years. We're ready to move in together."

"Wow. Sam's definitely not going to like to hear that you're dating. But he's going to epically lose it when you take this step. The emotional equivalent of a thermonuclear blast. At best."

"Tough."

Mira laughed, caught off guard.

"Don't get me wrong. I appreciate everything Sam's done for me over the past few years. There were times the only thing holding me together was his willpower. He gave me all the support and all the time I needed to heal, and figure out how to live this new version of my life. You know, they say when you break a bone, it heals twice as strong."

Huh. Gib had said the same thing. Maybe it was something the grief counselors had drummed into Sam, and he'd passed on to his friends. Mira could imagine him coaching them on how to handle his mother at her most fragile. He wouldn't have left anything to chance when taking care of her.

"I shattered into a million pieces when Patrick died. But now I'm two million times stronger. Sam doesn't see that. He's still too busy protecting me. He can't see past the memory of me huddled on the couch, not moving, barely stringing two breaths together. I'm ready to move on. I already have, in most respects. But I still need Sam to let go."

Mira agreed. However, it wasn't that simple. "Worrying about you, watching over you—that's been his whole life for quite some time. You're asking him to go cold turkey."

Kathleen moved her hands restlessly on the

counter. "I've been giving him hints, trying to spread my wings. He ignores them. No matter how hard I try, I can't shake him. Do you think I wanted him to run me around to six different bingo games? I don't even like bingo. That's just an excuse I made up to cover up when John and I go out on a date."

"That is very cute." And now Mira very much wanted to meet this man who was willing to sneak around to spare Sam's feelings. John sounded like a keeper.

"This isn't all about me. Sam needs to get back to living his life for himself, on his own terms. I thought, I hoped, that by letting you in he was doing just that. Finally putting his own needs ahead of mine." Kathleen grabbed her hands, her grip strong from years of pummeling dough. "You've got your toe in the door, Mira. Won't you help me shove it open all the way?"

Mira wanted to help this friendly, sweet woman. Her motives were more than sound. But her trying to help in this situation would be as foolhardy as asking a toddler to mix the volatile ingredients for nitroglycerin. "I can't. I want to. I agree with everything you are saying. But I have an absolutely horrible relationship with my parents. The closeness you and Sam share is an absolute gift. One that I can't risk wrecking. I'm afraid someone else stirring the pot would only lead to heartache. The most I can do is try and drop a few hints. Give him a very subtle nudge or two."

Kathleen patted her hands, then let go. "Nudges are good. Almost useless with my son, as his head's as thick as a brick, but every bit helps."

"And I'll see what I can do about getting you a set of those handcuffs. As a neighborly gesture."

"I should hope so. I know what you're giving my son on a daily basis. Fuzzy handcuffs are the least you can do for me."

FIFTEEN

SAM STARED AT the inside of Mira's refrigerator. With every second he held open the door, he wished more and more he'd thought to pull on pants before trekking out to the kitchen. All the cool air lowered his chance of a repeat performance of transforming Mira into a screaming pleasure puddle anytime soon. Bracing himself, he opened the freezer to rummage for bread.

A high, shrill scream rent the air. Sam spun around and palmed a knife off the counter in one movement. Unfortunately it was a paring knife, with a blade no longer than his thumb, but it was better than nothing. And being completely naked, he had a whole lot of nothing.

The lights came on. Daphne stood against the wall in clingy white pajamas covered with big red roses. She had one hand on the switch, the other covering her mouth, and a horrified expression on her face. Sam dropped the knife. As fast as humanly possible, he lunged for an oven mitt and held it in front of him. For all the infinitesimal coverage it provided. Still better than flashing his bits and pieces to one of his closest friends.

"Hey, Daph. Didn't hear you come in."

The eyebrows that had parked high on her forehead with shock drew together into annoyance. "With all the noise you two were making, you wouldn't have heard if a spaceship crashed into the living room and five-legged aliens hopped out to invade the world."

Sam tried to play it cool, have a normal conversation with her, as if the situation wasn't as uncomfortable as his first prostate exam. "Really? All the movies you watch, the best you can come up with is a five-legged alien? No tentacles or razor-tipped claws?"

"We are not going to stand here and discuss alien anatomy."

Better than discussing all of his own exposed anatomy. "I'm just saying, if they want to invade Earth, they should be ferocious in some way. Maybe fangs on their elbows?"

Daphne stomped her foot, shod in a fuzzy slipper shaped like the head of the lobster from *The Little Mermaid*. "Why are you naked in my kitchen?"

"Well, if you truly were listening to our 'noises,'" Sam made air quotes with one hand, "then you can probably figure out why I'm naked. And I'm in the kitchen because Mira's hungry. Thought I'd throw together a *croque monsieur* for her."

"Stop showing off, chef boy. Call it a grilled cheese sandwich like the rest of the world."

"That's like comparing a plain roast beef sandwich to the glories of a cheesesteak. Tell you what. Stop being so pissy and I'll make you one, too."

"Sam Lyons, you are bare-ass naked. I don't want you so much as breathing on a single one of my pans." She tossed him the purple afghan from the back of the couch. "For the love of all that is good and holy, cover yourself up."

Mira padded into the room, tightening the sash of her long, red robe. "I heard a scream."

Daph whipped around so fast her long ponytail smacked her in the face. "Yes, you did. I scream when I'm surprised by unexpected, naked men in my house."

"Sorry, Daphne." But Mira didn't look sorry. With her tousled hair, flushed cheeks and kiss-swollen lips, she looked like a satisfied, sexed-up woman. The primal caveman in Sam stood up and roared with pride at pleasing her. "We didn't think you'd be home so soon. Weren't you and Gib and Milo headed out to grab drinks at that new place on Southport?"

"Yes."

Sam peered over his shoulder at the clock. Still early enough that Daphne's story didn't add up. "You're not a one-drink girl. When you post up at a bar, you're there for the duration."

"Anything worth doing is worth doing right."

"So what happened?" Mira asked, walking her over to perch on the stools lined up at the gray granite breakfast bar.

"Milo caught the sniffles. You know how he carries on like he's got tuberculosis after a single sneeze. He stayed home to take enough supplements to choke a wildebeest."

"What about Gib? You guys hang out all the time."

Her cheeks filled with the same color as the roses on her pajamas. "Sure. I know. But tell that to one of Chicago's most eligible bachelors. Women were crawling all over him from the moment we sat down at the bar. He's got his hands full. In fact," the corner of her mouth skewed down, "he probably hasn't yet noticed that I left."

"He's letting this magazine feature go to his head." Mira crossed her arms and shook her head. "You were there with him. Ergo, he shouldn't have even noticed the random, bed-hopping candidates throwing themselves at him."

"It wasn't a date. He can look all he wants. Hell, he can do way more than just window shop. Because he's certainly not coming home with me."

"Doesn't matter. Being in a bar with a friend is like being in the army. You never leave a man behind." Sam edged out from behind the counter. The afghan was a loose knit, but he thought he'd bunched it up enough to keep him decent. From the front, anyway. "Want me to get him back, on your behalf? Short-sheet his bed, or put hair-removal cream in his shampoo?"

Daphne rolled her eyes high enough her pupils completely disappeared. "No. You know why? Because you're not twelve and at sleepaway camp for the first time."

Geez. Didn't he at least get points for trying? "Sorry. My options are limited. We're good friends. It's not like I can deck the guy for wanting to score. But I will tell him that he acted like a royal douche. How's that?"

"Satisfactory." Daphne shuffled over to peck Sam on the cheek. "You're a good guy, Sam. No wonder Mira's all hot and bothered for you." Then she curved her fingers into a claw and ruffled the hair across the top of his chest. "Of course, the way you look without a shirt might have something to do with it, too."

He swatted away her hand. Like it wasn't eight hundred degrees of weird already having a conversation with her half naked. Daphne was like a...well, not a sister. More of a little brother, actually. They watched Bears games together and told dirty jokes. On his birthday they'd had a contest to see who could eat more hot wings in a row before caving and reaching for beer. She'd come within one wing of beating him. For the most part, except for nights like the party Gib threw for Ivy and Ben, he even managed not to notice her fairly perky breasts. So to have her touching him was wrong and creepy and almost incestuous. "Cut it out," he ordered. "How would you like it if I ran my hand across your chest?"

She giggled, unfazed. "Probably not as much as Mira does?"

"That's enough, Daph." Mira hip-checked her away. Then she slid in and wrapped an arm around Sam's waist. "See, if you'd stayed at the bar you could've hunted up your own man instead of pawing at mine. Didn't you see any contenders?"

Daphne pursed her lips and scrunched up her nose. "Nope. Well, none who were available." She rummaged in a drawer by the sink and came up clutching a giant Toblerone bar. Waving it triumphantly overhead, she said, "This shall be the only thing sharing my bed tonight. And I know I am guaranteed satisfaction."

"That makes two of us." Mira grinned and dipped her hand beneath the afghan in the back.

"Seriously, make tall, dark and hairy next to you throw on some clothes before he touches anything in my kitchen. And try to keep your shouts of ecstasy under wraps, okay? This chocolate will only go so far in blunting my envy." She waved good-night and headed back down the hall.

Sam waited impatiently until her door closed. Then he let the afghan fall to the ground. He picked Mira up and set her on the counter, moving to stand between her legs. The way her robe gaped open gave him all sorts of ideas. He followed through on idea number one by palming her petal-soft breast. Immediately her nipple rose to a point, which he rolled between his thumb and first finger. "I thought she'd never leave."

Mira grabbed his hand and lowered it to her thigh. "She didn't. She could come back at any moment. Which means we can't do this."

"We can. It'd be easy. You're at a really good height to line everything up." To prove it, he cupped his hands around her ass and scooted her forward until they touched. "See?"

Huh. She didn't immediately wrap her legs around his waist, so he assumed she wasn't sold on the idea. Clearly he needed to sweeten the pot. Sam nibbled her ear, then caught the lobe between his teeth and gently bit down. Sure enough, she shivered from head to toe.

He'd already spent a considerable amount of time and energy learning what Mira liked in bed. What made her toes curl, what caused her soft and sweet sigh, and what made her clench around his finger, all hot and slick and wet. Just thinking about it pumped blood from all of his extremities straight to his dick. Good thing he had a strong grip on Mira to keep him steady.

"Sam, I can't piss off Daphne. She's a terrific roommate. Plus, I think your friendship would be irrevocably scarred if she caught you having sex in her kitchen. She seems rather proprietary about it."

He moved down, licking alive a trail of nerve endings in her neck. Not wanting to rush things, he paused at the hollow of her collarbone, right where her pulse fluttered blue just beneath the surface. A little light suction there and she squirmed against him. Smooth legs moved restlessly against his thighs. Exactly like she did in the middle of sex. God, he had to have her now. Right now.

No matter how much he tried to stay in control, keep his passion checked to see to Mira's needs first, she was his undoing. The mewling, sexy noises she made, her unbelievably soft skin, the way she moved against him, fueled his lust to levels he'd never before sustained for so long. Mira was both gasoline in his bloodstream and the match that set it aflame.

"You're driving me crazy," she whispered.

"Good."

Grabbing hold of his shoulders, she pushed him away to arm's length. "Just hold that thought until Daphne falls asleep, okay?"

"See? This is why we should've stayed at my place," he grumbled. "No scheduling sex around roommates." Sam wanted Mira on a twenty-four-seven basis. The need for her was like a low-grade fever, heating his blood no matter where he went or what he did.

"Yes, but no bathtub, either. Remember, that's why we came here tonight. I promised you a bubble bath for two. The tub even has Jacuzzi jets."

"Bribe accepted." He picked her up and carried her back to the bedroom. Just inside the door, he stubbed his toe on something and ended up dropping her on the bed. "Son of a bitch, that hurts." Sitting down, he gave a vicious kick with his other foot to the offending bag.

"Stupid thing. What do you have in here—concrete?"

"Ooh, pull it up. I need to sort through the mail I brought home from the store."

Sam propped himself against the mound of pink pillows, one arm draped across a raised knee. "You've got all this to keep your attention, and you want to read the mail?"

"No, in my list of prioritized tasks right now, mail does not supersede screwing you cross-eyed."

"Good to know."

"But I told you, we can't do anything until Daphne falls asleep." She dragged the bag onto the bed and pulled out a big stack of envelopes. Spreading them across the white comforter, she began pushing them into piles. A colorful postcard of a field of lavender caught his eye. There'd been a memorable weekend in Provence a few years ago with a picnic basket, a blanket and this blonde…who he totally wouldn't think about now that he was lying next to Mira. Sam picked up the card and flipped it over. Then he swore in a low, steady stream of invectives while he shoved his way up the bed to lean against the headboard.

"What's wrong?"

"The mailman mixed in some of my mail with yours."

"And that's really a reason to curse a blue streak at him? Don't get mad at the postman, Sam. They've got that whole workplace rage thing going on—you don't want to rile them up."

"I'm not mad at our mail carrier. I'm mad at my fucking selfish ingrate of a sister." Sam read the short card again. It didn't get any better the second time. The shiny, sun-dappled scene slipped from his fingers.

He felt like a giant mixing bowl, full of disparate emotions and reactions. Should he punch the pillow until it exploded in a flurry of feathers? Scream his frustration loud enough to piss off Daphne? Give in to the crushing despair, cover his head and curl up in a ball? For now, he pulled his legs up, crossed his arms over his knees and dropped his head. Then he took a few deep breaths. Tried to steady himself, so as not to scare Mira.

"Bad news from your sister?"

"Yeah. Bad news for me, anyway," he mumbled.

A heavy silence occupied the room for a few minutes, as present as a third being. He felt Mira pick up the postcard from where it perched on his feet.

"Diana finished her pastry training—"

"Six months ago," he barked, cutting her off.

"Ultimately, that's good, right? It means she's qualified to do whatever you need in the bakery."

Sure. The kid always had a light touch with all kinds of dough. She could keep up with him pretty well before haring off to Europe. "Keep reading."

"Sounds as if she's fairly enamored of this Italian count. Do they still have counts in Italy? I thought they got rid of the nobility after World War Two."

"Doesn't matter. Everyone uses titles over there,

even if they're several generations dead. You can even buy one, with enough money."

"It does matter." Mira's eyes widened. "What if she's being scammed?"

"For what? The grand Lyons family fortune?" The words tasted as bitter as rancid milk. "All we have is the bakery, and I guarantee they know how to make their own damn biscotti over in Italy."

"Your sister is flitting around Europe with some strange man, and you don't care?"

"My sister is fucking flitting around Europe!" he shouted, raising his head to glare at her. "She's got no job, no responsibilities, and is living in the back pocket of some rich guy. No, I'm not worried about her. Let's flip that coin. Aren't you going to ask if she cares about me?"

"What do you mean?"

Sam nipped the card out of her hand and waved it in the air. "Did you see anything in here about when she planned to return? When she plans to stop living the high life? When she'll stop playing, come home and finally set me free?" He ripped it in half, and then kept ripping, taking out his anger until it was nothing but a colorful pile of confetti on the bed.

"Set you free?" Mira repeated his words in a low, shocked murmur. "From what? The bakery? The thing you love with a passion, and trained for all over the world?"

"I trained to be a chocolatier."

"And you make chocolates. We're selling them in the store."

"No, I dabble. I steal time when I can. The bulk of my day is spent decorating wedding cakes, icing cookies, but not hand-molding chocolate." Sam rolled onto his knees. He'd hugged the dream close to him for so long, he wasn't even sure how to form the words. How to talk about the future his sister denied him with every single day she stayed overseas.

"What aren't you telling me?"

Now that he'd popped the cork on his secret, it all poured out. "I want to make art. I want to make amazing, sinful flavors enrobed in rich, beautiful chocolate. The kind of thing that makes you catch your breath when you look at it, and makes your eyes flutter shut when you taste it."

"If you can cook it half as well as you describe it, you're in business."

"Well, I'm not. Not yet. The best way for me to break into the gourmet chocolate business is by exhibiting at the Fancy Food show here in Chicago. I'd get immediate name recognition, unparalleled nationwide marketing just by manning a booth and handing out samples for three days. It's my shot." One he'd dreamt about for years.

The way some women planned their wedding day, down to the tiniest detail, before even landing a prospective groom? Sam lulled himself to sleep at night planning his exhibition booth. The color of the draping. The multitiered trays to show off the product. And of course, a constantly changing list of which flavors and designs to showcase. Of course there had to be a standard dark chocolate ganache truffle, for the purists. But what else? Port-soaked figs enrobed in chocolate? Blackberry sage, or pear and honey truffles? Or maybe hazelnut praline?

"When is it?"

"January. But the registration cutoff is in a week. And it's not cheap. The only way I can justify the expense is if I can immediately expand into a full-fledged business and hit the ground running as soon as the show ends."

Her eyebrows drew together as she pondered his story. "So you're saying you'd quit the bakery completely?"

See? Mira *got* him. He didn't have to talk in circles explaining himself. She understood what he needed to do, and why. Better than anyone else ever had. "Not completely. But yeah, most of my time would shift to chocolate."

"That's why you want Diana back here." She drove her first finger straight down into the pillow for emphasis. "To carry most of your load in the bakery."

"If she doesn't take my place, I can't do it." Sam wasn't a figurehead, sitting in a glassed-off office counting his profits. Sam *was* Lyons Bakery. "I can't abandon our family business, let it crash to a halt."

"Of course not." Mira ran a soothing hand back and forth on his thigh. It didn't stop him from pushing off the bed and pulling on his boxer-briefs. He needed to pace. Thinking about his sister worked him up too much to sit in one place.

"Diana's got to be back and in place before I throw away thousands of dollars on exhibitor registration. We came real close to going under." He braced his hand against the doorjamb while he remembered long, shaky nights of trying to make the numbers add up. "It took me a year to pull us back from the brink. Even though things are better now, we're still treading water pretty damn fast. An unbudgeted outlay like that, not to mention all the extra for ingredients and manpower? Too big a risk to take without a guaranteed reward."

"Did you ever tell Diana there was an end date to her European adventure?"

Would've been smart. The sort of thing his dad would've insisted on before she even boarded the plane. He hadn't thought of it. Hell, there were a lot of things he would've done differently, in hindsight. But Sam didn't have any experience in parenting an angry, grieving teenager. As just her brother, he knew he didn't have the right to order her around. His feet started him on another circuit between the fuzzy pink throw rugs in front of the door, the dresser and the bed.

"No. Damn it, she had her fun, and plenty of it. She didn't stick around and help pick up the pieces when Mom fell apart. The minute things started going downhill, she bailed. Claimed that if I got to train in Belgium and Switzerland, she deserved the chance, too."

"That sounds like a reasonable point," Mira ventured in a quiet voice.

"Except the difference is that she didn't bother to go to college first, like I did. She treated the Alps like her own oversized college quad. We'd get postcards from different ski resorts. Places with so many consonants in their names you couldn't say them without spitting. She'd bop from town to town, usually following whatever man turned her head that week. We used almost all of Dad's life insurance money to pay for her grand tour."

Mira leaned back against the pile of frilly pink pillows. "Which leaves one burning question. Between all the schussing and the screwing, did she ever show up to class and learn how to bake?"

"Probably. Diana's a whiz in the kitchen. She shadowed Dad from the time she was old enough to lick the beaters. If she put her mind to it, she could be better than me. Put her within three feet of a pastry chef, and she'll absorb every trick up their sleeve. Girl's got mad skills with flour and yeast."

She scrambled out of bed to pick up the pile of paper he'd mounded onto the fuchsia afghan at their feet. "Let me get this straight. This postcard you shredded doesn't make any mention of Diana returning soon, let alone by next week. If she doesn't magically appear, your dream of starting a new business is dead in the water." The tiny strips of paper slowly floated through her fingers into the wastebasket.

"Exactly." Sam stopped pacing. He didn't need it anymore. Just knowing that Mira sympathized, saw his side of the problem that he'd kept locked away from anyone else's scrutiny, calmed him. Their relationship was good for him. Well, not just good. Had to be said that the sex was eye-crossingly fan-fucking-tastic.

In Mira, he also got a partner. The kind of connection he'd seen between his parents. For two years, he'd pretty much kept his head down, focusing all his energy on his mom and the bakery. Sure, his friends had stood by him, but he hadn't connected to anyone with this level of emotional intimacy. Being able to let it all out and lean on someone relieved about two thousand pounds of pressure inside his skull. He'd fallen for her harder and faster than a failed soufflé.

God, out of practice didn't begin to describe his relationship with, well, relationships. Sam hoped he wouldn't accidentally do anything to epically screw it up. At least if he did, it wouldn't be a secret. Mira had proven from day one that she had no problem letting him know exactly where he'd stepped wrong.

Mira cradled her elbow with one hand, and tapped the first finger of the other against her cheek. "What did your mother say when you told her? Did you ask her if she could ramp up her hours and commitment back up to the level they used to be? Explain that you need her to at least fill that gap until Diana eventually wends her way home?"

"No."

"No to what?" she asked, with a gentle kick to his calf.

Sam spread his hands, palms up. "All of it. My mother doesn't know. Period. She can't know about any of this."

"You're going to quit the bakery, open a chocolate shop, and keep it all a secret from your own mother?"

"Of course not. But I'm not going to lay any of this on her shoulders until it's decided, one way or the other. She doesn't need that kind of stress."

"You're an idiot."

Whoa. What happened to her understanding? How did the most supportive girlfriend ever suddenly change gears and turn on him? He sat back down on the bed. "What's with the name calling?"

"This isn't a case of the caring son sheltering his sick mother from the big, scary world. Your mom's fine now. She's not going to collapse with an attack of the vapors from hearing that her son wants to aim for the stars. That's the sort of thing every parent *longs* to hear."

Riiiiight. Because Mira's parents were so excited about all of her life choices? Talk about a double standard. "No. That's the sort of thing parents dream about when they're staring down at a newborn. Messy, ugly life, the reality of it, is a whole different story."

She eased down beside him, threading her fingers through his hair in a rhythmic pattern that sent good chills up and down his spine. "Maybe so. Sometimes. In the past couple of years, the Lyons family's taken more than its fair share of licks. But the unlucky streak doesn't have to continue. What if this is what your mom needs to move forward? A sense of making a difference, helping her son to follow his own path?"

"No." How many times did he have to say it before she truly heard him?

"Sam, you're on the cusp of throwing away your dreams. Don't you owe it to yourself to at least consult with your mother before that happens?"

"You've talked to my mother a couple of times. Don't think that gives you any great insight into her. Pride's taught her to put up one hell of a front. I'm telling you, she couldn't handle my stepping back from my duties. Not unless Diana slid in and took my spot. I. Will. Not. Burden. Her." He spoke each word slowly, with great emphasis, so there would be no mistaking his intent.

She stared at him, her expression unreadable. One minute ticked by, then another that felt like a year as the silence grew. Damn it, this is why he hadn't told anyone. Showing off his possibly unreachable goal was a lot like showing off dirty underwear. People

were guaranteed to turn up their noses and say something about it.

With the brightness of the flashlight app on his
iPhone, Mira tilted her head and smiled. "How about
that bubble bath?"

Huh? He thought they'd been headed down the
road toward a full-blown fight. Instead, she'd jammed
on the brakes and made a U-turn. "You mean, we're
done here?"

"I think you've made that quite clear." Her smile
dimmed, just for a second. At least he thought it did.
She had it back in place so fast, Sam wasn't sure. "I
promised you a bath, not a browbeat." Mira skimmed
her hand down his arm. "Let's go lather that frown
off your face."

"I'd rather use the bubbles to put a smile on yours."

"The two plans are not mutually exclusive." Taking
his hand, she led him out of the bedroom. He couldn't
help but think he'd narrowly averted stepping on a
minefield. Trouble was, Sam couldn't figure out how
or why. He did know that he'd better figure it out before they went much further. Bubble baths couldn't
cure everything. But if Mira wanted to pretend they
did, though, he'd be ten times a fool not to play along.

SIXTEEN

EVERYONE KNEW THE classic stereotype of a boss: demanding, driven, nitpicky, consumed by the bottom line. Mira didn't think that Ivy, with her ponytails and propensity for the color pink, looked like she embodied the stereotype at all. Heck, the sunlight filtering through the restaurant's stained-glass windows even dappled a muted halo around her head.

But on the inside, behind the cotton-candy, smiling exterior, a detail-oriented bean-counter drove all of Ivy's business decisions. Which is why Mira brimmed with confidence that she would green-light this new idea for A Fine Romance.

She scooted her chair across the brown-and-cream checkerboard floor, barely hearing the squeak in the busy noontime buzz of the Berghoff restaurant. The entire El ride here, she'd been bursting to tell Ivy her plan. Restraint prevailed, though. They discussed the very serious issue of whether or not to have a groom's cake at Ivy and Ben's wedding. Also covered was the equally serious issue about what color her wedding-night lingerie should be, and if they should bother with a save the date. Basically, Ivy exhibited early symptoms of morphing into a complete bridezilla. The upside was that with half an hour already devoted to her wedding, Ivy would be able to fully focus on business talk over lunch.

Mira looked around at the wood-paneled room. It definitely lent a serious tone to lunch, only slightly mitigated by the strong scent of smoky knackwurst and vinegared sauerkraut that seared the back of her throat with every inhale. Men in suits packed almost every table. She and Ivy still hadn't quite figured out how to balance their tight friendship and a more formal employer/employee relationship. At least this atmosphere was ripe for business. Mira cleared her throat.

"Over the last two months, you've said repeatedly that you didn't know what to do with the second floor of the store."

Ivy jabbed her straw at the ice in her root beer. "Because the storeroom only takes up a quarter of the space. All the rest of it sits there, expansive and open. I swear it's just taunting me."

It was doubtful the brick walls and wood floor had it in for Ivy. At least, Mira hadn't heard anyone mention that her building was haunted. But if their mere presence pissed her off, all the better. "It doesn't have to stand empty much longer. I came up with a plan."

"Not now," Ivy groaned. "You've got more than enough on your plate. I told you not to worry about it until after the opening. We'll figure it out then."

"And I appreciate you not pressuring me. Probably the lack of pressure is what relaxed my brain enough to make the leap." Mira leaned forward, elbows on the table. "We should open a matchmaking service."

A double eye blink. A long, slow sip of a soda. Another double blink, finished off by a definitive head shake. "I'm sorry, I think I zoned out for a minute there. It isn't remotely possible that with two new employees and a highly publicized grand opening party in two days, that any sane person would recommend starting another entire business. Or drop it on me out of the blue."

Crap. She'd considered writing up an official proposal memo. No time to work up a complete business plan, but Mira could've at least bullet-pointed all the pros on a snazzy piece of letterhead. Clearly just springing it like any friendly piece of gossip hadn't been smart. Mira tried to regroup.

"It wouldn't be a separate business. It's a natural offshoot. We sell romance. In order to need romantic things, you need a date. We find people dates, we end up giving ourselves more customers. It would be a symbiotic relationship."

Another firm head shake. Ivy looked like a horizontal bobblehead doll. "You have a full-time job managing the store. I have a full-time job at Aisle Bound. We can't open a third business."

Why wouldn't she hear her out? If she had sent an email, Ivy undoubtedly would've read through the entire thing. Mira intended to plead her case all the way to the end. "It wouldn't cost much. Practically zero overhead—you're already paying for the space, whether we use it or not. We'd start slow. Mixers once a week."

Ivy threw up her hands. "Mira, I swear to God, you might as well be speaking Igbo."

"You made that up."

"I did not. Igbo's a real language, spoken by the Igbo people in Nigeria. In sixth-grade world cultures class I wrote a report on them. The name stuck with me."

It took every ounce of self-control for Mira not to roll her eyes. "Okay, then, consider this plan to be as real as the Igbo people. Chicago's filled with eight million people. Hard to work your way through even half that number. You see someone cute on the El, and there's no way to know if they are single and ready for a relationship. So many singles are looking for a way to whittle down the choices to a manageable group."

"That is their problem, not ours."

Mira ignored the ill-humored comment and continued. "Throw some café tables and chairs up there, and every Thursday night we could have a mixer. Serve Helen's amazing food. Or, work out a good deal with a nearby restaurant. Maybe a just-starting-out caterer that would be grateful for a steady gig. We'd give people someplace safe to mingle and maybe hit it off."

"You expect random people to walk in off the street and hang out on our second floor? We're going to get a soup-kitchen vibe going awfully fast."

That snarky little salvo proved Ivy's mind was welded shut tighter than a vampire's coffin at high noon. "Of course not." Okay. Wipe out all memories of she and Ivy dressed as twin mermaids at Halloween. Or the night they drank too many French martinis and jumped into Lake Michigan fully clothed. If Ivy wouldn't listen to her as a friend, she'd flip into full business mode. Bury her with details.

"Everybody would have to register with our Find a Romance service first. We'd run credit and background checks, be sure we're not offering up a buffet to a predator. The basic level of membership gives them entry to the weekly mixers. Maybe we could partner with a wine store, do tastings. Every week could be a different theme. Wine tasting, chocolate tasting, sports around playoff season. There's a million ways we could go. Anyway, the second tier of membership would get you one-on-one matchmaking."

"Can't be done. Not at this late date. You're leapfrogging about six months into the future."

Getting through to Ivy on this issue was proving harder than defending her master's thesis. But she'd survived that three-hour inquisition to graduate with honors. Persistence and patience proved to be the key. "I disagree. We can advertise the weekly mixers at the grand opening. Let them take shape for a couple of months while I find a qualified matchmaker. A licensed counselor would probably be best."

"If we were brainstorming ways to utilize the second floor, this would be worth adding to the list. But it's too much, too soon." Ivy leaned back to give the waiter room to deposit their plates of wurst. "Over at Aisle Bound, we're still in the thick of fall wedding season. I don't even have the spare brain cells to consider this from all angles. Let's back-burner it until after New Year's, at least." She dug into the steaming pile of hot German potato salad with gusto.

Mira, on the other hand, couldn't blithely start eating. She had a battle to win. "You're turning your back on almost pure profit, at least at the start. We'd charge people more than enough to cover the background runs and still pocket a good amount. The tables and chairs wouldn't set us back much. Once we're ready to move on to the matchmaker, she'd only be part-time. There are kinks to be worked out, but I guarantee it would work. People want to find love."

"I can't take on one more thing right now. I can barely steal time to plan my wedding."

"Your wedding's been planned since you were twelve."

Ivy brandished the tines of her fork. "Don't be glib. I'm serious."

"So am I. And you wouldn't have to be involved at all."

"There's where you're wrong. A Fine Romance is my store. My name on the lease, the incorporation papers, your paycheck. Nothing moves forward without my approval."

Whoa. They'd just taken a sharp detour from discussing a single idea to defining their entire working relationship. She should probably just redirect back to the topic at hand. But Ivy's comments were akin to waving a red cape, and Mira was just bullish enough to plow ahead. "You want to micromanage me? Do you want to start doing a walk-through every day to see if I've arranged the displays correctly? Straightened out the corners on the cash? Double-check the deposit slips before I go to the bank?"

Ivy kept eating, staring straight down at the plate. "You oversee the store. I oversee the big picture."

Was she serious? After she'd spent a solid hour on the phone last summer begging Mira to be the manager? Saying the only person who could take the job, who could give her peace of mind with her utter competence, was Mira? A ball of hurt and anger sat heavy in her stomach, as though she'd just inhaled all three of the sausages on her plate in a single gulp. "Don't you trust me?"

Squaring her shoulders, Ivy finally looked up. "I've

taken enough risks this year. I let a reality television crew tape me. I fell in love and got engaged in three months. I built a second business from the ground up. In a nutshell, I need to let the dust settle."

Now Ivy was the one who might as well be speaking some unknown tribal language. "How does all that even matter? I told you that I'd take care of every aspect."

"Really?" Ivy pushed back her plate and white-knuckled the table's edge. Her changeable hazel eyes clouded to a serious brown. "Every start-up requires money. If you're so gung-ho, why don't I see you reaching into that trust fund of yours, offering to cover the costs?"

Talk about playing dirty. Mira couldn't believe Ivy would throw her family angst into her face. Those who knew you best sure knew how to skewer you best. "You know I can't touch that money."

"No. You have no-strings-attached access to the interest until you turn thirty. And it's a safe bet that a month's worth of your interest could pay the mortgage on the store, Aisle Bound and my new condo combined." Ivy leaned forward, her eyes heavy-lidded with anger. "I know that you *won't* touch that money. There's a big difference. It's sitting there, waiting for you, and you refuse to dip into it for anything. After the hurricane, you could've whipped out that black AmEx your parents gave you and checked right into the nicest hotel in town. Instead, your almighty pride and stubbornness kept you in a Red Cross shelter for almost a week."

"My choice," Mira forced out between gritted teeth.

"At least you have a choice." Her voice rose, then dropped to a furious whisper. "I've thrown almost every penny from *Planning for Love* into getting this store off the ground. I didn't want to do a second season. But I signed a contract two weeks ago to live my life in a fishbowl for another three months. Not because I want the limelight. Not because I like being on television, and seeing my monthly breakouts in HD. Because I need a cushion. A chunk of money that will see A Fine Romance through the first six months before we can begin to hope to turn a profit."

"Is that the real reason why you hired me? So the Parrish family fortune could be your emergency parachute if we hit a bumpy couple of months?" The possibility rocked Mira to her core. And she knew their friendship could be irrevocably tarnished if she waited around to hear Ivy's response. She held up her hand and shoved back from the table. "Never mind. Don't answer that. It's clear we both need to cool off. So, with my boss's approval," she inclined her head to Ivy, "I won't waste any more of the company dime on lunch. I'm headed back to the store."

Where she had every intention of designing a flyer for the first Match-N-Mingle event. The name had popped into her head mid-argument. At least one good thing came out of this disaster of a lunch. Like a lone dandelion poking its yellow head out of a stinky, putrid pile of manure.

As Mira shrugged out of her coat, her arm went too wide and jammed her finger hard against the display case. She hissed in pain. Looked around at the quiet store and remembered that neither Helen nor Hays were on the schedule for the afternoon. "Son of a *bitch* that hurts." She shook out her hand. "This day is a one hundred percent, certified clusterfuck."

The heel of her pump had snapped off in a grate on the way to the El. She got off four stops early to pick up a replacement pair, and buy a zippy new outfit for the grand opening party. Retail therapy always cheered her up. Or rather, it used to cheer her up. Until Mira's pile of new clothes were snatched out of her hands because her credit card was declined.

Right now on the scoreboard she boasted an epic fight that might cost her a friend, which in turn might cost her a job. A job she might not have for long anyway, if the store flopped or a local morning show decided to focus in the next few days on her run of bad luck with managing stores. A boyfriend like a mussel shell, only opening up so far and then cracking when pushed further. One who shared his problems, but didn't want her to share her opinion in return.

No money in the bank, and no pretend money left to spend on her credit card. Unless…Mira scrabbled through the stack of mail she'd dropped on the counter. New credit card offers came about once a week. Maybe she'd get lucky and find one to tide her over.

A thick, cream envelope caught her eye. With her name in a dark swirl of calligraphy, it looked like a wedding invitation. Intrigued by the randomness, she ripped it open. A thin, plastic card slipped out. Reading the accompanying note took less than a minute. It also took less than a minute after that for all her frustration and rage to unleash in a choked-off scream.

The connecting door to the bakery slammed open. Sam stormed through, eyes wild. "What's wrong?"

"What isn't?" she answered grimly.

In two giant steps, Sam made it to her side and ran his hands gently over her body. "Are you hurt? Bleeding?"

"No." Embarrassed at screaming? Yep. Annoyed that Sam caught her in the middle of a temper tantrum? Yep. Wishing a giant carton of Ben & Jerry's Strawberry Cheesecake would magically appear before her? Yep to the umpteenth degree.

He parked his hands on her ass, snugging her close. The fact that Mira hadn't even enjoyed her super-sexy boyfriend feeling her up, albeit while checking for bumps and bruises, proved she'd spiraled to a dark, unhappy place. "Want to tell me what's bothering you, sweetness? 'Cause you're only supposed to howl like that when you're naked and under me."

"Bad afternoon. Ivy and I got in a fight. A big one. An I'm-not-sure-we're-still-friends kind of a fight. An I'm-not-sure-if-I-still-have-a-job kind of fight." She leaned into him, absorbing the comfort of his hard muscles. Of knowing he'd take her side, because that's what boyfriends did. Having him in her corner steadied Mira, smoothed off the jagged edges of the emotional wounds Ivy had both stirred up and inflicted. A girl could get used to this.

Sam kissed her cheek. "Of course you're still friends. And of course you still have a job. Arguments are rough. But people make up. You'll both apologize, hug and put it behind you. Would I be a sexist dog if I suggested shared ice cream on the couch and a viewing of *Pride and Prejudice* would fix it all?"

"Yes," she said in a particularly aggrieved tone. Why let him know he was probably right?

"You've been burning the candle at both ends. You're worn to a nub. Chances are you blew things up bigger than they really are."

"So what—you're telling me I just need a nap?" Mira knew she sounded testy. Maybe total exhaustion spurred a bit of an overreaction. But things were still dire.

"An early night, after a proper dinner, wouldn't be the worst thing in the world. I could bump up ravishing you on my schedule," he said with a double squeeze of her ass. "Preview week's over, so the store's closed until the big grand opening. Cut yourself some slack. Maybe you and Daphne could relax by going shopping tomorrow."

That drove her blood pressure straight back up into a borderline stroke. "My parents sent me a Bloomingdale's gift card today." Mira picked up the note and the card, waving them under Sam's nose. "To wish me good luck and help me buy an appropriate outfit for the grand opening. Can you believe that?"

"I guess. Why? Is it something insulting like twenty-five dollars?"

She huffed out a breath that fluffed her bangs. "Try twenty-five hundred."

Sam plucked the card out of her hand and stared in wonder, as though it were an actual pile of cash. "Damn. What are you supposed to buy—mink-trimmed panties?"

"Don't you see what an insulting gesture this is?"

"No."

"It says they don't think I can afford to buy a new outfit for myself." She grabbed the card back and skittered it along the counter.

"Can you?"

Not according to the store who'd cut up her credit card into tiny pieces half an hour ago. "Well, not one that costs a thousand dollars," she hedged. "I'm not destitute, for God's sake. There's a roof over my head, and working utilities. I'm not living on ramen noodles." Although she did have some on the pantry shelf. And cans of tuna, because it was cheap, too. Yogurt for breakfast and peanut butter sandwiches for lunch kept her grocery costs pretty low. Ivy never needed to know that every single time she opened a can of tuna, Mira's resolve slipped another notch. Or that the last time she had ramen for dinner, she went so far as to look up the password to her untouched trust-fund account. Just in case...

"Yeah, but a couple of months ago you were in a Red Cross shelter." Sam ran his hand through his hair, standing the black thickness straight up like a miniature Mohawk. "Pointing out that you're rebuilding from scratch isn't an insult."

"It's their way of sending a message. They know this store will flop, just like the others did. I'll run it right into the ground, and I'll need the family money to bail me out."

"You sure they're sending that message? Or were you already thinking it yourself?"

Back against the wall, Mira slid to the floor. She hugged her knees to her chest. When did her baker boyfriend decide to moonlight as a shrink? At least with a real shrink she wouldn't be sitting on the floor. "I've had a string of failures. Why should this store be any different? Why should I kid myself that it will succeed?"

"Because you've worked too hard for any other outcome to be possible."

She shook her head. "I work hard every time. Look what it gets me. No house, no car, no savings in the bank. Blood, sweat and tears, but nothing to show for it."

"Okay, before you go completely off the rails, you should just stop." Sam held up his hands at eye level, palms facing her. "Stop wallowing, stop whining, and just stop. Maybe you do need that nap, after all."

"Even if a miracle happens and the store flourishes, it'll take a long time to get in the black. There's certainly a cap to my salary. It isn't as if there's any place for advancement from store manager. I won't earn my first million this year to satisfy the terms of the family trust." Heck, working here, she wouldn't earn her first million in ten years.

"You knew that when you signed up for this gig." Sam eased to his knees beside her. Today the scent of carrot cake and pecan pie clung to him.

"I was drowning. Homeless, jobless, and Ivy tossed me a life preserver. I didn't have the luxury of worrying about the Parrish family legacy." Every day that ticked closer to her birthday, she felt it. Mira felt the weight of turning her back on generations of her family. Of a financial legacy they'd all protected, kept safe for the future. One that she'd basically thumbed her nose at for the last ten years. Ever since she'd informed her parents that she wanted to be respected for who she was, not the size of her bank account. That she wanted to be able to respect herself, and her choices, first and foremost.

She'd tried to sign away all her rights to the family money, to be strong and independent, but her parents' lawyer wouldn't let her. And, having given up access to the family fortune, Mira couldn't afford to go hire another attorney. So she'd lived with eschewing the money in principle, knowing that by her thirtieth birthday, all temptation would be permanently removed.

"So now that you've committed yourself to this store, and to Ivy—what? You'd back out? How would that get you to a million dollars in the next year? Unless you win the lottery, that's a fucking unreachable goal. There's no way to make it happen."

Mira was so tired. Maybe her quarter-life crisis was hitting a few years late. Maybe Sam was right and she really just needed one solid night's rest. Did the why really matter, or just the absolute knowledge that she was drained to the core? Tired of working twelve-hour days. Tired of trying her hardest and still not ending up where she wanted to be. Tired of scrimping and saving and still not being in the same place as her peers. Being strong and independent was freaking exhausting. Was it really so wrong to want life to be a little bit—okay—a lot easier?

"There is one way."

"Join a high-end escort service?"

It stung, but Sam's gibe wasn't far from the truth. "Close. I could marry someone suitable. That would solve the problem entirely. I'm sure my parents have a string of candidates just hovering in the wings."

His face shuttered closed so fast she couldn't glimpse even a second of his true reaction. "You're bluffing."

Bluffing, babbling, brainstorming—why label it?

"I call it exploring my options out loud. It would sure be easier."

"Okay, if you're not bluffing, then I've got to ask what the hell you and Ivy drank over lunch. How many beers did you throw back?"

"None. I left without touching a bite." Big mistake. Near starvation on top of her exhaustion probably wasn't helping her frame of mind. It would be nice if she could talk Sam into cooking dinner for her. He might be a certified pastry chef, but he sure knew his way around the rest of the kitchen, too. The other night he'd made them a *boeuf bourguignonne* and warm spinach salad for dinner. She thought her taste buds had died and gone to heaven. Later that night, he'd given her a completely different reason to scream the Almighty's name.

"Then you must be experiencing short-term amnesia. There's no other explanation."

"For what?"

"For forgetting that impassioned speech in your bedroom the other night. You know, the one where you told me not to toss away my hopes and dreams without a fight?"

"I remember." Mostly she remembered how their whole conversation felt like she'd been talking to a patch of the concrete her family sold. Mira didn't think she'd gotten through to him at all.

"So why the double standard?"

"You're talking in riddles, Sam." Thoroughly dispirited, she ran her palm across the glossy wood floor. It kept her from reaching out to Sam, from giving in to the urge to stroke his leg. The hard-as-

Plexiglas tone in his voice and the shuttered glaze to his eyes pretty much screamed *hands off.*

"Why are my dreams worth chasing, but yours get shoved under the carpet?"

"Because you *have* dreams, Sam. Big ones. Dreams that can and should blossom into a beautiful reality. I don't."

"Give me a break. You're one of the most driven people I've ever met. Next time we all go hit the lanes, your bowling nickname should be Pile Driver."

Mira bit her bottom lip. "Sure, I work hard. I keep reaching for that golden ring with my eyes shut because I don't know what it looks like. Is my dream to manage a store? Manage a corporation? I don't know. For years my only goal was to do the opposite of what my parents wanted. That's not really a fleshed-out life aspiration. When it comes down to it, all I really want is to be happy. And wouldn't that look stupid on a business card—Mira Parrish, Happy Person."

Finally Sam thawed a little, scooting closer to touch her side. "I think it's great. That's all most people want. They're just too scared to admit it. Life doesn't have to be some huge complication. Happiness is a great goal. An honest goal."

"Most importantly, it is achievable." Not the way he meant, however. No matter how hard she worked, the store could tank tomorrow. Or she could work herself to the bone for six months, scrimping and worrying the whole time—and *then* have it tank. That very real possibility did not, in any way, make her happy. "I could reach it tomorrow if I relent and get married. I think it's safe to assume my parents would give me a mixed assortment of eligible men far nicer than a box of Godivas. I'm sure I could be happy enough with an appropriate man." Well, not *sure*. But pretty darn close to throwing in the towel on struggling for something better. What was so wrong about taking the easy route? Aside from the fact that it was caving and Mira wasn't positive she'd be able to look herself in the mirror with any modicum of respect the rest of her life.

"No." The shutters fell away from Sam's eyes, revealing a frantic desperation that shocked her. "You'd be content, at best. Cows are content. Weeds are content. What about your independence? Caving to your parents means tossing that away. What about your chance at true love?"

Love didn't enter into the equation at all. The choice to fulfill her family's legacy, carry on the name and the company and yes, live in the style she'd quite enjoyed for her first twenty-two years, was about business and generational responsibility. Not something as pie-in-the-sky as true love. "Ivy's the one who believes life's like a fairy tale. Not me. There are no guaranteed happy endings."

"You don't believe in true love? Or you don't believe it's out there, waiting for you?"

"You make it sound like love is tangible."

"It is. It's sitting right next to you. I love you, Mira."

Her mouth went instantly dry, like she'd licked the floor of the Sahara. "If this is your way of convincing me to follow my wholly unclear dreams, I'd say that's cheating."

"I love you," he repeated. A soft smile teased at the corners of his full, sensuous lips. Sam's version of five o'clock shadow—one that showed up by two—darkened his jaw and lent him a hint of bad-boy roughness. In short, he was everything she never realized she wanted in a man, in a sexilicious package. And he loved her? How could the universe be so cruel as to dump this in her lap today? It complicated everything exponentially.

Sam took her hand, and kissed the back of each finger in turn. "Look, I know you're already juggling a million things right now. You don't have to say anything. We don't have to discuss it. I just figured that if you were about to decide the next step in your life, you ought to have all the facts."

"Oh." So utterly romantic that she wanted to squeal in glee. And practical. But Sam was right. She couldn't respond now. Letting slip how crazy in love with him she was wouldn't be fair to either of them.

"Every time Diana and I tried to take a shortcut in life, my mom would give us the same speech. She'd ask if we wanted to do things the easy way, or the right way? You could take the easy way. But would it be right for you?"

A heavy, smothering blanket of unease tightened her chest when she tried to think about it. When she first left grad school, it had been so easy to be righteous and declare her independence from the shackles of the family trust. But living these years without it wore her down. If A Fine Romance didn't succeed, Mira didn't know if she had the strength to start all over again. To persevere. Not when there was a far easier solution within reach. "I don't know."

"Just please, don't make any snap decisions," Sam begged. "Get through the grand opening. Put it out of your mind until then. The what-the-hell-do-I-do-next part, I mean. Feel free to dwell on how I love you."

His declaration of love would undoubtedly scroll nonstop through her mind like the CNN news ticker at the bottom of the TV screen. "Oh, I'll be dwelling, all right."

"Good." He flashed a wicked grin. "I plan to make a multisensory presentation later to show you just how much I love you. Your only job is to lie back and enjoy it."

"Now *that* I can commit to, on the spot."

SEVENTEEN

Mira pulled her hood up to protect her ears from the steady wind. It might land her on Glamour's infamous back page with a black box across her face as a fashion disaster, but she didn't care. Huddling into her coat like a scared turtle was the only way she'd found so far to combat the icy wind off Lake Michigan. Living in Florida had lessened her cold tolerance to an embarrassing level. She told herself every morning not to pull out the puffy winter coat until at least October. There might only be two days left in her self-imposed stricture, but a person could die of hypothermia in two hours.

The smart thing would be to go inside, get out of the surprise cold snap. Except that she'd already walked around the block three times to avoid going inside. Specifically, to go inside Aisle Bound and apologize to Ivy. Not for trying to push the matchmaking idea. That was pure gold. But neither one of them handled the discussion—and the ensuing argument—well. As much as she hated to admit it, Sam had been right. After sleeping for an amazing nine hours and carbo-loading on pasta, Mira was ready to either run a marathon or deal with Ivy. An apology for her behavior seemed in order to salvage their friendship.

Lights blazed from the floor-to-ceiling windows of Aisle Bound. The display showcased Daphne's amazing talent, in the form of a multitiered arrangement of pumpkins carved with a happy couple's name, dates and location. Orange gerbera daisies and sunflowers twined their way between the levels. Wheat sheaves fanned out in a sunburst behind. Inside, Mira could see Ben lounging on the white sofa, feet on the glass coffee table. His concession to the weather was to add a Cubs hoodie to his preferred uniform of cargo shorts. She'd waited until after dark, hoping Ivy's staff would be gone for the day. Having Ben as a witness didn't bother her enough to give her an excuse to stomp around the block again. Squaring her shoulders, she pushed through the door.

Ben dragged his eyes up for a split second, then resumed thumbing the keyboard of his phone faster than a thirteen-year-old girl at a boy-band concert. "Hey, Mira. You nervous about tomorrow night's big opening?"

"Do you want me to go into detail about the nine distinct bullet points of anxiety currently haunting me? Or will a simple *ohmygodyes* be enough for you?"

Her rushed and slurred delivery teased out a snicker, and he tossed his phone onto the lavender throw pillow beside him. "Sounds like you need a glass of wine and a foot rub. Why isn't Sam taking care of you? Doesn't he know the rules to being a good boyfriend?"

"Whatever you think the rules are, I guarantee the women of the world have a very different list." Mira eased down the hall toward Ivy's office. "I'm too wound up to be around Sam. I'd probably bite his head off."

"Like the female praying mantis does to her mate

after having sex? Or the way you and Ivy went at each other yesterday?"

"She told you?"

"Of course. I know that one's in the rulebook. Tell each other everything." He winged up a sandy eyebrow. "Didn't you tell Sam?"

"Of course," she mimicked, with a twist of her lips. "I just wish nobody knew how poorly we dealt with each other."

Ben leaned forward, resting his forearms on his tanned thighs. "Between you and me, I think your dating service idea's a winner. Full to the brim with potential."

A flush of validation spread through her. Or a stress-induced early onset menopause hot flash. "Thanks."

"Don't mention it. Seriously." He pointed his thumb and finger at her like a gun. "I didn't share my opinion with Ivy, and for the sake of our super-fancy upcoming wedding, I'd like to keep it that way."

"I understand." Mira mimed zipping her lips and throwing away the key.

"You two going to kiss and make up?"

"That's my plan."

His face lit up, hope etched in every inch of his raised brow. "Really? Because if you promise there's going to be actual girl-on-girl action, I'll need to break out my camera and record this."

"You're such a pervert, Westcott," she said, not bothering to hide her grin.

"Package deal. That is, it comes with my package, if you know what I mean." Ben gave her an exaggerated, lecherous wink.

The over-the-top sexist teasing steadied her. Gave her a couple of minutes of normalcy and peace before heading into the eye of the hurricane. "If you hear shouting, call for backup and run like hell." Mira walked the last few feet to stop in front of Ivy's closed door. She didn't want to give Ivy the chance to put her off for another few days. So she knocked with her right hand and simultaneously opened the door with her left.

"Hi."

Ivy's head popped up faster than a Whac-A-Mole. She spread her hands across the piles of fat bridal magazines covering every inch of her desk. "Oh, it's only you."

Great beginning. Annoyance flared. Mira tamped it down, remembering her mission. Her apology could only stem from cool, professional detachment. Not heated-up pissiness. She smoothed the front of her deep yellow sweater. "Sorry to interrupt."

"Don't be an idiot." Ivy beckoned her with a frantic wave. A wild glint in her hazel eyes looked out of place in her pristine office. "Come in and shut the door. Fast."

Curiosity erased the last vestiges of her sputtering temper. "What's going on?"

Ivy leaned back in her chair. She wore a dark purple cardigan over a lighter camisole that matched the bow around her ponytail. Kind of the way Purple Honker would look dressed up as a cheerleader. "Ben made me promise not to start looking at wedding dresses until after the store opens. He says that I only have a finite attention span. Apparently dress shopping is going to turn into a giant black hole, rendering me incapable of any extra tasks."

"Well, we both know he's right." Cautiously, Mira eased down into the white brocade armchair. The epic fight that probably started her down the road to her first ulcer seemed not to have fazed Ivy one bit. Mira didn't want to dredge up all that ugliness again. But she also didn't want to sweep the incident under the rug as if it never happened at all.

"Of course he's right," Ivy hissed. "But yesterday I cracked. I pulled every magazine from the last two years off the bookcase. Told Ben I had a late phone consult with a nervous bride."

Devious, underhanded wedding planning. Classic Ivy. Mira bit back a grin. "And tonight's excuse?"

"Supposedly I'm working up a proposal for a small March commitment ceremony. Two gay men, both of their dachshunds to be included in the ceremony, and they want it held at that crazy Mexican restaurant with the cliff divers."

"Huh?" What on earth was Ivy talking about? No restaurant had cliff divers. Mira wasn't sure she was following the zigs and zags of this overly intricate fib.

"Casa Fiesta. They run commercials every eight seconds on television. You haven't seen one yet?"

"Daphne and I watch lots of movies. And so far, Sam and I don't watch anything but each other."

"Nice." Ivy gave an approving nod. "The Casa's sort of an entertainment complex more than a restaurant. Big waterfall, mariachis, flame jugglers and a puppet show. Seats close to five hundred people. They had their first date there."

"Your imaginary gay couple?"

"Yes. Chauncy and Rick."

Mira wished for a glass of water, and the chance to go back in time by about three seconds. If anything in the world ever demanded a spit take, it was those two names joined in pretend couplehood. "Those are the worst fake names ever. They sound like porn stars."

"What do you want me to do? Go buy a baby name book to come up with something more appropriate for my wholly fake clients?" Ivy closed the magazines one by one and stacked them neatly in two piles. "I'm desperate. I can't bring these magazines home. Planning fake weddings is my only way to look for my dream dress."

Mira mentally drew thick black lines across her entire prepared apology. She and Ivy had a bigger-picture issue to hash out. "You and I love Mexican food. How many gallons of guacamole do you think we've eaten together?"

"Not enough?"

"Exactly. Why haven't you taken me to this spectacularly tacky Mexican restaurant yet? It sounds like it's the perfect place for us to do a girls' night."

"You're right—you'd love it." Ivy marked a page with a purple stickie and closed the last magazine. "I want to take you there. We just haven't gotten around to it yet. We've both been busy."

Technically a valid excuse. However, true friends didn't make excuses to each other. They carved out time for one another, no matter what. Until Mira moved out here, they'd been the truest of friends. This friendship apathy was as insidious and miserable as a cold virus.

Mira drove her point home with the sharpness of

a syringe full of antibiotics. "Why are you using the most elaborate lie I've ever heard to hide from your fiancé and drool over dresses? Why not just tell him you're going out to lunch with me? Don't you see the bigger problem here? You work with me, but you don't play with me anymore. I can't wait to go dress shopping with you."

"Really?" Ivy stopped lining up the magazine stacks to stare at Mira.

"Of course." The thought of arguing over brides-maid dresses filled her with icy dread. And argue they would, because she and Daphne would fight to the death to prevent being crammed into Ivy's favorite shade of cotton-candy pink. The wedding dress shopping, however, would be wonderful. Worthy of at least two purse-packs of tissue. "I'm sure the allure will tarnish after the first fifty you try on and discard, but for now, I can't wait."

"I like that idea."

Mira reached across the desk to grab Ivy's hand. "It's only been one day, but it feels like we've been fighting for an entire month."

"I know. I hated it. The whole thing had me so upset I turned down sex with Ben," Ivy confessed, her voice dropping to a whisper. "And he's *fantastic* in bed."

"He looks as though he's got some moves," Mira conceded. His body looked lanky under clothes, but in his running gear, his lean muscles bunched with purposeful grace. Ivy lucked out. Finding a guy with such a great sense of humor, buckets of charm and those California surfer good looks? Now that was a Triple Crown winner. "But my guy's full of his own talents. He not only knows how to make chocolate sauce, he knows how to use it."

Ivy gasped. "Sam got you to eat chocolate again?"

"Yes. Well, his chocolate. I haven't branched out yet beyond Lyons Bakery. I don't want to be put off by inferior cocoa products."

A smile bloomed across Ivy's face. "I've missed talking to you like this."

"Me, too. That's my point. We let our friendship fade once I moved here. We've managed to stay tight while living thousands of miles apart. Then once I move literally into your neighborhood, we both dropped the ball. Do you realize we haven't done one thing together?"

"No. Wait." Ivy scrabbled through the pages of her desk calendar. "You came to the viewing party for *Planning for Love*."

"True. But I wouldn't categorize you throwing up for three hours straight and then passing out exactly quality time."

Guilt had Ivy chewing on her bottom lip. "I threw up on your shoe, didn't I?"

"A little bit."

"Forgive me if I don't offer to let you return the gesture."

"I can let it slide." Mira straightened in her chair. "I can't let our friendship slide. The minute I got here, our dynamic changed. We didn't know how to integrate being friends and being colleagues. So we didn't. We're both Type As. Without consciously choosing, we knew the store opening had to be prioritized. To make it work, we back-burnered our friendship."

Ivy rounded her lips into a circle of dismay. "No. No, I can't believe it." She folded her hands and closed her eyes.

Great. Yet another idea of Mira's that Ivy dismissed out of hand. So much for their five-minute détente. Funny, she'd been so sure she'd figured out where it all went wrong. Instead, maybe they'd passed the point of no return. Well, if the friendship was dead, she might as well try to salvage her job. "Sorry." After one cold, quick nod Mira braced her hands on the armrest to rise.

"No, I'm sorry." Ivy jumped up and rushed around the desk. She crouched beside Mira, pulled her back down and enveloped her in a hug. "I really did turn into bridezilla. I've been so caught up with Ben that I didn't carve out any space for you. We've wished for years that we lived in the same city again. I can't believe I've been wasting this opportunity."

Well, that was the thoughtful, loyal Ivy she remembered. Hopefully she wouldn't disappear again. Relieved beyond measure, Mira hugged back. And felt truly at home for the first time since moving to Chicago.

"You're pissing me off, you know." Ivy sniffled and sank back onto her heels.

This time, Mira didn't jump at the bait. "Really? I apologize, we hug for a minute and you decide to go at me again?"

"That's the thing. *You* apologized. *I* was supposed to be the bigger person and apologize first. You stole my moment. With a one-word apology. Bigger is better sometimes, you know."

"Don't try to take credit now. That's like claiming

you know the answer to a *Jeopardy!* question, without screaming it out loud before they say the answer. You've got no proof."

"Wanna bet?" Ivy grabbed her bag from around the corner of the desk and pulled out a box. "To help officially smooth things over."

"You mean *after* apologizing for having your head in the sand?"

Ivy rolled her eyes. "Yes, after that. I had a whole, elaborate groveling scene worked out. We were going to meet at the Nature Museum, in the Butterfly Haven. Oh, Mira, you'll love it there. It's this beautiful greenhouse filled with one thousand butterflies. Every single day you can watch a butterfly emerge from its cocoon into a tropical paradise."

Her voice had slipped into a hushed, describing-their-dream-wedding-to-a-client tone. Mira had to nip it in the bud. Otherwise, Ivy would spend the next ten minutes effusing over each color of butterfly, their wingspan and probably far too much scientific trivia. "Okay, but what happened to the groveling?"

"I was going to bring you this present tomorrow." She passed it over, then dropped her hands in her lap.

Mira plucked at one end of the deep purple ribbon. "I'm sorry too, you know. Truly. Blindsided you, and then bickered with you. Not my proudest moment."

"And I'm sorry I aimed below the belt. Which puts us back on even footing. So open your present."

Swiftly she pulled off the ribbon and opened the box. Even in the dim light from Ivy's desk lamp, the pendant in front of her glimmered. Mira lifted the chain to let the silver-and-red enamel butterfly dangle freely.

"Ivy, it is gorgeous."

"Yes, but also meaningful." She rolled off her heels to her feet. When Ivy began to pace across the small space, Mira was shocked. Her black pencil skirt narrowed down to a fashionable but tiny tube at her ankles. It was a wonder Ivy could even totter, let alone walk. Especially in those platform pumps.

"When I came up with the idea for a romance store, I worked on it for a few years, every chance I got. If I somehow, miraculously, came up with the seed money, I still couldn't come up with a way to run the store and still devote myself to my Aisle Bound clients. How could I let a total stranger, no matter how qualified, be entrusted with shaping my dream into reality? And then I thought of you."

Mira executed a half bow.

"You took this larvae of an idea. Through back-breaking work and sweat and tears, you worked a metamorphosis. You turned my pages of plans into a beautiful, sparkling jewel box of a store. This necklace is to thank you."

The sentiment was even more beautiful than the necklace. Hence the cotton-ball-sized lump of emotion clogging her throat. Reluctantly, Mira returned the necklace to the box and handed it back. "I can't accept this."

Ivy began a sort of reverse tug-of-war with the box. "Of course you can."

"No. Not yet. We've already had some negative press. For a boutique store like this, word of mouth can make or break us." Which is what woke her up in a cold sweat every single night. "There's as much a chance of our success as of our failure."

Ivy perched on the edge of the desk, jaw agape. "You don't really believe that. God, even casinos have better odds than fifty percent. Channel the power of positive thinking."

Could she truly be that naïve, even after running her own business for years? This wasn't an uplifting episode of Oprah. A fancy vision board couldn't turn the tide of bad publicity. "Ivy, don't patronize me. Slapping a smile on my face won't change the facts. If we go under in a month, it would be entirely my fault."

"Bullshit."

Neck stiff from staring up at her friend, Mira moved to the chair. "Don't swear at me, either."

Ivy kicked back into pacing mode. "What do I excel at? Planning. I planned eight ways from Sunday for this store. I ran projections, I modeled, I spread-sheeted, I made tiny shoebox dioramas of the inside, I researched similar stores around the country. I left no stone unturned. Then I hired you. You, who can keep up with me in the list-making department, and can probably lap me when it comes to organizing. Plus, you have an artistic eye for display. There is every reason in the world for A Fine Romance to succeed."

In Ivy's world view, whatever love didn't conquer, planning could. Hearing the facts laid out like that really did reassure Mira. She'd gotten so caught up in imagining the worst-case scenario that she'd ignored all the reasons she initially accepted the job. Why Ivy had been able to convince her with a single phone call that the concept behind A Fine Romance was brilliant and eminently doable. "Wow. I feel like that was a locker-room speech. Either you should pat me on the ass or I should pour Gatorade over your head."

"No more apologies. No more moping." Ivy wiped the back of her hand across her forehead and collapsed into her chair. "In fact, no more business talk at all. Let's get to the fun stuff."

Fun with Ivy. Exactly what she'd been missing since moving to Chicago. The perfect antidote to the anxiety and stress poisoning her thoughts. "The guy with the scary arm veins on the new season of *The Bachelor?*"

Ivy shuddered. "Definitely not. Daphne mentioned you haven't spent many nights at home recently. I want to hear all about Sam." She leaned forward, elbows on the desk and palms cupping her chin. "Does all that quiet thoughtfulness hide a growling monster in bed?"

Oh, yeah. In bed, Sam had all the roaring passion and strength of a lion in heat. Or a jaguar. Heck, he channeled the entire Large Cats exhibit at the zoo. "Do you really expect me to answer that?"

"Aw, come on. Toss me a few sexy scraps. Kiss and tell a couple of things."

Instead of a stroke-by-stroke replay, she'd give Ivy a better tidbit. A thing she desperately needed to bounce off of someone. "Sam told me he loves me."

"Really? That's no scrap. You just tossed me an entire porterhouse steak full of gossip. Well, go on. What did you say?"

Mira bit her lip. Telling Ivy wouldn't sound any better than when she'd replied to Sam. "Oh."

"Oh, what?"

"That's basically it. Just oh."

Ivy's elbows slid to the side, slamming her hands down against the blotter. "Did you forget how to use your words? Or did you decide to let your actions speak for you, and you jumped him?"

"Sam is giving me time to mull my response." Thank God. The minute those three words slipped past his lips, Mira had felt the panic of a prison escapee, trapped in the middle of two zillion-watt searchlights. Overreaction? Sure. Which is why she calmed down considerably ten seconds later. That kicked off the non-stop searching of her heart and her head for the right response.

"Do you need it? Do you love him?"

As if that solved anything. Of course, in Ivy's eyes, permanently shaded by rose-colored glasses, it solved everything. "I do love him." She'd known deep in her heart for weeks. Even if she refused to admit it except late at night when her subconscious tangoed with her conscious mind. "And it's all your fault. I started to fall in love with him when you forced us to go on that Chicago River cruise."

"Fault? That's an odd word choice. You should be throwing me a parade. Spelling out *Thank you, Ivy* in fireworks over Lake Michigan."

"Before you ask me to rename a street in your honor, let's be clear. Sam's not perfect. He's thoughtful and sweet and challenging and yes, makes the earth spin when we're in bed."

"I knew it." Ivy grinned, her hazel eyes bright with joy for her friends. "Two of my favorite people—you totally deserve each other. Both of you with just enough imperfection to keep it interesting. Like the kick of a little cayenne in a Mexican chocolate cookie."

"You don't understand. He's loyal to a fault and

he believes in me. Hands down, he's the most fun I've ever had. It's wonderful. Sam's wonderful." The more she thought about it, the more amazed she was that Ivy and Sam never tried dating. How could any woman who truly knew him, resist him?

"So?" Ivy prompted.

"So—he's loyal to a fault. A big fault." Jitters skittered up her spine, forcing her up, out of the chair. Mira retraced Ivy's pacing route. "He's pressed the pause button on his entire life to concentrate on his mother. She doesn't need him anymore, not to that extent, but he refuses to see it."

"A problem, but not insurmountable."

"And he believes in me." Mira threw her arms up in the air. She knew how to handle indifference. Her parents grounded her in that area early. But Sam's total, unquestioning support threw her for a loop. "What if I fail again? What if I let him down? Or you? Or my parents?"

Ivy tugged the wrap off her ponytail and scrunched her fingers through her hair. "Geez, Mira, if I'd known you were throwing a pity party, I would've brought in some appetizers and a couple of bottles of wine. Maybe loaded up some Norah Jones on the iPod."

"Very funny."

"You're really worried about your parents? How about you worry about *them* letting *you* down? Because parents who don't want the absolute best for their children are losers. They should've rewritten the stupid strictures on that trust years ago."

Mira agreed. Unfortunately, she didn't get a vote. "But they haven't."

"Yet the world keeps turning. You can't let me

down, because you've already exceeded my expectations. And the only way you could let Sam down is by not being honest with him. It all boils down to only one person, Mira. You only have to worry about letting yourself down."

"News flash—that is a very real possibility."

"Well, a little nervousness will keep you fresh. Keeps you from stagnating in your comfort zone like algae. Speaking of which, let's talk about this matchmaking plan of yours."

Guiltily, Mira remembered the flyers she'd designed in a spurt of anger. Now that she and Ivy were reconciled, putting them up without her permission simply wasn't an option. "I don't want to fight about it."

"Neither do I. The more I thought about it, the more I realized it is a good idea. Smart. Opportunistic. It just pushed me way out of my comfort zone, without any warning. But we've got to compromise. You can't advertise it at the grand opening." She flicked through the pages of her calendar, lips pursed. "Take another month or two to work up a full business plan, do some comparative modeling. We could roll it out right after the New Year."

Mira knew that waiting was the appropriate choice. Rushed plans often turned into failed plans. Taking the time to do it right would be worth it, in the end. "Even hype it as a New Year's resolution—the chance to finally find true love."

"Exactly. And then that automatically feeds off of the desperation women feel as Valentine's Day approaches. We'll be off and running in no time." Ivy came around the desk, arms outstretched. "Let's hug on it."

Much calmer and ridiculously grateful for it, Mira squeezed her friend. "I've changed my mind. I would like to wear that beautiful butterfly tomorrow. As a good-luck talisman."

"And I've changed my mind." Ivy grabbed the box off the desk and tucked her arm behind her. "You don't need luck. When the accolades come pouring in and the cash register rings nonstop, I don't want you to think for a second it has to do with luck. Once we successfully open, then I'll hand it back to you."

"Fine." Mira pretended to pout. "Do I at least get the opening-day tiara you promised me?"

"You'll just have to wait and see."

EIGHTEEN

Sam stared at the tall, circular display case. Inside were the top tiers of all of this weekend's wedding cakes. A traditional white fondant, covered in white roses. Chocolate buttercream icing with alternating white and dark chocolate diamonds, like an Italian harlequin. Thick cream cheese frosting clustered with marzipan pumpkins. And one entire cake that was simply a single red rose, petals unfurled, full and lush.

Solid work. Good cakes. Each one good enough to be photographed and put on the website. Even the one his mentee Javon made. It was the first time the seventeen-year-old had done an entire wedding cake without any supervision from Sam, and the kid had rocked it. Sam knew he'd get a minimum of five referrals from each of these weddings. He didn't care.

Dropping to a crouch inside the daily bakery case, he took another inventory. Pecan caramel brownies dipped in chocolate. Raspberry-filled cupcakes. Slices of apple strudel. The snickerdoodles his mother taught him to make at age five. Cream puffs. Éclairs. Individual fruit tarts. Chocolate raisin whiskey shortbread bars. All strong sellers that flew out the door as fast as they baked them. Looking in these cases, he saw the entirety of his days. How many people could do that? Could literally see exactly how they'd spent their day? Be able to measure precisely how profitable each day had been? Watch the smiles as he handed over a favorite sweet to a toddler—or a grown man—grinning in anticipation? Sam just didn't care, though.

Pushing to his feet, he walked to the back kitchen. The rubber seal on the door snicked as he pulled it open. Leaning with one hand on the doorjamb, he stared at the tidy triple line of truffles on the shelf. Truffles created for the grand opening next door. Champagne and raspberry truffles, each topped with a carefully piped red heart. Those, he cared about. Not that it mattered. Not anymore.

He heard knocking, but didn't bother to turn around. There was no baker's code requiring Sam to respond to whatever imagined cake emergency had someone banging on the front door at nine o'clock on a Thursday night. They had to be high to imagine he'd open up his business three hours after closing to sell a couple of doughnuts. Come to think of it, anyone jonesing to get into a bakery this late probably *was* high. Well, just call him a crusader on the front line of the drug wars, 'cause he'd be damned if he'd enable their munchies.

Frustration made him want to slam the door hard enough to bounce it off the hinges. But the rubber pressure seal that kept in all the cool air would only give him a soft squish. Oh well. Just one more unfulfilled desire to add to his list.

"Hey there, handsome." He spun around to see Mira's beautiful face framed by a fuzzy blue scarf smiling at him. The connecting door was open a tiny sliver. "Why didn't you open up when I knocked?"

"Didn't know it was you."

"Fair enough, since I didn't expect to find you here

so late." She eased through the door sideways, then quickly shut it behind her. "I don't want you to see the store."

"I saw it ten hours ago."

"Yes, but a lot can happen in ten hours. Things change."

"Don't I know it."

Mira rushed at him. Cold air clung to her jacket as he automatically folded her in his arms. And then clung a little tighter when she boosted herself up to wrap her legs around his waist. "Feeling frisky?" he asked. Hopefully not. In his current foul mood, the only company he was fit to keep was with a case of beer.

"Feeling anxious. Good anxious. Night-before-Christmas kind of anxious. Right-before-graduation excited. Staring-at-the-pee-stick-for-a-plus-sign nervous."

Just when he didn't think it possible, his mood turned ten shades darker. About as black as the sludge left when he changed the oil in his car. Turning, he deposited her on the nearest table. And then took a couple of steps back. "Wait. What the hell? You think you're pregnant?"

"After the way we've been double-teaming it with your condoms and my birth control pills? Of course not." Laughter pealed while she swung her feet. "Don't be so literal. In case you're worried, there are still about eighty or so shopping days until Christmas, too."

"Oh. Okay." Sam released the breath he didn't realize he'd been holding. Crisis averted. Not that a child with Mira would be a disaster. The thought of dealing with the sudden *idea* of a child was what threw him for a loop. He'd reached the end of his rope for the day. Maybe for the week. No more surprises, no more giddy, gorgeous girlfriend. Sam needed to be alone. "Shouldn't you be home? Resting up for your big day?"

"I went home. That lasted all of maybe ten minutes. Daphne's over with Gib watching the Bears', and I quote, 'attempts to claw their way into a championship.' The apartment was too quiet. If I stayed home, I probably would've done something crazy to cut the tension." Hopping off the table, she shrugged out of her jacket to reveal jeans and an electric blue sweater that, under different circumstances, would've kick-started his libido into overdrive. "Maybe paint hot-pink polka dots on the walls. Or rearrange all the furniture. Either would give Daphne just cause for kicking me out. So I came back for one last look at the shop. If nothing else, I figured the walk might smooth out my jitters."

"Did it?" How could he get her out of here? Sam didn't want to hurt her feelings. He just didn't want an audience while he licked his wounds. If he took the time tonight to, well, flat-out sulk, then he'd be able to paste on a good attitude for tomorrow's big opening.

"Nope. Which is why I'm so delighted you're still here. You'll probably need five hits of espresso to catch up to my adrenaline buzz. There's no way I could sleep tonight. Waaay too amped up." Mira bopped a little closer, hips swaying. "So why not stay up with me? All night? I promise to make it worth your while. We could play strip poker." She toyed with the bottom edge of her sweater, edging it up enough to flash her belly button. "Or I could just strip. Your call."

"Surprise me."

She cocked her head to the side. Slid her fingers out from beneath her sweater. "You know how all of your friends think you're so quiet? Reserved? Close-mouthed? I've been telling them for weeks that they're nuts. That you throw words at me with the focused regularity of a senior citizen force-feeding quarters into a slot machine. Until tonight. Suddenly you've clammed up. I'm finally seeing the infamous Sam Lyons restraint."

"Welcome to me." Untying his apron, he lobbed it high to land in a heap on the back counter.

"I don't like it. The Sam I know doesn't hold back his words, his emotions. He's passionate. Which means that something's wrong." Hands planted on her hips, determination burned like the blue flame of a Bunsen burner in her eyes. "You might as well tell me now. No secrets, remember? We promised. So, spill."

"There's no secret."

"Excellent. Glad to know you're a man of your word. Let me rephrase. Tell me why you're moping."

Sam sighed. He loved Mira. He loved everything about her. He especially loved this playful, bouncy side of her. But right now he'd give every dollar in the cash register for her to go away. "Can we talk about it later? After the opening? That's where all your focus should be right now. On you. Your big day. My stuff can wait."

"No, it can't. I would never de-prioritize you like that. Besides, there's nothing I can do at the store. Come on. Whatever's going on with you, I bet I can help. Consider what a good distraction you'll be. In fact, if you want me to sleep at all tonight, you have no choice but to talk to me."

Christ. If their roles were reversed, he'd probably be just as tenacious. How could he blame her for caring? Sam pulled the giant calendar from the wall. Trying to get his mother to use the computer to book appointments had felt like a root canal straight to the brain. After two months, he'd given up and stuck with the decades-old tradition of scribbling down everything in the daily blocks. He flipped to January.

"See that?" Sam stabbed his finger at the stupid little square around January 8. It jammed his knuckles upward and hurt like a son of a bitch. At least now he had a rational reason to swear a blue streak. So he did.

Mira grabbed for his finger. "Let me kiss it and make it better."

He yanked his elbow back before she managed to make contact. "You can't make it better. You can't fucking fix it."

"Sam, what is wrong with you?"

"My mother." Sam made the same ta-da motion a magician would make after producing a rabbit out of a hat. Every single person in his life had poked and prodded to get him to admit it for at least a year. Even Mira knew him for—what—a week, tops, before pestering him about his relationship with Kathleen. "There, I've finally said it out loud. My mother is my problem. Freud can rest easy in his grave knowing that he was right. You can blame everything on my mom."

"What sort of blame are you tossing around?" she asked cautiously.

"My mother," he snapped out, "apparently went out and snagged herself a boyfriend."

"Oh, she told you about John? I'm glad."

No way had he heard her correctly. "Wait. You knew?"

"Your mom told me about a week ago. I think she really likes him."

Sam stalked over to her and glowered down all over her bubbly enthusiasm. "You knew and didn't tell me?"

"Do not even go there, Sam Lyons." Mira shook her finger at him. "Every time your mother comes up in conversation, you shut it down. And you shut me out. You've made it crystal clear that my opinions on your mother, and her impact on your life, are unwanted and unappreciated. You can't have it both ways."

The force of her righteous anger reeled him backward until he collided with the sink. "Tell me how you really feel, why don't you?"

"Sorry. No, actually, I'm not. I held my tongue before. Decided to bide my time and see how this thing between us played out. But now it seems that we're in a relationship. You can't pick an entire section of your life and declare it off-limits. So yes, I knew about your mother's boyfriend. And if you'd like to discuss how your mom dating again makes you feel, then I'm listening."

Maybe she had a point. Two-way street and all that. Besides, once he told her the situation, he knew Mira would back him one hundred percent. "I don't want to talk about my mom dating. It's not you," he held up his hand, palm out, to prevent another flurry of words, "it's that I'm not sure yet how I feel. My knee-jerk reaction is that she can't possibly be ready yet, or be well enough. But I'm going to sit on that, let it settle for a few days before I try to figure out my real reaction."

"Well, if you aren't freaking out about John, what's got you so worked up?"

He stabbed at the calendar again. "Thanks to her new man, my mother wants to escape what she shudderingly calls the frigid Chicago winter. They're going on a romantic getaway—her words, not mine— a weeklong Caribbean cruise. She'll be gone the same week that the Fancy Food show runs. Without her here, I won't be able to do the show. We can't afford to just shut down for three straight days. That's it. Mom gets a tan, and I lose the opportunity to start my chocolate business."

Mira folded him into a hug. At first, he couldn't relax enough to enjoy. But soon, her warmth spread through him, melting the anger faster than a double-boiler melted squares of baking chocolate. "You poor thing," she murmured. "That must've been a huge, two-pronged shock."

See, Sam knew he could count on Mira to understand. To have his back. To prop him up. Having his own personal cheerleader right next door was one hell of a silver lining to the night. "I didn't handle it very well," he admitted, sniffing deeply the vanilla scent of her hair.

"Not surprising," she said dryly.

"Mom stormed out."

"Not surprising," she repeated, rubbing his back in slow, soothing circles.

Sam jerked his head back. "What?"

She eased her hands around to lay flat on his chest. "You're her kid, Sam. Yes, a grown man, but still her kid. You don't have a say in who she dates, or when. If you acted half as put out as you are now, I'm not surprised at all that your mother left. But I'm sure she'll still move her trip."

As fast as Mira pissed him off about one thing, then she darted to another. He could barely keep track. "What do you mean? Why would she do that?"

"Didn't you ask her to? Shift the dates so that you can do the Fancy Food show?"

Okay, he'd given her way too much credit. Clearly she didn't understand at all. "Of course not."

Now Mira was the one who pulled back, all the way out of his embrace. "Did you tell her anything about wanting to exhibit at the show?"

"No."

"Why on earth not?"

Sam grabbed another beer from the six-pack he'd dumped in the sink. He'd need the hoppy buzz in his system to survive the rest of this interrogation. "I told you the first time I mentioned it that I wouldn't upset her until it was a done deal. Until I registered. Diana not coming back made it complicated enough. But now, with Mom planning to float through the ocean, that's it. There's absolutely no way I can do it."

"Sure there is. Tell your mom about your plans. Vacations can be shifted around, even if they've already booked the cruise."

Her endless optimism on his behalf was a stark contrast to the scorched-earth mindset she had about her own problems. Weird. "No. It's hopeless. I can't ask her to do that."

"You can't just give up, either."

"You don't understand." In a long, steady gulp, he drained half his beer.

"Make me."

Sam stopped and really thought about it. Why the hell not? He'd never told anyone this story, but it was probably the only way to get her to drop the topic for good. Then they could go back to the comforting portion of the evening. The part where Mira made sympathetic noises and tried to cheer him up. Preferably in bed.

"When Dad lay in his hospital bed, between heart attacks, he knew time was running out. So he wrote me a note. One of the nurses gave it to me when I got there, too late." He slipped his wallet out of his pants, then pulled out a well-worn and creased piece of paper. "Read this."

Mira unfolded it to stare at the shaky block printing. "'Take care of Cupcake.'" She looked up at him, quizzically. "Do you have a secret family recipe for cupcakes?"

"No. I mean, yes, we do, as a matter of fact." He lowered his voice to a whisper. "The secret is mayonnaise. Don't tell anyone."

She crinkled her nose. "Ewww. Don't worry."

"Cupcake was Dad's nickname for my mother."

A single tear welled at the corner of her eye. "That's adorable. Perfect for a baker. And it's a beautiful note. So touching that he put her first, even as he…well…" She trailed off. "Do you always keep it with you?"

Slowly and carefully he refolded and wedged it behind his emergency twenty. "Of course. It reminds me every day of my duty."

After a noise suspiciously close to a snort, she crossed her arms over her chest. "What duty?"

"Don't you see? Dad passed his responsibility on to me. I'm wholly responsible for her now."

"For your mother?" Mira sounded incredulous.

"Yes."

"No, you're not. She is her own person. You can check up on her, and worry about her. You can even go the extra mile to make her happy. But unless you're about to have her declared mentally incompetent, you aren't responsible for her."

This is why he hadn't told anyone. Until the two-ton onus of familial guilt squeezed against your heart every day, you couldn't understand. One of those walk-a-mile-wearing-my-chocolate-covered-apron things. "I can't ignore my father's last, dying wish."

"You can't take his place, either. And he wouldn't want you to ignore your own life."

God, he loved her, but Mira Parrish's single-minded pursuit of his happy ending was driving him to drink. Sam tossed back the rest of his beer and slammed down the bottle. "My life doesn't matter," he burst out. "My hopes, my dreams, it all has to take second place. My mother has to come first. The entirety of her happiness comes first. Always. I owe my dad that much."

Confused blue eyes squinted at him. "Why?"

"Are you kidding?" He spun away from her, driving his fingers through his hair. "My selfishness took me to Europe. My selfishness kept me a continent away when my father needed me the most. It kept me from saying goodbye to him. If he'd asked me to build a tower to the moon out of cream puffs in that note, I would've done it."

Mira grabbed his arm. When he didn't budge, she angled around in front of him. "Sam, are you listening to yourself? I mean, there's selfless, and then there's just plain stupid. You can't subsume your life to your mother's. Kathleen wouldn't possibly want that for you."

Here's where he drew his line in the sand. "She. Can't. Know."

"Don't yell at me. I'm not going to rat you out."

"Sorry." He didn't even realize he'd raised his voice.

"I can't believe I have to say something this basic, but here goes. Don't throw away your dreams for your mother's sake."

"She deserves it. Death stole her chance at sharing the easy years of retirement with my dad. And she gave up two decades of her life to raise me and Diana. The least I can do to even the score is make her life as trouble-free as possible."

Mira spread her arms wide at her waist. She wore the same condescending look his tenth-grade geometry teacher got whenever he asked a question more than once. "Why not let her decide?"

"Because she'd give up everything for me. It's why she fought with Dad for a year for my chance to go to Europe."

"I'm sorry, I don't want to get morbid, but this whole *me second* attitude is going to last how long? Until your mother dies? She seems pretty spry. She's easily got another twenty-five years in her." Mira blinked at him for a moment, waiting for a response. When he simply stared back, her lips thinned. Everything about her body hardened. If she'd been a hedgehog, spines would've popped out. "Are you going to wait that long to marry? Start a family?" Her words weren't loud, but very deliberate. "Because you can't have a child unless you're willing to put it first in your life, and it sounds like that spot's already reserved."

Sam hadn't thought about it. On purpose. For the past two years, he'd only existed by maintaining a one-day-at-a-time mantra, like an addict used to get through recovery. Through days filled with worry about his mom, his sister and throwing every ounce of energy into keeping the bakery afloat, planning for the future had been a luxury he couldn't afford. And planning for love was more Ivy's style than his.

Now that Mira threw it in his face, however, the truth couldn't be avoided. No matter how much he loved her, nothing had changed. Mom still came first. Mira appearing in his life didn't erase his dad's request. Wow. No wonder he didn't risk thinking about the future. Apparently he didn't have much of one. Sam braced his palms on the sink behind him. Suddenly he didn't feel so hot.

"I can't let my father down. I have to honor his request. That's the only answer I have to your questions."

"That's a shame. But it's your choice. It's plain to see there's no point fighting about it." Mira stepped forward and rose to her tiptoes to kiss his forehead. "Goodbye, Sam."

One lousy fight and she wouldn't share the sheets with him? "You're not spending the night?"

"No." She squared her shoulders, backing up almost to the door. "Don't you understand? This is the *big* goodbye. I'm ending this, Sam. I can't stick around to watch you throw away your life like this. Throw away our future. Trust me, I'm not angling for a proposal. But at our age, if there isn't the slightest chance that the road we're exploring ends in marriage, we're just wasting our time. I can't believe all you're giving up."

Ten minutes ago she'd practically crawled up him like ivy on a drainpipe. Just like that, they were over? This is the reward he got for sharing his big, painful secret? Panic cramped his gut faster than the night he ate an entire bowl of buffalo chicken dip. "You're the one giving up. I didn't ask you to break up with me."

"And I don't want to." She fisted her hand at her stomach. "Do you get that it physically hurts me? That you're willing to give up on us to take care of a woman who, as far as I can tell, can take care of herself?"

Un-fucking-believable. The woman he loved, who filled his life with as much sweetness as sugar and chocolate, really gave up on him over his mother issues? Why wouldn't she take a chance on him? Try to work through things? Then it hit him. She'd never said those three little words back to him. If Mira didn't love him, of course she didn't want to make the effort. The pain he felt honed itself into a sharp arrow, and let fly.

"You don't know anything about my mother."

"And maybe you don't know as much as you think you do," she shot back. "Sure, Kathleen hit a rough patch. Did you single-handedly bring her back from the brink of a nervous breakdown? Probably. But now she's better. Did you know that when you break a bone, it heals twice as strong? Your mother is happy, healthy and in an exciting new relationship. She's let go of you. Why can't you let go? Why can't you grab my hand instead? Start our life together?"

He wouldn't roll over to an ultimatum. "Because— I can't. I have to be there for her."

"Naturally. In general. But not every hour of every day, in every way. Let her live her own life again. Start living yours."

"I'm not letting Dad down. I'm sorry you think it has to be this way."

"I'm sorry, too. You're such a wonderful man, Sam. I wish you could see that the choice you're making is the only one that could let your father down." Mira sucked in a deep breath. "I can't put my life on hold for the next twenty years. I won't live half a life. You're the one who urged me to stand up to my parents and strike out on my own path. Find my own bliss. Watching you toss away your dreams is about as far from bliss as I can image." She walked to the door then paused, hand on the knob. "Please don't come to the opening. I don't think I'll be able to bear seeing you for a while."

How was he supposed to bear *not* seeing her?

NINETEEN

THE INSISTENT BLARING of his cell phone cut through Sam's headache like a hot knife through icing. Groaning, he patted in the general area of the nightstand. He managed to knock off the radio, a book and a full glass of water before finding the phone just as it stopped ringing. Then the landline started. This time, he skipped the groaning and went straight to swearing. Rolling to the foot of the bed—and his stomach rolling in somersaults with him—Sam grabbed for his sweats, then hotfooted it to the kitchen, where he slapped the phone off the hook.

"Hello?"

"Hey, you gotta come downstairs. Right now." Ben sounded serious. But not dead-body serious, so Sam couldn't think of any reason to throw on more clothes and comply.

"Not a great time for me. Catch you later?"

"No. Now." His voice lowered to an urgent, near-growl. Still not dead-body serious, but a hell of a lot closer. And given Ben's laid-back personality, very out of the ordinary.

Sam sighed. It couldn't be more than dawn o'clock. "Give me two minutes. I'll meet you out back." He hung up, threw on shoes, a shirt and dry-swallowed four aspirin. Maybe they'd kick in by the time he got some coffee brewed.

It took all his concentration to tiptoe down the stairs so his mom wouldn't hear him. Even though they weren't speaking right now, if she saw his hangover pallor and bloodshot eyes, she'd read him the riot act. Better to lie low until he hit the shower and choked down some toast. The jingle of the front door bell told him the bakery already had customers. Sam crept down the hall, feeling like an idiot. A grown man shouldn't have to sneak out of his own apartment. Why couldn't he own his stupid hangover? Take a weird, masculine pride in it, like jock itch and ulcers.

By the time he unlocked the back door, he'd cracked both eyes open. Not at the same time, but it felt like progress. Sam braced himself against the early morning chill as he opened the door. Then two hard blows to the chest, immediately followed by a rush of icy water, snapped his eyelids open. Shiver or shriek? Before he could decide, one more hard bump lashed right against his gonads. At least the shock of the cold water helped diminish the nut-cracking pain. Sam staggered backward, landing on his ass.

"What the fuck is going on?" he said from between chattering teeth.

Backlit by the pearly dawn, Ben and Gib advanced, each in sweats and hoodies. Gib had both arms crossed, but Ben hefted a bright red, tightly filled water balloon in one hand. "Give me one good reason not to use this," he said.

Had he lost his mind? "Give me one good reason why you would," Sam demanded. He curled his knees up to his waist and curled onto his side. Still hard to breathe from shock and pain, but it protected him from another hit. "It's still six months until April

Fool's Day. We stopped playing Humans vs. Zombies back in June once wedding season ramped up. What the hell did I do to deserve a sneak attack?"

Gib kicked the door shut with his foot. "What you deserve? If we doled out what you deserve, you'd be black and blue for a week." His crisp accent honed the knifelike anger in his voice to a lethal point.

"Seriously, I'm clueless here. And epically hungover, so cut me some slack. The bartender over at McGee's mixed me something just short of toxic last night."

"Good. If you're already in pain, it makes our job easier." Ben set down the water balloon and dropped into a crouch. "You're an idiot, Lyons. A first-class, no-holds-barred idiot."

Gib spread his legs wide and crossed his arms. A hip-hop artist pose, the kind that popped up mid-video right before the half-dressed women swarmed him. "We warned you the consequences would be dire should you break her heart."

His neurons weren't firing at full speed yet. Figuring out why they'd come at him felt like a pop quiz. "Who? Mira?"

"You treated anyone else like shit recently?"

"How did you—" Sam pieced together their outfits, the time of day, and figured it out. "She was supposed to go running with you this morning."

Gib snapped off a nod. "Yes. But after you shredded her heart into confetti, she wasn't exactly in the mood."

"Why'd you mess with her?" Ben demanded.

Sam didn't have the energy to bluster or lie. "I love her."

"Right. You love her so much you broke up with her."

"Hey, she dumped me." And that stung like battery acid on a slow drip into his heart. "Take that into consideration. Maybe I'm the one who deserves some sympathy. A little hey-we're-on-your-side attitude."

"We're not choosing sides." Gib sighed, then extended his hand to help Sam up. "That's the problem. We know you're both hurting."

"Especially since there are tiny gnomes hammering their way through my skull as we speak."

"We get the hint." Gib gave him a swift once-over. "You look like shit."

Sam squeezed out the hem of his shirt. "You're the ones who drenched me."

"I'll go grab coffee from up front and meet you upstairs." Ben tossed his balloon in the trash and ambled down the hall. Dripping at every step, Sam led Gib to his apartment. Once inside, he grabbed a towel and changed into another pair of sweats. "Why'd you decide to go with punishment by water balloon?" he called out from the bedroom.

"Ben wanted to borrow a fire hose, but we figured that would probably break a couple of ribs. Then he wanted to downscale to a Super Soaker, but we were too pissed off to wait for a toy store to open. Ben used his key to Aisle Bound and grabbed some balloons out of their supply closet."

Sam came out and flopped full length onto the navy couch. The cushions bunched around him as tightly as a chalk outline around a murder victim. Just because they'd gotten him up didn't mean he had to stay vertical. "I hope he left Ivy a note. You know she'll notice they're missing."

"Yes. Her attention to detail is wondrous to behold." Gib sat in the blue plaid wing chair, legs crossed as though ready for a tea party. "Now explain yourself. Explain how, if you truly love Mira, you can treat her so shoddily."

"It's complicated."

"You've tried that line on us before." The door snicked behind Ben as he handed out steaming mugs. The smell alone began to rejuvenate Sam. He inhaled deeply, savoring the spike of dark roast that woke up all of his nerves not already on alert from the water bombing. Nothing would make this morning even halfway good, but coffee made all mornings tolerable.

"We let you whitewash the situation once." Ben kicked Sam's feet out of the way and sat on the end of the couch. "But now we need to know what the hell is going on in that messed-up brain of yours."

Sam had held his dad's parting request close to his chest for years. When he finally shared it with someone, Mira used it as ammunition against him. Which meant he was in no particular hurry to unburden himself of those details again anytime soon. "Look, I'm having a crappy week, okay? Things at the bakery are jamming up on me. Diana's not back from Europe."

Ben snorted, blowing ripples across his coffee. "That's no surprise. Did you expect her to be?"

"No." He'd hoped, but deep down Sam never actually expected her to materialize, apron in hand, ready to work beside him. Stupid, in retrospect. Naïve. "I had a plan—an idea, really—to change things up at the bakery. Diana was the lynchpin."

"Do it anyway."

"Can't."

"Wanna bet? It's about time you shook up your life. You're a smart guy, and you've got even smarter friends." Ben grinned. "Between the three of us, we can figure out a solution. But you might want to start by telling us the problem."

Tempting. For a second, Sam thought about giving in, blurting out his dream to become a chocolatier. What good would it do, though? Besides making him think about something he needed to put firmly in his mental rearview mirror. He gulped his coffee, not caring that it seared his gullet on the way down. That pain was a lively distraction from the crushing headache and twisting in his gut.

"How about I just explain my sudden, depressing lack of a girlfriend? Will that be enough sharing for you two to leave me in peace?"

"If you're going to be all stubborn about it, yeah." Ben rotated his hand in a get-the-hell-on-with-it motion.

"Mira and I are in different places. She doesn't want to wait around for me to catch up. So we're through."

"Simple enough. Make up with her," Gib ordered.

"Can't. She wants a future. That's the one thing I can't promise her."

Gib leaned forward, cradling his mug in both hands. "But you love her? You're sure of it?"

"Yeah." No doubt at all. Sam wanted to spend the rest of his life with Mira. Just like he was sure he wanted to spend the rest of his life making chocolate. Oh, and how incredibly sure he now was that neither goal would ever be in his grasp. Kind of like the dream he had at age five of tunneling through the earth to play with kids his age in China.

"No wonder you drank enough to pickle yourself last night." Stalking to the kitchen, Ben slammed cupboards as he gathered bread, jam and peanut butter. "What makes you think someone else even half as wonderful will ever come along? Someone who not only puts up with all your shit, but loves you back?"

"What makes you think I have that now?"

Gib shook his head. "You've lost me."

"Mira never said she loved me." He thought he'd been willing to wait, let her come around to it at her own pace. And now he'd never hear those words spill out of her soft, pink lips. Not directed at him, anyway.

A whistle erupted out of Ben, arcing with a rocket's trajectory. "You said it first? Just dumped it on her, unwanted, like a flaming bag of shit on her doorstep?"

"Why wouldn't I? Love's not a game to me. There's no winners or losers."

Ben slapped a PB&J in his hand. "I'd say you're firmly in the loser camp today, my friend."

Knowing the bread would settle his stomach, Sam forced down a bite. "Love shouldn't have to be strategized, or timed out. I fell in love with Mira, so I thought she ought to know. I thought it would be easy."

"What—love or women? Because you're completely off your rocker if you think either is *easy*." Gib spat the word out like a bite of six-day-old salmon. "Sex is easy. Everything else is tortuous and painful and complicated."

"Hey. Baron von Bitter over there. Shut it. I'm getting married in less than a year, remember?" Ben patted his hand over his heart. "Allow me to wallow in the beauty of the love I have for Ivy. At least until I pay off the engagement ring."

"Sorry. Perhaps you should leave the room while I finish educating Sam."

"Try again. I'm not going to let you blacken and wither his heart against true love just because you have yet to fall."

"Lucifer fell. Look where he ended up." Gib twisted in the chair to dig his wallet out of his back pocket. "Mira is a wonderful woman. Smart, beautiful and an ass like an almost ripe summer peach."

Jealousy and panic jockeyed for the pole position at the front of Sam's mind. "Don't even think about making a play for her. For Christ's sake, there's a code about this sort of thing."

Eyes blazing, Gib shot to his feet. "I would never shag your woman. Bloody hell."

Even half-dead and half-awake, Sam realized he'd overstepped. "Sorry. My brain stopped working pretty much the same time Mira told me not to come to her opening."

"I'd say it stopped working sooner than that, or you wouldn't have mucked it up so badly. Here." Gib opened his hand to let a business card flutter slowly to Sam's lap.

"Dr. Debra Rubin? Who's she?"

Gib sat back down, crossing his ankle over his knee. "My psychiatrist."

It took all of Sam's limited mental capacity to prevent a full-out spit take. Only his strong desire to avoid scrubbing dark roast out of his cream Berber carpet made it possible. His life was bad enough now without throwing a brain excavator into the mix. "You see a shrink? I thought Brits didn't talk about their emotions."

"Generally true. Unless paying someone a considerable sum to listen. In which case frugality kicks in, causing me to sing like a canary."

"Why are you seeing a shrink?" A sardonic grin tightened Ben's mouth into an almost straight line. "Performance issues? Can't, uh, let's say, salute the queen with the same regularity now that you're looking at thirty in your rearview mirror?"

"Hardly." Gib's tone was about as warm as a winter night on Pluto. "That will have to wait for another day. This is Sam's turn to be under the microscope. We're not blind, Sam. We've watched you put your life on hold to take care of your mother. Is that what you meant when you said you didn't have a future to offer Mira?"

Right. Because he so wanted to poke at the pulsing, raw wound Mira left on his heart. "I'm not paying you anything, so according to your rules, I don't have to answer."

A wave of his hand said that Gib wouldn't allow him to plead the Fifth. "Doesn't matter. I know I'm right. The point being, your actions were all very noble, but the time to martyr yourself has passed. Your mother's let go. She's even seeing a very nice man."

And the hits just kept on coming. Sam threw back the last of his coffee and sat up, dropping his feet to the ground. "You know about John?"

"Everybody knows about John." Ben held up a

hand, then continued. "Everyone but you, I mean. Kathleen didn't know how to break it to you. Clearly, the inability to talk to each other runs in the family. She made us all promise not to say anything."

"Unbelievable." But while Sam wanted to be mad at his mother, he just couldn't. She'd kept her secret to spare his feelings. Probably. Now that he thought about it, maybe he could get good and mad at her. They worked together five days a week, sometimes more. They spoke every night. How did she manage to look him in the eyes for months on end and not share news this huge?

"You need to let your mother go," Gib said.

"Do you hear yourself? For God's sake, she's not an injured squirrel I nursed to health and have to release back into the wild." He'd about reached his limit for their well-meaning interference. Sam pushed off the couch, walked to the door and rested his hand on the knob. No need to be subtle with these two.

"Let me restate. Kathleen has become a really very bad habit."

"A crutch, holding you back," Ben added.

Why wouldn't they take the hint and leave? Or just shut up? If Mira couldn't get him to back away from his mom, the opinions of two men with not even half her charms certainly weren't going to be able to sway him. "I'm headed to the shower. These clothes are hitting the floor in about thirty seconds. In other words, thanks for the coffee, now get the hell out."

Gib didn't budge. "For a while it looked like Mira was on track to break you of that habit. If you truly love her, you'll dig yourself out of this rut. Consider Dr. Rubin to be your emotional tow truck." He used that wing chair like a throne from which to toss out ridiculous edicts. Well, like all rulers with an over-inflated sense of importance, he'd get deposed real soon.

He stopped halfway down the hall. Turned around to glare at the friends dumping shit all over him. "I don't need a tow. I'm not fucking broken."

Ben laughed. Laughed like a loon. "Of course you are. We all are. We've all got cracks running through our psyche. The trick is to find the right woman to help glue you back together."

Gib drummed his fingers on the armrest. "I'm really starting to regret bringing you along, Westcott. Sounds like Ivy's rose-colored glasses are on permanent loan to you."

"So what if we're coming at this from two different directions? Bottom line is the same. Kathleen re-tied the apron strings around Sam a couple of years ago. Now it's time to untie them."

Sam was so tired. Tired of having the same fight over and over, but with different people. "She's the most important woman in my life."

"Is she?" Gib asked.

"She has to be. I don't have a choice."

TWENTY

"HEADS UP, BEAUTIFUL boss-lady," Hays called out as he came down from the second floor. He carried a tray full of the signature sweet Helen had finally chosen for the store—dark-chocolate-covered coconut macaroons. Mira's newly rediscovered love of all things cocoa bean meant the cookies were a serious threat to her waistline.

"Third refill?" Mira asked. She'd tried to keep count, but it was impossible. Sure, she wanted to keep a firm grasp of every tiny detail. That wish hadn't lasted five minutes past opening. They'd opened the store during the day, then closed for two hours prior to the party in order to regroup, restock and buff the place up. Reporters, bloggers, stylists and shoppers kept her running from the get-go.

"Fourth. This crowd has a real sweet tooth. If we run low, do you think Sam would help us out with whatever cookies he's still got on the shelves?"

"No." The word snapped out faster and with more vehemence than she would've preferred. Mira didn't plan to tell anyone about breaking up with Sam until after the opening. Of course, that plan derailed pretty much at inception when Gib and Ben walked in on her bawling her eyes out at dawn. Luckily, Daphne had, well, gotten lucky and not come home. She and Ivy were still in the dark, along with Hays and Helen.

Her friends and colleagues overflowed with excitement about tonight. The bad timing of Mira's crushing breakup would not affect it. Period. If Gib or Ben breathed a word, she'd string them up by their balls. The grand opening of A Fine Romance was nothing less than the realization of a dream for Ivy. It had to be perfect. Unsullied. Drama-free.

"Hays, I'm sorry," she said with an apologetic pat to his arm. "I'm about ten steps past frenzied. While you were upstairs refilling the tray, I finished an interview for the WGN nine o'clock news. Helen's kids arrived just in time to come to the rescue. Noah's helping her with the food, and Lucy is bagging. Both of them are just as friendly as their mother, thank heavens."

Cranking his head to the side, Hays stared around Mira down the hall. "But if you're back here with me, then who is on the register? Or does everyone get to take home their selections for free tonight? Like party favors?"

"Are you kidding? I exalt in a hefty markup. Nothing is ever free." Not even a smile, for her self-control and stamina were sorely taxed by every single one she doled out. "Ivy's at the till. I figured I'd let her have some fun for a while, watching the cash roll in hand over fist. Or, rather, watching the credit card receipt tape grow longer."

"So you're a television star now?"

"Hardly," she said dryly. Doing the interview had been equal parts fun and nerve-racking. Sort of like driving for the first time, when knowing what to do from training manuals in no way translated to the glorious scare of mashing the gas pedal into the floor.

Back then, she'd driven right over the concrete marker at the end of the parking spot and taken out the muffler. Tonight's interview hopefully went better.

"Well, you look like a star in that outfit. I bet that after it airs, we have men by the dozens hanging out, waiting to catch a glimpse of the glamorous Mira Parrish."

The red silk blouse, the same deep red as the store's logo, did cling to all the perky curves of her Miracle Bra in a very gratifying fashion. At least, watching Sam's reaction to the tight blouse would've been gratifying. Had he been here, and actually in love with her. Which he most certainly was not. Not here, and not in love with her, despite what he said. If he truly loved her, he'd be willing to fight for her. For them.

"I worried the black T-strap stilettos were a bit over the top." But with the calf-length pencil skirt, her outfit evoked the glamour—and more important, the romance—of the forties. Perry Como and Ella Fitzgerald crooned over the sound system to help get people in the mood. "Fun, though. Even if my feet already throb. It isn't fair. Why is it only women who have to suffer to be fashionable?"

Hays looked down at his own wing-tips, high-waisted pin-striped pants and crisp white shirt topped with dark red suspenders. "Oh, I suffered. Halloween's right around the corner. I had to fight off two other guys at the vintage store in order to grab these pants. I took an elbow right in my pancreas."

It steadied her jitterbugging nerves to tease him a little. "Do you even know which side of the body your pancreas is on?"

"Sure I do. It's the side with the elbow-shaped

bruise." He winked at her and hurried back into the melee. Only an hour into the grand opening reception and there were people wall to wall. There'd been another questionable article this morning, this time in the weekly alternative paper. Nothing that flat-out predicted the store would flop. Just a very broad hint that if it didn't succeed, the finger of guilt should rest firmly on Mira's shoulders. So either people didn't believe the article, didn't care, or they'd come to watch her flame out. Fine with her, as long as they spent money. And then maybe raved about it to at least ten of their friends tomorrow.

Mira took a deep breath. So far, so good. No reason why she couldn't take a luxurious two-minute break. She'd been driving herself all day. Obsessing over details finalized three days ago, and rechecking everything for the umpteenth time. It distracted her from knowing Sam was on the other side of the Dutch door. They'd kept it closed today, in the whirl of final preparations. That excuse wouldn't fly tomorrow, though. She'd just have to suck it up and do her best to ignore the proximity of the man she wanted with all her heart. The man who simply didn't want her enough.

A familiar, shrill laugh switched her into crisis mode. She'd recognize that laugh anywhere. Mira knew that for certain, as she'd heard it in absolutely every corner of the globe. Despite Helen's invitation, despite her parents' note, she never fully believed they'd actually show up. Because the threat of epically bad publicity and losing her boyfriend at the same time wasn't enough to deal with? Seriously, how many puppies had she run over in a previous life to deserve this?

"Where's the brilliant mastermind behind this store? Fabulous idea." Her dad's voice boomed, easily heard over all the party chatter. If there was one thing Hale Parrish excelled at, it was making an entrance. Wearing a knit vest under a navy blazer with a sporty—for him—pale blue ascot, he looked like he'd just walked out of a party at Cannes. No doubt each piece alone cost more than her entire outfit.

"I'm right here." Ivy gave a little wave from where she manned the cash register. They'd strategized about whether or not to play up the store's connection to Ivy. Given her current "hot" factor from being spotlighted in *Planning for Love*, Mira had no problem urging Ivy to take all the credit. Free, positive publicity was worth a lot more than her pride. "I'm so glad you like the store."

Dad frowned. "You shouldn't try to take credit for someone else's hard work, young lady. I'll speak to my daughter and see that you're reprimanded."

Mira didn't know whether to be thrilled her father actually sounded proud of her, or appalled that he'd insulted her boss. She finally managed to slither between three women blocking the aisle, each holding an astronomically expensive vase. "Hi, I'm here. No need to threaten anyone, Dad."

"Oh, Mr. Parrish. It's a pleasure to meet you after all these years." Ivy shot Mira a what-the-heck's-going-on look before turning on the full force of her charm. "I'm Ivy Rhodes. Mira and I were roommates in grad school."

"Hale Parrish." He stretched out an arm to pull

the scary skinny woman in a little black dress to his waist. "And this is my wife, Elizabeth." They did a round of handshakes. It said a lot about their family dynamics that her parents chose to shake hands with a stranger *before* hugging the daughter they hadn't seen in over a year.

"Ivy's the one who hired me, and first envisioned the store."

"Thank you for rescuing our daughter." A sardonically hearty laugh rolled out of her dad. "We'd written her off as snakebit. Didn't think anyone would hire her again."

Still no hug or greeting, but at least he'd fallen straight into the habitual role of belittling Mira's endeavors. And it felt as hypocritical as ever, coming from a man whose entire résumé could be summed up in two words—professional partygoer. The closest he'd ever come to a paycheck were the monthly installments from his trust fund. Well, if he was following old patterns, then she would, in an effort to keep the peace. Dutifully, she nipped forward and kissed both of her parents on the cheek. "Mom, you look beautiful. Younger than ever."

Her mother air-kissed back in the general vicinity. "You look tired, darling. Clearly they're working you too hard. Come for a facial with me tomorrow morning."

"Nobody's pushing me, Mom. *I* run the store. And since we just opened tonight, I kind of have to be here tomorrow." Two beaming customers pushed their way up to the counter to check out.

"Well, when you're tired of 'working,'" her mother made air quotes with her fingers, "let me know, and we'll send you a ticket to catch up with us wherever we are. How does Christmas in Austria sound?"

"Delightful." And for a few seconds, she remembered the feeling of schussing down the Alps after ridiculously handsome blond men in thick sweaters. Yes, it had been fun playing all over the world with her parents. Fun—but not satisfying. Nowhere close to the utter fulfillment Mira had felt as people actually stood in line to get in to this reception. She and Ivy had both welled up as they'd cut the big red ribbon across the doorway. That moment defined her.

Mira certainly couldn't change her parents or make them understand. However, she could stand her ground, make her own way. Cashing a trust-fund check would never give her that feeling of self-worth. Never again would she question her decision to forego the family's buckets of money. Anytime she wavered, from stress or exhaustion, she could think back to this night and remember that money hadn't brought her this level of happiness (if she ignored the sucking emptiness in her heart over losing Sam). Hard work and good friends had. Just like that, she closed the door on any claim on the Parrish fortune.

Calmer and grounded, she screwed on a determined smile. "However, I hope December will be a very busy time for the store. I'm afraid I won't be able to join you."

"Well, contact our lawyers if you change your mind. They'll know where to find us." Hale spun on his heel back toward Ivy. "I recognize you. From that wedding show!"

Ivy looked up as she swiped a credit card. "That's me. As you make your rounds, you might also recognize my partner, Daphne—Mira's roommate. And my fiancé, Ben, shot all the footage. We're a tight-knit group, and we're all here to support Mira tonight. Oh, and I think in last week's episode we highlighted some of Sam's wonderful chocolate truffles. He runs the bakery next door."

Her mother's eyes, identical to Mira's, widened. "I remember him. Tall and dark and rather brooding?"

Ivy laughed. "Some of the time. He wasn't too happy about being filmed that day."

"He's quite good-looking. Darling, a television star who makes chocolate? You should date him."

The bitter irony burned through Mira. Could it really be that easy? Now that she'd turned her back on the money and on the man who didn't love her enough? And were they really going to have this conversation in the middle of her grand opening? Taking a quick peek at the rest of the room, it looked busy but not out of control. Helen had the food under control, and Hays had a group of six women eating out of his hand. Guess she had five spare minutes to finish off her family drama once and for all.

"Seriously, Mom? Because you saw him once on television, you think Sam Lyons is an *appropriate* man for me, according to the terms of Grandfather's will?"

Hale shuffled his feet, then cleared his throat. "Your mother and I came to terms a few years ago with the fact that we'd need to relax our standards as to the word *appropriate*. A man on television, artistic, talented and with his own business sounds like a good catch for our Mira."

"Funny you should say that," Ivy broke in. "As a

matter of fact—" She clammed up after Mira clamped her hand in a death grip on Ivy's arm. "Ow!"

"We're distracting Ivy. And I certainly don't want the person handling money distracted. Why don't we move this conversation back to my office?" Mira suggested. No way would she let Ivy tell her parents that she'd dated Sam. It would open a Pandora's box full of pestering. Besides which, she could barely even think his name without choking up a little. She'd deal with her parents tonight. She'd deal with losing Sam every lonely night after this one.

Then she remembered the cramped size of her office. If her parents saw it, they might drag her out of the store. Better to finish this in the hallway. "Look, I know that lowering the criteria for my potential husband is, for you guys, quite the affectionate gesture. But I don't buy that you'll accept any halfway decent man. Be honest. You don't have some Ivy League, hedge-fund broker waiting outside to meet me?"

Elizabeth pouted in a practiced, pretty way. "Now, darling, we only want the best for you. To have a life untroubled by worry or responsibility. Does that make us such terrible parents?"

"Of course not." In their own, shallow way, they just wanted to hand over her trust fund. Mira squinted at her mother in suspicion. "On the other hand, I don't hear you denying it."

"This is a store opening, isn't it? Any potential shoppers are welcome? Word of mouth can really build a small business."

"Yes."

"The son of a friend of ours lives here in Chicago. When he's not racing. He's on the America's Cup team. I think. Greyson races some sort of boat, anyway. We had dinner with him in Monte Carlo and he's a perfectly delightful man. He knows oh so many people here in town, and he promised to tell all his friends about your little store. If you're willing, he'd like to take you out for drinks later. To celebrate your big night." Elizabeth pointed at a tall, super-tan man flirting with Helen's daughter. "He's right over there."

Wow. Sooo many things wrong with that offer, even when made out of love. Mira didn't want to be set up. She definitely didn't want to be set up with a man who "did" Monte Carlo with her parents. Or with a man who spent months at a time at sea somewhere. She especially didn't want to be set up with a man who looked to be her own age, but found it acceptable to flirt with a college sophomore. Last of all, she didn't want to be set up with anyone because she loved Sam. Even knowing he didn't love her enough to take a chance on a life with her, she still loved him wholeheartedly. This was the moment of truth. Her chance to lay down the law to her parents. Mira clasped the butterfly pendant at her neck for moral support.

"Thank you for taking the time to flush out a potential suitor. Look, you're welcome to browse the store, but you are no longer allowed to browse for potential husbands. Love will always be more important to me than money. I'll find my own man, the right man for me, in my own time."

They both blinked at her, like a pair of sleepy owls. "It would be nice if we could believe that," Hale said.

"Much like the facial, the offer for Greyson will still be on the table if you change your mind. Even after we leave. We'll give him your number. Just think about it, darling. How on earth are you going to find a man cooped up in here all day? Shopkeeper isn't a particularly alluring profession."

She'd said her piece. Whether or not they accepted it was out of her hands. Mira looked at her watch. Almost time for Ivy's big speech. "I can't believe you came all the way to Chicago for the opening. Thank you." Because even with the jabs, she knew it meant a lot that they were here. The equivalent to normal parents driving a kid to college, or going to a track meet. Mira sincerely doubted her parents even knew that she'd run track in high school.

"Well, we went to New York earlier this week for the opening gala at the Metropolitan Opera. *Turandot*. Beautifully sung, and with exquisite costumes. As long as we were in the States, it would've felt selfish not to come see you."

They'd never win a parent of the year award. Or even parent of the century. Not even back in that century when parents sacrificed up their thirteen-year-old virgin daughters to volcano gods. But they were here. Mira put that in the win column, kissed them both again and walked back into the party.

"Helen, if you stay another minute, I'm firing you. Your family's waiting to take you out. Go." Sam watched through a tiny crack in the connecting door as Mira toed off her shoes. She probably needed a foot rub right about now. God, what he wouldn't give to be able to pull her legs into his lap and start rubbing. Of course, at this point, he'd be happy if she just listened to him without slamming the door in his face.

"You sure you don't want to come with us? I think

Noah has a tiny crush on you. He'd be over the moon if an older woman paid him some attention."

"Thanks, but I want to stay here for a while. Soak in all the wonderful things that happened tonight."

Two local news stations had carried promos at six for the store, and live stand-ups at nine. He'd watched them all, thrilled for her. Hungrily staring at the television screen for every second of her poised interviews. Every customer that came out raved about the place. By morning it would be the hottest new boutique in Chicago. All of Mira's hard work paid off, and turned the tide against the previous bad press.

"Including your parents' appearance?"

Sam almost fell through the door in shock. The Parrishes came to support Mira?

"Surprisingly, yes. You were right to invite them. This time. But don't go adding them to the store's mailing list or anything."

"You got it." Helen gave her a big hug. "A Fine Romance might have started out as Ivy's, but now it is all you. It sparkles like a ten-carat, cushion-cut diamond because of you. Be proud." Hefting an insulated food carrier off the counter, Helen headed out the door. Mira locked it behind her. She took a few steps forward.

"Well, it's just you and me now." Slowly she walked from the front of the store, trailing her hand over each display case like a coach patting the asses of the defensive squad after a good game. After a detour to grab a sparkly tiara from beneath the counter, she stopped at the kitchen area and sank onto a stool. Lower lip trembling, her head began to droop toward the tiara in her lap. Sam guessed she was about one good sigh away from bursting into tears. It was now or never.

Holding a doily covered silver tray in both hands, he kicked the door open. Probably a lot harder than necessary. It slammed against the wall and jolted Mira upright.

"Sam?"

"You told me not to come to the opening." He spoke in a rush, worried she'd cut him off before he got it all out. "I stayed away all night. But now that it's over, we need to straighten out a few things."

She shook her head from side to side, giving a clear keep-away signal before speaking. "I'm exhausted. Can it wait?"

"No. It really can't." Sam refused to be waved off before saying his piece. "I can't take the chance that you're miserable for another second because of me."

"Too late."

"Hear me out. Five minutes?"

Mira nodded. Or did a head bob from sheer exhaustion. It was all the green light he needed. "I talked to my mother."

"There's a shock. The phone line between you two's a second umbilical cord."

Okay. He'd expected her to be a little pissed, to not make this easy for him. "I asked her if she missed Dad taking care of her."

"Interesting."

Illuminating was more like it. Swiped his feet right out from underneath him. "She laughed in my face. Said that she was the one who'd worn the pants in the family. She'd taken care of him from day one. And as much as she missed him, it had actually been a little bit of a relief to only have to worry about herself."

"Is this when you informed her that you've actually taken over this caretaker position?"

"I tried. Mom just laughed even harder. When she finally caught her breath, she said that ever since she got out of the hospital, she'd been *letting* me take care of her. Thought it was part of my grieving process for Dad."

She focused on the tiara, slowly running her finger over each rounded point. "How'd that feel?"

"Like a slap in the face. Like I'm Han Solo in *Empire Strikes Back*, frozen in a block of carbonite for the past year." Like he'd missed the exit he was supposed to take on the road of life, and was now stuck going nowhere. "So I let it all out. I told her about my dream of being a gourmet chocolatier, the expansion and the Fancy Food show."

"That's a lot of sharing. You must be worn out."

Another direct hit. Sam absorbed the blow. If it meant she'd keep listening to him, he could take it. "As you predicted, Mom wouldn't let me give up my dreams for her sake."

"I do like to know I'm right. Thanks for telling me."

"I know I deserve all these little digs, but would you please be quiet? I'm getting to the good part."

She ran an imaginary zipper across her lips. Smartass. God, he loved that about her.

"I couldn't see the forest for the trees. The solution was right in front of me all along. The juvenile work-release program's been going great. We called the head caseworker, and he's going to assign us more kids. Javon's going to play a much bigger role in the bakery. He just passed his GED, so he was about to leave the program anyway. We're hiring him full-time, and Isaiah part-time. The store doesn't have to be run by just the Lyons family. We can create an extended family by nurturing these boys who have nothing."

Mira raised her hand. She still annoyed him without even trying. "What?"

"I think that is a beautiful idea. Generous and life-changing and wonderful. I bet your dad would approve."

"Thanks. That's what Mom said. Right before she pulled up the exhibitor registration form on the computer and made me fill it out on the spot. I'm in. I'm going to the Fancy Food show, and I'm starting my own chocolate line."

The corners of her lips lifted. Not a full-blown smile, but into soft approval. "That's really great, Sam."

"I realized that I couldn't give up on my dreams after urging you to follow yours. What kind of a hypocritical idiot would that make me?" Gib and Ben had certainly helped him to realize just how much he was on the brink of throwing away. Good thing he'd come to that conclusion before having Dr. Rubin chip away at his wallet for a few weeks. "We're both on the same path, and I want us to walk it together."

And the lips curved right back down. "No."

"Mira, haven't you heard me?" Wait, he knew what the problem was. He owed her a wheelbarrow full of groveling. Gib and Ben told him that she'd been crying all night. It made Sam sick that he'd been the reason. "I'm sorry. I was an idiot. I thought I was being selfless, but I was actually being a self-centered fool. Give me another chance, and I'll apologize every day until my hair turns gray. You can remind me three times a day of how stupid I was. I'll even set an alarm to remind you."

She slid off the stool and looked to be about two seconds from walking away. "It's too late. You can't decide to run after me just because your mom released you from your dad's imaginary onus. I won't be your consolation prize."

For such a smart woman, Mira really wasn't connecting the dots. "You're missing the point completely. I opened up this whole can of worms with my mother because I already missed you so much that I could barely breathe. I talked to her so that she could help me find my way back to you."

"Oh." She fell back onto the stool, as if her legs simply wouldn't hold her up anymore.

"Here." He picked up the tray and presented it to her. This was his last, best shot to make her change her mind and stay with him. Forever. "I made this for you. Just for you. It's a brand-new flavor I've created. I call it Fiery Love. Dark chocolate, because that's your favorite, with a little heat from chili pepper and Chambord. Try it. A small bite," he cautioned.

Her face giving away nothing, Mira nibbled at the edge. She scraped it against her teeth and wrinkled her nose. Licking her thumb, she looked down at the remaining half truffle. A gold semicircle peeked out of the middle of the brown, creamy ganache.

"It's delicious." Carefully she reversed the truffle

and, hanging on to the ring, sucked off the rest of the chocolate. "Sam, this is a diamond ring."

He grabbed it, cleaned it off with a napkin left over from the party until the burnished gold leaves surrounding the stone shone. "Not just any diamond. My father gave this to my mother as an engagement ring. When I told her that I'd do anything to show you how much you mean to me, she told me to use this. Thought it might prove that you are absolutely the most important woman in my life."

Mira hitched in a shaky breath. "Kathleen is a very smart woman."

"So are you. You're crazy smart. You can finish an entire Sudoku while you're brushing your teeth." Singing her praises came easy. There was so much he loved about her. "Mira, you totally get my passion for chocolate. You don't let anything get in the way of your goals. You bounce back faster than a Super Ball. You're thoughtful and loyal and funny and so beautiful I practically drool every time I look at you, and—"

"Sam, stop."

"I can't. I can't stop until I convince you to marry me, and be the sweetness in my heart forever. Say you love me," he begged, because right now, he wasn't above begging. He'd crawl on his knees over broken glass to hear those words come out of her lips.

"I love you," she said, laughing breathlessly.

It couldn't be that easy. He'd barely begun to grovel. And Gib, with all his vast experience, swore up and down that women were complicated. "Just like that?"

"I've been too scared to admit it. Scared to love you when the store might fail and I'd be stuck marrying some bore my parents chose. I told you that all I want out of life is to be happy, and you make me deliriously happy."

Sam was ready to turn backflips that she loved him. But they couldn't move forward until she answered the next question. Because they couldn't have a future if the shadow of her parents and the promise of an easier life hung over them. "What if the store fails?"

"Then I'll find another one." She leaned over to whisper in his ear. "It won't, by the way." Then she stood up, her eyes shining like the midday sky. "But my love for you is worth so much more than a measly hundred million dollars."

Holy shit. "How much?" If he'd known she was worth that much, Sam never would've had the balls to urge her to throw it all away.

"Doesn't matter." Mira dismissed her lost fortune with a wave. "Let me finish. I have to air the doubt I felt, and then it'll be done. I was scared to love a man who didn't love me enough. There has to be equal footing in a relationship."

"Then we're out of luck, because I love you way more than you could ever love me."

Her competitive streak flashed in her quick smile, but it was nothing but love brimming over in her eyes. "Not a chance."

He held up the ring to her finger, ready to slip it on. "Prove it. Say yes, and spend the rest of your life trying to prove you love me more. It won't work, because I'll always love you more, but I dare you to try."

Mira slid her finger through the gold band, happy

tears slipping down her cheeks. "You know I never back down from a challenge."

That was worth sealing with a kiss. And Sam kissed her, reveling in the sweetness of her lips and her love. He'd make damn sure every day of her life with him would be a fine romance.

* * * * *